THE CROWN AND THE COLLAR

KINGDOM OF CLAWS
BOOK 1

THE CROWN AND THE COLLAR

DOMINIC N. ASHEN

4 Horsemen
Publications, Inc.

4 Horsemen Publications, Inc.
1497 Main St. Suite 169
Dunedin, FL 34698
4horsemenpublications.com
info@4horsemenpublications.com

Cover by Oxford
Typesetting by Niki Tantillo
Edited by Tilda M. Cooke

Library of Congress Control Number: 2023941333

Paperback ISBN-13: 979-8-8232-0284-8
Hardcover ISBN-13: 979-8-8232-0286-2
Audiobook ISBN-13: 979-8-8232-0283-1
Ebook ISBN-13: 979-8-8232-0285-5

To Zach, my own smiling ray of sunshine. I love you.

TABLE OF CONTENTS

Map Key

1. Lamplight Farm
2. Two Pines Farm
3. Blue Moon Farm
4. Blacksmith
5. Schoolhouse
6. Market
7. Church
8. Townhall
9. To St. Kizis
10. To Blackport

WESTON

"Fields of Green,
Hearts of Gold"

ST. KIZIS

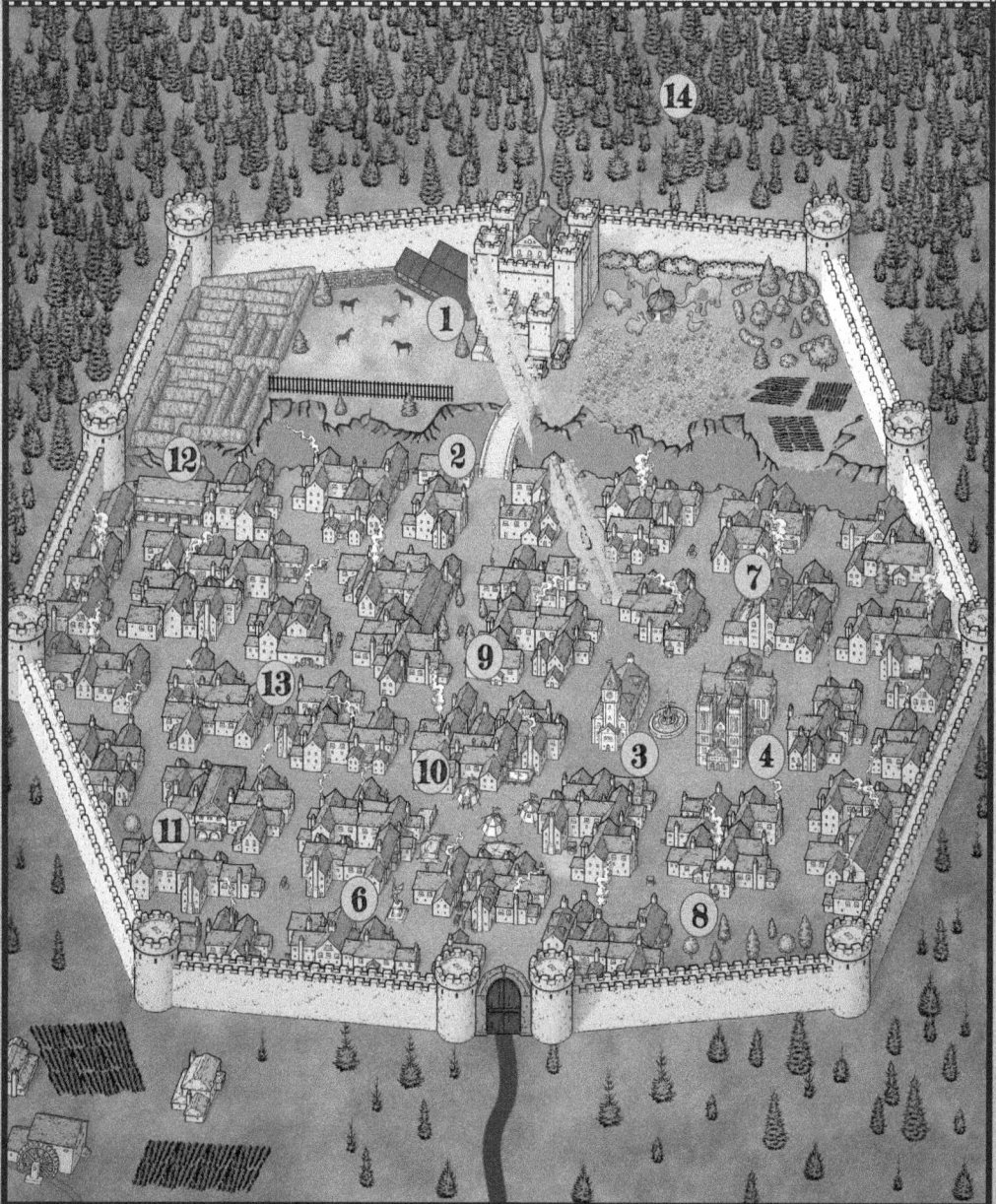

CAPITAL OF LITKALAA

"Sub Lunam Surgimus"

Map Key

1. St. Kizis Castle
2. Concourse Bridge
3. St. Kizis University
4. St. Kizis Cathedral
5. Coleman's Bakery
6. Statue of St. Olaf
7. Mammothbone Tavern
8. The Lady Luciana Memorial Garden
9. Park
10. Marketplace
11. Theatre
12. Merchant's Guild
13. City Guard HQ
14. Blackclaw Pack Kingswood

CHAPTER 1

"I think that's everything for this one."

"Okay, I'll go help Daddy finish with the other cart."

It's Astraday, which means it's time for another day at the Weston market. It's early in the morning, just after dawn, and I'm doing what I've done every Astraday morning for the last six weeks: helping my parents load this week's harvest so we can cart it into the town square. It's hard work, but it has to get done.

I don't really mind it though, even when I have to wake up extra early to take care of the animals. Things are usually pretty busy during the week, so I really look forward to when I finally get to go into town and catch up with everyone. It's one of the only times I get to see some of my old school friends these days.

"Just gotta load the last few crates on," Daddy tells me, already lifting one onto the back.

"Do you think these will sell well?" I ask, handing him off another crate.

"I think so. *I* can't stop eating them." He grabs two of our newest crop from the next crate I hand over, tossing me one and eating the other himself.

It's a small fruit, bright red in color and *very* sweet. I bring it up to my mouth and bite in, loving the way the sweet flavor bursts on my tongue. They grow on the mainland in the forests farther to the south. "Strawberries" is what they've been named, though I'm not really sure why. They don't look like straw or anything, but gosh are they good.

"We're not gonna sell *any* if you two keep eating them all!" Momma tells us both, hand on her hip. "Finish loading up and let's get moving!"

"Yes, ma'am."

"Yes, ma'am." Daddy and I both answer, sharing a grin as we load the rest of the boxes.

After we finish, I run up and hop onto the front cart with Momma. Once I'm in my seat, she whips the reins once, and we're off, our horse-drawn carts following one after the other on the dirt road. As we round the mill and the town comes into view, I'm already wondering what kind of day to expect.

If it's anything like it has been the past few weeks, we'll sell almost everything we've brought. It's been a good season so far, with all of our harvests having great yields. Most of the crops aren't native to Litkalaa, and my family was actually the first to cultivate some of them here: radishes, carrots, onions, and now strawberries.

I like living on a farm. I mean, I've spent my whole life on one, so I guess I don't really know anything else. We wake up early most days, and spend almost all day in the fields and stable. It's a lot of hard work, but the reward of watching something you planted grow from nothing but a seed really does feel amazing. I know it sounds cheesy, but I love it.

Lamplight Farm isn't the biggest farm in Weston, but we are one of the oldest, and one day I'm going to take over for my daddy, just like he did for his daddy. Even if I didn't want to stay on the farm (which I do!), there isn't a whole lot else to do around here. Weston is a small village located on the (you guessed it) western side of the island of Litkalaa. If I'm remembering it right, it's also one of the earliest villages built, founded over two-hundred and fifty years ago. But other than that, we aren't really known for much of anything.

"Peter, look." Momma nudges me with her elbow then points ahead. "Aren't those royal carriages from the capital?"

Just on the outskirts of town are three black carriages, each bearing the crest of the royal family: a black wolf head over two crossed swords. The vehicles are big and fancy looking, painted in red and black, each one pulled by two brown horses. They're large and muscular, and put our horses Abby and old Kino here to shame.

"What do you think they're doing here?" I ask, my mind racing.

"I don't know. I didn't hear about anything." She shrugs. "Maybe they're just passing through?"

"Maybe..." I bite my lip, eyeing them as we pass by.

Kino pulls us through the open gates and into the village. Most of the buildings look the same with wooden walls and roofs, though a few of the older homes are thatched with straw. Old memories are stirred up when I see the schoolhouse, the red paint on the walls having long since faded. They're *mostly* good memories. I'm not the smartest, and I was never really very good at it, but I miss school sometimes. I dropped out when I was sixteen, three years ago. I had to, for my family.

My parents had me a little later in life than a lot of my friends' parents, when they were both in their thirties. They're both in their fifties now, and every year it gets harder and harder for them to do things around the farm. Daddy's actually been talking about maybe hiring someone to help us out, but I'm not sure how he'd pay them. Sales have been good, but not *that* good.

I shake off the thought; none of that matters right now. I wave to a few people as we pass the church on the way to the town square. It's a good thing we're not very religious because working on a farm doesn't leave you a lot of time for church. We always make sure to say a prayer to Father Sun and Mother Moon on the solstices and equinoxes, but I know Momma and Daddy wish we did more.

We pull into the square and make our way to our usual spot west of the center fountain. Wooden stalls have been set up courtesy of the village council for us and other merchants. I help Daddy unload while Momma brings the horses to the nearby hitching post so they can rest. Daddy has a bad habit of pushing himself, so I try to do most of the heavy lifting when I can, stacking the heavier crates closer to the stand.

Ronald Lambert, my father, is about 5'8" and 140 lbs. He's got blue eyes, brown hair that's already starting to gray (including his beard), and while he's not out of shape, he did just turn fifty-five. My mother, Mary Lambert, is four years younger at fifty-one. She's two inches shorter and a little stouter, weighing a little more than Daddy does. She wears glasses over her brown eyes and usually keeps her dark blonde hair pulled back in a tie. My hair is just about the same color as hers, though I hear it get called "dirty blonde" more often than not, and I have blue eyes like my dad. I'm only nineteen, but I'm *way* taller than both of them at six feet even, and I weigh almost 250 lbs. *Most* of that is muscle—I've got a bit of a tummy. Momma says I've always loved eating.

We only have about twenty minutes until customers will start arriving, so the three of us quickly get to work. We empty the first few crates in no time, filling the stand's shelves with our best-looking offerings. Daddy always takes a little extra pride in the way he sets everything up. He says it's like a puzzle, making sure the colors all blend together in a leafy rainbow.

Before I even realize it, we've started. I swear, I go to grab another crate of radishes, and when I turn back around, the streets are full of people, Weston citizens making their way to each of the market stalls, including ours. It's practically a routine at this point. They come over, maybe make some small talk, pick out some fruit or vegetables, pay, and then leave.

"Hi, Peter!" Violet, one of those old school friends I mentioned earlier, steps up to the side of the stall with a wave.

Violet Ferrier is my best and probably oldest friend. We're the same age, or I guess she's technically older by a few months. She's a short girl with dark brown skin, brown eyes, and black textured hair that reaches her shoulders. Like I said before, we went to school together, although unlike me, she's smart and actually finished. Her father is the town blacksmith, or at least he was before he got sick, and she's been trying to pick up the slack.

"Hey, Violet," I answer her with a smile. "How are you? How's your dad doing?"

"He's alright," she lies. He's been really weak lately and tired all the time, but no one, not even the village doctor, can figure out what's wrong with him. "Did you see the royal carriages on your way in?"

"Yeah, I did." I look over at my parents to make sure they can handle the customers while I step farther off to the side. "Why? Do you know what's going on?"

"I heard the prince is here!" she whispers to me loudly, looking around like she just revealed a big secret.

"Prince Makseka?" I pull back, not believing her. Why would the crown prince be in our dinky little town? "Are you sure? Why?"

"That's what Monica said. And I dunno." She shrugs, still smiling and leaning in to speak low again. "Maybe he's looking for a consort."

There aren't a lot of things to do in a small town like this. There's drinking, card games, and gossip, and you can do all three at the local tavern. Gossip is probably the most popular, and the only one I really partake in (I don't really like the taste of beer, and I'm not very good at cards), and the royal family is a very popular topic in particular.

Like a lot of other countries, Litkalaa is ruled by a king and a queen. But unlike most of those countries, Litkalaa's rulers and royal family are all werewolves. Actual cursed-to-turn-into-monsters-during-the-full-moon werewolves. Or at least that's what they say. I've never met or even seen a werewolf myself before.

I remember the story from school. A long time ago, there were two groups of people living on the island: a tribe of werewolves, and a faction of non-werewolves. The wolves had been living here for hundreds of years, but this new faction had migrated to the island from somewhere in the east, across the ocean, to establish a new kingdom here.

The werewolves lived in the forests to the north while the others built their cities on the plains in the south. For a long time, the two groups lived in peace, not bothering each other or even interacting much, until the day the new kingdom came under attack. It started with seaside towns being raided, but eventually, these attackers started moving inland.

They soon learned the raiders had far more men and firepower, and that they wanted to control the island. The attacks became more and more frequent with them losing more and more land to these invaders each time. Finally, just when everything seemed lost, their king traveled north to beg the leader of the werewolves for help.

The werewolves were not worried about these invaders. Not only had they not yet been attacked, the thick forests of the north provided a lot of natural defense. Still, the werewolf chief was not heartless and did not want to see these outsiders wiped out. So he agreed to help them, on one condition: their king would step down, and the werewolf king would rule in his place. He would even marry his queen, tying their two families together. Not having any other choice, the king accepted.

And *that's* where this consort business comes into play. Because you see, the human king didn't go away after stepping down. In addition to marrying his wife, the werewolf king claimed the former king as his consort. A consort is almost like the king's second wife, with some, uh, key differences ... like being a man. Ever since then, it's been a tradition for all members of the royal family to claim and collar a consort. From what I've heard, it became so popular that it even started to spread outside of the royal family with a lot of nobles and other upper class people taking consorts of their own.

"Are you blushing?" Violet teases me.

"What? No." *Oh gods, am I?* I quickly turn away, stacking a few of the empty crates back on our carts.

"I always heard Prince Makseka was really good looking." She keeps talking like I'm not trying to ignore her.

"People say that about all the royals. So what?" I try to play it off, but I know she's messing with me. Prince Makseka is only about five years older than us, and to say that only a few of our school mates had crushes on him would be a serious understatement.

"Sooooo..." She just gives me a knowing look, swaying on her toes a little.

"Peter, go grab us some more strawberries, please." Daddy touches my shoulder, rescuing me with his request. "Hello, Violet. How are you doing?"

"Hello, Mr. Lambert. I'm well. Thanks for asking." Violet puts on her best talking-to-parents voice. "My father says hello."

I take my time getting the fruit for Daddy, Violet's words bringing back even more old memories. I used to maybe be a little ... obsessed with the royal family. Specifically the consort and collaring stuff. Like I said before, consorts can be men or women, and well... I like men. I'm gay, or at least I'm pretty sure I am, because I've never been interested in women. It's not something I really talk about a lot. Some people can be weird or even mean about it. Violet was the first person I told, then some of our other friends, and eventually I got the courage to tell my parents. I was scared about how they would react, but all they did was hug me and tell me they'd love me no matter what. I'm less nervous about it these days, but I still don't know anyone else like me, at least not in Weston.

But no one bats an eye when one of the royals takes on a consort of the same gender. Kind of the opposite, actually. There are a *lot* of books on the subject, romance novels, about the forbidden love between a royal and their consort. Like the prince who risked war to bring his kidnapped love home, and the knight who fought through an army of demons to free his consort from a deadly curse. I used to sneak them out of the library and take them home, where I would read them over and over and over. I'd even hide them under my mattress, worried my parents might find them.

But that was years ago, and I haven't read one of those books in ages. While I *might* have crushed on the prince myself when I was younger, I don't give that stuff much thought at all these days. I have other responsibilities to worry about. Speaking of... I shake off the old memories and finally grab the crate of strawberries Daddy asked for. Thankfully, Violet is nowhere to be seen, so I can go back to work without feeling embarrassed.

Sales are pretty steady the first couple of hours. All our regulars stop by and catch up with us while they shop. Mrs. Osbourne's grandchildren are going to be visiting from Eastport for a week, and she needs a good recipe for pie. Mr. Plakard needs to repair his fence after last week's rainstorm knocked part of it over and asks Daddy if he knows where to find some cheap lumber. And the Rizzo family just got a new pet dog and want to know what they should avoid feeding it.

We help out everyone with the questions we know the answers to and direct them to others for the ones we don't. Daddy always says we're a community and that it's important to support each other. Just as I'm handing

Mrs. Marrow her change, I notice something happening on the other side of the town square. A lot of people are gathered around one spot in particular, and I can see those in the back whispering to each other. The crowd eventually parts to reveal the source of the commotion: Prince Makseka.

My breath catches in my stomach when I see his rugged face. I've never seen him in person before, only heard about what he looks like from stories and rumors but... wow. Violet was right—he is really, *really* good looking. Hot even. He's tall, maybe even taller than me, with wide-set shoulders, muscular looking arms, and a natural tan. He's got short, jet-black hair, and his face is covered in a dark layer of stubble, right below his bright blue eyes. He's dressed up like you'd expect a royal to be, wearing a red shirt over a black pair of pants with a small red cape on his shoulders.

Standing around him are four knights in full armor—his bodyguards from the royal court, no doubt sworn to protect him. Not that he needs it. I've heard he's just as strong and fast as any other knight, and I'd bet that would still be true even if he wasn't a werewolf. There is another man with them, older and shorter, with graying black hair and dressed in similarly fine-looking robes, walking next to the prince. It seems like he's trying to talk to the prince, but the prince either doesn't hear him or is pretending not to, the shorter man getting more and more flustered.

The people gathering around to stare and whisper are sure to give them all a lot of space, parting around them automatically as the group moves through the market. The prince stops at the various stands, talking with the owners who can only speak back nervously. I don't even realize that he's coming our way until we lock eyes, and he smiles. I look away in a panic, already feeling my face start to heat. *What was that?*

"I told you, it really is Prince Makseka!" Violet says excitedly, joining me by the carts I'm trying to hide behind until my heart stops pounding. "What do you think he's doing here?"

"How should I know?" I almost snap at her. *Why do I feel so nervous?* Anyone would after almost meeting the prince... right?

"Maybe I was right about the consort thing too," she replies with a nudge to my side, before looking over my shoulder with wide eyes and then grabbing me by the arm and shaking. "Oh my gods, he's coming this way!"

"What?!" I look up and see that she's right. He's coming right toward us, his eyes locked onto our stall.

"Quick, get over there!" Violet tells me with a stronger shove than you'd expect from someone so short.

"Good morning," Prince Makseka greets as I stumble to the counter. "Is this your stand?"

"H-Hello, Your Highness," I stammer nervously. "Everything for sale is ours, b-but the stand belongs to the town. Th-the council sets them up for us and the other sellers to use on days like today." *Why am I explaining this to him?*

"I see. Well that sounds like a great way for your village to support its economy. I'll have to make sure my father thanks them for it." He flashes me another smile as he looks over the rows of fruits and vegetables. "Did you grow everything here yourself?"

"I... I helped?" I answer, confused as to why he's asking me these questions, or anything really. "I live on a farm right outside of town with my family. Lamplight Farm. It's just me and my parents."

"Good morning, Your Highness." Daddy steps forward and manages to not stumble all over himself like me.

"It is a pleasure to meet you," Momma tells him next, holding her dress and taking a small curtsey.

"Please, no need for the formalities." He waves them both off and shakes his head. "Just pretend like I'm any other visitor just passing through your village."

"We appreciate your visit, Your Highness," Daddy says next, ignoring the request to be informal.

"We have some farms near St. Kizis, but would you believe I've never actually seen one?" He picks up a radish as he talks, still aimed at me. "All the space you'd need for all the fields and animals, and having to tend to all of them... It must be a lot of hard work."

"I-It can be," I admit, swallowing nervously. "You have to wake up really early most days, and you spend a lot of time outside, no matter the weather."

"But you like it?" He puts the radish back down as he asks.

"I do." I nod, feeling my heart start to beat faster again. "Sir," I quickly tack on. *Are you supposed to call a prince "sir"?*

"Sir, huh?" He smiles with a warmth that reaches his eyes before he continues. "Well, I won't pretend that I'm familiar with a lot of physical labor, but it looks good on you."

"Th-thank you?" I'm not actually sure what I'm thanking him for, but I can feel that I'm starting to blush again.

He leans in close, smiling again (at my nervousness?), and... *Did he just sniff me?* He reaches for a strawberry and pops it into his mouth. His eyes grow when the sweet flavor hits his tongue. "Oh wow, that is *really* good. What are they called?"

"S-Strawberries, sir," I answer him, not even caring that he didn't pay for that. "Th-they're new."

"They're very good." The way he says it makes me think he's not talking about the fruit. "Is this everything you've grown, or do you get to keep any for yourselves?"

"This is most of it," I start to tell him. "We keep some of everything for our own pantry, and sometimes if a crop looks ugly or weird, we'll feed it to one of our animals instead of selling it, but this is everything else from our last harvest." *Seriously, why am I still explaining all of this to him?*

"Are you out here every weekend, selling your crops?" Part of me feels like he can't actually be this interested, but his face and tone say the opposite.

"We actually only started a few weeks ago," I start to explain. (*I mean... he asked.*) "We had to wait for the first of our spring crops to be ready for harvest. We will probably keep going until the end of fall."

"How long are you usually out here for?" He turns to look at some of the other stands, and I only just realize how *everyone* nearby is staring at the two of us talking.

"Usually most of the morning and part of the afternoon," I answer. "We will be here at least a few more hours today, unless we manage to sell everything. Sir."

He chuckles, turning back to face. "I probably should have asked this sooner, but what's your name, Sunshine?"

"I, uh, it's P-Peter." I almost choke on my own spit. *Sunshine?!*

"Peter." He rolls my name around on his tongue, and I feel my chest start to pound again. "It's nice to meet you, Peter. I think I'd like to buy your stuff."

"You'd like some strawberries, Your Highness?" Daddy steps forward quickly, already prepared to do business.

"No, sir. I mean all of it." His eyes move from Daddy to me with a pleased expression. "Everything you have here."

"I'm ... sorry?" Daddy is as confused as I am. He wants to buy *everything*?

"Your Highness, no." The older man who has been standing at the prince's side finally speaks up, an exasperated look on his face. "We cannot purchase all of this man's goods. We have no need for them."

"Oh come on, Kamo," the prince tells the old man with a sharp slap on his back. "We have a huge castle full of soldiers and servants, and even the stuck-up people in the court have to eat sometime. Are you telling me Mona won't be able to find a use for all this in the kitchens? She'll *love* it. Especially these." He pops another strawberry into his mouth. "*So* good."

"Your Highness, I just do not think we need to—"

"I've already made up my mind, Kamo." He looks at me again with a grin, his lips red from the fruit's juice. "Now pay Mr. Lambert here so me and the others can start loading everything into the carriages."

The older man sighs, looking like this is an argument he's had before. He adjusts his glasses as he turns to my father. "How much will it be for everything you have for sale here?" Kamo waves his hand over the stands.

"Well, let me see." Daddy and Momma start to count everything on the counters, doing the math in their heads.

"Don't forget about what's in those carts either!" Prince Makseka calls out, stepping around to the side of our stand.

"Th-thank you so much but ... why?" I dare to ask him. "Why did you do that?"

"How could I not buy everything from someone like you?" He shrugs, but the way his eyes move down my body makes me shiver. "Besides, I figured this way, you and your family will be able to go home early today. I'm sure you could use a day off."

"That's very generous." I don't bother to tell him that there is no such thing as a "day off" on a farm. I don't want him to change his mind. I'm glad my parents are handling the money because I can't even imagine how much it must be. Probably more than our family has seen in *years*. "Thank you so much, sir."

"There's that 'sir' again." He grins as he picks up the first crate of crops, the royal bodyguards behind him doing the same. "It was really nice to meet you, Peter."

"I-It was nice to meet you too, Your Highness." I stare at the back of his head as he turns and walks away, afraid that I might start shaking.

"Peter, get over here and help me get the rest of the crates for Prince Makseka." Daddy's gruff request snaps me back to reality.

"Yes, sir," I reply, my body moving automatically.

As I help my parents unload the last of our crops and my brain starts to work again, I wonder what the hell just happened. I see Violet standing off to the side, looking like she's ready to explode with questions, but I ignore her for now. I try to focus on the work and clear the silly thoughts from my head, but every time I close my eyes, all I see are a pair of blue eyes and a warm smile.

Chapter 2

"I can't believe that just happened."

"Me neither," I respond. "It *did* happen though, right?"

"Believe me, I had to stop myself from biting into the gold right in front of him," Daddy confirms. "It was real."

We're headed back to the farm several hours earlier than we normally would be after a day at the market, Momma driving the cart behind us. Both of them are completely empty, except for the crates we used to carry the crops, which are also now empty. We've had good days before, but we've never sold *everything*—not until Prince Makseka.

I still can't believe it. Why was he even there? He was just ... wandering around the market. Until he saw me. Then he kept asking me all those questions until he decided to just buy everything. He was probably the one person at the market who didn't need a single thing there!

The way he kept looking at me, his eyes, his smile... They're burned into my brain.

He and his knights got everything loaded pretty quickly—must be all that werewolf strength—and then returned all of the empty crates. Which makes me think that one of those carriages must now filled with loose fruits and vegetables just rolling around on the floor. I guess it's not really my problem. He can do whatever he wants with his food.

We make the turn at the mill, home just ahead in the distance. Lamplight Farm isn't the biggest, but we're still a decent size at fifteen acres. About half of that is empty fields of grass, but the rest is still a lot of land for the three of us to work. We've got a small stable for our two horses, a decent sized barn for our three dairy cows, and a small wooden chicken coop. The farmhouse where we actually live is an old wooden building with two floors, covered in a layer of faded blue paint.

"I don't know what you did to get the prince's attention like that," Momma says as we park the carts next to the farmhouse, "but I think it just paid for a new roof."

"Whatever it was, you'll have to do it again the next time we have a royal in town," Daddy jokes as we step off.

"I'm going to put this away," Momma tells us, hugging us both before she steps inside. "It feels dangerous carrying around this much money."

While Momma stashes away today's earnings in the safe, Daddy starts to pull the empty crates from the carts, stacking them in the shed near the fields so they'll be ready for the next harvest. They're light enough that he can handle it on his own, so I unhook Bess and Kino from the carts and bring them to our small horse stable.

We've had these horses for as long as I can remember, and they're both getting up in years, but they're gentle-natured and hard workers. I get them both in their stalls and make sure they've got fresh water and plenty of forage to eat. Before I leave, I feed them both an apple, a reward for all the work they did today.

My stomach starts to rumble after I leave the stable, so I head back to the farmhouse for lunch. Momma usually packs us sandwiches and a few snacks to eat while at the market, and I join her and Daddy at the dinner table to eat. When we're finished, we each head off to take care of what we need to on the farm.

Even though we woke up early to finish a few things, since we normally expect to spend most of the day in the marketplace selling, there's still plenty to be done around farm. The chickens and cows were taken care of this morning, so with the horses fed, that should be all of the animals. I think that just leaves some hay bales in the barn that need to be stacked.

"Good afternoon, ladies," I greet the cows as I enter the barn. "Don't mind me. Just moving some hay."

"Mooooo," Holly greets me in return, coming up to the edge of her stall with her sisters Molly and Polly at her side.

"Yeah, it was a *really* good day," I start to tell them about our morning as I pick up the first bale, starting a pile in the corner. "You'll never believe it: *Prince Makseka* was at the market today. Just wandering around like it was nothing."

"Moo?" Polly asks while I grab my second bale.

"Yeah, he came up and started asking me all these questions about the farm." I move another, already starting to feel the familiar burn in my arm muscles. "He seemed really interested for some reason, and then he bought *everything*. That's why we're home so early."

Okay, I know the cows can't *actually* understand me, and no, I can't understand them either, but that doesn't mean they don't like being talked to. They're friendly girls, always eager to say hello. Sometimes I feel like they understand me anyways, and even if they can't, it's just nice to have someone who listens, you know?

"Moooo." Sounds like Molly wants to hear more about the prince.

"He was really nice, actually," I tell her as I pull off my shirt, already soaked through with sweat, tucking it into the waist of my pants. "Not that I expected him to be mean. He was maybe a little weird, too. Kept asking me about what it's like living and working on a farm, how much I liked it. And then like I said, he bought everything we brought with us. Down to the last onion."

"Moo?" Holly seems skeptical.

"No, that was the other weird part. Even though Momma and Daddy were right there, *I* was the one he kept talking to." I finish with one pile and move onto the next. "I'm not sure why he was so interested in hearing from me. They've been doing this a lot longer, especially Daddy."

"Moo." Polly always did get to the right to the point.

"Yeah, okay, he was nice to look at, too," I admit, stopping for a second, pointlessly trying to wipe my brow with my shirt. "He's really tall, and he has these bright blue eyes I noticed from all the way across the square. I don't think he'd shaved in a couple of days, but it looked really good on him."

"Well, that's a nice thing to hear." The voice makes me yelp in surprise and drop the bale in my hands. Turning around, I see Prince Makseka leaning against the barn door. "Though I swear, I shaved just yesterday."

"Your Highness!" I blurt out, probably a little too loudly. "What are you doing here?"

"I happen to have it on good authority that you were given the rest of the day off, so I thought I'd come and see what your farm was like for myself." He steps farther inside the barn, his icy blue eyes scanning my body again. "Though it kinda seems like you're still working anyway."

"I... I'm sorry, sir." *Why am I apologizing?* "There's just a lot of work to be done on a farm." I gesture to the half-finished stack of hay bales.

"I can see that." Instead of looking there, his eyes are glued to my sweaty, shirtless torso, my chest hair matted to my skin.

"W-Would you ... like a tour of the farm, sir?" I'm right back to feeling that mix of nervousness and being drawn in, just like in town.

"I would." He nods once, stepping closer. "I really enjoyed meeting you today. So much that it made me start to consider some things."

"What kind of things, Prince Makseka?" It feels like he wants me to ask.

"Please, call me Max," he says before his expression turns more serious. "How much do you know about consorts to the royal family?" He looks almost worried about what my answer might be.

"I... I know a little," I lie, the question making goosebumps break out over my body. "I've read a few stories and heard about some other things from other people in the village."

"Well, I can promise you that only about half of them are true," he teases, putting back on his charming smile. "But I'm glad you're at least a little familiar because I have another question to ask you."

"Sir?" My throat suddenly feels very dry.

"Would you do me the honor of becoming my consort?" he asks, taking a step toward me.

"I... You... What?" There is no way I just heard him right.

"I want to claim you as my consort," he repeats, stepping closer.

"But... But why? We just met today. Why me?" Everything around us has gone dead silent. Even the cows are watching the two of us closely.

"To start with, Sunshine, you're gorgeous." He grins at me cockily. "But even if I didn't find you incredibly *attractive*, you also seem kind, and gentle, and you're obviously a hard worker. I think I wanted you from the moment our eyes met across the town square. And your scent?" He leans in and inhales through his nose, a pleasant smile crossing his face. *I knew he was smelling me at the market!*

"Th-thank you, Your Highness." I reel in my shock enough to force the words out. "B-But I'm sorry, sir. I c-can't be your c-consort."

"What?" His head swings around at the obviously unexpected answer. "Why not?"

"Well, my... my family. The farm." I look around the barn and over at Polly, Holly, and Molly. "My parents are getting older, and they can't do as much around here as they used to. They need my help. I quit school to be here for them. I can't just leave."

"Of course you'd be selfless too." He sighs, wearing a sad but still hopeful smile. "But maybe we can find a solution for that. Come with me."

"W-Where are we going?" I follow as he turns and strides swiftly out of the barn.

"To talk to your parents," he answers without ever looking over his shoulder. *What is he going to say to them?*

We reach the main house, walking in through the already open back door and through the kitchen. Seated around the dinner table are both my parents, Kamo, and two of the royal knights, with the other two on our couch. The knights and Kamo all stand when we enter, my parents hastily doing the same.

"Is everything alright?" one of the knights asks Prince Makseka, looking concerned.

"Yes, I just need to discuss a few things with Mr. and Mrs. Lambert here." The prince takes a seat in the only empty chair at the table. Everyone else returns to their seats as well, leaving me to stand awkwardly behind him. "So, to cut to the chase, I have asked your son if he would do me the honor of becoming my consort."

"You did what?"

"You did *what?!*"

Kamo's question sounds a lot angrier than my mother's. The knights all look surprised, their gazes moving between me and the prince, while Momma and Daddy are a mix of shocked and confused. Just like I was when he asked me. And mostly still am.

"I would like your son to come back with me to the capital, live with me in the castle, and claim him as my consort," Prince Makseka explains in the simplest terms possible. "Unfortunately, he told me that he can't because you need him to keep the farm running."

"Yes, he's a big help around here." Daddy seems hesitant to answer. Both my parents are looking at me confused and worried, like neither knows what to say.

"That's something I can understand. He's obviously devoted to this place and to the two of you." He nods. "So what I would like to propose is that in exchange for bringing your son home with me, I compensate you with a monthly stipend you could use to hire a farmhand to work in his place. Would a thousand gold cover it?"

I feel like the air is knocked out of me. *One thousand gold a month!?* That is the kind of money we could only dream of. We'd be able to get new equipment, new horses, fix up the house... With money like that, every month, my parents would never have to work a day themselves ever again!

Both of their eyes go just as wide as mine, sharing a look. Daddy starts to speak for them both. "I... I'm sorry, Your Highness, but there is no amount of money that could replace our son. I'm afraid I have to—"

"Wait," I cut Daddy off, all eyes in the room turning to me. "Your Highness, could... Could I have some time to think about it?"

"Of course," Makseka agrees with a too-quick nod, hope plastered across his face.

"Your Highness!" Kamo, who glares at me and my family in annoyance, puts his foot down. Literally, he stomps on the floor. "You cannot honestly be considering making this boy—"

"Do you think you get a say in this, Kamo?" The prince challenges his "keeper" with a cool look and a cocked eyebrow.

Chastised, Kamo takes a deep breath before continuing. "All I mean to say, my prince, is that we cannot delay our return to the castle any longer. We have already wasted enough time in this village and need to return home. The king and queen are expecting us."

"My parents aren't going to miss me if we stay one more night." The prince scoffs and rolls his eyes. Then he stands and turns to me. "I can give you until the morning. Would that be enough time for you to make a decision?"

"Yes, sir," I agree even though I know that's not nearly enough time for something this big. "Thank you. I promise I will give you an answer in the morning, Prince Makseka."

"I told you: call me Max." He gives me a smoldering look before taking my hand and kissing the back of it while Kamo and his knights stand, the group of them moving to the front door. "I'll see you in the morning. Sleep well tonight, Sunshine."

My parents and I are at a loss for words after he leaves, standing in silence in the dining room.

"Is today real?" Momma shakes her head and falls back into her seat.

"I need a drink." Daddy steps into the kitchen, returning with a bottle of whiskey and glass.

"What... What should I tell him?" I ask nervously as I sit down.

"You tell him no," Daddy tells me as he fills a glass.

"But ... he offered us so much money, Daddy." A thousand gold a month... I still can't wrap my head around it.

"And you are our son," Momma asserts, taking my hand. "All the gold in the world couldn't replace you."

"But Momma..." I know what she's saying, but I still shake my head. "With money like that we could finally hire some help around here. We could expand the fields. You could both *retire*."

"I don't care." Daddy takes my other hand. "You're our boy. This is your home. Nothing and no one is ever going to change that, even the dammed prince."

"We love you," Momma says with a squeeze to my hand.

"I love you both, too," I respond, even though my mind is still reeling. "Is it okay if I go into town for a little bit? I kind of want to talk to some friends about this."

"Go right ahead, son." Momma nods with a smile. "Just make sure you're back in time for dinner."

"Yes ma'am." I stand and hug them both.

I jog upstairs to my bedroom to replace the shirt I took off in the barn—I need to remember to grab that or it'll smell like the cows for days. Once I'm redressed, I head back downstairs and out the front door, walking down the dirt road away from the farm. Here, away from everyone else, I feel like I finally have the space to breathe.

What... What the heck just happened? Why was the prince at my house? How did he even find it? Okay, so maybe it's not actually that hard to find. But why would he want me to be his consort? I'm nobody, just a dumb hick. He talked to me for maybe fifteen minutes. What could he have possibly seen in me?

I head straight to Violet's house, knocking on the door way too hard. She looks surprised to see me when she answers, and behind her I can see two of our other friends, Monica and Ricky. Suddenly, I'm a little more hesitant to ask for advice.

Monica and Ricky are the same age and went to the same school as Violet and I. They've also been a couple for a few years now. They're fine, but the way they baby talk to each other can get a little gross. Monica is the daughter of the town baker, with brown eyes and mousy brown hair that she keeps in a ponytail. She's a nice girl, usually very quiet and shy, at least when she's not around Ricky.

Ricky is ... fine. Okay, honestly, he can be kind of a jerk sometimes. Don't get me wrong, I like the guy. He can just be kinda ... snobby. Which is saying something in a small town like ours. His family owns another farm in town, about twice the size of ours, and he lives there with his parents and two younger siblings. He's a few inches shorter than me with a slimmer build but just as much muscle, and he has light brown hair and green eyes.

"Peter!" Violet pulls me inside and leads me to where our friends are sitting. "I am *so* glad you came over. I was just telling them about what happened with the prince at the market this morning. I didn't have a chance to talk to you before you left!"

"I might have some more news about that..." I grimace as I take a seat on a chair next to the couch.

"Oh my god, what happened?" she asks with excitement as she takes her own seat on the couch next to me.

"He came to the farm," I start to tell them about my afternoon.

"What!?" Monica jumps up from the other side of the couch to move closer to me. "Why was he there? What did he want?"

"He... He asked me to be his consort." I let the words spill out of me. No point in beating around the bush.

Violet lets out a high-pitched squeal and clamps her hand over her mouth. "*WHAT?!*"

"Holy shit, seriously?" Ricky asks from his spot on the middle of the couch.

"Yeah, he said he ... really liked meeting me at the market and..." I can feel myself start to blush, and I trail off, remembering his words. *He called me Sunshine. He said he wanted me from the moment our eyes met.*

"You?" Ricky continues to sound shocked. "What did he see in *you*?"

"What the hell is that supposed to mean?" Violet defends me, slapping Ricky on the arm.

"Honeybun, that wasn't very nice." Monica turns and pouts at him.

"Aww, I'm sorry, pumpkin. I didn't mean it like that." *Might be nice if he apologized to* me... "I only meant that it doesn't make sense for the prince to want *anyone* from Weston as a consort. There's nothing special here."

"That's what I thought..." I ignore the way his words bring me down. "It doesn't matter because I told him no."

"You did *what?!*" Violet is scandalized.

"I told him that I couldn't leave the farm, that my parents need me here," I explain, even though that was far from the end of it. "So then he offered my parents money. *A lot* of money. Enough for them to hire some farmhands to replace me and then some."

"How much?" Ricky asks and is smacked on the arm again. "Oww. Sorry."

"A lot," I repeat, not wanting to tell them *everything*. "And I'm supposed to give him an answer in the morning."

"This is amazing!" Violet claps her hands together in excitement.

"No, it's not!" I look at her like her head just exploded.

"What are you talking about?" She fixes me with a stern look. "You can't tell me you've never thought about this before."

She knows I have. We used to talk about it all the time. Moving to the city, being swept off my feet by the prince, getting to live in the castle ... and then the other, more private things that take place behind closed doors. It was one of the only ways I knew boys were even *allowed* to like other boys.

"That was different." I curl in on myself. Ricky and Monica both know, but it still feels weird to talk about with them. "Before, it was just a fantasy. It was never going to be real. What am I supposed to do: just say yes? Leave the farm, my family, all of you?"

"Yes!" Monica exclaims, jumping up again. "I... I mean..."

"She means it's an opportunity," Ricky explains for her. "One you should really think about taking."

"Come on. Isn't there at least some part of you that wants to say yes?" Violet fixes me with a knowing look.

"Maybe." I sigh and shake my head. "But I still can't do it. I can't just leave everyone. This is my home."

"Yeah, alright." Violet sighs, disappointed. "I understand. But I still think you should—"

A series of loud coughs suddenly rings through the house—Violet's father. She mumbles a small apology as she exits the room to take care of him. Violet is an only child like me, and her mother died when she was really young, so it's just been her and her father most of her life. She's the only one here to take care of him.

He first got sick a few months ago. It was just a small cough at the start, but then he started coughing up blood, and since then he's gotten much weaker. He's always tired, and he's lost a lot of weight. Violet has tried to step in for him, but her blacksmithing skills aren't nearly as good as his yet. She comes by the farm about once a month to reshoe the horses, and after paying her, my parents always send her home with a box of food. She's having an even tougher time than we are.

The three of us sit quietly and awkwardly until she comes back, no one mentioning her father or his mystery illness. We hang out for another hour or so, talking more about the prince and some of the other things that happened at the market today. The girls in particular needle me for more details, pushing me to admit what I found attractive about him. I tell them a little bit, like about his eyes, and his stubble, but after I look out the window and see how late it's getting, I say my goodbyes and head home.

I'm glad I had the chance to talk to Violet and the others, but I'm not actually sure if it helped. It seems like they just wanted to talk about all the fun and scandalous bits, and not the "leaving behind everyone and everything I've ever known" part. I sigh to myself when I reach the farm, no closer to making a decision one way or the other. I head for the open back door, pausing when I hear my parents talking inside.

"I can't believe we're even considering this." *That's my mom.*

"We're not considering this." *And there's Daddy.*

"He is!" Momma corrects him.

"Well, can you blame him?" Daddy counters, trying to see things through my eyes. "The prince did offer us a *lot* of money."

"Money that would go to us, not our son." She makes a good point, but it's one that makes me lean toward saying yes. "If he accepts, it's only because of us."

"We raised a good son, Mary," Daddy tries to console her.

"Too good." I can hear her sad smile. "We can't let him do this. We're supposed to make sure he lives a better life than we did, not the other way around."

"I don't want him to leave either, hun. He belongs here with us." I won't lie. It feels really good to hear my parents want so badly for me to stay. "But that's a decision he's going to have to come to on his own."

"I know. Why do you think I'm making fried cod and scrunchions for dinner?" *That's my favorite!* I knew I smelled something good.

"We'll have to hope that'll be enough," Daddy jokes with a sigh. "It would be a lot of money, though."

"What are you saying?" Momma sounds annoyed now.

"Not that we should take it. But you can't blame me for thinking about what we could use it for," he defends himself, sounding wistful. "We could hire those farmhands like we've been talking about for years. Replace all our old equipment. And you know the horses are getting up in years. Just like us."

"All the new horses in the world aren't worth our son," Momma says with finality. "He was our *miracle*, Ron. We thought we would never—"

"I know, hun. I know." Daddy sighs again.

As good as it is to hear my parents' words, I also can't help but think about everything they could use that money for. They'd never have to work again. With even more to think about, I quietly take a few steps backward, making sure to stomp my feet when I step onto the porch this time so they'll be sure to hear me arriving.

"Oh good, you're back!" Momma calls over her shoulder as she stands over the stove. "Dinner's almost ready."

"It smells great, Momma." I lean over to kiss her on the cheek.

"Son, I want to make sure you know you don't need to say yes to the prince," Daddy tells me as I join him at the table.

"I know that, Daddy." I nod, pulling in my seat.

"But you're still considering it," Momma says as she sets a plate for each of us on the table before grabbing her own.

"It's just ... so much money." It would change our lives forever.

"We're doing just fine on money," Momma insists, even though I know that isn't entirely truthful.

"I know we're okay," I lie with her. "I'm just trying to think about the future."

"We're the parents here." She reaches out to take my hand. "You let us worry about the future."

As nice a thought as that is, it's not realistic. What the future holds is them getting older, and my needing to take care of them, on top of running the farm by myself. I can't even wrap my head around that. At least if I accepted the prince's offer, I'd know they'd both be taken care of, even if I wouldn't be here to do it myself.

We spend the rest of dinner talking about the work we need to do on the farm. Daddy wants to till the east field tomorrow so we can put down our first batch of potatoes for next season. The conversation feels a little like they're just trying to distract me, but I go along with it anyway.

When I am finished helping clean up after dinner, I decide to call it an early night and head up to my bedroom. My parents both hug me longer than usual, and I can tell they both want to ask me about my decision, but they don't. I'm glad because I still have a lot to think about.

I flop down on the bed once I'm upstairs and in my room. I keep thinking about what Momma said about the future. And it's not that I don't want to do those things—I really do love the farm, and I love spending time with both of them—it's just going to be a lot of work. Not to mention expensive. And ... would saying yes to Prince Max really be all that much worse?

I mean, if I say yes, I'll get to travel outside of the village and see a real city. I'll get meet new people and try all sorts of new things. *I wonder what the food is like?* But if I stay here, then I know exactly what my future is going to be. Staying in this small town, on this farm, in this old house ... alone forever.

I know I'm making that sound like a bad thing. I don't mean to. I've just never really thought about the possibility of doing anything else. I know I'd basically be signing the rest of my life away to someone else, but ... maybe it wouldn't be so bad? Like Violet said, it's not like I've never fantasized about it.

That brings up another memory. I roll over to the side of the bed, sticking my hand under my mattress and feeling around. When my hands land on an old book, I pull it out, running my fingers across the worn-down cover and creased edges. This was one of my favorites.

It tells the story of a prince and the love he had for another prince of a country far, far across the ocean. The two had met only briefly, shortly before war broke out between their two nations. After learning that his love is being held captive by his tyrannical father, our hero travels to the country in secret, seeking to free him. The story is filled with all sorts of action and drama, and I swear I must have read it over a dozen times. In the end, our hero manages to defeat the evil king, end the war, and rescue his love—who he of course claims as consort. I'll let you figure out the rest.

I slowly flip through the yellowed pages, the details of the story coming back to me like an old friend. I used to eat this stuff up, constantly day-dreaming about what it would be like if I could meet a prince of my own. And now I have ... so is it really so crazy if I take a chance and say yes?

I can already tell I'm going to have a hard time sleeping tonight, no closer to making up my mind one way or another. I lay there, trying to read, trying to think, trying to sleep, but none of it takes. I turn and look out the window at the night sky. The house is quiet, my parents already in bed themselves. With a sigh, I roll out of bed and throw on some clothes.

I don't always sleep great, so sometimes at night I'll take a walk around the farm to clear my head. And I could really use it tonight. I can't believe I'm actually considering telling him yes. I can't believe that this is even a thing I can say yes *to*. It's a fantasy I used to think about a lot... but that's all I ever thought it would be.

I stop and lean against the fence, looking up at the moon. It's only about half full, the moonlight pouring over the fields. Almost on cue, a wolf howl fills the air. One that sounds almost lonely. If I say yes, I wouldn't just be the prince's consort. I'd be a werewolf's consort. And I have no idea what that means. But maybe I'm ready to find out.

CHAPTER 3

"I'm going to tell him yes."

"Son, no!"

"We told you: you don't need to do this."

"Please, just listen to me," I start, hoping my explanation will be enough. I was up most of the night and part of this morning thinking about what I was going to say to my parents. "I know you don't want me to do this, but it's just too good of an opportunity to pass up. I know money has been tight for a few years now, and it isn't getting any better."

"You let *us* worry about money," Daddy tries to correct me. "That's not your responsibility."

"But someday it will be." *A day that is closer than any of us want to admit.* "And the truth is, I actually think this could also be kind of a fun experience. Getting to leave the village, seeing the capital..."

"You make it sound like a vacation," Momma interjects, frowning. "More like being sold off. You're going to *belong* to the prince."

"Well, everyone says Prince Makseka is supposed to be kind. And... I don't think he's terrible to look at, either," I admit, too embarrassed to meet either of their gazes. "It's not like I've been getting a lot of dates around here." *I've had exactly zero.*

"Well, if... If that's really your decision, son," he tries to give me his blessing, right as Momma bursts into tears.

"I can't believe you're leaving us," she manages between sobs.

"Don't cry, Momma. It'll be okay." I immediately move to comfort her with a hug. "I promise that I'll write to you all the time, and I'm sure I'll be able to come visit." Not that I have any way of knowing that, but I don't think the prince would keep me from my family.

"I just never imagined that you'd ever leave Weston." She sniffles, squeezing me tight. "You've always been my little boy. This is where you belong—with us."

"I know, Momma, but I'm all grown up now," I assure her. "I gotta make some of my own choices."

"You picked some choice to start with." She pulls away, wiping her eyes on the back of her hand. "Alright, you better get upstairs and start packing. I have a feeling the prince won't be long, and I have to start breakfast."

"Yes, ma'am." I laugh at her quick shift in personality. "I love you."

"I love you too. Now go." She shoos me out of the kitchen and into the living room.

"Son..." Daddy follows me as I make my way upstairs.

"I hope you're not going to try and get me to change my mind." *Not after I made that little speech and everything.*

"I'm not. I just want to make sure you know how much we're going to miss you." He hugs me. "You can always come back here. This will *always* be your home."

"I know. I'm gonna miss you too. I'm gonna miss the farm, the town, everything." I have to break our hug before I get too emotional—Daddy hates crying—and turn to my closet to find my old backpack. "Who knows? Maybe the prince will get sick of me on the ride there and decide to send me back."

"It's gonna be hard to believe something like that could happen." The loud clattering of pots and pans from downstairs has us both looking at my bedroom doorway. "I better go see if your mother needs help ... before she burns the house down."

With Daddy gone, I look around my room and start to think about what I need to pack. Some clothes obviously and my toothbrush. I should probably shave too; I want to make sure I look my best! But what else? I take a little too long deciding on which clothes to bring with me, trying to figure out which count as my "nicest" clothes.

The outfit I end up wearing is one I haven't had on since we went to church last year for the winter solstice, a white shirt with black pants that are just a little too tight. After I fold and stuff some of my other shirts and pants into the bag, I pick out a few books too (not any of the steamy ones—the last thing I need is for the prince to know about those). I'm also thinking about bringing along some old letters and birthday cards, and maybe... Oh wait!

I return to my closet, digging through my box of old keepsakes until I find what I'm looking for: a folded piece of paper, yellowed from age. I carefully unfold it, revealing a charcoal drawing of me and my parents. The three of us are on a bench with me in the middle, all of us looking as happy as could be. We had it sketched at the village's annual harvest festival almost ten years ago.

I love this picture and carefully refold it so I can pack it with my other things. I have a lot of good memories of that day. All the candy apples, dancing to the music with Violet and my mom, getting lost in the corn maze... I really am going to miss this place. When I got into my bed last night, I don't think I realized it would be the last time I slept in it.

Not that I got much sleep. Even after my walk, I spent most of the night tossing and turning, unable to stop thinking about what the morning would hold. What I'd need to say. Including some last minute things I want to ask the prince about before I actually tell him yes. I yawn, buckling my bag closed and throwing it over my shoulder, wishing my bedroom a silent goodbye as I leave.

Back downstairs, the smell of something delicious draws me back to the kitchen. When I enter, my eyes are immediately drawn to the mountain of food on the table. There's a big stack of flapjacks, a giant bowl of scrambled eggs, more sausage than I've ever seen at once, and a plate of mom's home-made biscuits.

"This looks amazing, Momma," I praise as I eagerly take my seat, an empty plate in front of me. "How did you make all this so fast?"

"Your father helped," she says as she takes her own. "I don't know what kind of fancy chefs they have in the castle, but I guarantee they won't hold a candle to your own mother's cooking."

"I know they won't, Momma." I smile, already piling flapjacks onto my empty plate.

We make sure that our last meal together is a nice one. There's only minimal crying on Momma's part. We avoid talking about how I'll be leaving any minute now and just treat it like every other breakfast we've had together. I'm gonna miss this so much.

I'm just finishing my fourth flapjack when a knock on the front door stops us mid-conversation. We all share a look; we know the prince is here. After quickly swallowing down the last few bites on my plate, we move to the living room, where Daddy answers the front door.

"Your Highness, good morning. Please, come in." Daddy steps back, holding the door open.

"Thank you, Mr. Lambert," Prince Makseka greets as he and his entourage enter. "I hope you and your family are doing well this morning. Especially you, Peter," he says to me, a look of expectation on his face.

"I-It is good to see you, Your Highness." *Guess I'm back to stammering.*

"I believe you have an answer for me?" He stands in front of me, waiting.

"I do b-but... I was wondering if I could ask you a few questions myself, first?" I dare, already nervous about his answers

"Alright, go ahead." He nods, though behind him I can see Kamo huffing.

"If I say yes, will I be able to come back to Weston? To visit my family?" I told myself last night that if his answer is no, then mine would be the same.

"Of course," he answers right away, and I let out the breath I was holding. "We could even have them come and stay at the castle sometime. Soon, even."

"Really? That would be great." Even as relief floods my body, I prepare for my next request. "There was one other thing. I know your offer to my family was already incredibly generous, but... I have a friend. Her father, he's very sick. He has been for a while now, but we don't know what the illness is or how to help him."

"Your local healer wasn't able to figure it out?" Makseka tilts his head to the side as he asks.

"No, sir." I shake my head. "Dr. Connor said there was something wrong with his lungs, but he's not a magic user and wasn't able to figure out more than that."

"I see." He chews his lip for a moment. "Well, I'd be happy to send one of the castle's physicians to come and take a look. Magic or otherwise, they should hopefully be able to help."

"Really?" I confirm with a little too much excitement. "That... That would be amazing, sir."

"Of course. Was there anything else?" I answer the question with a shake of my head. "Does that mean you have an answer for me now?"

"Yes, Your Highness." I nod. "I accept. It would be an honor to be your consort." *I think that's what you're supposed to say.*

"Fantastic." He grins wide and then quickly takes both my hands in his. "Now then, I don't want to rush you, but we were due back in St. Kizis ... yesterday. Are you ready to leave?"

"Actually, sir... I need to run into town," I say, worried and not quite anticipating that we would be leaving *immediately*. "There's someone I need to say goodbye to in the village."

"Your Highness, we have been here long enough. We cannot—"

Prince Makseka puts one hand up to silence Kamo without turning around. "Can you be fast?"

"Yes, sir." I nod frantically. "I promise I will run right back."

"Then that's fine. Go right ahead," he says with a warm smile. "I'll be here waiting for you when you get back."

"Thank you so much." I make an awkward little bow before rushing out the door.

I run down the road as fast as I can, past the three carriages parked outside the farm. People stare as I rush into the village, not stopping until I reach Violet's door, pounding on it frantically. She looks annoyed, still half-asleep when she answers, at least until she sees that it's me.

"Peter? What are—"

"I said yes," I blurt out before she can finish. "I told the prince yes. I'm going to be his consort."

"Oh my god!" Her face brightens into a smile. "That's amazing!" Her smile falters for a second. "But I guess that means..."

"Yeah. I'm leaving." I nod. "Right now, actually. I just didn't want to go without saying goodbye."

"I'm going to miss you." She leans in for a hug. "You better write to me all the time. I want to know about *everything* that goes on inside the castle." She pokes me in the stomach.

"I will." I rub at the spot she poked. "I have more to tell you though. Before I said yes, I told him about your father. How he's sick, and how we haven't been able to find him help. He said that he's going to send a doctor from the castle! I know it's not a guarantee, but they still might—"

I'm cut off when Violet rushes forward to grab me in another hug, her voice breaking. "Thank you. Thank you so much."

"I just hope they can do something," I tell her, not letting go as she sobs against my chest.

But eventually, I know I have to. "I have to go, Violet. He's waiting for me to get back."

"Okay." She nods, sniffling. "Write to me as soon as you can though. I mean it! I want all the details about the prince and all the royal drama."

"I will. I promise." I smile at her request for gossip. "And I'll be back to visit. Tell the others I said goodbye. And your father, too."

"I will." She adjusts her now-askew headwrap. "Now get back to your prince."

With a final wave goodbye, I leave the town, running all the way back up the dirt road. I'm winded by the time I make it back to the farm and realize with a grimace that I'm also sweaty. Maybe I'll have time to change?

Everyone is still in the living room, waiting for me when I enter, out of breath. The prince stands when I approach, obviously eager to see me again. But then he sniffs the air as he moves toward me, and his face shifts to suspicious.

"Good to have you back," he says cooly. "Did everything go alright saying goodbye to your..." Another sniff. "Girlfriend?"

"Girlfriend?" *How'd he know Violet was a girl?* "Not a girlfriend. Just a friend. My best friend, the one whose father needs the doctor."

His face softens when he hears my answer, his shoulders even drooping a little. "Sorry. When I smelled her on you, I just thought..." He trails off and shakes his head. "It doesn't matter. Alright, it's a long trip back to the castle, so you'll need to be ready for at least two days of travel."

"I'm already packed," I say with confidence before looking down at my sweaty shirt. *So much for changing.*

"Wonderful," Kamo interrupts. "Then if everything has been taken care of, we can leave. Your Highness?"

"Give him a minute to say goodbye to his parents, Kamo." Prince Makseka rolls his eyes and turns to me. "Sorry. Take your time, really. We'll be outside." He walks over to my parents. "Mr. and Mrs. Lambert, I want to thank you for your hospitality. I promise I will take good care of your son."

"Thank you, Your Highness," Daddy says with all the composure he can muster while Momma remains silent, probably afraid of what she might say.

"Momma... Daddy..." I start as the royals leave. Before I can continue, Momma wraps her arms around me and bursts into tears.

"I c-can't believe you're l-leaving us..." She sobs into my chest.

"Momma, please don't cry." I rub her back, trying to console her and not cry myself. "You heard him. I'll be able to come back whenever I want. You and Daddy will even be able to visit me at the castle!"

"It's just hard to lose you, son," Daddy explains as he joins our hug. "Remember, you always have a home here, no matter what."

"I know." I squeeze them both tightly. "I love you both, and I'm going to miss you so much."

After we share a few more minutes of teary-eyed goodbyes, it's finally time for me to go. I throw my bag over my shoulder, and my parents follow me to the door outside. As they wait on the porch, I say one final goodbye to the farmhouse, turning toward the carriages, the prince, and my new life.

"There you are." Prince Makseka flashes me a bright smile as I approach.

"Yes, sir." I drop my bag on the ground. "I'm ready to go."

Before I realize what's happening, one of the knights comes up and picks up my bag, bringing it to the rear carriage. Figuring that's where I'll be riding, I start to follow her until a shoulder on my hand stops me. I turn and see the prince watching me with a look of confusion.

"Aria is just loading your bag with some of the other luggage," he explains before patting the side of the middle carriage. "You're riding with me."

Up close, I can see that it's actually bigger than the other carriages, bigger and with more detailing. Kamo holds open the door for the prince, revealing the plush red seats and fabric lined walls inside. After climbing in, the prince turns around to offer me a hand up.

"This is so nice," I say as I sit down, in awe of the interior. I've never sat on anything besides a hard wooden bench before, and none of those carts had a *roof*.

"I know this is all really sudden," Prince Makseka says as he takes the seat opposite me. "I'm really looking forward to getting to know you on the ride."

"Your Highness, I am sorry to interrupt." Kamo pokes his head in through the still open door. "If you will remember, before we left the castle, there were a number of matters that required your attention. Studying for your upcoming university examinations, reviewing the trade deal with Lutheria you pushed for, as well as completing the report for your father on the results of this outing to Blackport..." He holds a large stack of papers in both hands, holding them for the prince to take. "You will need to read through these by the time we arrive. Some require your signature."

"Ugh, seriously Kamo?" He flips through the thick stack with a frown. "This is a week's worth of work at least."

"I am sorry, Your Highness," Kamo apologizes, but I swear I see the hint of a smile on his face. "But as you know, we were due back at the castle yesterday. It cannot be helped."

"Alright, sorry gorgeous." Prince Makseka gives me an apologetic look. "The responsibilities of a prince never really end. I'll try to get through these as fast as possible."

"It's okay. I understand." I nod. Looks like I'll be in charge of entertaining myself.

I wave goodbye to my parents on the porch as we pull away from the farm, Momma holding on sadly to Daddy's side. I watch as we pull away from the village, the familiar sights fading in the distance. Soon enough, the outside is filled with forests and hills that I've never seen before, and I'm glued to the window.

"Is it really that interesting?" The prince's question startles me.

"Sorry, I've never been this far outside of Weston before." I feel embarrassed and turn back to the new sights and sounds. "This is all new."

"No, the look on your face as you were watching the landscape... It was cute. Endearing even." He looks bashful himself for a moment before looking out the window himself. "I wish I could see it through your eyes."

"How's the reading coming?" I ask, eyeing the stack of papers that he's barely managed to work through.

"Mind-numbingly boring," he complains, flipping through them. "I'm sorry. I was looking forward to spending this ride getting to know each other."

"Well... We'll still have time for that when we reach the capital, won't we?" I try not to sound disappointed.

"I'll make sure of it." He nods. "And if you think all this is great, you'll love when we reach the city. I can't wait to show you around."

"That sounds nice," I tell him with a small smile.

After that, the prince goes back to reading, and I go back to staring out the window. At some point, my lack of sleep finally catches up to me, and I pass out, waking to the prince gently shaking my shoulder.

"Morning, sleepyhead." I see him smiling down at me. "We just stopped for lunch. I would have woken you earlier, but you looked peaceful."

"I guess I needed a little extra sleep." I try not to feel embarrassed as I rub the sleep from my eyes.

"Come on. Let's get out and stretch our legs and get something to eat." The prince leads the way out of the carriage.

Outside, I see the knights and Kamo have already exited their own carriages. One of them, a dwarf with dark skin, passes around what look like sandwiches pulled from a leather bag. I try not to stare, but I haven't seen many dwarves before, let alone a dwarf werewolf. There are dwarves, elves, orcs, and all kinds of people living on Litkalaa, but humans outnumber them all by a lot.

As the prince is speaking with Kamo, I sit in the shade of a tree and take a bite, figuring out that the meat is chicken, which is a little dry, but I remind myself that not everyone's sandwiches are gonna be as good as Momma's. As I eat more, I start to feel a little homesick.

"Is it true you've never left Weston?" I look up to see one of the knights, the woman who took my bag, standing over me.

"Yes." I nod, wiping the crumbs from my face. "This is the farthest I've ever been from home."

She looks a little surprised by that info but doesn't say anything else, joining her fellow knights. They are all seated together, being spoken to by Kamo, though they don't seem to be paying much attention. Finished with the advisor himself, Prince Makseka comes and sits with me, sandwich in hand.

"Do the others not like me being here?" I ask shyly. "That's the first time any of them has said anything to me."

"Oh no, it's not that. They just know I haven't gotten a chance to talk to you much and don't want to get in the way." He waves off my worries. "They're all pretty friendly once you get to know them."

"Do they come with you a lot?" I imagine the prince would only travel with the most trustworthy people. "Do you leave the castle very often?"

"They're my personal guard, though I don't get out nearly as much as I'd like to," he tells me after swallowing a bite. "There's always an event to prepare for or dignitaries to meet with or any number of other princely responsibilities to take care of. Although..." He leans in close, making sure that none of the others are listening. "Sometimes, I like to sneak out into the city. Not all the time. Just when I need to get away for a bit."

"Really?" I have to admit, I'm a little scandalized. "Isn't that dangerous?"

"Enh." He shrugs away my concern. "I'm always in disguise, so it's not like anyone knows who I am."

"What's it like there, in St. Kizis?" I'm really eager to learn more about it.

"Different from what you're used to, I'm sure." He takes another bite. "There are farms on the plains around the outside of the city, much larger than any of the farms they had in Weston. But things are packed together pretty tightly inside the city's walls, with more people than you could possibly imagine. There are a few small parks, but it's mostly buildings and roads everywhere you turn."

I try to wrap my head around all of that as I eat my sandwich. The city sounds big and exciting but also like you could easily get lost. And I still don't know what it will be like in the castle. But before I can ask more, Kamo has called the prince back over, and I am alone again.

We don't stop for long, and once everyone has eaten, we're back on the road for more of the same. Which means me entertaining myself (and trying not to nap) while Makseka pores over his papers with a frown. When the sun starts to set, we stop again, this time to set up camp for the night.

Dinner is more sandwiches, but there sadly isn't a lot of talking this time, with everyone heading to bed so we can get a move on early in the morning. The prince has a tent of his own, and I'm surprised when I'm given one as well. It's not as fancy or big, looking just like the ones the knights share, but it's still nice. There's even a cot that for once isn't too small for me.

I lay there all night, once again unable to sleep as thoughts of my future flood my mind. I can't stop thinking about the city and what it will be like living in the castle. I think about how Momma and Daddy are doing without me, if *they're* able to sleep. I wonder if I'll ever actually have the chance to get to know the prince I agreed to basically give my life to.

Morning comes sooner than I want, with me having gotten even less sleep than I did the night before. Breakfast is only a few small sweet rolls, Kamo pushing us to get moving fast so we can arrive at the castle as soon as possible. I try to help the knights with breaking down the tents and packing up, but they won't let me, insisting that it's not work for a consort. Not really having an answer to that, I frown and leave them to it, climbing back into the carriage after the prince.

"Are you okay?" He looks at my exhausted face. "You look tired."

"I'm sorry." I grimace. "I didn't sleep very well."

"Was it the tent?" He sounds apologetic. "It takes some getting used to."

"No, it wasn't that." I shake my head, though I guess that was part of it. "I was just up too late thinking."

"Are you feeling nervous?" I can't help but nod yes to the direct question. "Well, don't be. I know this is a lot, but I promise, you'll feel much more relaxed once we get to the castle."

"Yes, sir, Your Highness." I hope he's right, but for now, I'm still a bundle of nerves.

There's a little more small-talk after that, but soon he's back to his papers, now more than halfway through the pile. At some point, I nod off again, waking a few hours later when the carriage drives over a bump in the road. As I wipe my eyes, I look out the window to see grassy plains stretching out ahead—and a farm!

It's huge with acres of fields full of crops and livestock. They look like they're being tended to by dozens of farmhands, all working together. I can only imagine the amount of people you'd need to work that much land. And if there are as many people living here as the prince said, they must need the food.

I sit up, poking my head out of the window so I can see the city ahead. St. Kizis is large, which makes sense since it is our country's capital. There is a large stone wall surrounding the outside, the roofs of some of the buildings visible over the top. Behind those are the castle, elevated by the hill it sits on. I know from stories that the castle sits on the border of the city and the forest behind it, the domain of the royal werewolves. They say that on the nights of the full moon, you can hear the howls for miles. Unable to help myself, I lean farther out of the window to try and see more, banging my knee against the wall and getting the prince's attention.

"Oh great, we're almost home." The prince puts down his papers, peering out the window with me.

"You were right. It's amazing," I tell him, still in awe. "I've never seen so much farmland."

"Believe it or not, even all of this isn't enough to keep everyone in the city fully fed," he comments as we pass a windmill. "We have to have a lot of things imported from villages like yours."

"Hard to believe that we could ever compare to a place like this." I wouldn't even know where to start running a place that big.

"Places like your village have lots of things to offer," he says with a smile. "But just wait until we're inside."

I don't have to wait long. About fifteen minutes later, the carriages slow to a stop as I hear a loud creaking sound that must be the city gate. When we start moving again, the sound beneath us changes as the carriages cross from dirt onto stone.

The clip clop of the horse's feet on the city streets is loud, and the ride gets bumpier, but I am too drawn in by the sights around us to pay them much attention. There are so many buildings here, all crammed together, some two or three stories high. They mostly seem to be made of the same peach-colored brick with shingled roofs that vary in color between blue and gray.

And more than the buildings are the people. So many people, all staring as we pass by. Some point at us as they speak excitedly to one another while others watch with less-than-pleased expressions. Some children try to run alongside us, jumping up to try and peek into the window and see who might be inside.

"Like what you see?" Once again, the prince surprises me, and I blush as I realize how closely he's been watching me. *By now he probably thinks I'm just some dumb hayseed.*

"It's..." *Big, crowded, exciting, scary.* "...very different from Weston. You were right. There are so many people here."

"I really can't wait to show you around." He scooches closer to the window on his side. "Look there, see that bakery?" He points at a building whose sign is a baked loaf of bread. "That's one of the places I like to sneak out to. I go there almost every week. They make the *best* cupcakes."

"And nobody there knows you're the prince?" I still can't believe he does that.

"If they do, they're really good at pretending," he says, looking a little cocky ... which looks good on him.

The prince points out a few other locations as we ride up the winding road to the castle. A nice restaurant, his favorite tavern, the home of one of his friends—who doesn't know his real identity. Eventually, the carriage stops again and there is another gate-opening sound—we must have reached the castle. Another stone wall passes us outside as we cross over a moat until we are inside the castle walls and come to a final stop.

"Come on." The prince is already standing, papers forgotten on his seat. "We have a lot to do before the day is over. Tons of people to introduce you to."

People like the king and queen, probably. I stay silent, my nerves getting the better of me as I exit after Prince Max. We seem to be in a large garden (or I guess it's called a courtyard?), one that looks like it's been well tended to. I even see a couple of gardeners trimming a hedge at one side. The large doors of the castle's main entrance are right in front of us, the tall stone towers hovering above ominously. *Welcome to your new home, Peter...*

CHAPTER 4

"**C**ome on. Let's head inside."

The prince manages to break the trance the castle puts me under. To my left, the knights are unloading the carriages. I feel like I should help, at least to take my own bag, but before I can, Prince Makseka is bounding up the stairs without looking back, and I decide it's better to follow him for now. Hopefully I'll be able to get my stuff later.

The giant wooden doors are automatically opened by the two guards standing outside them as the prince approaches. The room we enter into is *huge*, maybe bigger than the entire farmhouse. The floor is a shiny, polished marble, and on the walls are large windows stretching all the way from the floor to the ceiling. And speaking of the ceiling, hanging above us is a sparkling crystal chandelier.

A plush red rug runs through the center of the room and leads up a large staircase in front of us, with guards stationed on either side at both the top and bottom. There are other guards posted in other locations around the room, outside of the different doors and hallways I can see on the first and second floors from where we are standing. This place is so over the top that I'm left speechless.

"I know. It's a lot, right?" The prince looks at me over his shoulder, where I'm standing with my jaw hanging open. "When you grow up around it, you kind of forget how ostentatious it all is until you leave and come back to it." *I think that's a fancy word for saying fancy?*

"I've never seen anything like it." I keep getting drawn back to the way the crystals above us catch the sunlight.

"I'll make sure you get a tour of the whole castle later," he says with a grin and reaches for my hand. "Now come on. I want to introduce you to my—"

"Your Highness." Kamo's voice cuts in from behind us. He catches up, handing the stack of forgotten papers to the prince. "I have been informed that your parents are currently busy entertaining visiting diplomats. As some of these papers are still incomplete, why don't you take care of them while you wait until they are available?"

"Yeah, I guess you're right." He sighs unhappily, accepting the stack and facing me with a frown. "Sorry, looks like you'll be stuck with me and these papers for a little while longer."

"Actually, sir, you can leave your future consort with me," Kamo corrects him. *He can?* "I will make sure he is properly prepared for when you present him to the king and queen."

"Prepared?" The prince is wondering the same thing as me.

"Well, sir, there is a *traditional* way to introduce a potential consort to the ruling king," Kamo explains. "It will only take a few hours, by which time your parents' business should be concluded. I will have a servant inform you when we are finished, and then we will await your arrival in the throne room. You are too young to have seen any past consort presentations, but I assure you, I only want to see that this is done properly."

"Alright, if you're sure," the prince agrees, then turns to me, taking my hand and kissing the back of it again. "Sorry to leave you, Sunshine, but I'll see you soon. Just stick with Kamo. He can be a lot too, but he'll take good care of you."

"O-Okay." I nod, feeling anxious again. I was just getting used to being around him.

"Thank you, Your Highness." Kamo bows as the prince turns and makes his way up the stairs.

Without another word, Kamo turns to the left and walks quickly from the room and down an open hallway. He's moving so fast that I stumble to keep up as he leads me down hall after hall. Before long, they all start to look the same, and I get worried that I might lose him around a bend. Eventually, the silence gets to be too much for me.

"Um, excuse me, Mr. Kamo, sir?" I call ahead, not even sure if he knows I'm still behind him. "I was wondering where—"

A loud sigh prevents me from saying more as the man comes to a stop.

"I know this is all new to you, but we do not have the time to explain all of the intricacies of becoming a royal consort to *you*." He adjusts his glasses as he turns around. "For now, all you need to worry about is doing what I tell you when I tell you. Am I understood?"

"Y-Yes sir." His tone leaves no room for argument, and it's pretty obvious that the guy doesn't like me.

"Good." He turns on his heel and continues walking forward. "You will be presented to the king and queen in a few hours. There is a certain protocol that will need to be followed, but before that, we will need to make you presentable."

Presentable? I mean, I guess what I'm wearing isn't up to his standards. That's fine. I'll wear whatever they want me to; I want this to go well.

Finally, we come to a stop with Kamo opening a door that's carved with images of waves and seashells. He leads me inside to a room covered from floor to ceiling in shiny white tiles. There is a large pool in the center, sunken into the floor and filled with steaming water. Along one wall is a long table under a mirror and some chairs, and there is a set of shelves next to an open door that leads to a toilet. We're in a bathroom. The fanciest bathroom I've ever seen. We only have an outhouse on the farm.

There are also two people in here with us, a man and a woman, and from the way they are dressed, I think they must be servants. They look to be around my age, maybe a little older, the woman's hair long and red while the man's is short, curly, and brown. They're both wearing what looks like long sleeveless white robes that are cinched at the waist with their arms bare. Kamo doesn't come to a stop until he's standing in front of them.

"Daniel, Hannah," Kamo greets them both in turn. "I trust there have been no issues in my absence?"

"Of course not, sir." Daniel shakes his head, then peeks around Kamo to me. "Who's this?"

"This is the prince's intended consort," he says with a sigh. Daniel and Hannah both look shocked. "He will be presented to the king and queen later today. I need the two of you to get him ready."

"We can certainly clean him up and do something with his hair," the woman, Hannah, offers.

"No-no." He waves her suggestion off. "I need you to prepare him according to the *old* standards for consort presentations."

"Are you sure, sir?" Hannah narrows her eyes in confusion.

"Don't question me. It is my job to make sure all of our rituals and customs are still being followed," Kamo answers snootily. "I will return to collect him in two hours. You have until then to prepare him. I trust you will succeed."

"Of course, sir. He'll be ready." Daniel nods. "Is there anything else we should know?"

"You do not need to worry about dressing him," Kamo informs the two of them. "I will have his outfit with me when I return."

"Understood, sir." Hannah nods as well. "We will see you in two hours."

"You are to obey them just as you would me—or anyone else I say, for that matter," Kamo tells me with a pointed finger before turning and leaving me in the bathroom.

"Alright, everything off." Daniel wastes no time, gesturing to my body.

"In front of you?" I can't help but feel a little scandalized.

"We see naked people in here every day," Hannah says a little more gently. "I promise it's nothing we haven't seen before."

"And we're gonna see it one way or another, bub." Daniel shrugs. "No real point in hiding it now."

"O-Okay." I feel a tightness in my throat that forces me to swallow.

I begin to undress, deciding to start with my shoes and socks before anything else. Once those are off, I try to do everything I can to block out the two people staring at me right now, but my hands still shake as they reach for the buttons on my shirt. Daniel takes it from me after I pull it off while Hannah collects my socks and boots. They do the same when I slide off my pants next, and then continue to stare as I stand there awkwardly in my underwear. Like they're expecting me to...

"E-Everything?" I look down at my flimsy drawers.

"Yep." Hannah nods. "Need to know what we're working with."

"Besides, you're gonna have to get in the water, and you don't wanna get 'em wet, right?" Daniel's words offer me little comfort.

My hands hover around my waistband as I gather up the nerve to remove my underwear. I don't think I've been completely naked in front of anyone since I was a kid at the doctor. I don't even know these two, and they just expect me to... I take a breath and try to stop freaking out. *Just get it over with. It's not like you know the prince, and you'd still want him to...*

Before I can psych myself out, I hook my thumbs into my waistband and shuck them off, holding them out for someone to take with my eyes closed. I can feel my whole body starting to shake, and I can't help my other hand from doing what it can to cover my dick. When I feel someone take the small cotton shorts from my hand, I dare to peek an eye open.

"Not bad." It's Hannah looking me over, and her words make me blush.

"It's a shame we're gonna have to get rid of all that hair." Daniel looks at me with a frown, sounding disappointed.

"What's wrong with my hair?" The hand that was holding my underwear goes to the top of my head.

"Not that hair." Daniel shakes his head and gestures lower. "Your body hair."

"Consorts are *traditionally* kept shaved from the neck down," Hannah says with a slight grimace.

"You're going to shave me?!" My hand moves to join the other one in covering my crotch.

"As fun as that might be, we don't really have the time," Daniel answers as he walks toward a shelf of bottles and jars, retrieving one and turning around. "Instead, we're going to use this."

"What is it?" Besides a large glass jar filled with something white.

"Depilatory cream." I give Hannah a confused look at that word. "It gets rid of your hair."

"Do... Do we have to?" I look between them, pleadingly.

"Afraid so," Hannah says with an apologetic frown.

"Is it permanent?" *I don't know if I want to be hairless for the rest of my life.*

"No, but we'll cross that bridge when we get to it." Daniel smiles, opening the jar as he returns. He and Hannah each scoop out a large portion with their hands before holding it in my direction. "Go ahead. Take some."

"Me?" I look at the jar apprehensively.

"I mean if you want us to apply it to your crotch and ass, we can do that. I just figured..." Daniel shrugs, but my eyes go wide. *Even my...?* I can feel my cheeks clench uncontrollably. *They really do mean everywhere.*

Tentatively, I reach out and scoop out my own handful. It feels cold in my hand, is as white as a bottle of milk, and has the consistency of butter. I start to slowly bring it toward my crotch, hovering over it as I remove my other hand. Just as I'm gathering up the nerve to start applying it, two different sets of cold hands on my back make me jump forward and mash my cream filled hand against my crotch.

"Sorry, we probably should have warned you," Hannah apologizes behind me.

Sighing, I start to rub the smeared cream across my groin, the golden yellow of my pubic hair vanishing beneath the white. At the same time, Hannah and Daniel return to rubbing their cream-covered hands on my back. They might be letting me take care of my own privates, but I guess they're gonna help me with the rest. I'm not the hairiest back there, but I'm far from smooth.

I start to spread the cream lower, and then ... behind me, as they work in tandem on my upper body. Their hands go everywhere: shoulders, arms, armpits, chest... I shriek in surprise when I feel a hand slide into my butt crack, though it pulls away immediately.

"Sorry!" Daniel holds both hands up, looking guilty. "For a second I forgot that you already had that covered. My mistake."

I'm too embarrassed to say anything and remain silent while they finish their work. They move lower, getting my thighs, legs, and the tops of my feet. Then, after double checking that we didn't miss anything, they declare that I'm done.

"Now we wait about fifteen minutes." *I have to stand here naked and slathered in this stuff for fifteen whole minutes?!*

My hands move back to cover my crotch as I wait, humiliated. At least the cream makes it harder to tell that my whole body is bright red. I can hear Daniel and Hannah making small talk that they thankfully do not try to include me in. After a while, the cream starts to feel warm and tingly on my skin before long, but before I can ask about it, my time is up.

"Okay, that should be enough," Hannah declares my torture to be over. "Go ahead and get in the water and rinse off." She points to the bath at the center of the room.

I manage to hold off from covering my butt when I turn toward the pool, wanting to climb in as quickly as possible. There is a small ladder leading into the water, which is deep enough to reach the bottom of my chest. Like I thought, it's already warm, and I dunk my full body underneath it, head and all.

When I come back above water, I look down to see that the cream is already rinsing off and taking my hair with it. I run my fingers down my now smooth chest. The sensation is different, and not just because I'm missing my hair. My skin actually feels more sensitive. Seeing as there's no point in delaying things any further, I sink back down until I am submerged up to my neck, and begin running my hands over my body, removing all of the excess cream and hair.

My crotch in particular feels weird. I run my hand above my dick, where my pubic hair used to be. I remember being twelve and how excited I was when they first came in. Lower than that are my balls, which feel as smooth as a pair of eggs rolling around in my hand. And then even lower is my... Okay, I won't pretend like I've never played with my own butt before. I was curious to see what it would feel like! Which wasn't this—a smooth valley between two shaved peaches.

When I'm satisfied that I've gotten everything, I stand and turn to the tub's ladder, ready to get out. As I start to climb out, Daniel and Hannah both wave at me to stop, shaking their heads.

"Just go ahead and soak for a while," Hannah tells me. "You look like you could use it."

"The cream should have gotten everything, but we'll get any spots that were missed with a razor when you get out," Daniel says with a nod.

"...Thank you." I let go of the ladder and sink back down into the water.

The two of them go back to their small talk, leaving me with my thoughts. Thoughts that are currently about the prince, the castle, and everything else that's been going on. They've been friendly enough... Maybe these two would answer some of my questions?

"Is... Is this what you two do for work here?" My question catches both of them off guard, though neither looks put off by it.

"Well, not *this* in particular, usually." Daniel gestures in a small circle. "New consorts are a rare occurrence. You're technically our first!"

"We are in charge of a lot of the beauty and wellness needs of the royal family," Hannah explains. "We've been here about six years now. We trained under and assisted the castle's last esthetician. When she retired two years ago, the queen promoted us both in her place."

"We mostly work with the queen and the king's consort," Daniel continues. "But we also assist the king and the prince, as well as their guests and some of the others living in the castle, things like hair and makeup."

"Not clothing, though," Hannah adds. "Fashion is all Trixie's department."

"Do... Do you know a lot about the prince?" I hesitate to ask.

"Probably more than most people," Hannah guesses. "Why? What do you want to know?"

"Is... Is he nice?" *Ugh, that is such a stupid question.* "Do you think he'll like me?"

"I mean, you already know the answer to that," Daniel answers next. "I doubt he would have brought you back to the castle if he didn't."

"The prince is a kind man," Hannah informs me. "We don't see him often, usually just for a haircut every few weeks, but he's always been polite and understanding with us."

"I think he hit on me once. Ow." He rubs his arm at the small smack Hannah gives him. "I didn't say it was a bad thing!"

"I've never … done anything like this before." I bite my lip between my teeth. "I'm worried I'm going to screw something up."

"Listen, for all the pomp and circumstance that Kamo wants to play up, it's really not that complicated." Daniel is at least straight with me. "It's a relationship. You're either compatible or you're not. Oww! Will you stop hitting me!?"

"If the prince sees something in you, then I don't think you have anything to worry about." Hannah ignores her coworker's complaints. "Now, I don't think we ever got your name. I'm Hannah, and this is Daniel."

"I'm Peter." I didn't even realize I never told them. "It's nice to meet you. Thank you for talking to me. And helping me."

"That's what we're here for," she responds with a warm smile. Maybe I just made a couple of friends?

I soak for a little while longer, this time included in some of their small talk. After about ten minutes, they tell me to get out, and as I stand there, wet and naked, they closely inspect my body for stray hairs. My hands are fisted at my sides as they look at my crotch and butt, but thankfully the only stray hairs they find are on my thighs and lower back. They make quick work of those with a sharp blade before giving me the all clear.

"I love your hair color," Hannah comments as they finish. "It's light enough that you'll be able to get away with an extra day or two of not shaving."

"I have to *keep* doing this?" I ask, wary.

"Maybe, if this is what Kamo is pushing for." Daniel frowns. "But you'll have us here to help."

Satisfied, they send me back into the tub, this time with soap and sponge to give myself a good scrub. They tell me that the water is heated and filtered with magic, so I don't have to worry about any of my removed hair floating around. This time when I get out, I'm given a fluffy towel to dry off with, and when I'm finished with that, they apply an oil to my skin that they say will help with any irritation, along with making me "glow," in their words.

Once I've air-dried enough, they give me a nice fluffy white robe to slip on and steer me into a chair in front of the wide mirror so they can fuss over my hair. I don't really need a haircut, but they still insist on at least cleaning it up. They also make sure my face and neck are cleanly shaved, pluck my eyebrows, and trim and file my nails.

It's a lot of stuff I never really cared much about before, but when I look at myself in the mirror afterward, I can't deny that they did a good job. I look different, maybe a little *too* cleaned up, at least compared to what I'm used to. And after that, they declare their work finished! *Phew.*

I'm sitting in the chair, listening to Daniel and Hannah tell me about some of the latest castle drama (one of the cooks got caught in a closet with one of the maids—who is *married*!), when we hear the door open, signaling Kamo's return. All gossiping stops, and both servants gently lift me from my seat. As Kamo approaches, they move to stand behind me.

"Take off the robe so I can see." He gestures to my only covering.

My hands are back to shaking as I undo the tie at my waist, but I calm myself, letting the robe slip from my shoulders as it is caught by one of the people behind me. Kamo's eyes begin to scrutinize me, running up and down my naked body. I shut my eyes, willing myself to not cover up.

"Hmmm. Here." He holds out his hand, something gold-colored between his fingers. "Put this on."

I take the item, and realize that it's fabric—clothing of some kind. Like a pair of underwear but much tighter and covering a lot less. I look at Kamo to see if he's serious, but his scowl tells me to just shut up and put it on. I awkwardly bend over, stepping into what I think are the leg holes. It stretches around my thighs and butt as I pull it up, and as a thin strip of fabric slides up my crack, I realize the back has even less fabric than I originally thought— my entire ass is basically on display.

"I suppose that will have to do," Kamo says with a sigh, his dismissal making me shrink. "Now come along. The royal family will be ready any minute now."

He starts to walk away, intending for me to follow him wearing nothing but this … thing. I try to follow but stutter in my steps, a hand on my arm steadying me.

"Sir? Hannah starts, holding the robe. "Don't you think he could at least wear—"

"No," Kamo answers before she can finish. "He will be expected to wear however much or little as the prince will allow. Better for him to get used to it now. Now come with me. I'd rather not repeat myself a third time."

Hannah and Daniel both look sorry as I am made to exit the room. Kamo is once again walking fast enough to have me scrambling, which is made all the worse by what I'm wearing. I can feel the eyes of every servant or guard on me we pass in the hall. I do my best to ignore it, to focus on following Kamo, but it's enough to wish the ground would just swallow me up.

Eventually, after we climb two different sets of stairs, we enter what must be the throne room—which I figure on account of the two thrones placed on the platform at the back of it. Large red tapestries hang from the walls, each bearing the royal crest, and the floor is covered in the same thick red carpet

I've seen elsewhere. There are several guards, posted by the doors we entered through, at the sides of each throne, and at another set of doors behind them.

"Kneel here," Kamo orders as he leads me toward the center of the room, pointing at a spot on the carpet in front of the raised platform.

Just kneel? Okay... I sink down at the spot he indicates, feeling silly that I'm doing it almost naked. He quickly moves to adjust my positioning, fixing my posture and spreading my legs with his feet.

"Keep your hands behind your back," he says, stepping back to look me over, but then he freezes, his ears perking up. "This will have to do—they are here. Remain silent, and do not speak until you are spoken to."

He moves to stand in front of me, fanning out his cloak as if to hide me from view behind him. I can't see much from my position, but a second later, I hear the doors ahead of us opening, and what sounds like several people walking inside. *How did he know? Oh right, werewolf hearing.*

"Your Highness," Kamo starts to address who I assume is the king, "it is good to see you and the queen again after my time away."

"Good to have you back, Kamo." *That must be the king.* "This place runs much smoother with you here. Now, my son tells me there is someone here he would like us to meet?"

"Yes, Your Highness," Kamo says with a little bow. "It is my pleasure to introduce you to your son's future consort."

With that announcement, he steps aside to reveal me, and I can only stare at the floor in front of him. The room goes deadly silent, sending my nerves into overdrive. *Why is no one saying anything?* I gather up the courage to look up and see the royal family looking down at me. King Samoset and Queen Anna look as regal as I would have expected, the king in a fine pair of black slacks and a white long-sleeved shirt with a red cape over his shoulders and a crown on his head. His dark hair matches his son's, though with a shiny golden crown sitting atop it. The queen is wearing a long, dark green dress and the same type of cape, along with a smaller but no less majestic crown of her own. She has dark brown hair, but it's her blue eyes that really catch my attention, matching the prince's.

To the king's right is a man around their same age with light brown hair and eyes, and black pants and a green shirt that matches the queen's dress. The top of his shirt is unbuttoned, part of his chest exposed to reveal a golden chain around his neck—that must be Alden, the king's consort. Finally, on the queen's left is Prince Makseka. None of them look particularly happy, though Max at least looks more confused than upset.

"What are you wearing?" he asks, climbing down the stairs toward me. "And... Aww, what'd they do to all your fuzz?" I feel his hand ghost over my bare back and shoulders as he stands over me.

"I-I-I-" I look up at him in a panic, not sure what to do or say. I hear a noise of displeasure, and my eyes turn toward his family, who are now scowling at the two of us. The consort's hands are balled up into fists, and it looks like he might start shaking in anger at any minute.

"Leave us!" the king shouts to the room, making even Kamo jump in surprise. "Everyone!"

"And send in Enid, please," the queen tacks on, sounding less-than-pleased herself.

Oh gods, what did I do wrong? Panic fills my mind as I hear Kamo and the guards exit the room. I can still feel the prince standing at my side, but when another shadow starts to loom over me, I'm too terrified to look up.

"Here you go, dear." I jump when I feel the queen's hands, opening my eyes to realize she has just wrapped her cloak around my shoulders. "You must be cold."

Panicked again, I feel my mouth open, but no words come out.

"Son, what is the meaning of this?" the king asks from his spot near his throne.

"What do you mean?" The prince sounds offended. "I didn't ask for this!"

"I'm sorry!" I blurt, drawing all eyes back to me. "I... I don't know what I did wrong, but if you tell me, I can fix it. I can do better, I swear. Please don't reconsider the deal you made with my parents."

The room goes silent again, though this time I catch the look that everyone seems to share, not that I know what it means. Just as I start to worry again, the door behind the thrones opens, a stout, dark-skinned woman walking in. She has short black hair with small, deep-set eyes and is wearing a simple black dress with gold trim.

"Ahem." The queen clears her throat, offering me a hand to stand. "I don't believe we were given your name."

"P-Peter," I stutter, the queen smiling in response.

"Enid, could you please escort Peter to one of the castle's apartments?" she asks the approaching woman. "Make sure he is settled in and also get him some clothes?"

"Of course, ma'am." Enid nods her head as she offers me a hand up.

"I sh-shouldn't keep this." I start to take off the queen's cloak.

"I think you need that more than I do right now." Queen Anna stops me, hand on my shoulder. "Enid can return it to me later."

"Th-thank you." I look from her to her son, who's frowning but says nothing.

"Come with me, Peter." Enid leads me by the arm out of the room. As we turn into the hall, I share one final look with Max as the door closes, only to get a look that is confused and maybe a little worried in return.

Enid leads me through the halls and up the stairs at a much slower pace than Kamo. It's nice, but my mind is a little preoccupied with whatever just happened in the throne room to give it much thought. I'd like to ask my new guide about it, but she wasn't there and I wouldn't even know where to start.

"Here we are," she announces as we approach a door. "This is one of the nicer ones."

She opens the door and leads me into a room that is four or five times the size of my bedroom. It's huge with a massive four poster bed along one wall covered with dark purple sheets and a purple canopy above. There's a lounge chair, a dresser and wardrobe, and a small wooden table with a matching set of chairs. There's also a fireplace, a balcony, and I think an entrance to my own bathroom.

"Wow," I say, trying to take everything in. "This might be one of the nicest places I've ever been in."

"Well, it's all yours!" Enid tells me happily. "So why do you still look so mopey?"

"I... I think I might have messed up whatever was supposed to happen in the throne room," I tell her, clutching the cloak around me tighter in shame.

"Aww, I'm sure it can't be that bad," she tries to reassure me. "Give me a few minutes to go and find you something to wear, and then you can tell me all about it, okay?"

"Okay." I nod a little dumbly as the bubbly woman leaves the room.

Alone, I look around the nice room, worried that I might have screwed everything up before it even started.

CHAPTER 5

MAX

I watch silently as Enid, my mother's personal attendant, leads Peter from the throne room. Even if I couldn't see it on his face, I could smell his fear and anxiety as he kneeled in the throne room as soon as I got close. *And what was he wearing?* I feel awful. This isn't how I thought this was going to go at all.

It's only when I turn back to my parents that I realize how upset they all are. With me, specifically. At least we're alone, so we don't have to watch our words in front of anyone. Most of the people who work in the castle know what we're actually like, but it still feels like I can't really relax until I know I'm in good company.

"Son," my father starts with a sigh, "could you please explain what just happened?"

"Can *you* explain what just happened?" Papa, Dad's consort, asks *him*, sounding really, really angry.

"I thought you talked to Kamo about ending the 'traditional' aspects of consort presentations?" Mom asks next from my side.

"Don't look at me. It was one of the first things I did after taking the throne! You were both there!" Dad insists to both of his spouses. "He didn't do that at Kendra or Steven's presentations."

"Those were almost a decade ago," Papa points out. "And they were for the consorts of knights, not the crown prince."

"Perhaps he forgot?" Mom suggests, though it doesn't sound like she believes it.

"Maybe..." And from the way Dad shakes his head, he doesn't either. "I'm not sure why he would have suddenly brought these 'traditions' back now. Unless..." As he trails off, all eyes turn to me.

"I didn't ask for that!" I defend myself, my voice going a little too high. "All Kamo told me was that he was taking Peter to be 'properly prepared' before he was introduced to you. I didn't know that *that's* what he meant. I didn't even know that was a possibility!"

Okay, that last part is a little bit of a lie. I have actually heard about past consort presentations that were more ... revealing, like what just happened with Peter. My history tutor mentioned them once, but wouldn't go into much detail, so I had to hunt down the information in the library myself. It was *way* more interesting than anything Mr. Longfellow ever taught me about history—but I really thought it was just that, *history*.

"What did you *think* he meant?" Papa asks in that way parents do when they want to say that you should have known better.

"I just thought it was like when a foreign dignitary came through the palace," I answer honestly. "That he was taking Peter to get cleaned up, maybe put him in some nicer clothes. I figured there'd be some ... pomp and fanfare when he was introduced." I didn't plan for them to meet with Peter *kneeling in a gold thong*!

"Maybe you should start at the beginning." Mom tries to get everyone to calm down, taking her seat on her throne, while Dad does the same with Papa sitting on his lap. "We didn't even know you had been considering someone as a consort. When did you meet Peter?"

I can feel myself shrink before I even answer. "...Three days ago."

"*Three days ago?*" Three sets of eyes bulge out at that information.

"When did you... How did you..." Mom brings a hand up to her forehead and closes her eyes, taking a deep breath. "From the beginning, please."

"We were on our way back from Blackport," I get to explaining because I know stalling isn't going to make it sound any better. "We had just stopped in a village called Weston to rest for the night."

"I think I've been there, once," Dad interjects. "Small town, from what I remember."

"Very small," I confirm. "We weren't planning on staying, but then I learned about a street market taking place in the village square the next morning. I didn't think there would be any harm in delaying our departure by a few hours so I could see it. And that's where I met Peter."

"He's a merchant?" Mom asks, genuinely curious.

"A farmer," I correct her. "He lived and worked on a farm with his parents."

"So you met Peter at this market," Papa confirms. "How exactly did him becoming your consort come up?"

"It didn't, yet." I feel sheepish as I remember what I did next. "First I, uh, bought everything they had for sale."

Dad groans while Papa and Mom laugh. "And what happened after that?"

"Well, since they didn't have anything else to sell, they went home," I explain my plan. "I thought it would be easier to talk to him alone there."

"You followed him home? Aww" Papa seems to find that endearing. "Like a puppy."

"I waited a little bit before going, and I didn't *follow* him. He told me where he lived." *Well, he told me the name of his farm, and it wasn't hard to track him down after that.* "That's where I asked if he'd be my consort."

"You just asked him?" My mom sounds confused. "But you had *just* met him."

"Yeah, but Dad always told me that when I found the right person, I'd know." I bite my lip as I remember spotting Peter's blonde hair from across the village square. "And when I saw him in that market... When I *smelled* him... I just knew."

"While I'm sure your father *meant* well, he was also being a little overly romantic." She gives Dad some side-eye, who tries to sink into his throne. "There are other things that still need to be taken into consideration."

"This boy said yes after knowing you for only a few hours?" Papa seems just as skeptical as Mom.

"Well, no, not at first." *Oh gods, he's gonna hate this part.* "His first answer was no. He said that he couldn't leave because without him his parents would have no one to help them run the farm... So I offered to send them some money to make up for his absence."

"You did *what?!*" Papa stands, walking halfway down the stairs. "Is that what you think of me and your father? That he just walked down to the stables, offered my family some money, and moved me into the castle?"

"No, Papa, not at all!" I feel awful knowing I've hurt him like this. "I really thought I was doing a good thing. That I was helping."

"Son, you can't just offer people money like that." Dad shakes his head. "Especially not in exchange for their *son*."

"That's not what I was doing though!" I try to plead my case. "The offer was so that Peter's parents could hire farmhands to replace him. I thought he was telling me that it was the only obstacle to him leaving."

"How *much* money did you offer them?" Mom asks with some hesitation.

"...A thousand gold a month." All three of them groan at my revelation. "It's not like we can't afford it!"

"It's not about being able to afford it, son," Dad starts with a sigh. "That is a staggering amount of money to most people."

"So much that they might consider saying yes to something they do not actually want to do," Mom continues, grimacing.

"What? You think that Peter only agreed..." I pause, remembering the way Peter begged me not to go back on the deal before he left the room with Enid. "...Oh gods."

"Son..." Papa walks down the rest of the stairs and puts his hand on my shoulder. "Are you even sure he likes men?"

"Of course he..." I pause and think about everything he's told me. Beyond the occasional shy smile and wishful thinking about his nervousness, have I actually seen *any* indication that Peter is attracted to me? All I've smelt is fear and anxiety. "...Oh no. Papa, I didn't mean to... I didn't think I was..."

"Hey, hey, it's okay." Papa starts rubbing my back. "We're gonna figure it out."

"How do I fix this?" I ask all three of my parents.

"Well first, you need to talk to Peter," Dad tells me, standing from his throne. "Clear up any misunderstandings between you two."

"Which will be difficult to do with the offer you made to his parents hanging over you," Mom adds, standing herself, the two of them joining me and Papa. "And I'm afraid the only solution for that is to send his parents the gold regardless of his decision."

"I'll talk to the treasurer," Dad says with a sigh.

"You need to make sure he knows that there are no strings attached to his decision," Mom continues. "And that he understands exactly what his future holds if he chooses to stay. And go by the kitchens first. The poor thing is probably starving."

"If he went through what I did back then, he's probably also feeling confused, anxious, and humiliated," Papa tells me next.

"Was it really that bad, Papa?" It's not that I doubt him. I just wasn't there. I wasn't even born yet. "Why did you go through with it?"

"Because I loved your father," he answers simply. "And I knew I'd have him there afterward to help make me feel better."

"Okay." I nod to myself. "I'm going to fix this."

"That's my boy," Dad says as I leave the room.

"I'm not sure how that could have gone *worse*," a familiar voice teases as I enter the hall.

"You think you could have done better?" I challenge the young man who has likely had his ear to the door this entire time. "How much did you even hear?"

"Enough to wonder what could have possibly possessed you to try and *buy* someone from their parents," Oliver finishes, crossing his arms. "Seriously, Max?"

"I know, okay? Or did you miss my parents chewing me out?" I roll my eyes. "Are you going to help me, or what?"

"Of course, my prince." He bows dramatically.

I've known Oliver for five years now. Similar to what Enid does for my mother, and Kamo does for my father, Oliver is my personal attendant. He's also my best friend and probably the only person besides my parents who isn't afraid to speak his mind to me. When everyone around you just tries to kiss your ass, that's something you come to appreciate, even if he is kind of a smart-ass.

With my parents' words fresh on my mind, I'm determined to make things right with Peter. Taking my mother's advice, our first stop is down to the kitchens so I can get my boy something to eat. It's only when I get there and Mona, the castle's head chef and Oliver's mother, asks what I would want to bring him that I realize I have no idea what kind of food he likes.

"He's from Weston, right? Grew up on a farm?" I nod at Oliver's questions. "Then he probably won't want anything too fancy, so let's just keep it simple."

With their help, I end up filling a large metal tray with cheeses, fruits, some slices of ham, half a chicken breast, and about a dozen different kinds of bread, sweet rolls, and other pastries. Mona, Oliver, and the rest of the kitchen staff give me a strange look as I pile things on, but no one stops me.

"You sure this isn't too much?" I ask, looking over the hodgepodge of food on the tray.

"Oh it's *definitely* too much," Oliver assures me. "But I'm willing to bet he'll find that cute, and this way you can eat it together."

"Do I ... take it up myself?" I've never actually brought a tray of food to someone else before.

"Do you want him to know you're sorry?" Oliver asks and waits for me to nod. "Then yes, you take it up yourself."

So, with the large and unwieldy tray in both my hands, I make my way to Peter's guest apartment. Except as I start up the stairs, I realize that I am again missing some critical information, and have no idea which room Enid brought him to, or even what floor he's on right now. I grumble a few curses to myself, exiting the stairwell on the next floor to hopefully find someone to direct me.

Which turns out to be no easy task because the majority of the castle staff has been trained to avoid and even hide from us during the day. Kamo said something about remaining unseen and invisible while working. It's a weird rule, and not one that me or my family has ever asked for. It's actually something we've had to train *out* of our personal attendants. Do you know how weird it is to have someone clean your room and pick out the clothes you wear every day, and never talk to or even see them?

So I try to hunt down one of the castle staff to figure out where Enid took Peter. It's harder than I'd like—Kamo trained them well—and I have to use my hearing to pinpoint where some of the maids are hiding. It's a little strange, as I'm used to hunting things in the forest, not the castle. They're all nervous to be directly approached (though that doesn't stop them from giving the tray in my hands an odd look), and sadly, none of them know where Enid or Peter went.

I'm leaving one of the castle's many sitting rooms and am just about to give up when I catch a whiff of the most delicious scent—Peter's. It's still new enough that it stands out when compared to the dozens of others from the castle staff and my family. I follow my nose to the stairs, and then up to my own floor, the scent leading me down a long hall and coming to a stop at a door in the opposite wing. I can hear two people talking on the other side: Peter and Enid. It sounds like they're laughing. I don't want to interrupt, but with the tray in my hands, I have to awkwardly knock with my elbow, and as soon as I do, the talking inside stops.

"Oh, Your Highness!" Enid opens the door, surprised to see me—and all of the food I've brought.

I see Peter inside behind her, seated at the room's sitting table. He looks less nervous and just as surprised to see me. He's thankfully wearing more clothes now, just a simple white shirt and brown pants. I can't help but smile now that I see him again, passing Enid and setting the tray on the table in front of him.

"Thank you for helping him settle in, Enid," I tell her as I pull out the table's other chair. "And for keeping him company."

"Of course, Your Highness." She gives me a small bow. "I will leave you to your meal. It was very nice to meet you, Peter."

"It was nice to meet you too, Enid." He waves as the woman exits and looks up at me, the scent of his nervousness returning. "H-Hello, Your Highness."

"I told you to call me Max." I sit, trying my best to make him feel more relaxed. "Are you hungry?"

He looks over the platter of food in front of him, larger than the table it's set on. His eyes are almost just as large, flitting back and forth between all of the options. After what feels like a lifetime of silence with him not touching anything, I finally speak again.

"Do you not like any of it?" I ask, disappointed in myself. *Maybe he's a vegetarian?*

"N-No, it's not that." He shakes his head rapidly. "This all looks amazing. There's just so much that I'm not really sure where to start."

"Start with whatever you'd like." I try to relax; me feeling anxious isn't gonna help him feel any less so. "Don't worry if there's something you don't like or can't finish. I'll eat whatever you don't."

He looks surprised at that but still reaches a hand tentatively toward a roll, bringing it to his mouth. I grab a grape and pop it into my mouth, smiling as I smell his fear finally starting to dissipate. Now we just have to talk.

"So, I need to talk to you about what happened earlier in the throne room," I start, my eyes cast down.

"I am so, so sorry, Prince Makseka," Peter blurts, the roll in his hand dropping to the floor. "I-I don't know what went wrong, but I swear I can fix it. I—"

"Whoa, hey, slow down." I put my hands up in a calming gesture. "I'm the one who needs to apologize to you. Shaving off all your hair, making you wear that flimsy costume, and then having you kneel there almost naked in front of everyone? I had no idea that's what Kamo meant by 'preparing' you, and I can't even begin to tell you how sorry I am. None of that should have happened."

I don't tell him that, loss of his body hair aside (I like my men fuzzy!), I actually thought he looked incredibly sexy kneeling there for me in nothing but a thong. I'd just prefer that he be doing it for *only* me. But I'm not sure him knowing that will actually help anything right now. Especially not seeing as it happened *in front of my parents.*

"Everyone seemed really upset." He worries his lip with his teeth.

"They were, but not at you, I promise." *It really could not have gone worse.* "They were angry at what they knew you had gone through. And at me, a little bit. That *was* the tradition at one time, but one that my dad said he thought he had stopped after *his* consort had to go through the same things. I'm still not sure what possessed Kamo to bring them back." *I hope Dad really chews him out. I know I will.*

"What... What *was* supposed to happen?" He's not looking up at me, and I can sense his hesitation.

"I just thought he was going to help you clean up, maybe give you some new clothes," I tell him honestly. "If I had any idea what he was planning, I never would have let him take you away."

"So you're not going to send me back home?" He finally meets my eyes, lip still between his teeth.

"That's actually what we need to talk about next." *Even though I really don't want to.*

"I swear, I can do whatever you need me to, sir." Even if I couldn't smell it, I can hear the desperation in his voice. "Just tell me what to—"

"Stop, please," I say as gently as I can. "It's something else I need to apologize for. I never should have offered your family that money the way I did. It wasn't... I wasn't trying to *buy* you. I thought I was taking care of a problem that was keeping you from leaving. I thought I was *helping*. Saying it out loud makes me hear how stupid and arrogant it sounds. I'm so sorry."

"I-I'm sorry. I don't really understand." He looks down bashfully. "A-Are you sending me back, then?"

"No, not unless you want to leave." I shake my head. "And even if you do, I'm still going to send your parents the money I offered. That happens no matter what you decide."

"Really?" He looks up hopefully. "That's... Thank you so much."

"Not sure I deserve a thank you," I admit with some sadness. "I'm just trying to fix how badly I've already fucked this up."

"I... I don't think you messed up *that* badly." He offers me a small smile. One I don't deserve.

"No, I did," I insist. "I mean... Do you even like men?"

He goes silent, his body turning red, and I take that for my answer.

"See?" I try not to sound disappointed. "I understand why you wouldn't want to stay."

"No!" He reaches across and touches my hand—the first time I think he's touched me at all. "I mean, no, I don't want to leave. I... I *do* like men." Relief floods my system when I hear that. "This place is just really new to me, and there's still so much I don't understand. I've never been anywhere like this before. I'm just..." He shakes his head, forgetting whatever he was going to say. "I'd like to stay, but ... could we slow things down a little bit?

I thought I had an idea, but I'm not sure I understand exactly what being your consort means anymore."

"Of course." I put my hand over his, happy to at least have a chance. "We can go as fast or slow as you want. I'll answer any questions you have about being my consort, or anything else you want to ask about. Whatever you need. Is there anything I can do for you right now?"

"No, I think I'm okay right now." He laughs, but then I can tell that something comes to him. "Actually ... do you know where my bag is?"

"It wasn't brought to you?" I ask, a little surprised.

"Should it have been?" I can tell he's serious.

"Yes, one of the servants should have brought it up once everything was unloaded. They're usually better about stuff like that." *Yeah, for you, because you're the prince.* I curse myself and stand up. "Alright, you sit tight and fill your belly while I go find your bag."

"Maybe you could go after we eat?" he suggests, looking up at me from his seat hopefully. "This is way too much for me to finish on my own."

"Yeah, okay, I can do that." I sit back down with a smile, eager for what I'm sure will be one of the strangest and most memorable lunches of my life.

CHAPTER 6

PETER

I felt a lot better after talking with Max. I'm still trying to get used to calling him that—it just doesn't seem right. After we finished our lunch, he ran right off to get my bag. He looked so pleased with himself when he handed it over—if he had a tail, I bet it would have been wagging. I thanked him and then he left not long after, saying he knew it had been a long day and that I hadn't gotten much sleep.

It's odd being alone in this room. I mean, it's a nice room. It just feels a little *too* nice for someone like me. I was paranoid about making a mess the entire time I was eating. I'm glad the only thing that ended up on the floor was some bread—I feel weird even sitting on the bed.

When the sun starts to set, I notice that the torches set in the walls aren't actually torches, but torch-shaped glowstones that light up on their own. I've never actually seen them in person before, magical crystals enchanted to act as lights. Not long after, Enid, the nice woman who brought me to my room, comes back to ask me a few questions about the kind of food I like, returning later with a covered plate holding my dinner. It's smaller than the massive tray the prince had brought me but still pretty big. There's some sliced ham, mashed potatoes filled with herbs, a small salad, and some soft buttery rolls. There's some wine as well, but I've never really had it before, and I'm not sure I like the taste.

"Thank you, Enid. It smells great." It's true, but I also just want her to like me.

"I'm glad you like it." The older woman smiles at me warmly. "Are you settling in alright? Do you need anything?"

"Everything has been great so far," I lie a little, but I really am feeling better after talking with the prince. Though the smell of the food does make me think of something. "Actually ... could I get some paper and a pen? I'd like to write a letter to my parents."

"Of course," she answers with a nod. "I'll be right back."

She brings me a large stack of paper along with a pen and some ink. I thank her, and after finishing my meal, I get to writing. I don't tell them everything—gosh, I hope they *never* find out about me kneeling almost-naked in front of the king and queen—but I talk about the city, and the castle, and just make sure to let them know that I'm okay. I wish I had more to say, and even think about asking if they've thought about what to do with the money yet, but I hold off. I'll have more to say in a day or so, I'm sure.

When Enid comes back a short while later to collect my dinner plate, she takes my letter as well. I realize then that I've never actually mailed a letter to anyone before—everyone I knew lived in Weston. Enid tells me not to worry, asks me for the name of the farm and my village, and promises to make sure that it will get where it needs to go.

After that, there wasn't much left to do but sleep. Enid showed me that the lights turn on and off with just a touch, and after I finish with those, I get ready for bed. To my surprise, everything I need to brush my teeth, including a new toothbrush, is laid out for me on the counter next to the wash basin, complete with a faucet and actual running water. Then I finally have to make peace with messing up the very nice sheets on the bed, which feel even more comfortable than they looked. Unlike the previous two nights, I don't have any problems sleeping.

I don't remember my dreams, but I know I slept well, only waking when someone knocks softly on the door to my room. Expecting Enid, I'm surprised when a new person walks in instead. It's a man, younger than Enid though still a little older than me, with shoulder-length dark brown hair. He is dressed similarly to some of the other castle staff and is carrying a tray in one hand.

"Good morning, sir," the man says as he sets the tray on the table. "We have not had the pleasure to meet yet, but I am Oliver, Prince Makseka's personal attendant."

"It's nice to meet you, Oliver," I say as I straighten the clothes from yesterday that I threw on in a hurry.

"The prince wants to make sure you are having a comfortable stay." He pulls out one of the table's chairs for me to sit in. "The royal tailor will be visiting after your breakfast, and then the prince has asked that I give you a personal tour of the castle grounds."

"That sounds nice." I take the seat, not used to having my chairs pulled out for me. "Will the prince be there?"

"The life of a royal is sadly a busy one, but he will do his best to join us." My good mood deflates a little hearing that. "Please, eat, and we can begin whenever you are ready."

He lifts the lid of the tray, revealing a breakfast of a large omelet and a glass of orange juice. I cut into the omelet with a fork, marveling at the long string of cheese that follows my hand up to my mouth. It's light, fluffy, and filled with some kind of ham. It's a little odd eating with someone watching me who *isn't* eating, but I manage. When I'm almost finished, there's a knock on the door, which Oliver opens.

" 'allo!" an elf woman greets in an unknown but very thick accent as she enters.

She's tall, and thin, with extremely curly black hair that she has tied into a short ponytail. She's the first elf I've seen in a long time, so while she looks young, I have no idea how old she might actually be. She's wearing glasses and a simple black dress, and in her arms are several different items of clothing, a cloth bag thrown over her right shoulder. She quickly unloads the items onto the room's couch before straightening her dress and turning to us.

"It is so wonderful to meet you." She walks forward and greets me with a short curtsey. "I am Trixie, zee royal tailor."

"It's nice to meet you, too." I give her an awkward bow in return.

"I am zee one responsible for the clothing you are wearing." She gestures to my current outfit. " 'as it been fitting well?"

"Oh, yes, thank you." I run my hands down my white shirt. "Everything has been really nice."

"Zat is wonderful to hear." She claps her hands in excitement before reaching into a pocket and pulling out some measuring tape. "Now I already 'ave some idea of your size, but I would like to get some specific measurements, if you do not mind."

She steps forward and before I realize it, she's wrapping the tape around my chest, waist, and arms. She at least gives me a little warning before she drops to one knee to wrap it around my thigh and then down my leg and up my inseam. It's weird, but I try to remind myself that she's a professional. I mean, Daniel and Hannah both saw me naked yesterday.

"Excellent." She claps her hands again before turning back to the clothes folded over the chair. "Now, I 'ave just zee thing for you today."

She sorts through the clothes she brought with her, picking out a pair of brown pants and a blue shirt and handing them to me. She then hands me a belt, socks, and shoes that were all pulled from her bag, which seems like it should hold a lot less than it does. After pushing me to get changed in the bathroom, she approves of her selections, and before I can tell her no, she assures me that my closet will be filled by the end of the day. Then it's time for Oliver to give me my tour.

We start outside on the castle grounds. Oliver tells me that they hold over half a dozen different gardens, and he is happy to show me around all of them. Some are home to many different flower species from all over the world, all gifted to the royal family over the years. Another is filled with giant hedge sculptures—Oliver calls them "topiaries"—all trimmed to look like different life-sized animals, some that I think I've only ever seen in picture books. There's even a garden with a hedge maze that I think I'd like to explore sometime.

It's all fascinating, and I find myself paying extra attention when Oliver explains to me where each of the plants originated and how they're maintained. Maybe two hours in, I'm surprised and happy to see Prince Max, who comes right over to ask how I'm doing. But as soon as I finish answering him (I'm well. Oliver has been showing me the gardens), he's gone again, and it's back to just me and Oliver. I see him a few more times over the course of the morning as we walk between the gardens but never for very long.

We have lunch outside—or at least I do, while Oliver sits by politely. I offer to share with him, but he insists that he will eat later. I'm not sure when, seeing as he's supposed to be carting me around all day. Not once do I ever see him slip away for anything. I'm not even sure when he's using the bathroom.

I have dinner in my room again, alone. It was a nice day, really, but I still find myself a little disappointed. This isn't quite what I expected when I came here. After I finish my food, I sit and wait, hoping that Max will stop by to say hello before bed and talk, but the only person I see is the maid who comes to collect my dinner tray. I thank her, and then decide to just call it a night.

Everything repeats the next day, only this time Oliver is showing me around *inside* the castle. Specifically, I'm shown some of the royal family's different art galleries and collections. Giant paintings done by artists whose names I've never heard, elaborate sculptures that look almost lifelike, even a selection of creepy old antique dolls. They've got *a lot* of stuff.

Just like in the gardens, the prince makes the occasional appearance. He always asks how I'm doing, how I slept, how I'm liking the palace so far. But before I can ask anything in return, he's gone. It starts to feel a little frustrating after a while. After another dinner alone, I find myself bored in my room, and end up going to sleep early.

That also means that I'm up early the next day, already waiting for Oliver to arrive. While things start pretty normally with breakfast, afterward when I'm getting dressed, I notice a few itchy red blotches on my legs, chest, and stomach. And now that I've seen them, I can't ignore how itchy they are—my hair is starting to grow back. I do my best to ignore it, but I can't help the occasional scratch.

I am prepared for another prince-less tour today, so I'm not surprised when Oliver tells me that today he's taking me to see more of the castle grounds. Apparently, the prince thinks I might enjoy seeing how they look after the animals they keep here. He isn't wrong, but it would still be nicer to hear it from the man himself.

The main point of focus are the royal stables where the fleet of palace horses are kept. It still smells like a stable. It's kinda comforting knowing that no matter how much money you have, that's one stink you really can't get rid of. They're big, strong creatures, obviously well fed and cared for. Most of them seem to have a gentle disposition with the royal family's personal mounts seeming to have a little more personality, though I didn't actually get to see them very much up close.

Surprisingly, there is also a small amount of livestock held on the grounds. They keep a number of cows, chickens, and even goats so that fresh milk and eggs are readily available. Similar to my family's farm, they don't do any butchering here, all of that taking place on the farms outside of the city. Just as Oliver is bringing me back inside for lunch, someone calls out to us and stops us.

"Oliver. Peter." I turn to see Alden, the king's consort, walking up to us. His clothes still look very fine, though less formal than when I saw him in the throne room.

"H-Hello, sir." *Crap, what am I supposed to call him?*

"Good morning, sir," Oliver greets him with ease. "Is there something I can assist you with?"

"No Oliver, thank you," he assures the man. "I just wanted to come down and see the horses. It's been a while. But how about you, Peter? How are you doing?"

"I-I am well, sir," I stammer out. "Oliver has been showing me around the castle. It's all been wonderful."

"I was just taking him inside for lunch," Oliver agrees with a head nod.

"I'm glad you're enjoying yourself," he tells me with a smile. "I wanted to apologize for how we met. I take it the prince has been talking to you about everything?"

"Yes, sir, at least when I see him," I answer honestly.

"What do you mean?" He's confused by that. "Where is he?"

"W-Well, he's been very busy." Why do I feel like I just got him in trouble again? "But he sent Oliver, who's been doing a great job!"

"Hmm. I see." He's still smiling, but there's a sharpness behind it. "Well, don't let me keep you from your lunch. It was nice to see you again. I hope you enjoy the rest of the day."

"Th-thank you, sir." I give him an awkward bow. "Please have a good day yourself."

"I will," he responds, still wearing a tight smile as we re-enter the castle.

Inside, Oliver brings me to a small lounge for another solo lunch. At least this time Oliver does not stick around to watch me eat, leaving to hopefully eat something himself. Today's lunch is some roast beef served over some spiced potatoes. There's also more wine, and after the way the last few days have gone, I tell myself "screw it" and down a glass, despite the taste. This has all been very nice, but ... I'm lonely. I also can't seem to stop itching, using my fork to reach a tough spot on my back. I sigh, pouring myself more wine and finishing my meal, and am surprised when it's not Oliver who comes to collect me, but Enid.

"Hello again, Peter." As she greets me, another maid is already clearing my lunch from the table.

"Enid, hello." It's nice to see a familiar face. "How are you today?"

"Busy as always, but still good." She's just as warm as I remember on that first day. "I'm going to be taking over for Oliver in showing you around this afternoon."

"Really?" *He didn't mention anything like that to me.* "Is everything okay?"

"Yes, he was just pulled away for a little while," she explains. "When you're a personal attendant to the royal family, things often come up unexpectedly."

"I'm starting to understand that." I try not to sound too disappointed.

"Tell me, do you like to read?" If she notices my downer mood, she doesn't let on.

"A little." I nod, not saying much more than that. There wasn't a whole lot else to do in Weston, but other than the uh, books I like, I wouldn't say I was a big reader.

"Well, today I'm going to show you the castle library," she tells me with excitement. "It's quite large. There are so many books that I'm sure you'll find *something* you like."

I follow her out of the lounge, climbing up a few flights of stairs to what I'm pretty sure is the floor my room is on. I'm starting to get a general idea for where things in the castle are laid out, but only a little. It's just so big, and I'm always learning about something new.

Enid wasn't kidding. The library is huge. I'm not positive about the size of the castle yet, but it has to take up a good chunk of the entire floor. The rows and rows of bookshelves reach almost all the way to the very high ceilings, most having a ladder attached so you can reach the top shelves. There are reading nooks with comfy looking chairs in every corner, and along one wall is a set of writing tables.

"What do you think?" Enid asks as she watches me take it all in.

"It's amazing," I repeat myself for I'm sure the hundredth time over the last three days. "I don't think I even knew that this many books existed."

"Peter?" I turn and see who else but the prince himself coming down the row. "What are you doing here?"

"Enid was just showing me the library." I point to the woman. "What are *you* doing here?"

"Certainly not *hiding*." Another voice answers for him—Alden. Everyone's heads turn to see the man walking toward us, wearing the same expression he did when I saw him by the stables—though now I can see it is clearly directed at Max. "Enid, dear, could you come with me? I need help polishing some of the queen's jewelry."

"Of course, sir," my escort replies automatically, the two of them leaving the two of us alone in the library.

"What was that?" I ask Prince Max, confusedly watching the door the two left through. "Are they really going to polish your mother's jewelry?"

"No." The prince sighs as what the consort actually said settles in.

"Wait... Have you been hiding from me?" I ask, scratching at the itchy patch on my chest.

"I... No. Not exactly." He looks bashful.

"What is it then?" Maybe it's because of the wine, but I'm feeling a little bolder than usual. "Did you decide that you don't like me after all?"

"What?" His eyes go wide at that. "No, not at all!"

"Then what is it?" I scratch my arm.

"I keep screwing this up." His shoulders slump. "After everything that happened that first day, I just thought you probably wanted some space."

"Oh. Thanks, but ... I was kind of hoping I'd be able to get to know you?" I offer, feeling a little less wound up by his answer. "Not to mention it's been kinda lonely."

"I'm sorry," he apologizes with another sigh, then watches as I reach down to scratch my leg. "Are you okay? You seem ... itchy."

"Ah, yeah... My hair's starting to grow back," I answer with a hint of embarrassment.

"Shit, I'm sorry." He winces. "That's another thing that's my fault."

"It's okay." Now that I know he's noticed, I fight to keep myself from scratching in front of him. "I'll be fine."

"It's still my fault." He frowns, then quickly looks like he's got an idea. "But maybe there's something I can do to help. Could I meet you up in your room in an hour?"

"An hour? Are you sure I'm not interrupting something?" I hate to admit but I'm still worried that he might just be trying to get rid of me.

"I'm sure." He reaches for my hand and squeezes. "I'll be there, Sunshine, I promise."

"Okay," I agree, nodding. "I'll see you in my room in an hour."

He lifts and kisses my hand (it's been a few days since the last one) before he makes his exit, leaving me alone among the shelves. I look around the room briefly, at least pretending to be interested, but I make my own exit soon after. I have to figure out the way back to my room on my own this time, and I don't want to risk getting lost and being late. I end up in the wrong hallway twice, but eventually make it, and then there's nothing left to do but wait. About an hour later, there's a knock on my door.

"Hello, Peter." I feel myself relax when I answer and it's Max on the other side. "It's good to see you again."

"It's good to see you too, Your Highness." I step aside and let him enter the room.

"Oof, I'm back to 'Your Highness?'" He pretends to be wounded. "I deserve that."

He leads me out onto my room's small balcony, the sun just starting to set.

"So first." He pulls a bottle of yellow-tinged liquid from his pocket. "Papa gave me this for you and your regrowing body hair. He said it should soothe the itchiness and also help prevent any ingrown hairs."

"The king gave this to you?" I can't help but feel embarrassed that the king of Litkalaa was talking about my *body hair*.

"Err, no. Papa is what I call Alden, my dad's consort." I look at him, dumbfounded by the information.

"You call him ... Papa?" *Is that a title thing?*

"Alden is essentially my second father, so ever since I was little I've called him Papa, to avoid confusing the two." He pauses with a sigh, chewing his lip. "He was the one responsible for us running into each other in the library earlier. And when he gave me the oil, he also lectured me for leaving you alone the past few days. He explained how confusing all of this has probably been for you. I'm really sorry I'm so terrible at this."

"I wouldn't say you're terrible." *Not that I'm sure I fully get what "this" is.*

"That's sweet, but no, I *really* am." He chuckles and shakes his head. "I'm sure you have a lot of questions about everything, but Papa thought that would be a good place to start. The outside world sees Papa as my dad's subordinate, or even his pet, but the truth is we're a family. Dad and Papa were together for a few years before Dad married Mom, and all three of them raised me together."

"I had no idea." *And neither does anyone else!*

"Yeah, sadly a big part of royalty is keeping up appearances," he answers with a frown. "Kamo can be pretty strict about that kind of stuff, but he's usually got the kingdom's best interest at heart. Still, that's not an excuse for what he put you through. Dad almost tore him a new one—and so did I."

"You didn't have to do that." I scratch again at my chest. "I don't want to get anyone in trouble."

"Don't worry. He needed to hear it. Dad says he can be a little too 'big picture' sometimes," the prince assures me. "But from what Papa told me, it's always been that way with royal consorts. One view for the public, and another for private. I can't remember them much, but I do know that my grandfather loved his consort very much before they died."

"I'm sorry you didn't get to know them better." King Nachek's consort, Yura, was said to be a great beauty. Sadly, she died alongside the then-king and queen when the boat they were traveling to Albion on sank about twenty years ago.

"It's okay. I was pretty young." He brushes off his sadness. "But my point is that regardless of what the outside sees, being a consort is a lot closer to ... marriage. That's the way it works for my parents."

"*M-Marriage?*" My mouth goes dry at the implication.

"Essentially, yeah," he says with a laugh and a nod. "Really arrogant, huh? Again, sorry for just ... blowing in and assuming you'd agree to everything. What a way to start things off."

"It could have been worse?" I offer, scratching at my belly. *I'm still stuck on the "closer to marriage" thing!*

"I guess you're right." He laughs. "You know, I had originally planned on dazzling you with everything around the palace this week, and on Astraday I was going to take you out here and kiss you. Cheesy, right?"

"Heh, y-yeah, cheesy." I try to laugh off the idea, ignoring the way my whole body heats up. "I've ... never actually kissed anyone before," I admit for some dumb reason.

"You haven't?" He looks over at me, a surprised but tender look in his eyes. "Would you... Could I kiss you now?"

"I... I think I would like that." I nod a little stupidly.

He smiles at my answer, turning and closing the distance between us. I feel his arm on my lower back as he pulls us together, our chests meeting in the middle. As he lowers his face toward me, I close my eyes on instinct, and a second later, I feel his warm, soft lips pressing to mine.

It's like everything around us melts away. All I can sense is the way he feels against me, his heartbeat, his scent and taste. I have no idea what to do, or if I'm even kissing back right, but all I want is for it to keep going. So when I have to reach up and scratch a particularly itchy patch on my stomach, I'm more than a little annoyed.

"Would you like to put on the oil?" the prince asks after I break us apart. "I could... I could help get your back, if you'd like?"

"I.... Yes. Please." I nod, my mouth going dry again. "That would be nice."

"Why don't you take off your shirt and lie down on the bed, on your stomach?" He walks me inside and points to the bed.

"Okay." I nod and move toward the bed. As I start to unbutton and pull my shirt over my head, I notice the prince staring and I blush. Before I can psyche myself out, I crawl onto the mattress and lay flat on my belly. With my head turned toward him, I watch Prince Max grab the bottle of oil and stand, approaching the side of the bed.

"Alright, this might be a little cold at first," he warns me as he uncorks the bottle.

I still jump when the cool liquid hits my back, though the prince makes sure to quickly warm it up with his hands, running them through the oil and over my skin. He starts at the center of my back and slowly spreads it to the sides. He moves up, running his hands over my shoulder blades, and I can't help the small groan that escapes when his fingers press into my muscles.

"You've never had a massage before, have you? You've got a lot of knots back here," he comments as he continues to work my back muscles. "Probably from working on a farm your whole life. Hmm... One second. I want to make sure I can get to everything evenly."

His hands leave me, but a moment later, the mattress dips as he climbs on behind me. He shuffles forward, straddling my legs and sitting right behind my ass. His hands return to my back, once again spreading the oil and kneading my muscles, making me groan.

"That's better," he comments as he works. "Papa said you should only need to do this every other day for about a week. Unless you decide you want to keep shaving your hair, in which case I can get you more of the oil."

"Oh... I hadn't really thought about that." And the truth is, I don't really want to, but... "Do you ... want me to keep removing it?"

"Actually, I kinda liked it more when you were all furry," he confesses a little timidly.

"Then ... I think I'd like to have my hair back," I admit, just as timid.

"Awesome." I can hear his grin even if I can't see it and smile into the sheets myself.

I hear him open the bottle again, dribbling more of the oil along my back. Max's hands start to move lower, making me shudder as he tickles over some of the more sensitive areas. I groan every time he stops to work out a knot from the muscles of my lower back, melting into a puddle on the bed. This feels so good.

As the prince continues to rub me down, I realize I can feel something pressing against the bottom of my ass. Something firm. *Is... Is he hard right now?* The thought makes my whole body flush, not to mention the fact that I've basically been grinding into the mattress almost since we started.

"Okay, I think I'm finished," he says with a hint of disappointment, his hands still on my back. "You'll need to stay on your stomach for a little while to let this dry... Um, if... If you wanted, I could ... go lower? Just so we can get everything all at once."

I immediately understand what he's implying, my thoughts going back to the hardness pressed against my butt. I've never actually been touched by another man like this. Hell, I've never been touched by *anyone* like this. I just had my first kiss on the balcony. I can't even describe how nervous I feel, but do I want him to stop? *No.*

"O-Okay." I nod as best I can. "Let me just..."

Max climbs off me for a second as I lift my groin from the bed. My hands reach underneath me to undo the belt and buttons at my fly, and then slowly and carefully, I drag them and my underwear down my backside. I tug them down as best I can, down to my upper thigh before going back to lying flat, leaving my ass on display while making sure to still hide my ... other bits underneath me.

"Gods..." I hear the prince whisper to himself, and I turn even redder than I was before.

He helps to tug them down to my ankles, and then a moment later, my legs are once more being straddled. I'm almost disappointed that he had to move lower, since I can't feel him against me anymore. At least until I feel him reach down and squeeze my right cheek, making me jump in surprise.

"Sorry!" he quickly apologizes. "Just, uh, wiping off some excess oil."

He uncorks the bottle for the third time a second later, splashing the cool liquid onto both of my cheeks. His hands return, slowly rubbing and squeezing my flesh as he covers my skin with the oil. He massages my glute muscles in firm circles, and on each pass, it feels like his fingers are moving closer and closer toward my crack and what lies within. As he works my muscles, I start to blush even harder. *Can... Can he see ... everything?*

I have to bite my cheek and grip tightly onto the sheets to keep myself from whining and pressing up into him. His hands eventually move down to my thighs, making me shudder again as he dips into the sensitive area between them. After that, his hands move back up over my butt to my back, and then back down, each time making me fight against the urge to press into them.

I have no idea how long we've been doing this. My eyes are squeezed shut, and my mouth is doing its best to use the bed to muffle any of my embarrassing noises, but I know some are making it out. Max's hands feel so good on my body, and I just want him to keep touching me. And from the way I occasionally feel him hard against my legs, he likes touching me too. I know that eventually though, this has to end.

"Alright," the prince says a little sadly, having come to the same conclusion, "I think that's everything."

He slides off my back, rolling onto his side next to me on the bed where I can see him. He's smiling, but his skin is flushed red, and there's a small amount of sweat on his brow. His eyes move down back, freezing for a moment when they reach my ass, and I blush again myself. Neither of us says anything about his obvious erection.

"Thank you," I finally remember how to use words. "That felt wonderful."

"Happy to help." He smiles. "And I can help you again next time, too, if you'd like."

"I would." I smile back, still too shy to even think about rolling over and revealing the rest of my naked body.

"So like I said, you'll need a little bit of time for that to dry," he comments, looking at my back and ass. "And you also still need to get the front side of your body."

"Yeah, I guess I do," I answer with a little sadness, figuring this is where our evening ends tonight.

"So... why don't we wait for that to dry, and then while you take care of your front half, I can I go downstairs and ask them to bring both of our dinners up to your room?" He smiles, running his hand down my back. "Then we can spend the rest of the night talking, and I can answer all your questions. Does that sound alright?"

"I think I like that sound of that a lot." And if the price for that is letting him stare at my butt while it dries? I think I'm willing to pay.

CHAPTER 7

"And here we have King Wematin, his wife Queen Kanti, and his consort, Talia."

"They were my great, great, great, great, great, great, *great* grandparents."

"Correct, Your Highness," Mr. Longfellow praises Max. "It is good to see that some of my lessons have stuck."

It's the early afternoon, a time I'd normally be in the fields harvesting crops. Instead, I'm in a hall containing dozens of portraits of Litkalaa's old kings and queens at different points of their reigns with Prince Makseka and his history instructor, Mr. Longfellow. Instead of his usual lesson, Max asked if the man wouldn't mind giving me a brief history of the royal family. I think he was also happy to have an excuse to get out of whatever the old man originally had planned, but I don't say anything because I'm actually excited to learn some of this.

After our *intimate* discussion yesterday (and maybe a little more kissing), I put my clothes back on and had dinner with the prince in my room. While we ate, Max told me about what life is like in the palace and what I should expect for myself. I had a lot of questions. Like what he had been up to when he was avoiding me.

His days are a lot less free than I expected. He might not have to work like I did, but he still has a lot of responsibilities. While the king and queen are usually the ones to entertain visiting nobles and other dignitaries, sometimes they have children closer to his age, and the obligation falls to him.

There's also his combat training, where he spends all afternoon and sometimes the evening running drills and sparring with the other knights, which is apparently tradition for all future rulers of the kingdom.

Then there are his studies. He doesn't go to school in the traditional sense ("attending the University of St. Kizis is not an option for security reasons") but instead has multiple tutors to teach him all sorts of subjects, complete with exams that the university approves. Prince Max asked about my own education, and I was embarrassed to admit that I was a dropout.

Mr. Longfellow has been walking us through this history lesson for a couple of hours now. He's an older man, no more than five and a half feet tall, which makes him the shortest werewolf I've met yet. He has a natural tan that is darker than Max's, and his head and face are covered in a forest of black and dark gray hair. He looked at Max a little suspiciously after he made his special request but still agreed anyway. He's been cheerfully walking us from painting to painting, explaining who is pictured and some of their accomplishments.

"King Hanun was only the third of the Blackclaw line to take the crown," Longfellow continues, explaining the royals in the next painting. "He was also the first to prioritize improving our relationship with the original werewolf tribes from which his line was descended, and Queen Nadine was the first of many queens chosen from the northern territory of Deepwater."

"What happened before that?" I find myself asking.

"Well, as is standard for many kingdoms, oftentimes marriages would be arranged for political reasons," Longfellow informs me.

"Like my mother," Max interjects. "She was a princess in Albion."

"That is correct, sir," Longfellow confirms, sounding a little nervous. "Not to say that these relationships were any less full of love and respect than other marriages..."

"It's okay, Mr. Longfellow," Max assures him. "I know Mom and Dad were married as part of an alliance. I also know they love each other a lot."

"Of course, sir." Longfellow bows his head. "Regardless, since King Hanun, all rulers of Litkalaa have sought to maintain good relations with the northern tribes, including your father."

"Not that they're big fans of us," Max mutters.

"What do you mean?" I know nothing about politics or werewolves.

"I mean, I've never actually met any of them myself," he admits before continuing. "But from everything I hear, they look down on us. They think living in the city—in a castle—has made us soft."

"So then, who does meet with them?" I ask him next.

"I know Dad has in the past, but really it's Kamo who handles most of that these days," Max explains.

Before he can say anything else, the bell that hangs in the city's cathedral rings five times, signaling the hour.

"Ah, with that, Your Highness, I am afraid our day has come to an end," Longfellow says with a hint of regret.

"Of course." Max nods his head. "Thank you for deviating from today's usual lesson for us."

"As always, it has been my honor." Longfellow bows his head. "I shall see you later tonight at the full moon gathering."

"See you then, Longfellow." Max waves as the man makes his exit down the other end of the hall.

"Is the full moon tonight?" I haven't been doing a very good job of keeping track of the date since I got here.

"Sure is." Max nods. "In a few hours, the pack will gather in the forest behind the castle like we do every full moon."

"Every month?" The moon doesn't really come into play much with farming, so it wasn't something I ever tracked very closely.

"Yep. Kamo is probably already in the middle of making preparations," he explains as we walk. "He actually handles a lot of the day-to-day stuff around here. He really only goes to my dad with the more important things, and Dad really tries to delegate as much as he can."

"Is the king also the Alpha of your pack?" I wonder how much cross-over there is.

"Alpha?" Max looks at me confused. "Where'd you hear that term?"

"Oh, uh, I think it was mentioned in some books I've read." *Why did I have to say that? Or anything at all?*

"Right." He wears a knowing smile. "I think I know the kind of books you're talking about."

"Sorry." I blush. *Great, now he knows what I like to read.*

"You don't have to apologize." He shakes his head. "It's just not a term we actually use. It's got kind of a weird history."

"What do you mean?" All I know about werewolves are some of the legends and rumors I'd talk about with my friends.

"Well, for starters, it was only made up like, sixty years ago," he starts to explain. "Some guy wanted to study wolves, so he captured a bunch of them, stuck them in a pen together, and watched how they interacted. Actual wolves, not werewolves."

"That sounds ... a little weird." *How many wolves are we talking about? And how big was the pen?*

"No kidding," he continues. "Since they were all strangers to each other, they'd just end up fighting for dominance, and they called the wolf came out on top as the 'alpha.' But that's not how wolf packs—or werewolf packs— work. Packs are families, parents and their kids, and once the kids are old enough, they go off to make packs of their own."

"That makes sense." Still, I feel silly. "I'm sorry for not knowing better."

"It's not your fault," he assures me. "I'm guessing you don't actually know all that much about werewolves?"

"Only what I've read." I admit, embarrassed.

"And I can only imagine what that might be," he teases with a grin. "You already know that we shift during the full moon, but we can also transform at other times. It's just that the full moon actually forces it on us, as soon as it crosses the horizon into the sky."

"What does it feel like?" I ask, immediately curious. "Does it just happen?"

"Not exactly," he answers after some thought. "It's kind of like a reflex? You just ... *feel* it coming and then your body does the rest. Happens even if we're asleep."

"Does it hurt?" I've never seen it in person, obviously, but the descriptions make it sound painful.

"It's not painful, but it can get uncomfortable." He grimaces at a memory. "You can really feel all your different body parts, inside and out, moving around and changing."

"What was your first time like?" I ask, on the edge of my seat.

"I can't actually remember," he tells me. "I was born a werewolf, so I've been shifting since I was a baby."

"Oh." I process the new information, trying to picture a tiny baby were-wolf. "Do werewolves always have werewolf children?"

"Mhmm," Max confirms with a nod of his head. "The curse passes from parent to child. It doesn't matter if only one of them is a werewolf, either."

"Are there a lot of ... mixed marriages?" *Is that the right term to use?*

"A few, but it's not very common," he tells me. "Most of the wolves in the kingdom marry other werewolves, and a few have gotten permission from my father to pass the bite along to their spouse."

"They have to get permission?" *How do you even control something like that?*

"Yep, and it's been that way with every king and queen," he continues. "My father has always been selective when it comes to giving people the bite, and he's taught me the importance of doing the same when I'm one day the king."

"Why's that?" Maybe that's a stupid question.

"Well, for one, it's dangerous," he starts, his voice turning serious. "Born wolves—myself included—can sometimes have a hard time remembering that it's a *curse*. A dangerous, deadly, magical curse. The changes it forces your body to undergo are drastic, and it can even shut parts of it down. Not everyone who is bitten survives."

"Is there a way to tell before you bite them?" That sounds pretty scary otherwise.

"Nothing obvious. It could kill someone in perfect health, while someone sickly might end up stronger than ever," he shares with a frown. "That's why Dad says it's important to judge someone based on their character, which is also another reason for being so strict. Could you imagine the kind of harm the wrong person could do if they got that kind of power?"

"That does sound dangerous." He sounds like he's speaking from history. "Has that ever happened?"

"Not in a long, long time." He shakes his head. "It's usually only the people closest to the king that receive the bite—members of the kingsguard or other high-ranking knights. Their children then tend to follow in their parents' footsteps and become knights themselves."

"There must be a ton of werewolf families by now then." At least it sounds that way.

"Fewer than you'd think." His voice turns a little somber. "Werewolf pregnancies are dangerous. A pregnant werewolf is still forced to transform on the nights of the full moon—but the baby growing inside of her doesn't, at least not until the later months of pregnancy. Sometimes when shifted, something happens where their bodies stop recognizing the baby as their own, like it's so different from the mother that it gets treated like a foreign object or something. And so then the body tries to ... end it."

"Oh my gods." I cover my mouth, horrified.

"I know," he says softly. "Once it's developed enough, the baby will start to shift with its mother, but when exactly that happens is up to chance. And the same is basically true for pregnant non-werewolves, just with the timing flipped. While they don't shift, their growing children eventually do and can lead to the same complications."

"Wow." I am dumbfounded. "That sounds so scary."

"It's why werewolf families aren't quite so widespread even all these years later, and why we're careful about who we bite." He brings it back to his earlier point. "A lot of people have refused it, or at least asked to delay it until after they've already had children so that they can avoid the risk."

"That makes sense." I might do the same in that position. "Are there any other differences between bitten and born wolves? Do you all have the same inner wolf?"

"Inner wolf?" He chuckles at my words. "Like an internal wolf spirit that shares my body? Another thing made up for stories. We don't have inner wolves; we *are* the wolves. It's a part of us. But no, there's not really a distinction between them, not in a physical sense. I think born wolves have an easier time with shifting only because we've been doing it since before we can even remember. Bitten wolves sometimes have a difficult time controlling it, let alone controlling themselves during a full moon. Which sucks, because that's actually why you're not going to be able to join us tonight."

"I'm not?" Not that I knew to begin with. "I didn't think non-wolves were invited."

"You don't have to be a wolf to be part of the pack." He smiles warmly. "Normally there are plenty of non-wolves there. Every wolf's family is considered pack and is welcome. Which I know makes us sound a little more like those 'wrong' wolf studies—but no one's calling my dad Alpha."

"Why can't I go this time?" Now that I know, I'm a little disappointed.

"During the last full moon, my father offered the bite to one of our knights, who accepted," he starts to explain. "When you're bitten, your body essentially shuts down for a few days, so much that you almost seem dead. But even though you can spend days unconscious, the transformation isn't complete until the *next* full moon."

"So this knight's first shift will be tonight?" I wonder if I've met them yet.

"Correct." He nods in agreement. "And first transformations are dangerous. I told you, bitten wolves can have a hard time controlling themselves. So the gathering for this full moon is strictly werewolf-only while my father and the rest of us make sure the new wolf can learn to control himself. No children or any non-wolves at all. Dad doesn't even want Papa there."

"That makes sense." My feelings are less hurt about being excluded since I'm not the only one.

"Still, I wish you could come." He takes my hand thoughtfully. "They're usually pretty fun nights... Plus I *have* to be there... Anyway, did you have any other questions?"

"Um..." I wrack my brain trying to think of some, but the only thing that comes to mind is one of the dumbest things I can think to ask. "I do, but they might be kind of stupid."

"That's fine," he responds with a chuckle. "I've heard 'em all by now."

"Okay." I nod, ready to further humiliate myself. "Is it true that you can turn into actual wolves?"

"Ha!" He barks a laugh. "No, we've only got the one giant half-man, half-wolf monster form."

"What about talking to or controlling them?" These are all things I've read in my stories back in the day when I had no clue about what was true and what wasn't.

"Nope," he answers with a laugh. "Animals don't 'talk,' not like a conversation, but we *can* understand things like their body language and even what the sounds they're making mean and use that to communicate. We do have a sort of affinity for wolves. Dogs too, actually. There are a few "real" wolf packs in the forest that are friendly with ours. I think they can sense that we're 'alike.'"

"Wow," I say, amazed. "I always wished I could talk to the animals back on the farm, just to know what they're thinking."

"I'm sure the cows miss you already," he teases before patting his stomach. "For wolves it's usually just 'I'm hungry' or 'I'm horny.'"

"Do you... Do you think I could see you shift?" I ask the question nervously.

"Oh! Um..." His eyes go wide at my request, but before he can say more, a set of doors opens at the other end of the hall.

"Max!" A dwarf clad in armor steps into the hallway, and I think I recognize him as one of the knights that was in Weston. He gestures in the direction he just came from. "The king is expecting us."

"Shit, I'm sorry." Max looks at me with a grimace. "Dad wants to talk strategy with me and the knights about how to handle the new wolf before we head out there. I gotta get down there. I'm already late."

"I understand." I try to hide my disappointment. "Sorry for keeping you."

"I have an idea though." His shy smile helps me to feel warm. "Tonight, when you're up in your room, step out onto your balcony at say ... a little after 7 o'clock? And make sure you look down."

"7 o'clock?" I confirm, not sure what he has planned. "Okay. I can do that."

Prince Max departs for the full moon gathering, leaving me to finish the walk back to my room on my own. I spot some sheets of paper and a pen on the small table in my room, which I requested this morning from the servant who brought me breakfast. I know I only wrote to my parents a few days ago. I'm not expecting to get a response for at least a few more days. *This* letter is for Violet.

I start by telling her about my days spent in the palace so far, leaving out the more humiliating parts of that first day. Gosh, if she knew I was basically naked in front of not just the prince but the whole royal family, I'd never hear the end of it. I ask her if the healer has arrived and for other updates on her father next. Max told me that one of the palace doctors was dispatched the day after we arrived. I really hope he's been able to do something, Violet could use some good news.

I also ask if she's noticed anything different on the farm or if she wouldn't mind going by soon to look. I don't know if my parents got the money yet, and I'm afraid to ask Max or anyone else in case they think I'm ungrateful, but I want to know what they are doing with it. Upgrades to the farmhouse, new farm hands... anything.

I fold up the letter when I'm finished, leaving it on the table so that I can remember to give it to someone tomorrow morning to mail out. With nothing else to do, I have to occupy myself to keep from getting bored. After Enid showed me the library yesterday, I went back this morning and picked out a few that looked like they might be fun reads. I did it mostly based on the titles, though. I've got *Frankenstein*, the story of a mad gnome scientist who manages to bring a dead body to life, and *Treasure Island*, which is about a young man who joins the crew of a brash orc pirate captain. There was also one with the title *Moby Dick*, but it turned out to be about some whale instead of what I originally thought, so I left it.

Not long after I start reading, dinner arrives and I eat about half of it before lying back down in my bed to continue. As the evening turns into night, I look up from my book when I hear the clock tower bell chime six times—the final time it will ring before the sun sets—which means I've got an hour until I am due to "see" Max. I think about reading a little longer, but without the bell tower to help me keep track of time, I'm a little more worried that I might miss something. So after setting the book down, I step out onto the balcony.

The vast forest sits behind the castle as the sun sets behind it in the distance. Even as high up as I am, some of the trees still seem to almost loom over me. It's dark inside, at least until I notice a few small pinpricks of light by the treeline—torches seem to mark the way within. I follow them with my eyes to find a few similar torches placed along a path that leads to the rear of the castle.

As I look down, I realize I can see people following the lit path and entering the forest. There are a few faces I recognize, some of the knights that originally came to Weston with Max, but overall it's people I've never seen. The groups of people entering the woods vary in size. Some people go in alone, and then others are in groups of three or four. I don't see any children, which is probably good. Going by what Max told me, they must all be werewolves, but I'm still a little surprised that none of them seem to be particularly well dressed. Although I guess that's probably because their clothes would just get destroyed in the transformation.

I start to see some more familiar faces, starting with Kamo who leads a small procession of people into the forest. I see a few more familiar faces among the guards, and bringing up the rear of the group is the royal family: king, queen, and prince. I think about shouting out to Max so he can see me, but I don't want the king and queen to think I'm rude.

I don't need to worry though because as he follows the others into the forest, he turns and looks up at me on the balcony, smiling and giving me a small wave, which I return before he enters the trees and is gone from my sight. Eventually, I stop seeing people entering the forest as the sun fully sets and the moon starts to rise. Everything is quiet, especially the forest, almost eerily so. The only sound is the wind occasionally blowing through the trees.

That's when the howling starts. It's just one at first, but soon dozens of others join it, an almost mournful sound that bleeds into the night sky. It isn't the only sound, though. Soon after, faint barks and growls can be heard coming from the forest, followed by yelps and other noises that almost sound like a fight has broken out. Is that the newly-turned werewolf? Do they have it handled? Will everyone (including Max) be okay?

Eventually all of the sounds die out, and it once again starts to feel like I'm alone, just me and the dark forest ahead. Max is due any minute now. So I wait. And wait. And nothing happens.

And then I see it. See him.

Walking out of the trees, just in front of my balcony, is a large, hulking figure. It looks as black as night, almost melding in with the shadows until it steps out into the moonlight. If it weren't for the two ice-blue eyes staring up at me, I almost might have missed it. Instead, what I see standing there on the grass just below my window is a werewolf.

He's covered from head to toe in thick black fur, and even from this distance I can tell he would tower over me by at least a foot, if not more. At the end of each hand is a set of sharp claws, and on either side of his head are a pair of long pointed ears. But what really catches my attention are his eyes, the same bright and brilliant blue that I have come to know pretty well over the past few days.

"Max?" I call down hesitantly. "Is that you?"

The werewolf lets out a single bark as he nods his head, and behind him, I can see a long black tail spring to life, flicking back and forth rapidly. I can't help but laugh at his visualized excitement. Excitement that he has about seeing me.

I have to admit, I'm even more curious now about what it looks like when he transforms. His chest and shoulders are broad and muscular, visible even under the black fur, and in his mouth, I can see a row of shiny white fangs. Between those, his muscles, and his claws, I bet he could do some real damage in a fight. He looks ... amazing. Terrifying... *Hot.*

"Thank you for showing me," I tell him, already wishing I could come down and get closer to see more.

He barks again in response, his tail wagging so much I almost forget he's not a dog. Behind him, two other werewolves exit the forest, one of them letting out a short bark to get his attention. I don't recognize them, but they're only focused on Max. After he notices them, Max turns back to me to give me a final bark, waving goodbye as he follows them back into the forest.

I stay on the balcony a little longer, listening to the sounds of the forest. Nothing more than the occasional rustling in the trees or the odd bark or growl, but I still wonder what the wolves within are getting up to. I try getting ready for bed, changing my clothes and lying down to sleep, but my mind keeps wandering back to the forest and what's happening within.

Tired of tossing and turning, I get up and decide to do what I usually do when I can't sleep: go for a walk. Of course, I don't have the farm to wander around anymore, so I'll just have to make do with the castle's halls. After getting re-dressed, I poke my head out of my room.

It's dark (duh) and really quiet. Not only have most of the servants gone home or to their own rooms for the night, but several of the castle's inhabitants are out in the forest right now. Still, I'm spooked when I turn a corner and see two guards standing outside the doors to the one of the stairwells.

They both give me a strange look after my reaction but don't say anything as I awkwardly turn around and walk back the other way. *Right, I'm not actually alone up here.* I'm a little more cautious now as I continue to wander, really just wanting the chance to think and clear my head a little.

I've only been here a few days, and my life is already so different. One of the reasons I wanted to leave home was to see all these new things, but after learning more about werewolves and what goes on in the forest, I realize I'm pretty clueless. Here's hoping Max is willing to be patient while I learn.

I wander the castle for another thirty or forty minutes, I think. I run into a few more posted guards, but I'm at least less jumpy now. I try not to go too far from my room, worried that I might get lost, but I'm also eager to learn my way around. Eventually, I find my way to the library, pleased with myself for figuring it out. I don't go inside, deciding it might be time to try to sleep again.

On the way back to my room, I pass a large window that overlooks the forest. I look out, and even though it's quiet right now, I can still hear the wolves howling into the night. With little else to do, I say a silent goodbye to them and the forest and return to my room, images of pine trees and black fur filling my head as I fall asleep.

CHAPTER 8

"Does the name Pythagoras mean anything to you?"

"I thought this was about math?"

"It is. He's credited with discovering a formula, the Pythagorean theorem. Does that sound familiar at all?"

"Ma'am, I'm not even sure I remember what a formula is."

It's been two weeks since the full moon, and a lot has happened. To start, I didn't see Max until almost two in the afternoon the "morning after," and he looked completely worn out. He said that he had just woken up, and that coming to see me was the first thing he did. I can't deny that hearing that made me feel pretty good. It also felt pretty good when he helped me apply the oil to my back again, which he did that night and every other night for the rest of the week. We never really talked about the night of the full moon, but I still appreciated that he shared his *other* appearance with me, even if it was from a distance.

After that though, things pretty much went back to normal. Or at least more normal than they were those first few days. I started seeing the prince a lot more while we got to know each other. He still had busy days, either with his lessons or training with the castle knights, but he made sure to see me at least once a day.

I'd tell him about life back in Weston and the trouble I'd get into with my friends, like sneaking out of the house and drinking crappy beer in our barn, and he'd tell me about what it was like growing up in the palace. It was mostly a lot of complaining at first, but I was still happy to hear it. I learned why he prefers to go by Max: he was named after his great-great-great-great grandfather, an old king who, in Max's words, "was a real asshole."

We'd usually have dinner together, and then after dinner he'd ... help apply the oil to my skin. It was another thing we never actually spoke about, which seemed silly considering what we were doing, but there was this tension between us. Like we were walking a tightrope and might slip at any moment.

It only lasted a week though. Not the oil. That ran out after the third night and Max had to get a refill. It was my hair. A week in and enough of it had grown back that I didn't *need* the oil anymore, so we couldn't really justify continuing our late-night massage sessions. So instead, now our dinners together drag on for longer and longer until one of us has to make an excuse about getting ready for bed and Max leaves, even though we both want him to stay.

The days that I wouldn't spend a lot of time with him weren't that lonely either because Hannah and Daniel started to hang out with me as well. I suspected Oliver may have been behind it, which was pretty much confirmed when they dragged him along to lunch with us one day. It's been nice getting to know them too. And Max isn't the only busy one anymore either because I have tutors now! A few of them. It was Max's idea and wasn't something I'd expected, but it was sweet how he set it up.

"So, I was wondering," he started during the late lunch we had the day after the full moon. "Would you ever want to start learning again?"

"Do you mean go back to school?" The question caught me off guard. "Aren't I too old for that now?"

"Maybe not an actual school, but what if you had tutors, like me?" he answered with a little excitement.

The first thing I felt was nervous. I had gone to a few of his tutoring sessions, but other than some of the history stuff, I don't think I understood any of it. I wondered if it was because he thought I wasn't smart enough. If he was asking me, then it must be something he wants me to do, right?

"Do... Do you think I should?" I asked, already prepared to say yes.

"Only if you want to," he clarified after seeing me starting to stress. "I remembered you telling me how much you liked school before. But really, you don't have to do it at all—it's totally up to you. I know you've been bored without much to do around here, and I thought this might be something you'd like."

The answer made me feel a little better, but I still had to think about it. I mean, would it even feel the same? It's not like I'd be going to a school or have classmates. I did really hate it when I had to drop out, and while most of my friends never made me feel bad about it, it did always seem like they weren't really that surprised when it happened. Like they expected it from me.

"A-Are you sure they'll be able to help me?" I pushed around the food on my plate with a fork. "It's been a really long time... I'm not sure what I remember."

"It's okay." He reached across the table and covered one of my hands with his. "They'll be able to help you no matter where you are with things. And again, it's only if you want to." He squeezed my hand as he said the last bit.

"I... I think I'd like it," I said with a nod. "If you're sure it wouldn't be too much trouble."

"No trouble at all, Sunshine." He smiled warmly before shrugging. "And if you change your mind later and want to quit, that's fine too."

<hr />

I haven't changed my mind yet! It's been fun or at least as close to fun as schoolwork can get. Most of Max's tutors—who are now also my tutors—are nice. Some more than others. Really, it's only Professor Harrod, who teaches writing and grammar, that's been kind of rude. I get along fine with Mr. Longfellow (who teaches history) and Mrs. Koplat (who does the sciences), and Miss Yadrow here is easily the nicest of them all. This is only our second "class," but she's a lot more patient with me than some of the others.

"It's alright, Peter," she assures me. "I have a test I want you to take."

The brown-haired gnome woman lays a few sheets of paper on the desk in front of me. I look over them and immediately get discouraged, already unsure of what a lot of the symbols next to the numbers mean. *I'm definitely going to fail this.*

"There's probably going to be a lot of things on there that you don't understand," she continues, seeing my confusion. "That's alright, just do the best you can. This will help me know where we need to start."

"Yes, ma'am." I nod more confidently than I probably should and reach for my pen to get started.

By the time I'm finished, it's been at least an hour and I feel like I only understood about half of the problems on the paper. I answered the others as best I could, but I'm sure I got most of them wrong. She walks back over to the desk when she sees that I'm done, and I hand her back the sheets with a grimace. She looks over them thoughtfully, not frowning nearly as much as I expected.

"This is good," she tells me, looking up with a smile. "I didn't expect you to get most of these, but it gives me a good idea of what you remember. I can use this to make a lesson plan that we can start next lesson."

"That sounds great, ma'am. I'm looking forward to it." I really am. I just hope I'm not wasting everyone's time.

"Well, that's all I have for you today." She hops up into her chair and begins to pack things in her bag. "I'll see you back here in a few days."

"I'll see you then. Thanks again, Miss Yadrow." After saying goodbye, I stand and leave what I've been calling the study room for the last week.

I take my time walking back to my room. I finished earlier than I expected today, and I've got a little bit of time before Max will be done with his own lessons. I can't say I know where *everything* is, but at least I'm not getting lost in the castle anymore, not even when I take the occasional late-night walk when I can't sleep.

I enter my room, spotting some blank sheets of paper on the round table I normally eat at, next to the pen and some ink. I'm still not used to the idea that someone comes in here when I'm not, cleaning up and stuff. I wouldn't say that I'm comfortable living in the castle yet, but some things are at least starting to feel a little less weird.

I asked Enid this morning if everything was alright with the mail. I still haven't heard back from my parents or Violet, but I didn't tell her that—just that I was worried my letters didn't reach home. She said that as far as she knew, everything was fine, and that she had dropped my letters off at the castle postmaster's office herself. Not wanting to seem like a pain, I just asked if she could get me what I needed so I could write another.

⟨∘∘∘∘∘∘∘∘∘∘∘∘∘∘∘∘∘∘∘∘∘∘∘∘∘⟩

Momma and Daddy,

I hope you got my last letter. I really miss you and hope you're both doing alright without me. Everything here in St. Kizis is still good. I actually just started tutoring lessons! It's still new, but I'm excited to start learning again.

Have you made any changes to the farm yet? I think about home almost every day. I'm even starting to miss waking up early and cleaning out the barn, if you can believe it. How are Polly, Holly, and Molly? And Abby and Kino? Do you think any of them miss me yet?

I know you guys have to be really busy with all the harvesting and planting for the summer. I really wish I could be there to help you. Let me know what's going on and when I can come visit. I miss you both.

Love, Peter

I read over my letter a few times. I feel like I should say more, but I'm not sure what. I'm worried that if I keep asking them for more info, I'll be bothering them. I just wish they'd write me back already!

I fold up the letter and leave it on the table to hand over when I next see Enid or another member of the palace staff. I step into my bathroom to relieve myself, and when I come back out, there's a knock at the door. I'm expecting it to be Max on the other side, so I'm surprised when I open it and see Alden, his "Papa" and the king's consort.

"Oh, hello, sir." I immediately try to bow, not liking how much taller I am than him.

"Good afternoon, Peter," he greets me with a bright smile. "I hope I'm not interrupting you."

"No, I'm not busy at all." I move back from the door. "Please, come in."

"I apologize for not coming to see you sooner," he tells me as he steps inside, taking a seat at the small table. "Max asked us if he could have a few weeks to get to know you himself before introducing you to 'all of the family craziness'—his words, not mine. How have you been settling in?"

"Well, it started off a little rocky," I admit as I take my own seat. "But since the prince and I have been talking, it's gotten a lot better."

"Good. I hope you don't mind that I meddled a little there," Alden confirms what I had already thought about me and Max's chance meeting in the library. "I'm sure *he* thought he was doing the right thing, even if it didn't make much sense. He gets that from his father."

It's a little odd hearing him talk about the prince and king that way, but there's still a lot I don't know about their family. That they even are a family. Though I probably already know more than most of the public.

"The other reason I came to see you was to extend an invitation," he says next. "The king, queen, and I would like you to dine with us tonight."

"Tonight?" I ask, my voice cracking a little. "You want me to h-have dinner with you all, tonight?"

"It's just dinner," he assures me with a chuckle after seeing my reaction. "Max will be there too."

"Yes, of course, I-I'd love to be there," I respond too quickly after realizing I hadn't actually said yes. "Is... Is everything alright?"

"Everything is wonderful." He pats my hand from across the table. "We just want a chance to get to know you too. Especially if you might be accepting Max's bite."

"Bite?" The term confuses me. "What about Max's bite?"

"It's part of the rite of claiming." He looks at me, confused. "Max *has* talked to you about the rite of claiming, right?"

"N-Not exactly..." Does he mean like a werewolf's bite? The idea sounds scary and a little exciting. "I-I know there's traditionally a collaring ceremony. I didn't know there was biting involved."

Alden's mood instantly sours. "It's actually separate from the collaring, and yes, there is biting involved, along with a few other things Max *really* should have told you about by now." He sighs to himself and stands. "I'm very sorry to cut this visit short, but I'm afraid I need to go speak with a certain irresponsible prince."

"I didn't mean to get him in trouble." I start to stand when he does.

"Don't worry. He'll survive." Alden chuckles again before pulling me in for an unexpected hug. "It was nice getting to meet you again. I'll see you at dinner. Don't worry. I'll send Hannah and Daniel to help you prepare."

"Th-thank you, sir." I wave awkwardly as he leaves. "See you at dinner."

Of course, I spend the next hour and a half pacing my room and stressing out over our entire interaction after he's gone. I can't believe I'm going to have dinner with the entire royal family tonight. And what was he saying about a bite? Eventually, I wear myself out enough to need to lay down, and just as I do, there's another knock at the door. With a sigh, I get up from the bed to answer it.

"Hello again, Peter," Hannah greets me cheerfully.

"Fancy meeting you here," Daniel jokes at her side.

"Hey you two." I step aside and allow them to enter. There's something nice about seeing some familiar faces.

They both head straight for the bathroom, each carrying an assortment of jars and bottles in their arms. They set them on the counter in front of the mirror, and while Hannah starts to organize them, Daniel grabs a chair from the main room and sets it in the bathroom. Then he pushes me to sit in it, and they start working.

My hair is trimmed, not that it really needs it. They don't shave my face this time, just clean up the edges of the beard I've been trying to grow out after I found out from Oliver that Max likes them. There's also no mention of removing my body hair—probably because I told them all about the fallout after last time.

"Alright," Hannah starts after running some kind of white cream through my hair and styling it, "I think you're almost ready for dinner. You just need—"

Another knock on the door cuts her off.

"That'll be Trixie with your clothes," Daniel announces, letting her in as Hannah and I follow into the main room.

"'allo!" the elf woman greets in her thick accent. "I brought some options, we are going to 'ave you in ze perfect outfit for tonight."

She sorts through everything she brought with her, laying the items she doesn't like on the seat of the chair. She picks out a black pair of pants and a blue shirt, holding each of them up to my body for a moment before nodding to herself.

"Change into zees." She hands me the clothing and ushers me toward the bathroom. "Afterward, we will 'elp you with ze finishing touches."

As the door closes behind me, I quickly get to work undressing. Knowing there are three people out there waiting for me is a good motivator. The pants are solid black and made from some of the softest material I've ever felt. They fit perfectly, hugging the muscles of my legs and thighs just right. My butt doesn't look too bad either. The shirt is a dark blue, like the ocean in winter, and when the light catches it just right I can see a leafy-vine like pattern that shimmers in a slightly darker blue. It covers my chest nicely and doesn't get weirdly tight around my stomach like some of my other shirts do. I even flex one of my arms, watching the fabric stretch around the muscle.

I tuck the bottom of my shirt into the pants and finish buttoning up, turning to look at myself in the mirror. Even with my hair done nicely and the fancy clothes, I still look like me. But I feel different. The longer I'm away from the farm, the more I start to wonder about who I am without it.

A knock on the door brings me back to the present, and after checking myself one more time in the mirror, I finally leave the bathroom, Daniel and Hannah complimenting myself and Trixie for her skill. Trixie then hands me a belt and shoes, both made of black leather that shines in the light of the room's glowstones. The buckle of the belt looks gold (*it's not real gold, is it?*), and I can see the outline of a wolf's head etched into it. Trixie looks me over to make sure I didn't miss a button or anything else, then attaches these two gold things she calls "cufflinks" through the button holes of my shirt sleeves. After letting Daniel and Hannah look over my hair one last time, I finally have the approval of everyone involved.

"Ze prince will be very pleased," Trixie compliments herself before there's a knock on the door. "And zat must be 'im!"

I quickly look down at myself, suddenly worried about every small wrinkle. She is of course correct. It's Prince Max on the other side of the door, looking as good as I've ever seen him. He's wearing a silk, red shirt with black buttons over a pair of black pants that look like my own. A small red cape adorns his shoulders, and a circlet of gold sits on his head—his crown. *I've never actually seen him wear it before.*

"You look amazing," he says a little breathlessly as he looks me up and down.

"Th-thank you." I immediately start to blush and look down for a moment. "You do too."

"Great job as always, you three," he praises the three people behind me who made this possible as he steps closer.

"It was our pleasure, Your Highness," Hannah says for the group.

"You look fantastic together," Trixie compliments again.

"We do," the prince agrees, smiling and then turning to his side to offer me his arm. "I believe we have a dinner to get to. Shall we?"

I nod and take his arm, feeling too bashful to actually say anything. I look back to wave goodbye to Trixie and the others, catching the knowing look they all share with each other. Then all my thoughts go to dinner and Max's family.

"Nervous?" Max asks as we walk up the stairs together.

"...Is it obvious?" I can't help but wince at the observation.

"You've barely spoken since we left your room," he says with a chuckle. "You have nothing to worry about. It's just dinner."

"Easy for you to say," I mutter. "You're not about to eat with the king and queen for the first time."

"So then don't think of them as the king and queen," he suggests with a shrug, like it's the easiest thing in the world. "Just think of them as my parents."

"I'm not sure if that makes it any better." Still, I do my best to calm my nerves.

We approach a set of double doors I haven't seen before, though that's not exactly odd—there's dozens of those around here. Two guards are posted outside, saluting as we approach and opening the doors for us. We enter into a dining room, or at least that's what I assume since the round table at the center has place settings and silverware. It's not as big as I expected, though I guess one of those almost comically large ones you read about in stories wouldn't make much sense for just the five of us.

Instead, there's only room for five people, and half the seats are already occupied. King Samoset sits at the head of the table with Queen Anna on his left and Royal Consort Alden on his right. They all look impeccable, smiling as we enter. Max steers me toward the table, pulling out the chair next to Alden for me, before taking a seat at the opposite end of the table from his father on my right.

"Max, Peter, thank you for joining us tonight," the king greets us, though I feel like it's mostly directed to me.

"Th-thank you for the invitation." That seems like the right thing to say. I really should have asked Daniel and the others when they were in my room on the rules for this kind of thing.

"We wanted to apologize to you for what happened during our first meeting—or at least the events leading up to it," Queen Anna says next.

"It's okay, m-ma'am," I stutter, my nerves getting the best of me. "I know it was a misunderstanding."

"That's one way to put it," Alden comments dryly.

"Regardless, we are happy to have you join us now," King Samoset continues.

As he speaks, two servants enter the room, one pushing a cart with a number of trays, a pitcher of water, and a bottle of wine. While one of them fills each of our glasses, the other places bowls of soup in front of each of us. Then I look down and realize there are more than eight different eating utensils, including three spoons, and I have no idea which to use.

"Just work from the outside in." Max leans over when he sees me looking at the three different spoons with worry. "Also, none of us actually care about that sort of thing," he finishes with a wink.

"I wouldn't say *no one*," his father corrects, holding up a fork. "I remember being younger and spending a long time with Kamo trying to remember the difference between a salad fork and a dinner fork."

"Can you tell me which is which right now?" Queen Anna challenges as she starts in on her soup.

"...I'm pretty sure this is a soup spoon," King Samoset says, following her lead.

"That kind of stuff really only matters when we're like ... hosting foreign dignitaries or something," Max informs me as everyone starts to eat.

We're having some sort of vegetable stew. It's not bad, but it could use some salt. The wine is … fine? I never really had wine before coming to the castle, and I'm still not used to the bitter aftertaste, but I do like the warm buzzy feeling it leaves me with.

"My son tells me you're from Weston," the king asks a short time into our meal. "A small village if my memory serves correct. How was it living there?"

"I-I liked it," I answer before second-guessing myself. "It's still pretty small, I think. But Daddy always said that being small made it easier to get to know your neighbors. You have to depend on each other."

"Your parents own a farm there?" Queen Anna follows up with her own question.

"They do. Lamplight Farm." I nod my head. "My great-great-grandfather built it himself, and my family has lived there ever since."

"That name sounds familiar," the king adds, though he's probably just saying that to be nice.

"I've always been fascinated by farming." As Queen Anna speaks, the two servants re-enter the room, and while the one with the pitchers refills our glasses, the other replaces our mostly empty soup bowls with one holding a salad. "I visited a few with my father in Albion when I was younger."

"Working a farm must be a lot of hard work," Alden says, looking for me to say more.

"It is." I nod, starting to feel warm from the wine. "You've gotta wake up early pretty much every day. You don't really get days off because there's always crops or animals to tend to."

"Perhaps you can help me in my garden sometime," the queen offers.

"I'd be happy to, Your Highness." Although even if I wasn't, I'm not sure I'm *allowed* to say no to the queen.

"I can't say I know much about plants, but I do know a thing or two about taking care of animals," Alden says next. "Specifically, horses."

"We had two horses on the farm." *Aww, I miss Kino and Abby.* "And some chickens and a few cows."

"Papa's family has worked as the royal stabler for a really long time now," Max leans over to tell me.

"Over one-hundred years," Alden confirms. "Before I was the royal consort, I worked there with my father and sister. She's the stablemaster now. I still go down to see her sometimes."

"I know a thing or two about horses myself," King Samoset adds. "I used to go down to the stable quite a lot when I was still a prince."

"Yes, but from what I've heard, you weren't there to see the horses, dear," Queen Anna teases.

"No, he was not," Alden confirms, sharing a silent laugh with the queen.

The family continues to pepper me with questions about farm life as the meal progresses. After the salad comes a plate of grilled fish, and I figure that's gotta be the main course until after *that* we each get an entire tiny chicken served to us. Then comes a plate of just different kinds of cheeses, and it's only when we are each served a slice of chocolate cake for dessert that I realize the meal is finally coming to an end.

"So you plant them in the fall, and they survive all winter unattended to like that?" The king is asking me about onions as we finish eating.

"Onions are a very hearty vegetable, sir," I explain. "Not everything survives but more than enough for your first spring harvest."

"Okay, I think we've asked him enough about farm life," Queen Anna announces with a small smile. "Thank you for joining us for dinner tonight, Peter."

"Thank you for having me, ma'am. And sir. And sir." I still don't know what I'm actually supposed to call them besides "Your Highness."

"You know, it's a lovely night," Alden comments off-handedly. "Max, maybe you should take Peter out on the western balcony to see the stars tonight. It's right around the corner. Don't worry. I'm sure the cool air isn't too *biting*." He really makes sure to emphasize the last word, locking eyes with Max while the king and queen both share a look.

"Great idea, Papa," Max responds with a wince, then turns to me. "You'll love it. You can see the whole city." He stands, offering me his hand.

"Okay." I nod and let him help me up, not quite knowing what else to say. Before we leave, I turn to his parents. "Thank you again for dinner, Your Highnesses."

"The pleasure was ours," King Samoset says as the two of us make our way from the room.

"Do you eat together like that a lot?" I ask Max once we're down the hall.

"No, just when we want to impress someone." He nudges me with his elbow before his expression turns serious. "So, there's something I need to talk to you about."

"Does it involve a bite?" I ask, remembering Alden's words.

"Yes." Max sighs. "I'm sorry for not saying anything sooner. I was worried that if I told you about it too early, you would have never even considered saying yes."

Before he continues, we turn a corner, and I see a door with large glass windows. Max opens it for me, leading me out onto what must be the western balcony. The floor is a round half circle of stone, big enough to easily fit a dozen or more people out here if they wanted. Max takes my hand as we stand at the ledge. I can see the entire city below us and the stars shining in the sky above. Alden was right. This is nice.

"Whenever a new royal consort is chosen, there's a public collaring ceremony. That part you probably already know about." I nod. None have happened since I've been alive, but I've read all about them, and from the way they're written about, they almost seem like a wedding. Even before I saw the way that Alden proudly wears his, I'd imagine what it would be like to have a collar of my own. "The rite of claiming is separate from that. It happens earlier, during the full moon, with just the pack. It goes back to an old werewolf ritual that's been around since before the kingdom was even really a kingdom. During the full moon, you'll be given a potion to drink, a mixture of wolfsbane and a few other things, and then ... I will bite you."

"Like a werewolf bite?" I remember him telling me that they could only pass on the werewolf curse on the full moon.

"In a way, but it's not exactly the same," he continues. "Because of the potion, the bite will still change you, but it won't fully transform you into a werewolf."

"What do you mean?" This sounds confusing.

"You won't be able to shift, but it will make you stronger and faster. You'll be able to hear and smell better, and you'll even heal a little faster," he explains. "You'll essentially be just as strong as we are when we're not shifted."

"Really?" That sounds like a pretty good deal.

"Yes, but you'll also get all of our weaknesses—like wolfsbane and silver. And there's something else." He starts sounding a little dejected. "It will also make you sterile."

"What does that mean?" I'm confused by the term. "Like, I'll be clean?"

"No." He winces. "It means you'll be infertile. You won't be able to father any children."

"...Oh." I try to process his words but... "I'm not sure I understand."

"Even with the potion, the bite still changes you enough that you're not really fully a human or a werewolf, but somewhere in between," he tries to clarify. "And as a side-effect, your body would be different enough from both that you won't be able to get someone pregnant—werewolf or otherwise."

"I... I didn't know about any of that." It's definitely not in any of those books I used to read.

"Yeah, it's not really something widely talked about," Max continues with a sigh. "It was actually seen as a benefit in the past because you wouldn't have to worry about a king or queen having a baby with a consort. But it's always made me uncomfortable."

"And it's permanent?" It sounds like a dumb question, but I still have to ask.

"Yes. Just like a werewolf bite, it cannot be undone." He pauses, releasing my hand. "I'm really sorry that I didn't tell you sooner. I understand if this means you're no longer interested in being my consort."

Truthfully, I don't know how I feel about it. I never really thought about having kids all that much before. I knew that even if I managed to find a boyfriend or something, we weren't exactly going to be having any ourselves. But knowing that I'll *never* be able to have kids is making me feel anxiety over something I never expected to happen in the first place.

"Could... Could I have some time to think about it?" I ask hesitantly, not sure how he's going to take it.

"Of course." To my surprise, he actually looks hopeful when I answer. "Take all the time you need. There is absolutely *no rush* on this."

"Thank you," I tell him, reaching out to take his hand this time. "And thank you for telling me."

"You should thank Papa. He chewed me out again for this," he responds with a sad smile.

I might have to do that and then some. I mean, Alden might actually be able to answer some of the questions I have. He might even be the only person alive who can understand what I'm going through right now. I just have to work up the courage to speak to him.

CHAPTER 9

"**...A**nd Raina, consort of King Matteu, was responsible for presiding over the inaugural Lavender Ball in 4691."

"Did any of them ever do anything ... bigger? More important?"

"I am afraid that the role of consort is one that, at least until recently, had been relegated to the background."

He isn't kidding. It's been two days since Max told me about the rite of claiming. Since then, I've been trying to learn as much about what life as a royal consort is really like. Their accomplishments, their relationships, anything.

And there isn't much! I spent all of yesterday in the library, and I couldn't find a single book written about them, and anytime I'd find a mention of them in any other book, it basically boiled down to who they were the consort of and what they looked like. It isn't making me feel very confident about saying yes. There isn't even much written about most of the queens, not once they were married.

Before today's history lesson started, I asked Mr. Longfellow if he wouldn't mind telling me about some of the consorts and their history. He's been happy to oblige, but so far all I've learned is that they used to throw balls and design gardens. It's like after they became a consort, they stopped being anything else. But I've met Alden, and I know that's not actually true.

"Yes, I'm starting to understand that," I answer the older man with a sigh. "Is there anything else you can tell me about them?"

"I am afraid that is about the extent of what I know," he says with a frown, adjusting his glasses. "As I said, until recently there was not much of a push to record the full histories of the kingdom's consorts. Was there something in particular you were hoping to learn about?"

"No," I lie, a little embarrassed about what I'm asking for. "I guess not."

"Then I suppose we can get back to our regular lesson." He turns to the chalkboard behind him and starts to write. "In 4534, Queen Hurit led the Litkalaan Army into battle against..."

Later that night (much, much later), I'm wandering the halls of the castle because once again, I can't sleep. I've mostly got a hang of the layout here now, at least on my floor. I don't get lost on the way back to my room anymore, and I know which halls are patrolled by guards and which are clear for me to be alone in and think.

I had dinner with Max after my history lesson, and it was just the same as always ... except for it being completely awkward! Max barely said anything the whole time, probably because he's still feeling guilty over not telling me about the claiming bite, and I've never been good at filling silences, so we mostly just sat there and said nothing while we ate. At least the food was good.

I feel bad that he feels bad, but it's not like I'm going to say yes without knowing more about what I'm agreeing to first. I already did that once! I just don't really know what to do. Okay, so maybe that's not *completely* true. I know exactly who I could talk to about this: Alden. I'm just not sure how to actually do that. Or I'm too embarrassed to ask, I guess.

I'll just walk up to him and say, "Hey sir, your son, who I still don't fully understand your relationship with, told me all about the rite of claiming and how he's going to bite me and take away my ability to have children. How are you?" *Ugh.* I know I'm being a little bratty here. Momma said I used to do that a lot as a kid, but at least I'm keeping it to myself this time.

I sigh as I pass a large painting of a past king—King Wematin, I think— the kind with eyes that look like they follow you as you walk by. This is the hall that leads to the library, so I pass it a lot. It's not so bad during the day, but it's dang creepy at night.

Around the next corner is a large window, moonlight streaming in through the glass. I pause when I reach it, looking out over the forest. Everything is so different at night. Peaceful. Even a little spooky. If the werewolves feel comfortable enough to spend every full moon there, I can only imagine what else might live inside.

Do I want to be one of them? Or I guess, half of one of them? Max told me how the bite is going to change me, but hearing it is probably a lot different than experiencing it. If I really want to know, I guess I could ask the one other human in the castle who's gone through with it...

I hear a noise behind me, coming from the hallway I just used to get here. It's faint, some kind of scratching or shuffling. I move back to the bend in the hall to see if I can hear better.

"H-Hello?" I call out. "Is someone there?"

I don't get any response, but the noise stops. I poke my head around the corner to see nothing but the dark hallway. The painting of King Wematin hangs on the wall, judging me as I talk to none but myself.

I swear I heard something... but maybe I'm just tired. I sigh to myself, shaking my head and starting back toward my room. If I'm hearing things, maybe I'm finally ready to sleep.

"Um, Oliver, I was wondering... Do you think it would be possible for me to speak with Al—the Royal Consort?" I ask the man as he is dropping off my breakfast, after working up the courage to last night.

"I can certainly see if he's available," the well-dressed man responds after thinking for a moment. "I'll be right back."

I want to stop him, not expecting him to do it *right now,* but he's already gone. I don't have any tutoring lessons today, and Max is busy training with the knights, so I've got nothing to do but wait for him to get back. That and eat my breakfast of eggs, fried ham, beans, and toutons covered in molasses, which I manage to just finish up by the time Oliver returns.

"Sir, the Royal Consort would be happy to speak with you," he tells me with a smile. "He is just finishing breakfast himself, so I can bring you to him now, if you'd like."

"R-Right now?" I nervously push myself away from the table. "Sure, I-let me just clean up first."

I probably spend too long in the bathroom washing up and brushing my teeth, but I want to look my best. When I exit the bathroom, Oliver is still there, but my used dishes are gone. I quickly change out of my sleeping clothes and throw on some shoes, tying the laces as fast as I can. Now, I'm worried about being late!

"I think I'm ready." I run my hands down the front of my shirt, "Do I look alright?"

"Absolutely, sir." Oliver nods confidently. "Right this way."

Oliver leads me from my room through the usual maze of hallways and stairs. We're going up, which means toward the royal chambers. *I'm not going to meet him in his bedroom, am I?*

We come to a room with its doors already open. I can see several of the castle's staff gathered around inside. Some of them leave the group, passing us on our way out of the room, and I can see that the person they were gathered around is Alden, who is still talking to some of the others.

"...we'll need to set the menus for when the dignitaries from Emberwood visit next week," he says to them while looking through a small book in his hands. "Oh, and the rugs in the north wing ballroom are due for a cleaning."

"We will take care of that right away, sir," one of the servants tells him with a nod, the rest dispersing with their orders.

"Sir, I have Peter for you," Oliver announces me as the others leave.

"Oh good, thank you Oliver," Alden tells the man before setting his book on a desk and turning to me. "Come and sit down. I have a feeling I know what you wanted to talk about."

He leads me over to a couch as Oliver leaves. Looking around the room, it's actually very similar to mine. There's a big desk, a bed, a bathroom, and what looks like a large closet. *Is this where he sleeps?*

"Is this room yours?" I ask first, dancing around why I'm really here.

"It is." He nods. "It's the room I stayed in when Sam was first courting me. But I don't think you're here to ask about my sleeping arrangements. Can I assume that Max finally told you the truth about claiming you?"

"Yes, sir, he did." I nod. "About the bite and how it would change me."

"Then I'm sure you have a lot of questions." He gives me a pat on the thigh. "I'm happy to answer whatever I can."

"What did it feel like?" I start with the most basic thing I can think of. "Being bitten."

"Well the bite itself hurts, that's for sure," he says with a grimace. "And I don't just mean the physical pain. The way it starts to change your body, it feels like you're on fire. I passed out. As far as I am aware, everyone does."

"Oh." *Well, that's not what I wanted to hear.* "And ... what about after?"

"Honestly, when I woke up the next morning... I'm not sure I've ever felt better." His frown brightens to a smile. "I mean, I was groggy at first, sure, but then I realized I could hear birds outside from miles away. Back in the castle, I could smell the servant coming down the hall with lunch, and

I found out how strong I was when I accidentally bent my silverware while eating it."

"Is it like that for everyone?" That doesn't sound too bad at all.

"Near as I can tell." He nods. "I've never heard of anything different happening."

"Were you ever jealous?" I'm starting to feel like I can be more direct. "Did you ever want to be a full werewolf instead?"

"Not really." He shrugs. "It was never something I had thought about before, and it's not like the king was going to offer it to me. But even if it was an option, I'm not sure I'd say yes. The risks are too great. A claiming bite and a turning bite are functionally the same, the difference is that the potion you drink during a claiming actually protects the body from the full effects of the curse. If your body rejects the bite, the worst that will happen is you'll spend a week in bed recovering. Not die."

"What about the other changes?" I start, not sure how to word this. "Did you... Are you sad at all that you can't have children?"

"Ah. Going sterile is a pretty unfortunate downside," he admits with a short laugh. "But I challenge the idea that I don't have children. I'm pretty sure you're currently being courted by my son, even if he does seem to be cocking it up left and right."

"I-I'm sorry." *Great, you offended him, Peter.* "I have to admit, I don't really understand how your ...*family* really works. It's not something I'd ever heard about before."

"Right, public appearances and all that." He laughs again. "Most of the country thinks I'm just the king's pet, or servant, or 'mistress'—or all of the above."

I allow my silence to confirm his words.

"I told you that I grew up working in the castle stables with my family," he starts to explain. "Well back then, King Samoset was still Prince Samoset, and he used to come down there to see me all the time. He actually had a bit of a reputation back then for 'spending time' with several of the castle's servants, so at first, I figured I was just his latest conquest. But it was fun, and I liked him, so I went with it."

"Then, unexpectedly, we started to grow real feelings for each other," he continues with a smile. "Which wasn't as great as it sounds. I was just a stable boy. I knew that no matter what we were to each other, one day, he would be expected to marry and have an heir, and I was never going to be an option for that. So I assumed our relationship was doomed—until one day, when Sam came to me and asked if I'd become his consort."

"What did you say?" I am completely enraptured by the story.

"That I needed to think about it," he says next. "I worked in the palace, so I knew more about what the life of a royal consort was really like than most people. Sam's father, King Nachek, had a female consort, Yura. She was a very kind woman, and Sam thought of her as a second mother. She never seemed unhappy, or mistreated, and even some of the more ... questionable traditions didn't make it seem like the worst life. I also understood that accepting meant that I could still be with Sam. I told him yes three days later."

His story doesn't sound all that different from mine, although at least he had more time to get to know King Samoset. "Did you ever regret it?"

"Nope." He shakes his head confidently. "There were a few times where I thought I might. Like when he met Anna and they became engaged. Sam's mother, Queen Odina, was from Litkalaa, but Anna is from Albion. Having consorts like this isn't really done anywhere else but here, so I had no idea how she would feel about me and Sam's relationship. I was happy to learn pretty fast that I didn't need to worry. She was a little confused by it at first, but she accepted me even quicker than I expected, as a part of Sam's and now her life. We've grown to be good friends in the years since. I got worried again when she became pregnant with Max—but again, there was no need. We raised him together, and she did everything she could to make sure I knew that Max was as much mine as he was theirs, even if the public doesn't."

"That sounds really nice." The story gives me hope but also makes me worried about something else. "I... I know Max is going to have to get married one day. Whoever she is, what if she isn't like Queen Anna? What if she doesn't..."

"Your relationship will be different from ours, just like ours was different from Sam's parents. Though I might be able to tell you something that may set you at least a little at ease," Alden steps in when I can't continue. "When it comes to romance, Max has more in common with me than he does his father. In his youth, Sam would get caught fooling around with the milk-maids *and* the stableboys, whereas Max has only ever been caught with the stableboys. Do you catch my meaning?"

"...*Oh*," I respond with realization.

"My worries over Anna were that Sam was going to fall in love with her and out of love with me," he explains. "Which is silly—love isn't finite. But seeing as Max is not interested in women, no matter who he marries, or even has children with, they aren't going to be able to hold a candle to you in his heart. Political marriages happen all the time among royalty—that's all Anna was intended to be at first."

That does weirdly make me feel a little better about the situation, although it still seems like it could be a problem down the line. "You and Queen Anna are still good friends?"

"Oh gods, best friends at this point." He scoffs. "Though I suppose that's bound to happen when you share a bedroom, bed, and *husband* with someone."

"You share a bedroom?" My first thoughts are to ask about their sleeping arrangements, which then leads me to some dirtier thoughts about what else they do in bed together (and how big that bed is, exactly), but I quickly tamp them down. "Why do you still have this room then?"

"I mostly use it as an office these days. I sort of unofficially took over managing the castle's staff after Sam became king. I needed *something* to do all day while Sam was in his boring meetings," he explains. "He gifted it to me when we were courting, and he insisted I keep it even after I moved into his bedroom. He thought it was important that I have a place that was just mine, somewhere I could go if I needed to get away from him or anyone else."

"Is it difficult sharing a room with two other people?" I've never shared a room with anyone.

"Enh, it's a pretty big room." He shrugs with a smile. "It took a little getting used to at first, figuring out where everyone's things go. We've got *two* bathrooms, so that we don't need to worry about who's using it when. But you may not have to worry about any of that."

"How was it at the beginning?" I press for more. "Before you became a family."

"Strange. I don't think we quite knew what to make of each other at first," he answers. "It was Sam who pushed the two of us to spend time together. And that's when I learned she wasn't who I was worried about her being, and she got to know me and felt the same. You know... Maybe you should talk to her next."

"The q-queen?" He's not serious, is he?

"Of course." He stands as he answers, offering me a hand. "I mean, if you say yes to Max, she's practically going to be your mother-in-law."

"R-Right now?" I take his hand and stand, not feeling like I have a choice.

"No time like the present." He starts to head toward the door.

"What if she's busy?" I ask as he leads me from the room.

"She's not. She usually spends Aquadays in her garden," he answers matter-of-factly as we set off.

I'm expecting us to go down to the ground floor, so I'm a little surprised when instead Alden leads us up one. We walk down to a set of double doors that lead out onto a large balcony, one that is full of plant life. There's grass underneath my feet, all kinds of flowers, and even trees. It seems like we're alone, but then I spot a figure bent over a flowerbed—the queen.

"Anna!" Alden calls out as we head toward her. "Get out of the dirt. I brought someone to talk to you."

"Hmm?" Queen Anna kneels up, looking back over her shoulder as we approach. "Oh, Alden, Peter. It is good to see you. What brings you to me today?"

"Well, our son finally got around to explaining the details of the rite of claiming to Peter, and some of what came after," Alden says, patting my back gently. "I've been answering his questions, but I thought there might be a few things you could add."

"I'd be happy to." She dusts the dirt off her gardening gloves before standing, pulling them off, and brushing off the front of her dress.

"Then I'll leave you to it," Alden says after giving Anna a hug. "I've got to get back to planning next week's dinners."

"I'm sure whatever you pick will be great. But please no more asparagus," she tells/pleads with him as he leaves. "Now then, would you join me in the shade, Peter?"

She walks us to a wooden bench that's placed under a large oak tree. It looks different than the kind I've seen in the countryside, so I figure it's not from around here. In fact, a lot of these plants and flowers are new to me.

"Do you like the garden?" she asks when she sees me looking around. "It was a gift to Max's grandmother, Queen Odina, from her family. She came from the northern werewolf tribes, and their druids and shamans built this addition to the castle as a betrothal gift. Its care fell to me after she passed."

"Yes, ma'am, it's lovely." I nod, still looking around—and once again avoiding what I came here to talk about.

"Now then, why did you want to speak to me?" She gets right to the point though.

"W-Well, Your Highness." *There are my nerves again.* "I was w-wondering about when you first m-met King Samoset and Alden."

"Ah, that was a very … *interesting* time," she says with a small chuckle. "I come from Albion, where my father is still the current king. I am the youngest of five children, which meant I was never going to inherit much of anything, let alone the crown. I knew from a young age that it was likely that I would be married off by my father for an alliance or other political gain."

"That sounds … horrible." I can't imagine growing up knowing you'd never get a choice in your future relationships.

"Only that aspect. The rest of my life was fairly easy," she continues. "I was pampered and sheltered in the castle until my father began to seek an alliance with Litkalaa. I had heard that the king there had a son that was around my age—Prince Samoset. I had barely just learned his name when it was decided that we would marry—before we had ever even met."

"You didn't even know him yet?" That sounds crazy.

"I'd never so much as seen what he looked like." She shakes her head. "But soon after, I was sent to visit the country to meet my betrothed. One of my brothers came along as a chaperone. It was … difficult at first. I thought he was handsome and charismatic, but I did not know anything about him, or this country, or what it would be like to marry a werewolf. And then I learned about Alden."

"How did… How did you react?" That had to be a pretty big surprise.

"Privately, not well, at first." She sighs. "In my country, it's not uncommon for people, especially royalty or other members of the upper class, to have affairs or even mistresses, but it's not quite so open, let alone publicly condoned. I didn't quite know what to make of him or who he was to Sam."

"But, completely unexpectedly, I started to actually fall for Sam. He can be a little thick, but he's quite charming when you get to know him." She huffs a little laugh. "From the way he tells it, he started to fall for me too, and as we continued to romance each other, there just came a point where I had to make a choice. I knew Sam loved Alden, and I knew Alden was not going to go anywhere. So I could either learn to accept him or spend the rest of my life being unhappy about it."

"Was it that easy?" I'm skeptical.

"No." She laughs again. "Sam helped a lot. He pushed us to spend time together, showed us how much we had in common. And we both loved him, so in the end it wasn't too hard. It actually became very, very easy. And I certainly did not mind the extra pair of hands when it came to raising Max. Even with a full-time nanny, that boy was constantly getting into trouble. These days, I love my life and my family, and I would not change it for anything."

That sounds really nice. I can picture the three of them late at night, fussing over a baby Max. Then the darker part of my mind creeps in again and wants me to ask about their sleeping arrangements, but I ignore it.

"How did you know it would work out, being in an arranged marriage?" It must be so strange to be told you're marrying a man that you've never met. "I mean, it feels like everything is moving so fast. It's hard to make a decision about something that is so … permanent."

"Believe me, I understand," the queen assures me with a pat on my leg. "I had no idea if it would work out with Sam. I did not have the option to say no, either. Had there been any problems, it's hard to know for sure what I would have done. If the issue was just that we were not a great match, I likely would have remained silent, probably dealing with it by focusing all my energy on Max. But if he turned out to be cruel or abusive? Then I think I would have found a way to leave, my father's alliance be damned. But I am happy to say I had nothing to worry about."

"I suppose you didn't." She seems like such a strong woman. I'm glad it worked out pretty well for her in the end.

"You know, you *do* have a choice in all of this, Peter." She gently places her hand on my wrist. "You are right in that this is a permanent decision you are making for yourself. And if it does not feel like the right one, if becoming my son's consort is not the right fit for you, then it simply isn't. There is no shame in that. But do not let fear cloud your judgment or keep you from something you may actually want. And do not be afraid to talk to Max about how he feels, either."

"Thank you, ma'am. I'll try to remember that." I sigh, not quite sure if I actually feel any better about things. "I have a lot to think about."

"I am sure you do." She nods her head. "I've always found gardening to help when I needed to think through a problem. Would you care to join me?"

"I'd love to, Your Highness." I jump at the chance to help the queen with her garden. "Thank you."

It's been ages since I've been able to get down in the soil, and I've actually really missed it. Maybe reconnecting with my roots will help me come to a decision. And if not, I'll at least get to clear my head for the afternoon.

CHAPTER 10

"As you do not currently have any official standing, it is imperative that you not speak before any of the gathered nobility unless you have been spoken to."

"How will I know who's a noble?"

"They will be announced at the start of the session, after the king, queen, and prince. Next, we will go over appropriate attire..."

I sigh as Kamo continues his lecture. It's been about a week since I learned about the claiming bite from Max. I felt a lot better after talking to his "Papa" Alden and his mother Anna, though not enough to agree just yet. I told him that I still needed more time before I said yes, but that I didn't want to go anywhere. He was happy to hear that, and since then things have thankfully gotten less awkward between us.

While the rest of the week was filled with our usual lessons and wandering around the castle, tomorrow is something special: I'm joining Max in court! He asked me yesterday, and I said yes, even though I didn't really understand what going to "court" involved. So today Kamo is giving me an etiquette lesson.

It's been going alright. There are a *lot* of rules, like where to sit, who to talk to, and even what to wear. I'm trying to remember things and take as many notes as I can, but I just know I'm gonna mess something up. So much of this just seems so ... stupid. But of course, I don't say that out loud.

"And that completes our lesson," Kamo finishes with a small sigh of relief from us both.

"Thank you, Kamo," I tell him, writing the last of my notes.

"Before you leave, there is something I need to say to you," he says as he composes himself. "I wanted to apologize for the events that transpired on your first day here in the palace. I had the kingdom's best interest at heart, but I was a bit over-enthusiastic in preparing you to meet the king and queen. I am sorry for the physical and mental humiliation you suffered as a result that day."

"Thank you, Kamo," I accept his apology without hesitation. "I really appreciate that."

"If there is anything else I can do to make amends, please let me know," he says while trying to hide a small grimace.

"I will." I ignore it, smiling. "I'll see you tomorrow."

I leave the lesson room with a little pep in my step. It was nice of him to apologize like that, even if it did sound forced. I haven't interacted with or even really seen much of Kamo since that first day, but I'm betting Max or his parents put him up to it. But I'll still take it. Momma taught me that holding a grudge only hurts you in the long run.

Max has a late training session with some of the knights tonight—the werewolves, specifically, which means I'm on my own for dinner. I take a bath when I get back to my room—I'm still getting used to having my own bathroom with running hot water. It's so fancy I almost miss the farm's outhouse. After toweling off and redressing, there's a knock on my door, and I open it to see Daniel and Hannah on the other side, each with a tray in hand.

"Peter!" Hannah greets me with a smile.

"Heard you were with Kamo all day learning about court etiquette," Daniel says next. "Thought you might like some company for dinner."

"Sure, please come in," I say, allowing the two of them to walk past me into the room and set down their trays on the table.

"So you're joining the prince in court, huh?" Hannah starts as she takes a seat.

"Yeah, tomorrow morning," I confirm, joining them at the table. "Though I'm still not sure I understand exactly what it is or what happens there. Have either of you ever been? Can you tell me about it?"

"Stuffy," Daniel answers without hesitation, uncovering the tray he brought to reveal a plate of sandwiches.

"We've never actually been ourselves," Hannah corrects with an eyeroll, reaching for one herself. "It happens once a month, sometimes more if there's something going on. The king gathers together the leaders of each of the island's provinces, and even the mayors of some of the bigger cities, all to go over the issues they're dealing with and resolve any disputes. Though more often, people just send representatives."

"There's also a lot of people who are there just to stand around and gossip. The whole thing is technically open to the public, so anyone can present their problems to the king," Daniel explains next. "But you've gotta jump through a lot of hoops to get in. Filling out paperwork, knowing the right people, and a bribe or two doesn't hurt either."

"That doesn't seem fair," I say before taking a bite of my sandwich, some sort of shredded chicken.

"Thuff involving rich people uthually ithn't," Daniel responds with a full mouth before swallowing.

"We usually see the king, queen, and consort a day or two before. They always want to look their best, but we don't have much else to do with it," Hannah continues. "But we both have a few side jobs outside of the castle with a few of the city's upper class who expect to attend, acting as stylists and cutting their hair and whatnot."

"Rich people are basically incapable of caring for their own appearances," Daniel adds, already halfway through his sandwich.

"Ooooo, I bet Trixie already has a nice outfit all picked out for you," Hannah says with a grin.

"So, how was it with Kamo?" Daniel asks next.

"Uh.... Okay, I guess," I lie. "I have a lot of notes to go through."

"I wouldn't worry about it too much," Hannah tells me when she sees me already reading over the multiple pages. "You'll be there with the prince, right? I'm sure he'll handle most things and help you out if you need it.

"Back to Kamo—was he a jerk?" Daniel is insistent.

"No, actually," I inform them. "He even apologized for what happened on my first day."

"The prince probably made him do that," Daniel points out.

"Yeah, probably," I admit with a laugh. "But I still appreciated it."

The rest of dinner goes nicely. I like the two of them, and I'm glad we're becoming friends. Afterward, when I'm alone, I go back to reading through my notes. I know Hannah is probably right, but I still want to try and remember everything I can.

Morning comes sooner than I'd like after staying up too late reading. Trixie knocks on my door bright and early, her arms filled with the day's outfit. It's a purple silk shirt and brown silk pants with a gold belt buckle, buttons, and other accents. It reminds me a lot of my outfit for dinner.

When Max comes by a short while later to collect me, I am impressed by his own outfit. He's also dressed similarly to the night we had dinner with his parents, but just … more. His shirt color matches my own and has a golden pattern on the silk in the shape of the royal crest, and a sash thrown over his right shoulder. His cape even seems longer.

"Wow, you look…" I start.

"I know. It's too much." He frowns and looks down at his clothing.

"I was gonna say great," I finish with a smile.

"Oh." I think *he's* almost blushing for once. "Well, you look great too. All ready for today?"

"I think?" I answer honestly as I join him in the hall. "I'm nervous I'm gonna mess something up."

"Don't worry. Just follow my lead," he tells me as we start down the hall. "Honestly, this whole thing is gonna be pretty boring. Half the reason I wanted you to come was to help keep me entertained."

"I'll do my best," I say with a smile, biting my lip.

We head downstairs in the direction of the throne room. I might not have the best memories of the last time I was here, but I'm sure whatever happens today will be pretty memorable in its own right. There is a large group of people gathered at the back door to the room: knights in their shining armor, Kamo, and the king, queen, and consort looking their best.

"Right on time, son," King Samoset comments as we approach.

"You look very nice today, Peter," Queen Anna tells me with Alden nodding in agreement at her side.

"Thank you, Your Highness." I blush slightly.

"Good morning, sirs, madame." Kamo bows to the gathered royals. "If everyone is ready, I will begin the pronouncements."

"Take it away, Kamo," the king gives his go ahead.

The older man nods his head before opening the double doors, stepping inside and to the right.

"Now presenting, His Royal Highness, King Samoset Blackclaw, Queen Anna Blackclaw, and the Royal Consort, Alden Blackclaw."

As soon as Kamo finishes speaking, the king and queen walk into the room arm in arm with Alden right behind them, all three flanked by a group of guards. As they enter, Max has the two of us step into their place near the door, taking my arm as the remaining guards move around us automatically.

"His Royal Highness Prince Makseka Blackclaw and his honored guest, Peter Lambert." *Honored guest?*

Before I have a chance to piece that together, Max leads us in with the guards. The room looks much different than it did last time. Not the layout or decorations—it's just full of people now. More than I've ever seen in one place before, all of them are staring at Max and me as he walks us forward toward two chairs to the right of his parents on the throne platform. I hesitate to call *these* thrones because apparently, one is for me. His parents are already seated, except for Alden, who is kneeling between their actual thrones, while the knights all stand in formation at our sides and behind us.

Kamo continues to announce to people, now reading from a small scroll he's pulled and unrolled from his pocket. Each of these people enters through the opposite end of the room, the way I came in the first time, walking down the center carpet until they reach the throne platform. Most of them have titles, Lord or Lady, and after bowing to the king, they turn and join the rest of the room, some taking a seat at one of several tables while others stand closer to the walls.

They're all dressed in their very best, some even looking fancier (and maybe a little weirder, especially in the hat department) than any of the actual royals. But what I notice more than that is the way they're all *staring at me*. Some are even turning to each other and whispering. It makes me want to sink into my chair and disappear.

I do my best to ignore them, which isn't actually that difficult since it's just Kamo reading names, one after the other. I pick a spot on the far wall and stare as he drones on ... until I hear him announce someone and their own consort. My eyes are immediately drawn to a young woman with a *collar and leash* around her neck, the other end in the hand of the older man who was just announced. I've never seen Alden in a leash, but I can't help but watch her as she is led around by it. *Would Max ever do that to me? Would I want him to?* The thought gives me a funny feeling in my stomach and a tight one in my pants.

A few more consorts are announced, men and women, some with leashes and some not, but each looking and walking elegantly as the first woman did. Finally, Kamo makes it through the entire list and announces that the proceedings will now begin. And just as Max warned me, that's when things get boring.

One by one, each of these people, nobles or representatives or whoever, come forward to speak to the king and queen, seemingly in the order they were announced. Some of their issues are large, like the city of Onglov needing help recovering from a flood after the dam in the Foxgrove River was breached, but most of their problems are small and even petty, like the man who just wanted to complain about his cousin being awarded more land than he was in his father's will. Some of the people don't seem to have any problem at all and just want to compliment and suck up to the king.

This goes on all morning and into the early afternoon. I manage to tune out most of it, only paying attention when I hear Kamo announce that lunch is about to be served. Instead of eating by ourselves, we move into a dining room, this one with the kind of ridiculously long table I expected to see when dining with Max's parents the other night. There aren't enough seats for everyone, so it seems like only the best of the best are invited to eat with the king and his family.

We are seated with them down at one end of the table. King Samoset is at the head with Alden and Anna on either side of him. Max is seated next to his mother, and I'm next to him. The other seats are all filled with nobles and other upperclass people, the man on my right giving me a stink eye. A few of the people around us try to talk with Max or his mother or Alden, but it's clear that who they really want to speak with is King Samoset. Even after the first course is served, he is continuously peppered with questions, requests, and praise.

"Is it always like this?" I lean over to ask Max under my breath.

"Pretty much," he responds. "At least it's more than halfway over."

"So much of what they're asking for seems so ... stupid." There are real people with actual problems in Weston, and I'm sure every other Litkalaan city. "Like, was that one guy really complaining about the title he received?"

"That's nothing. There was once a man who came in just to whine that the horse my father had gifted him was missing a tooth," Max says next. "He *literally* looked a gift horse in the mouth."

I laugh at Max's stupid joke, covering my mouth with my napkin. "So much of that seemed so pointless."

"You're not wrong, but Dad says it's important to appear open for your subjects to speak to," he starts to explain. I'm not sure how much I believe that, considering I haven't seen a single non-rich person here all day.

"We used to do this every other week, and my dad cut it down to once a month because he feels the same way," he continues to explain. "Most of the big problems are solved before they ever even reach the throne room. I told you that he delegates as much of his responsibilities as he can. He'd probably like to do even less if he could and let the people figure things out for themselves."

I think about that as we finish our meal—which takes about an hour and a half for all the courses to be served. Then it's back to work, I guess.

The second half of the day is a little less structured than the first and with only about half the amount of people. Instead of going back to the throne room, we're brought to what's apparently called a "drawing room." There are chairs and couches for people to lounge on, and servants walk around offering guests glasses of wine or ice water. Not a single drawing, though.

King Sam and his spouses are seated together at one of the nicer looking tables, already being pestered by more guests. Max has us sitting together in a quiet corner with me on one couch and him on another, as far from as many prying eyes as we can be here. The people around us are trying to talk to him, but thankfully ignoring me for the most part. I'm once again zoning out, at least until...

"Prince Makseka!" a particularly shrill voice cries out.

Max and I look up to see two people approach, a man and the woman the voice is attached to. She is wearing a *very* low-cut emerald green dress while he is in a fancy black suit, his bowtie the same emerald green. They both have brown eyes and light blonde hair and share several facial features, so they've gotta be related.

"Ah, Charlotte, Edgar," Max names them as they come to a stop in front of us. "I'm so glad you could make it."

"It is good to see you again, my prince," Edgar says with an overly formal bow while Charlotte curtseys.

"Your Highness, have you given any thought to who you will be taking to the Lavender Ball?" Charlotte asks, obviously fishing.

"Now, now, sister, I'm sure he would much rather discuss the upcoming Cornwall Jousting Tournament," Edgar interjects.

Max doesn't look like he wants to talk about either of those things or anything else with these two, for that matter. But seeing as I don't exactly feel like sitting around and being ignored for yet another conversation, I excuse myself to get some water. I stand, looking around the room until I manage to find someone with a tray of glasses, taking one with a "thank you."

I turn back to the corner I was sitting in with Max, not at all surprised to see Charlotte is now in my previous seat. With the way she's leaning over the arm of the couch, she's practically spilling out of her dress. *Does she not realize Max isn't interested in ... those?* I keep the thought to myself as I start to walk back.

"Who *is* he?" I hear a voice behind me say.

"I don't know, but it seems like they're letting just about anyone in here these days," another voice adds with a scoff.

I turn my head to find their source, but there are just too many people. Either way, I know they were talking about me, and I can't help but curl in on myself a little, trying to shrink my presence in the crowded room. I turn back toward the couches a little too fast, banging into someone and spilling my glass all over them.

"Would you watch where you're going!" Edgar angrily shouts after I douse him in cold water.

"Oh gosh, I am *so* sorry!" I panic and freeze. "Wait, please, let me get you a napkin."

"Unbelievable!" he fumes, the white shirt under his suit turning transparent. "I don't even know what someone like *you* is doing here, you oafish backwater peasant!"

"I—I—"

"What the hell did you just call him?" *Max!* I didn't even notice him coming toward us.

Neither did Edgar, whose look of fear I manage to catch right before he begins to slowly turn around and greets the prince face to face.

"Prince Makseka!" His voice is *way* too high pitched. "I apologize! I meant no off—"

"I'm not the one you should be telling that you're sorry," Max growls with a glare.

"I, ah," Edgar stammers as he nervously turns back to me. "I apologize for my outburst. I meant no offense; I merely allowed my emotions to get the better of me. It will not happen again."

I want to open my mouth and say something, but I'm still frozen in place. Almost all of the eyes in the room are on me again, and I would give anything for them to be anywhere else. With me not saying anything, and after looking to Max for approval, Edgar slinks off with his tail tucked between his legs to join his sister.

"Alright, I think we've had enough of this for today," Max tells me as he takes my arm. "Let's get out of here."

He walks us both out of the room, and even though I can't bring myself to look up, I can still feel *everyone's* eyes are on me. It's only when we're out in the hall with the door closed and away from everything that I feel like I can breathe again. I can't believe how badly that went. *Why do I have to be so big and clumsy?*

"I'm so sorry," I say to Max once we're alone, ready to beg for forgiveness.

"You have nothing to apologize for," he insists, squeezing my arm gently. "I can't *stand* those two."

"Were they your friends?" I ask with hesitation.

"Hardly." He scoffs. "I guess you could say we were childhood friends, but even then, the only reason we ever played together was because they were some of the only other children in the castle. Their father, Kristen Halfdan, is friends with my father."

"Was she...?" I keep thinking about how close Charlotte's boobs came to popping out of her dress.

"Hitting on me?" Max looks to me for confirmation. "Yep. Not sure if she's oblivious or just really hoping she can change my mind."

"They didn't seem all bad," I offer, not really believing myself.

"The Halfdans only talk to me when they want something." Max sighs as we start to climb the stairs together. "Or when they want to brag about something. Or when they want something to brag to their other friends about. I couldn't tell you a single thing about them that isn't fake. It's not easy finding *real* friends when you're royalty."

"It must be hard never knowing if someone likes you for you." It makes me miss my own friends.

"You know... That gives me an idea." I'm not sure if it's because he sees the sad look still on my face, but Max's mood seems to brighten pretty quickly. "Do you still have the clothes you wore here on your first day?"

"I do." I nod. They're in my bag with my other things, though I'm not sure what he's getting at.

"Good. Get them together for me," he tells me. "I'll meet you in your room in a few minutes, okay?"

"Okay." I nod again, even more confused by what he's got planned.

"Great!" And then we split up, Max presumably returning to his own room while I go to mine.

I get back to my room and changed out of the too-fancy outfit into something a little plainer, a little nervous that Trixie will have my head if I mess it up. Then I find my other clothes as requested, which are currently folded neatly on the table in front of me. I have no idea what Max is planning. I just hope it doesn't involve anyone from downstairs. Even after what Max said, the words still sting. *I guess they're letting anyone in. Backwater peasant.* When I hear the knock on the door, I'm happy for the distraction.

"Hey," Max greets me when I open it. He has removed his crown, cape, and sash. "Did you find your clothes?"

"Yep, right there." I point to the items folded on the table.

"Perfect." He walks over and grabs them, stuffing them into a leather bag he's got slung over his shoulder. "Are you ready?"

"Yes... Though I'm still not sure what for," I answer honestly.

"You'll see. Come on." He takes me by the hand, pulling me from my room.

"You know... I didn't expect to see other people with consorts like that," I mention the other thing that stuck out to me about today. "I didn't even know there *were* that many people with consorts."

"They're not *actual* consorts. Most of them aren't even werewolves," Max starts to explain. "But nobles like that want so badly to be a part of this life that they imitate us, 'claiming' consorts of their own, even if they're nothing like our actual relationships. It's a status thing."

There's certainly a much younger part of me understands why. I follow Max as we walk the castle halls, him greeting any servants or guards we pass on the way. At least at first. The path we're taking seems familiar, leading to the library, but about halfway there I notice Max walking a little more softly and looking around before turning any corners. When we finally reach the library, he pulls me inside and locks the doors behind us.

"Is there something in here you wanted to show me?" *Why did he bring me in here, and why did he lock us inside?*

"Yes, but that's only the start of tonight's adventure." He grins before marching through the bookshelves with purpose.

He turns left about halfway into the room, not stopping until he reaches the far wall of books. He turns again and continues down past a few more rows until he stops for a final time, turning toward the wall. There's a thin stone divider between each of the shelves on the room's four walls, and the one in front of us doesn't look any different from the others.

Each of the dividers has a metal candlestick sticking out of it, and Max locks his eyes on this one. He reaches up and grabs it, rotating it until the stick is pointing to the right. Then there's a *click* before the bookcase to our left suddenly swings inward and reveals a hidden tunnel.

"Oh my gods." I walk toward the now open entryway in wonder. "This castle has secret passages?"

"Of course. It wouldn't be a real castle without them," Max tells me with a wink. "Some of my earliest memories are of my Nana Yura showing them to me and the two of us using them to sneak around and play pranks on Grandma, Grandpa, and my dad. These days, I use them to sneak in and out of the castle when I need to get some air or see the city."

"This will take us out of the castle?" I ask as I walk a little closer. It's very dark inside.

"It'll take us downstairs toward the kitchens. There's an exit near there that will take us out into the forest," he says as he rummages through his bag.

"From there we'll be able to sneak into the city. Here." He holds out a small round glowstone for me to take.

"We'll need to be quiet," he keeps explaining as we walk all the way inside. "Most of the castle's rooms are magically insulated, but werewolf hearing is strong and there's a few tricky spots."

After we enter, Max pushes the bookcase back into place with another *click* before leading me through the passage. Though it starts as wide as a bookcase, it thins out as we navigate our way through the castle's walls. The light Max gave me is a big help, though trying to go up or down the stairs back here still feels dangerous.

Every so often the tunnel will spill out into a wider "room," where there's evidence of someone having been here long in the past: old clothes, the occasional chair, or the odd children's toy. Max points out a few peepholes on the walls where you can spy into the hallways, and some of the other hidden entrances to these tunnels tucked away in corners or behind furniture just out of sight. Eventually, I can smell food, signaling that we're near the kitchen.

"Okay," Max says as we reach another small room, reaching into his bag and handing me my old clothing. "Change into these. They'll be a lot less conspicuous in town."

I still have the clothes in my arms when I see that he is already starting to strip. I know I should get started, but I'm frozen—for a good reason this time—as I watch the muscles of his chest rippling as he pulls off his shirt. His pants are next, revealing an equally hairy set of legs, thighs, butt and... I turn away before I can get caught staring, even though I kind of want him to.

By the time I'm finished redressing, Max is in an outfit unlike any I've seen him in before. It's a simple tan cotton shirt, the kind with a couple of buttons near the collar, over some brown leather pants that have probably seen better days. Even his boots are plain and worn in. If it weren't for the dark gray cloak he has on over everything else, this could be something I'd wear on the farm.

"Like my disguise?" he asks as he pulls the hood over his head.

"I can hardly recognize you." At least from this distance.

"Good." He straightens his clothing and nods. "Okay, let me just make sure the coast is clear."

He moves along the wall, placing his ear against it and listening. When he's satisfied, he reaches around on the stones in front of him, pressing on different bricks until one sinks farther into the wall. There's yet another *click*, and then the portion of the wall in front of Max partially slides inward, revealing a thin passage leading to the forest outside. With an over-the-shoulder grin, Max squeezes through the thin passage on his side, urging me to follow until we are out and standing in the forest behind the castle.

"This way," Max quietly guides me away from the castle and into the trees before turning to the left.

I can still see the castle walls as we march through the woods, though I'm sure it's much harder to see us. Max moves with purpose, silently but quickly—you might even say wolf-like. We don't move in a straight line, curving our path inward until it's not the castle that I can see through the trees, but the large wall that surrounds the city.

"There's an opening around the corner that we can use to get in without anyone noticing," Max says as he leads me out of the forest and around a stone wall.

There's a break in the wall, just big enough to squeeze through that leads into an alley that runs behind the homes along the outside of the city. Garbage cans and old lumber litter the road around us, but just as Max said, there are no people. At least none that I can see.

"Alright, we made it," Max says with excitement as he leads me out of the alley and onto the city streets. "Time to explore St. Kizis!"

CHAPTER 11

MAX

I'm so excited as we walk out onto the St. Kizis streets that I could shout. I don't, of course, because when you're in disguise, you need to keep a low profile. Besides, I'm a little too busy watching Peter for his reactions to do much else.

He's next to me, looking at everything around us with wide, curious eyes. It almost makes it a little *too* obvious that he's not from around here, but I don't have the heart to tell him to tone it down. Not when he looks as excited as a kid in a candy store—which is a place I need to make sure I take him to while we're here.

I don't have our entire trip planned out. There are a few places I know I want him to see, but I want us to have plenty of time to just wander and explore too. Still, I point us in the direction of the university—I want our first stop to be the famed St. Kizis belltower.

"Wow," Peter breathes out a few minutes later when we're standing outside of the cathedral.

"Yeah, I'm impressed every time I see it," I admit, looking up at the tower with him.

The St. Kizis Lunar Cathedral is over three-hundred years old. It took almost fifty years to construct with countless workers, magical and non-magical alike. The centerpiece of the building is the belltower, which rises high over the rest of the city, its bell ringing out every hour before sundown. It's almost as tall as the castle, and the whole building is located right next to St. Kizis University.

There are deep arches along the outside of the building, each made with impressively detailed stonework. The walls of the tower are carved with reliefs of wolves and the moon while on the opposite end is the cathedral proper, a large sunroom where most of the sermons actually take place, featuring tall stained glass windows displaying images of non-werewolves and the sun.

"I can't believe it's that old," Peter comments after hearing the random facts I've been spouting off. "It's hard to believe anything could be that old or take so long to build."

"The priest in charge of starting construction wasn't even alive by the time it was finished," I share one last tidbit of information with a quick grimace.

"Aww, that's kinda sad." Peter frowns.

"I wouldn't worry about it too much," I reassure him. "From what I've read, the guy was kind of a dick to all the workers doing the *actual* construction work."

I walk with Peter from the cathedral's courtyard over to the university, passing a large fountain with a sculpture at its center. Father Sun and Mother Moon are back-to-back, surrounded by birds, wolves, and many other animals that you might find in the nearby forests. Water streams down their stone bodies into a small pool where several young children are playing and splashing around.

"So this is the university?" Peter asks when we reach the entrance to the grounds.

"That it is." I nod. "It's almost as old as the cathedral."

St. Kizis University is the largest college in all of Litkalaa. Students come from every corner of the island to attend classes here, and while not *officially* a religious institution, they share land and some staff with the cathedral next door. I hear the two have a fairly good working relationship ... for the most part.

"Have you ever been inside?" Peter asks me, watching students entering and exiting the large building ahead of us.

"I toured it with my parents when I was younger," I answer. "But going here, being a student, that was never an option."

"Not even part time?" He looks over at me with a frown.

"Nope." I shake my head. "It's okay though. Even if it were safe enough, it's not like I'd expect to have the same experience or get the same treatment as everyone else anyway. My parents had to specifically make sure my tutors knew *not* to just give me a passing grade because I'm the prince—most teachers aren't going to want to tell the king his son is failing math, you know? But what about you? Did you ever want to go here?"

"It was a nice idea when I was younger, but I never actually expected to get in here, or anywhere else." He looks down, maybe a little embarrassed? "I do know some people who attend, though."

"Friends?" I ask next. "Do you want to go in and maybe see if we can find them?"

"Oh, no, that's okay." He shakes his head very quickly. "I guess, maybe we used to be friends? There's no bad blood or anything, we just weren't close enough to keep in touch after they moved away, and I don't see a point in bothering any of them now."

"Alright then, in that case..." I take Peter by the shoulder and turn him to our left, pointing. "My favorite bakery is right around that corner. Let's get some cupcakes."

I lead us away from the school neither of us was ever going to attend and toward something much, much tastier. As per its name, Coleman's Bakery was built and is run by the Coleman family, and they sell some of the tastiest pastries in the city. I don't get to come here very often, but I try and stop in whenever I sneak out of the castle.

"Is that you, Alec?" the woman behind the counter asks as we enter.

"Mrs. Coleman, it's so good to see you!" I wave and try not to look surprised because I just remembered I haven't actually mentioned my "Alec" persona to Peter yet.

"Where have you been?" she asks me with her hand on her hip. "I feel like it's been ages since I last saw you."

"Sorry, things have been pretty busy with work lately," I quickly come up with an excuse. "Dad had some business out near Blackport, and I tagged along with him to help with a few things."

"Selling horses out in Blackport?" she considers my fake father's non-existent trade. "I'm sure he'll be doing some good business there. Now, who do we have here?" She looks to Peter.

"Oh, this is just my new friend... Larry," I answer after too long a pause.

"H-Hello, ma'am." "Larry" waves awkwardly at my left.

"I was just telling him about how amazing your cupcakes were, and I decided he needed to try them for himself." I manage to sell it anyway.

"Oh you sweet talker." She pats the glass display case to her right. "I just got done frosting a fresh batch."

Peter and I walk up to the case and gaze at all the wonderful baked treats inside. There are sweet rolls stuffed with jam and drizzled with honey, tasty looking pies, and at least ten different kinds of cookies. But the real treat is at the very top—rows and rows of elaborately frosted cupcakes. Some have sprinkles, some have chocolate chips or nuts, and all of them look amazingly delicious.

"They all look so good," Peter agrees, in awe.

"They are." But we've got things to do, so I'm going to make an executive decision. "Do you like chocolate?"

"I do." He nods.

"Two of the chocolates, please." I hold up two fingers on one hand for Mrs. Coleman while the other digs into my bag for the wallet pouch I keep with my disguise.

"One silver for the both of them." Mrs. Coleman tells me with a smile.

"You can't give me a discount every time I come in here," I say as I drop the money in her outstretched hand. "Otherwise Mr. Coleman is going to start getting the wrong idea," I flirt, ending with a wink.

She lets out a small giggle as she pockets the coin before stepping behind the display case and removing our cupcakes. She slides across the counter for us without getting even a single drop of frosting on herself, whereas Peter's and my hands are both immediately sticky with it.

"You boys enjoy, and don't you be such a stranger, Alec!" she tells me as she bids us farewell.

"I won't. Have a great day Mrs. Coleman!" I wave goodbye as we leave. "Come on. There's a nice park we can sit in down the street."

"Sure thing, 'Alec,'" Peter teases with a grin.

"The first time I snuck out of the castle, someone asked me for my name, and I panicked and said Alec," I explain the origin of my secret identity as we walk. "And it just kinda stuck. *Larry*."

The park I bring us to is small and technically nameless. There's not exactly a lot of room for a ton of greenery in the city, so we take it where we can get it. It's just the corner of a city block that's been covered in grass and a patch of trees, a small pond at its center with a couple of benches placed around its edge. There are a few children playing tag as we enter, so I guide us to sit on a bench on the opposite side.

"So, what do you think of the city so far?" I ask Peter before we both bite into our cakes.

"There are so many people here," he says with wonder, a little frosting on his nose.

"A lot bigger than Weston, huh?" There are barely a hundred residents, according to our last census. I *might* have looked up some things about Peter and his hometown in my spare time.

"Much smaller." He nods his head. "Pretty much everyone in town knew each other."

"Do you miss it?" I ask with some reluctance. I don't like thinking that I took him away from everything he cared about... even though that's exactly what I did.

"I do. Not that I'm not having a great time here," he quickly corrects. "It's just all I knew for nineteen years."

"I understand." *And feel guilty about it.* "What was it like growing up there?"

"Busy," he answers without hesitation. "A lot of my friends would probably say it was the opposite and complain about there being nothing to do, but I never felt that way. I grew up watching Momma and Daddy working on the farm, and as soon as I was old enough, I was out there helping them."

"I bet that kept you really busy." I *don't* mention how adorable I find it that he refers to his parents as "Momma" and "Daddy," or the way I caught him talking to their *cows* (seriously, so cute) but I do wonder what kind of work a kid does on a farm.

"Very, but I loved it." He looks down at his half-eaten cupcake, smiling. "All the hard work made me feel good. Accomplished. It's part of why I've felt a little ... bored sometimes, being in the castle."

"I'm sorry. I didn't realize." *Even though I should have.*

"It's okay. I have a lot more to do now." He smiles, talking about his own schooling. "I've been making friends with Daniel, and Hannah, and Oliver too. I mean, I wasn't *always* working on the farm. Sometimes I'd just hang out with my friends."

"Tell me about them." Even if I feel bad, I like seeing how happy he gets talking about them. I'm glad he's made some new friends, too—I'll have to thank Oliver when we get back.

"I was never really popular or anything. There were only a few people that I hung out with regularly." He licks some frosting off his thumb before continuing. "There's Monica. She's *really* smart and used to help me out a lot with my homework and studying. She has a boyfriend named Ricky whose parents own their own farm in Weston, even bigger than ours. But it's Violet who's my very best friend. I've known her since I was a little kid, and we were pretty much inseparable all throughout school. There were some people who actually thought we were gonna get married someday." He chuckles a little nervously.

"She's who I smelled on you the morning we left Weston," I say with realization.

"Mhmm," he confirms and nods, though I can tell he wants to change the subject. "So, what about you? Tell me about your own friends."

"Well, you've already met most of them," I admit with a frown. "The only *real* friend I have these days is Oliver. Everyone else is like Charlotte and Edgar: fake and only interested in what being my friend can do for them."

"That sounds pretty lonely," he sympathizes.

"Growing up in the castle was very different from Weston," I start with a sigh. "I was lonely, but with all the servants everywhere, never really alone. The only time I'd ever see other kids would be the children of other royalty visiting with their parents or maybe the child of someone on the staff who bought them into work that day."

"I can't imagine growing up without other kids to play with," he tells me, the frosting on his nose making his frown look more silly than sad. "That must have been hard."

"I dunno. It's not like I had a hard life or anything," I try to justify myself. It's hard to act like you had a crappy childhood when you know you're going to be king someday. "I was just lonely. Most of my 'friends' were the castle staff themselves, which comes with its own set of issues. For a long time, I thought that the only reason people are nice to me is because of who I am and that they were paid by my parents. Then I met Oliver."

"What did he do that was different?" He finishes off his cupcake, getting more frosting on his nose.

"He talked to me," I answer with a smile, reaching over to wipe the tip of his nose with my thumb. "Like, *actually* talked to me. He wasn't afraid to talk back or speak his mind or call out my crappy behavior. Believe it or not, I used to be even *more* entitled and spoiled than I am now."

"I still can't imagine using those words to describe you," Peter butters me up.

"Well, he doesn't hesitate to," I say with a chuckle, taking another bite of my cupcake. "I first met him when I was sixteen and he was eighteen. His father works as a guard in the castle, and his mother is the kitchen's head chef. I figured he was just going to be a pushover like the rest of the staff, but one of the first things he did was tell me off for being rude to the maid that had just made my bed. We've been friends ever since."

"That's nice." Peter smiles. "I'm glad you have someone like him."

"Me too." Though on the subject of me having friends and him not... "I'm really sorry for taking you away from your friends and family. I'm sure you miss them. Maybe we can go visit them soon?"

"I'd really like that, but..." He hesitates to continue, biting his lip. "I... I haven't actually heard from anyone since I left."

"What do you mean?" I could have sworn he mentioned writing them letters.

"Well, I wrote to my parents and Violet right after I got here, and I still haven't gotten a response." He curls in on himself as he talks. "I don't know if something is wrong or if they're mad at me for leaving... I've just been worried. Did... Did you send the healer to town, like I asked?"

"I did. She left the day after we got back to the castle." I nod my head, dumbfounded by this information. "We sent out the money to your parents on the same day, but the only thing I've heard back was her telling us that she would be staying longer to help look after the town. She said the local doctor was a bit overwhelmed and under-informed. But I don't really have any specifics other than that."

"Oh. Right. I understand." Oh gods, the sad way he's looking down at his lap is breaking my heart.

"We're just about due to send the batch of gold to your parents," I say, quickly coming up with an idea. "I can ask for the doctor to send back some updates at the same time."

"Really?" He looks over, his face a little brighter. "That would be great... Thank you."

"Of course. I just want you to be happy and comfortable while you're here." I pat him on the upper thigh and squeeze. "Since we're done with the cupcakes, are you ready to see more of the city?"

We spend the next couple of hours walking all over St. Kizis, with me pointing out the various sites to Peter as we pass. I show him the city's marketplace, the theatre, the merchant guildhall, and the headquarters for the city guards. There's also the old Concourse Bridge that leads over the moat into the castle, the Lady Luciana Memorial Garden, dedicated to one of my distant relatives, and the statue of St. Olaf, where people leave flowers in the hopes that he will watch over their deceased loved ones. When we're finished, the sun is just getting ready to set, and it's just about time for dinner, so I bring us to the last place I wanted to visit today: the Mammothbone Tavern, which is right near the alley we used to sneak into the city.

It's not the biggest tavern or the fanciest, nor does it have the best food, but that's why I like it. It's a quiet little hole in the wall where you can enjoy your evening in peace. We slide into an empty booth after we enter, and I order us both a mug of ale from the serving-boy.

"I know this place is a little different," I say, seeing the way he inspects our surroundings.

"I like it," Peter assures me. "It actually reminds me a lot of home."

"It has good beer, decent food, and no one will bother us," I tell him with a grin.

"Are you sure we aren't going to get caught sneaking out like this?" he asks with some nervousness.

"Nah, we'll be fine," I assure him. "Anyone who comes looking for us will just assume we snuck off somewhere together, and a couple of uneaten dinners sitting in our rooms aren't the end of the world. Plus, I told Oliver to cover for us before we left." I give a wink before downing some ale.

I order us two of whatever the kitchen is serving for dinner tonight when our server brings us our next round. After that, we both receive plates holding half a roasted pheasant over some potatoes and steamed carrots. As we start to eat, a bard begins to play his lute on the other side of the tavern, singing us tales of epic adventures.

We finish our food and down a few more beers as we listen to the performance. There's the tale of Bruno the Dragonslayer, and even one about my great-great-great-great grandfather Turok and his battle to protect the island from invaders. Then we hear a new one about a coming hero, or maybe one long past? It's not fully clear. Supposedly blessed by the gods, he possesses incredible speed and strength, and is either destined to be born in or die in a storm of blood and thunder. Each of the stories is far-fetched, but they make for good entertainment. When the last story is finished, and so is our food, I leave a couple of gold coins on the table before we make our exit.

"We should probably start heading back to the castle now," I inform Peter with a sigh as we walk away from the tavern. "Did you enjoy your visit to the city?"

"I did, a lot." He nods, and I see his hand tentatively reaching for mine before it drops back to his side. "Thank you for bringing me."

"The pleasure was all mine," I tell him, taking his hand with confidence.

"No, really," he continues as we enter the alley that will lead us back to the forest. "You didn't have to do any of this for me. It's not like those people in court were wrong—I am just some peasant who doesn't belong here."

"You really don't think very much of yourself, do you?" I ask after hearing him put himself down yet again.

"I... I'm nothing special." He shakes his head as we round the outer wall of the city.

"I happen to think you're *very* special," I tell him as we continue deeper into the forest.

"You'd be about the only one," he responds while looking down, fully accepting what he's saying about himself.

"I find that very hard to believe." I stop us, turning to Peter. "Can I kiss you again?"

"You... You don't have to ask if you want to kiss me." Hearing him say that is already more than enough for me, but then he decides to go one step further. "*Sir.*"

Blood rushes to my heads—both of them—a moment before I push Peter's back against a tree and kiss him. He gasps in surprise against my lips, but quickly relaxes, his eyes closing automatically and his hands coming up to hold my shoulders. I swipe my tongue against his lips, plunging in as soon as he opens them and pressing my body against his.

He moans into my mouth, his hands clutching me tighter as I grind my crotch against his. We are both already rock hard, and combined with that title he just called me, I'm feeling a little bold. I reach up with my hand, running my fingers through his blonde hair before taking it in a gentle grip.

He moans when he feels me grab him by the hair, and then again when I tug it to the side, baring his collar. I tear my mouth away from him only to plant my lips on his neck, nipping at him gently with blunt teeth. His whole body shudders when I bite firmly into his flesh, his arms sliding around my back to hold me in place against him.

He tastes so fucking good. Almost as good as he smells. I continue to bite and kiss everywhere from his neck to his collarbone, stopping for a few more minutes of kissing before I pull his head in the opposite direction so I can switch sides. Suddenly, the hands holding onto my shoulders squeeze me as Peter moans even louder until his whole body gives another big shudder, and he freezes. *Wait, did he just...?* I sniff the air once to confirm—Peter just came in his pants.

"I-I'm sorry!" he stutters and attempts to push me away.

"For what?" I correct as I hold him in place. "Because I just made you cum without touching yourself? Do you have *any* idea how hot that is?"

"I..." He looks completely mortified, still furiously blushing, so I kiss him again.

"Gods, to know that I was able to cause *that?*" I kiss him along his neck again. "I don't think I've ever gotten a bigger compliment."

"It's... It's embarrassing..." he says, clearly uncomfortable, but at least he's smiling now.

"Why?" I challenge him with a grin. "It's not like there's anyone else out here to hear us. Unless you want to stop and go back inside..."

He bites his lip and shakes his head no, hands still around my back. Satisfied, I lean back in for another kiss, once more grinding our groins together. Despite the mess he may have made, his erection doesn't feel like it went down even a little. I love this—I'm no virgin, but I've never fooled around out here in the forest before, and it's more than a little thrilling. At least, until my ears pick up the sound of someone or something trudging through the forest toward us, and I quickly pull back from Peter so that I can listen.

"Is everything okay?" *Shit, the poor boy looks worried that he's done something wrong again.*

"Yeah, everything's fine. I just thought I heard something." I pause, listening for whatever it was before, but only finding silence now. "It was probably nothing... but it *is* getting late. We should probably get back inside sooner than later. Besides, you probably want to change out of those sticky pants."

"If you think that's best," he agrees with a little reluctance and a big smile. "*Sir.*"

I growl again. "You keep that up, and I'm not even going to make it back to my room." I kiss him one last time before pulling him away from the tree.

"Is that a promise?" he teases as we start to walk.

I lead us back toward the castle walls where I search for the entry switch on the outside. I push the brick in with a *click*, causing the door to swing open again and allowing us to slide back within. Before I close it behind us, I listen out into the forest one more time for that strange sound, but there's still nothing. Satisfied once the entrance is closed, I pull a glowstone out of my bag and hand it to Peter. We can't all be blessed with decent night vision.

"So, I hope you don't mind me asking this, but..." I start as we make our way up the dark passageway, "are you a virgin?"

"I... I am." He's blushing so much that I could see it even without the glow of his light. "But I know how it all works. Where babies come from."

"There's no shame in being a virgin," I assure him. "It's not that uncommon, even at our age. Plus, I bet you didn't exactly have a lot of options back in Weston, right?"

"I'm not sure there was another gay person in the whole village," he answers with a sigh. "My parents still gave me the baby-making talk when I was pretty young, and well..."

"What?" I ask when he goes silent, turning to see him looking very bashfully at his feet.

"Well, we had a lot of animals on the farm, including dairy cows," he starts to explain, still too embarrassed to look up. "But dairy cows only start producing milk after they're pregnant. I was really young at the time, but I can remember when Daddy paid Mr. Johnson to bring over one of his bulls so it could..." I didn't think he could get any redder, but then he has to go and prove me wrong. "I, um, always kinda wondered what it felt like ... for the girls."

"Fuck..." For whatever reason, that little admission of his goes straight to my cock. "You were just a curious little thing, weren't you? Wanting to know what it felt like to get filled up like that?"

The dirty talk spills out almost automatically, but when I see his breath hitch in reaction to it, I know I've done my job. Without saying another word, I crowd him against the wall and kiss him again, hard. We make out there in the dark passage for a few minutes until the sounds of someone walking through a distant hallway reminds me of where we are and what we are doing.

"Well, maybe soon I can help you figure that out," I flirt after breaking our kiss.

"I... I think I'd like that," he responds, breathless. "Sir."

I swallow the growl I want to release, instead taking Peter by the hand as we continue our way back to the library. The room and the outside hall are both empty, so we're able to get back inside without any issues. It takes all my power not to follow Peter back to his room or invite him back to mine. Instead, I manage to bid him goodnight with a final chaste kiss, fully intending to spend the evening with my hand once I'm in bed. Maybe a few times.

CHAPTER 12

PETER

"Are you nervous about tonight?"

"I bet he's been counting down to it all week!"

A week after the painful day in court and my sneaky trip into the city with Max, another event is about to take place: the full moon. That means it's time for the werewolves of St. Kizis to gather in the forest behind the castle again. And this time, I get to attend too!

It also means that I have officially been living in the castle for over a month now. A month where I haven't heard from my parents or friends in Weston even once. I've been trying not to worry about it or take things personally, but it really is starting to get to me. The last time I asked him, Max said he was still waiting for word back from the castle healer that was sent to Weston.

I've been doing what I can to keep busy though. My lessons have been going well. Miss Yadrow said I'm just about ready to start on basic algebra, and I surprised Mrs. Koplat yesterday by already knowing the life cycles of a lot of different plants—though she did have to help me with the technical names for everything, like "germinate." I only had a short lesson with Mr. Longfellow earlier today, and afterward, I came down here to the spa to hang out with Daniel and Hannah.

"You're both right," I tell them. "I'm excited *and* nervous."

"Aww," Hannah sympathizes with me. "I wish we had something to tell you about what goes on during the full moon."

"It's not like either of us have ever been invited," Daniel says with a shrug. "But from what I hear, it's not nearly as exciting as you'd think."

"How would you know?" Hannah challenges with one eyebrow raised.

"I hang out with werewolves sometimes," Daniel defends, crossing his arms.

"Wait, are you still seeing that guard?" Hannah questions him, suddenly interested.

"We might have had another date last week," the brunette man says nonchalantly while pretending to look at his nails.

"So, I was wondering," I try and steer the convo back to the events of tonight, "even though you guys haven't actually been, is there anything you can do to help me prepare for it? Like, fix my hair or something?"

"Oh, sweetie, you don't need to worry about any of that," Hannah assures me. "I hear it's a pretty casual affair."

"Yeah, you shouldn't expect to hear from Trixie today either," Daniel adds with a shake of his head. "You're about to spend a lot more time up close and personal with the royal family than most people in the kingdom."

I know their words were meant to calm me down, but all they do is make me more anxious. Now I'm not just worried about saying or doing the wrong thing in front of the king and queen but also an *entire pack of werewolves*. I'm a bundle of nerves by the time I get back to my room, pacing back and forth while I watch the sun get lower and lower. I'm so nervous that I open the door not even three seconds after Max knocks.

"Hey there, Sunshine." *His smile always makes me feel a little calmer.* "Are you all ready for tonight?" He's dressed casually, almost like he was when we snuck out of the castle, which makes me glad I didn't try to change into something nicer.

"I think so?" I answer, unsure of myself and looking to the room behind me. "Is there anything I should bring?"

"Nope." Max shakes his head. "Everything we need for the night should already be set up."

"Then yes, I think I'm ready." *As I'll ever be.*

"Great." He smiles brightly as I step into the hall with him. "There's some people I wanted to introduce you to before the sun goes down."

Great, more people to embarrass myself in front of. I don't share my feelings out loud as we walk down to the ground floor together. Instead, I try to focus on the excitement I'm feeling at being let into this world instead of the nervousness. I still haven't made up my mind about Max claiming me or not—but maybe tonight will help to answer some of my questions.

When we're on the ground floor, Max leads us toward the back of the castle where the kitchens are. Before we reach them, we take a turn and approach a different room with a set of guards posted outside. They bow their heads to Max as he walks between them, opening to reveal the rest of his family inside.

The king and queen are seated on a couch together while Alden is kneeling at the king's feet, head leaning against King Samoset's thigh. While they're not quite as casual as me or Max, they are still dressed much less formally than I've seen them before. For a second, it feels like we've walked in on something too intimate for our eyes, though none of them seem overly concerned about it.

"There you are, son," the king greets us as we walk in. "Good to see you, Peter."

"We are happy to have you joining us tonight," Queen Anna adds with a smile. "Even though we may not seem like ourselves for most of it."

"Don't worry. I'll be there to explain things while they're all wolfed out," Alden tells me with a grin as he stands.

"Are we almost ready to go?" Max asks, sounding a little restless.

"Should be. We are just waiting on Kamo to—" The king is interrupted by the doors opening behind us.

"Ah, Prince Makseka, wonderful," Kamo says as he enters the room. "I've triple checked that all the preparations are complete, so we can proceed to the gathering spot whenever you are ready, sire."

"I think we can get started." The king looks at his spouses for confirmation before standing with Queen Anna. "Lead the way."

Without another word, the three of them follow Kamo back out of the room with Max and me right behind them. We exit the rear of the castle through another set of guarded doors and into the forest outside. I recognize the torch-lit path leading into the forest from my balcony and turn my head to the right, looking up to see if I can pick out which room is mine.

"So, tonight is gonna get a little weird," Max leans over to say under his breath, taking my hand and squeezing. "Just go with it. You'll have more fun than you expect."

"I will," I reply with a smile that isn't *entirely* forced, squeezing his had in return.

The path leads us deep into the forest, way deeper than Max and I ventured last week. If it weren't for the torches, I'm not sure the path would be obvious at all. After another fifteen minutes of walking, the path opens up into a large clearing. There are more torches set up around the perimeter with a large bonfire at its center. There are several tents, some benches and tables, and a few makeshift wooden shelters, some with leather hanging like curtains. Not quite what I would have expected for the royal family.

Many people are already here, milling about the camp. I see a few familiar faces from the castle, like guards and some of the knights, but there are plenty of new faces as well. There are men and women close to me and Max's age, some closer to his parents', and some even older than that, along with several children as well. Almost everyone turns to us as we enter, a few approaching with smiles, while most of the others just look at me strangely.

"Sam, it's good to see you!" a friendly older man says as he approaches, his hand in the air waving. "Did you have a chance to talk to..."

"Come on. While my parents say their hellos, we can say ours," Max says as he pulls me away. "You've actually already met them, unofficially."

We leave Max's parents and head toward a group with some familiar faces—the knights that Max was traveling with when he visited Weston. There are two men and two women, and I only caught one of their names before—Aria, I think. They watch me carefully as we approach, not quite closed off, but not exactly friendly yet either.

"Hey, guys. You all remember Peter," he introduces me to them, one hand on my shoulder. "Peter, this is Aria, Thomas, Ryse, and Gala. They're my personal guard and who I train with."

Ryse is the tallest of the group, even taller than Max, with black hair, brown eyes, and a rough patch of stubble on his face, like he hadn't shaved in a day or two. Aria is the next tallest with short brown hair and blue eyes—and since I already sort of know her, that makes her the least intimidating. Then comes Gala, who looks about as tall as I am with light blonde hair pulled into a ponytail and brown eyes, and then finally is Thomas, who as a dwarf is the only non-human in the group, and is also the shortest by at least a foot and a half with brown hair and brown eyes. They all look me over appreciatively, their smiles not quite reaching all of their eyes.

"It's nice to meet you all again," I greet them with an awkward wave.

"I'm kinda surprised to see you're still here, farmboy," Gala says in response, not quite scoffing.

"Ignore her. She's always crabby right before moonrise," Thomas says on her behalf. "We're happy to have you here."

"Yes, it's good to have you with us," Aria agrees.

"Mmm," is all I get out of Ryse, along with a nod.

"So, how are you liking your stay in the castle?" Thomas asks me as our group moves closer to one of the shelters.

"I bet it's way cushier than working on that farm," Gala adds dryly.

"I've been liking it a lot, so far." I don't let the attitude get to me. "It's not as busy, but there's still a lot of exciting things going on all the time. Like tonight."

"Excited for moonrise?" Aria asks me with a grin.

"I think so?" I look around, seeing that even more people have joined the gathering. "There are a lot more people here than I expected."

"Every werewolf in the city," Max informs me. "I wish you could've come last time."

"Right, that's why you made your little visit back to the castle last time after we got Jackson under control," Thomas says with realization.

"See that guy there?" Aria points to a knight, seeing my confusion. "That's Sir Jackson. He's the werewolf that was just bitten, who shifted for the first time during last month's full moon."

"He was a little wild last time," Max adds a little wearily. "Nothing out of the ordinary for a newly turned werewolf. The pack stayed with him all night, made sure he stayed in control and didn't run off to try and hurt anyone."

"He's been training with the wolf squad since then," Aria continues explaining. "Practicing his shifting and getting used to his new senses. He's been doing good so far, so there shouldn't be any issues tonight."

I smile and nod, though I hadn't even considered that something *could* go wrong tonight. But I am going to be spending the night in a forest full of werewolves. Maybe I should be more cautious.

"What happens now?" I try not to sound nervous.

"Well, I think just about everyone is here," Max answers after a scan of the area. "The sun is almost down, so my dad will say a few words soon and then—"

"Everyone!" King Samoset says loudly to the group, raising his hands and getting everyone's attention. "As always, I want to thank you all for being here again. This is a long-standing tradition, but it is always good to see everyone's faces, old and new. Now we only have a few minutes, so I'll leave everyone to get prepared. I will see you on the other side!"

After he's finished speaking, he turns to his wife and Alden, all three of them stepping behind one the leather curtains. A few others do the same, but almost everyone else starts to strip right out in the open. I almost panic before I remember why—they don't want their clothes to be destroyed. And I'm guessing that some people, like the queen, prefer more privacy for that sort of thing.

Max and his friends are not those people. I turn away for a second, and when I look back, Gala already has her top off, and the rest of the group is joining her, including the prince himself. I quickly find myself staring down at my feet, my cheeks burning.

"Aww, he's modest too," Gala teases as she finishes stripping.

"You'll get used to the nudity," Max assures me, smiling when I dare to lift my head up to look at him.

"Newly turned wolves can sometimes be a little shy, but most of us have been doing this for so long together that it's just not a big deal," Thomas explains. "But not everyone. Some people prefer to disrobe and transform in private. Even the queen."

"Yeah, Mom's never been comfortable with public nudity," Max admits. "Once you're shifted, you learn to stop caring. There's not really any other option."

After everyone seems to be just about done stripping down, they all gather their clothes together and place them under one of the nearby shelters. I have to be careful when I'm looking around, trying to keep my focus above people's shoulders. Then I see a few people start to transform.

"Is it starting?" I ask Max, not seeing anything from him or his friends.

"Not yet." He shakes his head. "Some people like to shift beforehand."

"Is it different?" I ask, unaware of that quirk.

"Not really." He shrugs. "You still freeze up when you feel the urge pass through you. Actually, it is going to happen any minute now, so why don't you stand over here?"

He guides me to a spot just off to the side where they've laid their clothes as the five of them start to spread out like the others. I move to where I'm asked, keeping my eyes focused on Max and not any of the other dozens of naked people. The sky is dark, and I can feel the energy in the air. Then, when Max and everyone else freezes in place, and I know it's starting.

They give a sudden jerk, some of them falling to the ground as the change begins. Their limbs grow longer, noses stretching into snouts as hair sprouts all over their bodies. It was hard enough trying to imagine Max transforming into that monster I saw below my window a month ago, but being around dozens of werewolves all shifting at the same time is freaking me out. I can *hear* them shift, their bones scraping together, their insides squishing as they move around. I have to look away and almost cover my ears at one point.

When it sounds like it's over, I dare to look up and am greeted with the sight of a forest full of werewolves standing in the clearing. A second later and they all raise their snouts to the sky, howling in unison. The sound feels like it runs through my entire body before everything goes silent and still, and everyone suddenly seems very tense. Then I hear a small bark, and everyone turns to see two of the smaller wolves—werewolf children, which are exactly as adorable as you think they are—growling as they roughhouse on the ground. That seems to break the spell, everyone turning to each other and starting to move around and interact. I see a few non-shifters among them, but for the most part it's werewolves as far as the eye can see.

Max, in his new hulking form, takes a few steps toward me carefully, stopping before he reaches me to leave me some space. He's even bigger up close, making me feel truly small for the first time in my life. He's covered from head to do in jet black fur, each of his fingers ends with a sharp claw, and his mouth has been replaced with a snout filled with shiny, sharp teeth. I know this should be scary, and there is a part of me that is anxious to be surrounded by literal monsters, but after looking up into those familiar blue eyes with a small smile, I close the distance between us and reach out a hand toward his chest. In response, I get a small *woof* and a lick across my face.

"Max?" I manage to not sputter, getting a huff and quick nod in return.

Behind him are his friends, and I realize for the first time that the color of everyone's fur matches the hair on their heads. I also notice that everyone's … *everything* is exposed and once again have to make a point of not looking below their shoulders. Though not before I get a good eyeful of what some of these werewolf men are packing, which is intimidating to say the least. *At least it doesn't look like a wolf's, I guess?*

There's a low bark behind Max—Thomas, judging from his height. He's about a foot shorter than Max, with thicker legs and a barrel chest. Just behind him, I can see an elf-werewolf, who seems particularly lithe and with extremely long ears compared to the others. I never even considered there would be a difference in the way they'd look.

The group of young werewolves starts to talk, or at least I think that's what's happening. There are some noises, but there's mostly a lot of movement and body language. I'm not sure what they're saying, but none of it seems negative.

"Max, Peter!" someone with an actual voice calls out.

Max and I both look over to find the source: Alden, standing next to two werewolves. One has black fur similar to Max's, though with some gray accents around his face, while the other is auburn—King Samoset and Queen Anna. Alden is waving us over, so with Max in the lead, we cross the sea of newly sprouted fur. I feel like I get a lot of strange looks as we move, though I'm probably also just *very* aware of my current surroundings at the moment.

"I thought you might like to be with someone you can actually speak with tonight," the brunette man says with a grin after we join them.

"Thank you," I tell him, glad I'll still get to use actual words tonight. "What happens now?"

"It varies," Alden answers while Max "speaks" with his mother and father. "But usually—"

King Samoset interrupts with a bark and a toothy smile.

"—the pack will go out to hunt, as a group or individually," Alden finishes, smiling at his furry spouse. "Then everyone sort of breaks out to do their own things for the night."

As if on cue, the king and queen step away from our group, letting out two short, loud barks and getting everyone's attention. There are several barks in response, and most of the pack begins to gather together around the king. As he leads most of the werewolves out of the clearing and deeper in the forest, Max pauses, giving me another lick and nuzzling against my neck before joining them. I wave at his back as he leaves.

Most of the pack seems to have gone with only a few werewolves remaining in the clearing, most on the younger side. There are about ten non-shifters too, not counting children. I think I saw a few leaving with the rest of the pack, but it was no one I'm familiar with.

"Peter, I'd like you to meet Kendra and Steven." I turn back to Alden to see him standing with two of the other humans. "They're both claimed, like me, by members of the kingsguard."

Both appear to be around his age. Steven is about as tall as I am with dark brown hair that has a few shocks of gray in it while Kendra's hair is an almost equal mix of gray and brown, wound in a simple braid that runs down her back. I notice now that they and most of the other humans have also changed their clothing. While they aren't naked, what they are wearing is much simpler—the men are both shirtless, and Kendra has a simple wrap around her top, all three wearing shorts that leave their legs exposed.

"It's nice to meet you both," I say, extending my hand.

"It's nice to meet you as well," Kendra tells me.

"We know very well that this can all be a lot to take in at first," Steven adds with a smile.

"Yeah, it's all very ... new," I try to say politely. "What do you usually do now while the others are off hunting?"

"Just relax, talk, tend to the fire," Kendra answers simply. "We normally just spend time with our wolves."

"Sometimes we'll join them for the hunt," Steven says next. "Though that is really more of a young person's game."

"There's no real goal for the night," Alden tells me, walking over to a pile of wood, picking up a long log and breaking it over his thigh, throwing both halves into the bonfire. "Just spending time together as a group."

"You're so strong," I say in amazement. *He snapped that like it was a twig.*

"Comes with the territory," he responds with a smile. "So does better hearing, better smelling, and better sight—at least at night."

"That sounds pretty great." I can only imagine the work I could have done on the farm with that kind of strength...

"It's not a bad deal," Kendra adds. "I still feel like I'm in my thirties."

"Could I..." I pause, hesitant for a moment, but when will I get another chance like this? "Would it be alright if I asked the two of you about being claimed?"

"Sure," Steven answers.

"Go right ahead," Kendra tells me. "I assumed that's one of the reasons Alden wanted us to meet."

"Correct," Alden confirms. "Ask away, Peter."

"Okay." I'm a little nervous, but at least I already asked my stupid questions to Max last month. "How did you know that you wanted to be claimed? I know about the 'side-effects' that come with the bite, so what made you decide that it was the right thing for you to do?"

"Well personally, I viewed those side-effects as a benefit," Kendra answers first. "I like being an aunt, but I never wanted kids of my own, and neither does Sir Dakota, my wolf. So it was actually a fairly easy decision for the two of us, and we haven't regretted it since."

I have to admire her confidence as she speaks, the way she seems to know exactly what she wants.

"It wasn't quite as simple for me and Wyome," Steven answers next. "She had already delayed her accepting the king's bite until after we had our two children, but even afterward we still occasionally harbored the idea that we might have more. But eventually, and I apologize if this is too much information, we decided that her claiming me was the right thing for our relationship. And just like Kendra, we've never once looked back with regret." He tilts his neck to proudly show off his collar, the metal shining in the light of the fire.

"But the point is, they still all talked about it together," Alden brings it back to communication. "Just like you and Max are doing."

I'm happy that I got the opportunity to talk to Kendra and Steven. For Alden and me, it seems like the main reason for being claimed is that it's the only way we can stay with our royal men. It's hard to imagine someone willingly giving up not just the ability to have children but also a lot of control in general to a werewolf, so being able to see their faces as they speak joyfully about their lives really sets me at ease.

I meet a few of the other non-shifters, the spouses or children of werewolves, some claimed and some not. It's easy to tell who's claimed and who isn't by the collars around their neck, but it's almost like the opposite of the people in court—no one here is trying to imitate the royal family; they were claimed by a werewolf because they wanted to be. They're all friendly for the most part, though I do feel a few of them eyeing me warily. The children don't seem to pay me much attention at all, too engrossed in their own games of hide and seek.

"So you do this every month?" I ask the others as we sit around the fire a little later.

"Pretty much," Steven answers. "It's usually a pretty quiet night."

"I know tonight is a new experience for you," Alden tells me. "There really isn't much more to it, but I don't want you to be worried if you notice anyone acting strangely. The full moon changes everyone here—even us."

"What do you mean?" I ask, already intrigued,

"All of our instincts are brought to the surface," he starts to explain. "Not the human, but the wolf."

"It affects you like that too?" I can't help but notice him saying "our." "What does it feel like?"

"It's a little hard to describe," Alden says, before trying anyway. "You already feel different after the bite—things like the urge to hunt or chase, wanting more physical contact, and even finding it easier to read someone's mood. It's all just overcharged."

"Not as much as it is for them, of course," Kendra adds some info. "But on full moons, we feel closer to them than we do our human halves."

"But at least we can still hold a beer mug," Steven says as he pours ale into a mug from a nearby keg.

"I just don't want you to be ... shocked if Max does anything that seems out of the ordinary," Alden finishes his thought. "It makes sense to him, at least right now."

I'm not sure I really understand what Alden is saying, but I'll try to keep an open mind. Steven offers me some ale of my own, but I turn him down, wanting to stay as clear headed as I can tonight. I spend the rest of the early evening with them and the rest of the people who stayed at our little camp, watching the werewolves and their children together and seeing how Alden and the others help out, like one big family. It's nice.

A couple of hours later, the first of the werewolves who left to hunt start coming back with their spoils. Some carry large game, like a dead buck in their arms or over their shoulder, while others are holding smaller animals in their claws or mouths. A few have nothing at all, but they don't seem too beat up about it.

I see Max's eyes before the rest of him as he exits the forest, something red and bloodied in his jaws. His eyes seem to lock onto me as he stalks forward, and if it weren't for the tail wagging behind him, I might be intimidated. Okay, *more* intimidated. You try being in a dark forest at night surrounded by werewolves! When he finally reaches me, he stops, crouching down and dropping whatever was in his mouth in front of me. It looks like ... a rabbit?

"Is... Is this for me?" I ask hesitantly. *Is this what Alden meant?*

Max huffs and nods his head, tail still wagging, as he leans forward to lick across my face. I do my best not to flinch or wipe myself dry right away, but that's going to take some getting used to. Max looks from me to the rabbit expectedly, but I'm not sure what he wants me to do.

"That's very nice, Max, but you know humans can't eat raw meat," Alden tells him as he approaches the two of us. As he bends down to retrieve the animal, Max makes a few grumbling noises. "None of that. Let me get this cleaned up and *then* you can feed him, okay?"

Max huffs, apparently in agreement, and allows Alden to remove the rabbit. After he leaves us, Max guides me toward his friends with a careful clawed hand on my back. The four of them watch me with curiosity like before, and when we come to a stop, Max allows them to approach and circle us, sometimes leaning in to sniff at me.

I hear some more werewolf noises before, without warning, Max takes a hold of me—and I'm suddenly in the middle of a werewolf cuddle pile. I don't know what the etiquette is for these things, so I just lay there and allow myself to be wolf-handled. This feels playful, not horny, and ends with me laying atop Max's chest with I think Aria at my back.

After laying like that for a while, everyone disentangles. I can sense something like a conversation happening between them. When Ryse suddenly tackles Max, I'm worried they're fighting over something, but I realize they're just roughhousing like the children were earlier. I sit back against a tree, just watching, and definitely *not* staring at the well-muscled and fur-covered bodies rolling around on the ground together... Nope.

"Here." I look to my left and see Alden holding a bowl of something steaming that he hands to me. "Rabbit stew."

Max belts out a happy bark when he hears that, looking up from his current wrestling match for only a second. I eat my dinner while I watch the wolves continue to play, not sure if there is any reason for it beyond burning off energy. When I finish, I return my bowl to Alden, turning to find that Max has followed me.

Carefully taking my hand in his, Max leads me into the forest. I look back at Alden, who only waves and smiles knowingly as we leave. It's eerie out here, and I'm not sure what he wants, but I don't feel unsafe. If there is any danger, Max will to protect me.

I don't know where we are headed, but it feels like we're walking uphill. After a while, the trees give way to another, much smaller clearing. There's not a lot to see, just some flowers and a large boulder, but when Max points one clawed finger up, I understand why he brought me here. The sky above us is completely clear, the stars and the moon shining brightly down on us.

Max lets go of my hands, taking a seat against one of the trees as he spreads his legs and pats the ground between them. Taking his cue, I sit down in front of him, leaning back against his chest. His arms wrap around me as he buries his face in my neck, inhaling deeply before slowly licking over my shoulder.

And then we just ... watch the stars together for the rest of the night. It's nice and peaceful, and I'm kept plenty warm by the furry furnace behind me. Before I even realize it, I'm asleep in his arms under the night sky.

I wake up the next morning feeling groggy, my neck a little sore because of my sleeping position. Even though it's daytime, I'm still surprised to look back and see a naked Max asleep behind me instead of a werewolf. I can't see the sun, so it's either really early or really late. Not knowing if I should wake him, I readjust myself so that I'm lying next to him, trying to keep his nude and no longer furry body warm.

"Mmmmf," he groans when he finally wakes up about fifteen minutes later.

I stand up and offer him a hand to do the same, watching as he stretches his limbs once he's vertical. He cracks the knuckles on both of his hands and swivels his neck around a couple of times before turning to me and smiling.

"Good morning, Sunshine," he says with a sleepy grin. "Hope you had a good time last night."

"I did." I nod and step close to him. "Thanks for letting me come. And for the rabbit."

"Oh gods, sorry about that." He shakes his head at himself. "*Oof.* I'm always worn out after the full moon, so I think today is gonna be all about napping. And food. Come on. Let's get back to camp so I can find my clothes."

"Coming," I say with a laugh, watching the way his hairy, round ass moves as he leads us back to camp and the castle. I can definitely get behind doing this every month.

CHAPTER 13

"**...A**nd shortly after their marriage, Queen Carlotta became pregnant with King Wyman's first child, Prince Delmar, joining her previous children in the castle."

"The queen already had children?"

"Oh yes, Prince Tristan and Princess Sophie, who were fathered by the former King Andrew before he became the new kingdom's first royal consort."

It's another quiet day in the castle. I've really settled into a routine in the month and a half that I've been here. Lessons, spending time with my new friends, I've even been helping the queen in her garden! I'm really grateful to have something physical to do again, even if I'm not getting the same workout I used to on the farm.

Today's lesson is history with Mr. Longfellow. We're actually talking about the founding of the kingdom, when the werewolves first joined together with the mostly-human group of island settlers. Or colonizers, as he called them. I was already familiar with the story from school, but I'm starting to see it through new eyes now that I know more about the royal family.

"As part of the agreement in becoming his consort, King Wyman agreed to raise the couple's former children as if they were his own," Longfellow continues. "It is such a shame the tragedy that befell them in the following years."

"What do you mean?" This is the first time I've ever heard about these kids or a tragedy.

"Well, you see, the kingdom was still very young back then," he starts to explain next. "The treaty had essentially forcefully combined two different populations, and there was dissent from both."

"What happened?" Though I'm not sure I actually want to hear it.

"There were the loyalists to King Andrew, who felt a grave insult was being done to him and his lineage, whereas among the werewolves were those who felt that there was no benefit to this alliance for their own people, that they were being used as cannon fodder to protect these weak humans," he continues seriously. "What started as protests eventually turned violent. One day, when the royal family was traveling home to the capital, their carriages were attacked, and the carriage carrying the young Prince Thomas and Princess Sophie was set ablaze and crashed. Neither survived."

"That's horrible." *Who would go after children like that?*

"It was." Longfellow nods solemnly. "And now that Consort Andrew was sterile, it also marked the end of the Durenholtz line."

Longfellow pauses after saying that, watching me in a way that makes me feel like he's looking for a reaction. When I don't say anything, he continues.

"Those responsible were arrested and hanged, but from what I understand, the king, queen, and consort were never quite the same after."

"I don't think I would be either." I honestly can't imagine what it must be like to lose not one but *two* children.

The rest of the lesson is less dark, but afterward, I can't shake the sad story from my head. What would Max's parents do if something happened to him? Heck, what about my parents if something happened to me? The whole thing just makes me shudder.

"Peter!" I look up from my thoughts to see Oliver coming down the hall toward me. "I was just looking for you."

"Is everything alright?" I'm not usually someone being looked for around here.

"Yes, the king has just requested to speak with you," he answers with a nod. "I am to bring you to him."

"What? W-Why does he want to talk to me?" I ask with some panic. "Are you *sure* everything's okay?"

"As far as I am aware," he says with slightly shaky confidence. "At least, it didn't seem like anything was amiss when he made the request."

"O-Okay." I nod nervously. "Lead the way."

We walk through the castle until we reach a familiar wing, the one I think Alden's "office" is in. Unsurprisingly, the room he leads me toward has guards posted outside, who watch but otherwise don't acknowledge us as we approach. Oliver knocks twice on the door before opening it and leading me inside.

It's a room similar to Alden's, though bigger and... I dunno, fancier? There are big elaborate paintings of landscapes on the walls, and the desk the king is sitting at is *huge*. I can see small statues on just about every surface, an ornate looking rug on the floor, and a very nice-looking fireplace.

"...and there has still been no word from Sir Hebert." Kamo is also here, speaking to the king across his desk. "And no success from any of the mage knights we've asked to scry, either."

"Damn, it's been almost two months now." The king shakes his head. "And what about the situation with Deepwater?"

"My last two attempts at correspondence have gone unanswered," Kamo tells him with a sigh. "But I will continue to try."

"Thank you, Kamo." As Kamo makes to leave the room, King Samoset finally looks over to me and Oliver. "Peter! Thank you for coming to see me."

"O-Of course, Your Highness." *Like I'd tell the king no.*

"Did you need anything else, sir?" Oliver asks him next.

"No, that was all, Oliver. Thank you," the king dismisses the man, who leaves us in the room together.

"W-Was there something you wanted to talk to me about, s-sir?" I ask nervously now that we are alone.

"It was pointed out to me by all three members of my family that I am the only one among them who has not actually spent any time getting to know you yet," he answers with a smile, pushing his chair away from his desk. "So, how has your stay in the castle been?"

"I-It's been g-great, King Samoset," I say without thinking. "No problems at all."

"Please, Peter, have a seat and take a breath," he tells me with a laugh, gesturing to a chair on the other side of his desk. "I know it can be intimidating meeting the king, but I promise I don't bite."

"S-Sorry, sir." I clamber into the seat awkwardly.

"And please, you can call me Sam," he tells me next. "I get enough 'sirs' and 'Your Highnesses' from everyone else."

"Y-Yes, sir," I answer automatically and then wince when I hear myself.

"Habits can be hard to break," he assures me with a chuckle. "It took almost two years and a *lot* of pinches to my side from Anna and Alden to get me to stop cursing around baby Max. And that still didn't stop his first word from being 'fuck.'"

I snort out a laugh, not at all surprised by Max's choice of first word. Just like with the others, hearing the king talk about his family like that helps put me at ease—which was probably what he intended.

"Was Max a lot of trouble when he was little?" I decide to ask more about our common link.

"I feel exhausted just remembering it," he answers flatly. "Always running around the castle, hiding in rooms, and getting into all kinds of trouble. And once he figured out how to shift outside of the full moon, he was quite literally a little monster."

"He must have been a handful." I can't even imagine how you raise a small werewolf.

"We managed, and we made sure his nannies were *also* werewolves," King Sam explains. "He eventually grew out of that phase and started to actually behave instead of ripping all of his clothes off and going feral."

"Did you—" I cut myself off trying to hold back another laugh. "Did you ever want more children?"

"Yes, Anna, Alden, and I all did but..." He trails off with a small frown. "Anna had an amazing pregnancy, and Max was so perfect and healthy when he was born... I just didn't feel it was worth the risk. Why tempt fate?"

Before I can say anything to that, the doors to the room behind me swing open.

"Your Highness, the delegates—" It's a castle worker I haven't met before, who pauses when he sees me. "My apologies. I didn't mean to interrupt, sir."

"Come in, Jeffrey," the king tells him. "Is everything alright?"

"Actually, sir, the delegates from High Ridge and Eastbrooke have arrived early," the man says with some hesitation, naming two of Litkalaa's territories.

"Already?" The king rolls his eyes. "They're not due for another hour."

"I understand, Your Highness, but I'm afraid they've already started to argue," he continues with a grimace.

"I guess I better get in there then." King Sam sighs as he stands. "I am sorry, Peter, but I've got to help negotiate a trade deal between those two. "

"It's okay, sir. I understand," I answer, standing as well.

We both go our separate ways after exiting his office, my thoughts on Max and his family as I return to my own room. I'm surprised when I get back and find people already in it: Max and Oliver. Whatever they were talking about, they stopped as soon as I came in, and are now both just staring at me.

"Hey, guys," I greet them, stepping into the room. "What's going on?"

"Come sit with me for a bit?" Max asks, patting the empty space next to him. "I've got something I need to talk to you about."

"Is everything okay?" I ask with some worry as I take a seat.

"This is gonna be tough..." he starts, mostly to himself. "I finally heard back from Dr. Hiram, the healer we sent to Weston. I'm sorry it took so long. It was really hard to get her to tell me the details of who she's been treating. I had to use my title to throw my weight around."

"What... What is it?" I look from him to Oliver who looks uncomfortable but stays silent.

"It's about your friend Violet's father," Max bites his lip before continuing. "Dr. Hiram thinks she's figured out what is wrong with him. Do you know what cancer is?"

"I... I think I've heard the name before?" *It sounds awfully close to the month of "Cancea," I guess...*

"Well, Dr. Hiram thinks your friend's father has it in his lungs," he finishes, still frowning.

"That's good though, right? That they know what's wrong?" I ask with hope.

"It is *good* because now they can figure out how to properly treat him, but..." Max still seems crestfallen. "Cancer... It's not like other diseases. It doesn't react to healing magic the same way."

"I don't understand." It's an illness, isn't it?

"It's really complicated," Max struggles to explain. "It affects different parts of the body by growing these ... tumors, and they don't stop growing. Sometimes it can even spread."

"But, if they know what's wrong, can't they just ... magic it better?" I still don't understand. "Wasn't the whole point of sending them so they could fix it?"

"Cancer doesn't respond to healing magic like other diseases," he repeats. "There's no 'damage' to heal away, and there's a very specific way to use magic to treat it."

"Oh..." I try not to sound depressed.

"But it's not hopeless!" Max quickly adds after seeing how *completely* devastated I am. "Dr. Hiram thinks the guy has a great shot at beating it, and is already working with the local doctor to figure out treatment."

"That's... That's good." I try and fail to sound hopeful.

An awkward silence fills the room after that as I try to make sense of what I was just told. Violet's father is sick with a disease that magic can't even fix. No wonder she hasn't responded to my letters; she's been busy dealing with that.

A cough from Oliver has me and Max both looking up. With the prince's attention, Oliver looks from him to the window and forest outside, then back to Max. Max can only look at him confused, which Oliver responds to by rolling his eyes and giving him a look that says, "You know what I'm trying to say."

"Peter, why don't we get out of the castle for a bit?" Max offers after a second. "Get some fresh air and clear your head."

"Okay," I answer, not sure what exactly he's got planned.

<hr>

"I'm really sorry about your friend's dad," Max tells me a little later when we're walking through the forest. "I know it wasn't the news you were hoping for."

"It's okay," I answer, looking down as we walk. "It's not your fault."

"I know, but I still wish I could fix it for you," he says with a sad smile.

We're walking somewhere in the forest behind the castle. I thought we might have been going to the city, but I'm glad we didn't. This is much more peaceful. We didn't even have to sneak out this time—we just walked out past the guards at the rear gate.

I don't know what to do. I want to be able to do something for Violet, to help her. I know it was me and Max who sent the healer in the first place, but I still just feel so useless. *I'm a terrible best friend.*

"I just wish there was something I could do," I voice my frustrations out loud.

"I know how you feel," Max responds. "You want to fix something so badly, but you're stuck, barely even able to watch."

"What do you do when you feel like that?" I ask him next.

"Distract myself," he answers with a tired smile.

"How?" I will seriously take just about anything right now.

"Usually by coming out here." He stretches his arms out as we walk. "Going for a run or even a hunt. Burning off some energy usually helps."

"That does sound nice." I know exactly what he's talking about. Maybe not the hunting, but back on the farm, whenever I was feeling down, I could just spend a day in the fields and forget about my problems for a little.

"So, wanna do something right now?" He looks at me suggestively.

"Here?" I look around at the forest.

"Yeah!" he answers cheerily, and then points ahead of us. "There's a small river not too far that way. I'll race you there."

"But aren't you super-fast?" This doesn't seem like a very fair race.

"I won't use my full speed—promise." He holds up one hand as if making a pledge.

I was never the fastest runner, but it does usually take a while for me to tire out. *Hmm...*

"Okay!" I decide after thinking it over, and before Max can realize, I take off.

"Hey, no fair!" he calls out behind me with a laugh.

I feel a little giddy myself as the trees start to rush past me. I can hear Max close behind me in pursuit. I know if he wanted to, he could easily blow right past me, but the fact that he hasn't pushes me to run faster. I just hope I'm still headed in the right direction.

It's a few more minutes before I can see the river in the distance, just past more of the trees. My lungs are burning with the strain of running for so long, but I don't care. I can hear Max right behind me, but I think I might actually win!

"Who knew the crown prince would be so easy to beat?" I taunt behind me.

"Maybe I'm not aiming for the river anymore!" he shouts back from my side, making me look over and see the wolfish grin he's wearing—right before he tackles me.

The initial shock wears off when Max wraps his arms around me, taking the brunt of the impact as we fall to the ground. We roll together on the grass until we come to a stop with the prince on top of me. He looks down with a playful glint in his eyes, moving his arms to rest beside my head.

"Sorry about that," he apologizes, not sorry at all. "It's a wolf instinct; when you see something running, you just want to *chase*."

He emphasizes this last word with a roll of his hips, and I feel the hard lump in his pants grinding against me—and it starts to wake up my own lump. I can feel his full weight on me, and it's not a feeling I mind. Without thinking about it, I wrap my hands around Max's neck.

Something changes in Max too, his expression turning more serious— right before he leans down to kiss me. I let out a squeak of surprise when he pushes his lips against mine, relaxing a moment later. His tongue presses against my lips, and I open, and then we are kissing on the forest floor.

I hear myself moan into Max's mouth, unaware the sound is coming from me until it's over. Our hands start to roam over each other's body, Max's on my chest and arms. As our kisses grow deeper, Max relaxes on top of me. If it weren't for the sound of the river, I might even forget we're outside.

Max lifts himself up, reaching for his shirt buttons, which makes me do the same. When he sees that, he rolls off me entirely, pulling off his shirt before moving onto his pants. We don't stop until we're both naked, staring at each other's bodies as we lay on the grass.

Max is ... really nice to look at. It's not the first time I've seen him naked, but it is the first time I feel like I can actually look without it being weird. His chest is broad and muscled, his stomach flat, and he's covered from the neck down in a forest of dark, curly hair. Seriously, he's even hairier than I am. His thighs are thick, and what's lying between them is equally impressive in its size.

He's doing the same to me, his eyes wandering up and down my body. I feel myself blush but fight the urge to curl in or cover myself up, wanting him to see me the same way I see him. He doesn't look unhappy about it, his eyelids heavy as he looks over me from head to toe. My own cock has grown the same as his, and the shame I feel from being on display like this seems to only makes me harder.

Whatever he sees, he must like because he quickly climbs back on top of me. I automatically spread my legs for him to fit between them, moaning when his cock rubs against mine. He kisses me again, and I immediately wrap my arms around his back, squeezing him to me tightly. He growls into my mouth, humping forward as we make out.

Our kisses start to get rough, Max nipping at my lips with his teeth. His mouth moves from mine to my ear, his hot breath making me shudder as his tongue traces over the shell. From there he kisses his way down my neck, sucking and softly biting into the flesh. My fingers scrabble at his back as the sensations overwhelm me. And then he switches sides.

"I am so glad all of this grew back," he says as he starts to kiss his way down my chest, nuzzling into my body hair as I blush again.

He stops at my nipple, running over it with his tongue before sucking it into his mouth. I squirm, the sensation new but not unpleasant, and he makes sure to repeat it on the other side as well. He moves from there down to my stomach, his stubble tickling me and making me jump. He thankfully doesn't spend too much time there, moving even lower to my ... crotch.

"Nice to see you're big everywhere," he comments as he reaches for my cock without hesitation.

I jump when his fingers wrap around me, my hands digging into the ground at my sides. No one else has ever touched me like this before and I have no idea what I'm supposed to do. I must look terrified to him, but he only gives me is a cocky grin before lowering his mouth over me.

"Oh gods," I say out loud.

His eyes wrinkle as he smiles up at me with his mouth still full. He doesn't stop until he's got almost my entire dick in his mouth—which at nearly eight inches is a very impressive feat. He pulls back to the head before sinking back down two more times. Then he pulls off me, using his hand to stroke me as he catches his breath, and then he's right back to swallowing me down.

He is so good at this. Probably because he's had a lot of practice. That thought makes me start to consider my own lack of experience and whether or not I'll be able to give Max even half as good as I'm getting. Then a hand starts to stroke my balls and all other thoughts go out the window. Max keeps bobbing up and down, his cheeks hollowed out as he stares into my eyes with a hungry look.

"I'm... I'm going to cum soon," I warn when I feel the end drawing close ... and then whine when Max pulls off entirely.

"Don't want to finish just yet," he says as my wet cock pulses in the air.

He moves to lay next to me on the grass as I compose myself, my hands still at my side. I'm afraid that if anything so much as brushes against it, my cock will explode all over my chest and stomach. And if Max doesn't want me to cum yet, neither do I.

"That was... Gods," I try to say as I calm myself down.

"Thanks," he says, wearing that same cocky grin and tracing a finger over my chest. "The pleasure was all mine."

"That *can't* be true," I reply, still breathless. "But..."

Before I can talk myself out of it, I quickly climb over Max's body and kiss him again. Following his lead, I lick my way down his body, trying to pay special attention to all the same areas. He's surprised at first, but then I feel his hand on the back of my head, not pushing or guiding but just resting there. I make my way down his chest and stomach until I'm eye to eye with his... Wow.

It's impressive, that's for sure. He's bigger than me in just about every other way, at least an inch or two longer and almost thicker than my hand can go around. And I know I'm not exactly small, so that's saying something. I reach a hand out, gently taking his dick in my hands and slowly stroking up and down the shaft. It twitches as I hear Max's breath hitch, a bead of precum appearing on his head. Once again, before I can talk myself out of it, I lean forward and lick it.

It's an odd taste, at first. Not bad, but not like anything I've had before. Okay, that's a lie. I *have* tasted my own once or twice—I was curious!—but this is different. Salty and earthy, with a slight sweetness? I suck the whole head into my mouth on my second attempt, seeking out more of this new flavor as Max moans, the hand on my head gently tugging on my hair.

I start to lower myself more, trying to take as much of him into my mouth as he did. Which doesn't work. I don't think I even make it a third of the way down before I feel the urge to gag and pull back quickly. Max's hand strokes over my head, never pushing, like he's just letting me know he's there. After taking a few breaths, I try again.

I still can't take him deeper than a few inches, but that doesn't stop me from trying. I gag, a lot, so much that I feel like I must be drooling a ton of spit onto Max, but when I look up (through watery eyes) all I see is an encouraging smile. So I keep at it. Can't get better without practice.

Max starts to shift and pulls away from my mouth, and I'm worried I did something wrong, but then he adjusts us so that we're both lying on our sides facing each other, now head-to-toe. Or face-to-crotch, I guess. With it hanging in the air in front of me, I lean forward and get back to work on improving my sucking skills.

I moan around Max's dick when I feel him wrap his lips around mine, nearly humping forward against his face. *How is he so good at this?!* I try to focus on what I'm doing, reaching one hand up to hold Max steady and stroke some of his length that I can cram in my mouth. But Max's hands start to roam around my lower back and butt, squeezing and digging into the flesh with his fingers.

When one of his hands starts to try and delve deeper, I know I'm a goner. I groan as loud as I can with a stuffed mouth as I cum. My cock pulses as I fire off the first shot straight over Max's waiting tongue, so much that I'm sure the shots that follow are filling his mouth to the brim. The head of Max's prick slips from my mouth after I'm finished, laying down on the grass while I try to compose myself.

"That's... It was... *Grood*," I try and fail to explain how amazing that felt.

"Heh, sucked ya stupid, huh?" Max jokes as he pulls off, licking his lips.

"I... You..." *I'm just going to stop trying to talk for a little bit.*

While I do that, Max moves again, sitting up and adjusting so that I'm now laying between *his* spread legs. His cock is still hard and pointing straight up, the end slick with my spit. Determined to finish what I started, I situate myself on my stomach and get back to work.

Sadly, I'm still no better at this than I was a few minutes ago. My lips are already sore from being stretched around his thick shaft for so long, and I'm pretty sure I'm gonna have a sore throat in the morning, but dammit, I'm making him cum! Maybe sensing my determination, Max takes some pity on me and takes himself in hand, while still leaving the first few inches open for me to suck and lick on. We start to work together, his hands occasionally bumping up against my chin when our rhythm is off-sync, but I can see the way he starts to breathe harder, and when his hand starts to move faster too, I know he's about to finish.

"I'm gonna cum," he confirms through gritted teeth.

His hand attempts to tug me away, but I keep myself in place as he begins to fire off. The first shot surprises me, hitting the roof of my mouth, and the spurts of cum that follow quickly fill me up. It's a struggle to swallow everything, and I can feel it dripping down the sides of my mouth, but still, I manage.

"Wow." Max sounds breathless as he lays on his back. "Great job."

"Not as good as you did," I say, wiping my hand with the back of my mouth before squeaking in surprise when Max grabs me by the arm and pulls me to lay down next to him.

"Well lucky for you, we have plenty of time to practice," he says with a sleepy smile before leaning in to kiss me, probably able to taste himself. "But for now, why don't we get cleaned up before we head back?"

After a little more cuddling and some sleepy kisses, we manage to pick ourselves up, daring to wade in the river. It's freezing of course, so we only go in deep enough to wash off the areas that actually need it. Sadly, I lose my footing and slip, Max laughing as I tumble into the water. I splash him as revenge, the two of us playing together in the water until we realize the sun has almost set. We finally drag ourselves out and start the walk back, naked and still wet. We'll put our clothes on when we're close to the castle, but right now, walking together naked in the forest? It feels right.

CHAPTER 14

"Prince Makseka, I am sorry to interrupt, but your father is requesting your presence."

"I better go see what he wants," Max tells me as he stands. "Be right back."

He walks away with the attendant, leaving me alone on the couch in the corner. My second time in court with Max and his family has gone about as well as the first. I think there were even *more* eyes on me this time, thanks to the scene we made with Edgar Halfdan before our loud exit at last month's event. I'm trying to ignore all the stares and whispers, but it's hard.

It doesn't help that we're back in the same room it happened in. I saw Edgar and Charlotte earlier, but they've both kept their distances from us all day. In fact, it seems like a lot of people have, with fewer of them trying to approach Max to talk. Up until now, it's been nice, since last time Max was the only one who actually talked to me anyway. But now that I'm alone, it feels a bit too much, so I stand up. *I need some water.*

"—can't believe the prince is considering someone like *him* as his consort," I overhear a snooty voice say as I pass.

"Where is he even from?" someone else says next.

"Some unsophisticated rustic town in the west, I think," another voice adds.

"Eww, really?" a *fourth* person asks. "What's so special about him?"

"Hell if I know. He certainly doesn't belong *here*."

I can't help myself, scanning around me to try and see where the voices are coming from. I can see people looking at me, but not who is actually speaking. Not that I need to. Their faces say it all. *I'm not wanted here.* Already feeling my breath getting tight, I look around for Max, only to find him cornered against a wall by Edgar and Charlotte. Max and Charlotte don't see me, but Edgar does and smirks.

I don't bother saying anything. I just leave, doing my best not to rush out of the room and cause another scene. I head straight for the nearest bathroom, happy when I find it empty. I'm hot and sweaty, and my heart feels like it's pounding against my ribs. I turn the tap on one of the wash basins, filling my hands with some cold water and bringing it up to my face.

I stand there, the cool water dripping down my chin and into the basin. What doesn't soak into my shirt, at least. I've felt this way before. Back in school, when I'd have to speak in front of the whole class, my stutter would always get worse, and sometimes I'd even start shaking. I know how to fix this; I just need to calm down and *breathe.* I start to take deep, steady breaths, and after a minute or two, my heart finally starts to slow down.

"Towel?" I jump when I hear the voice.

"K-Kamo?" I sputter, my heart once again hammering in my chest.

"Apologies if I am intruding." For once, the man's gentle tone doesn't sound forced.

"Th-thank you." I take the small white towel he offers me, drying my face and hands. "You're not intruding. I just needed to get out of that room."

"Yes, I noticed," he admits with a frown.

"Was I that obvious?" *Great, I caused another scene anyway.*

"Not to everyone," he tries to assure. "I had been watching you."

"Making sure I didn't talk to anyone I wasn't supposed to?" Even *I'm* surprised by the amount of bite I put into that.

"No, I am pleased to say you have been following the rules of etiquette I passed on to the letter," he responds with a small chuckle. "It was more out of concern. I ... have been in your shoes before."

"You have?" I ask as I toss the damp towel into a small basket.

"Contrary to what I appear, I have not always been the well-mannered stick-in-the-mud you see before you." He makes a little flourish, gesturing to himself. "Honestly, I came from an even poorer background than yourself."

"Really? So then ... how'd you end up here?" I realize too late how rude that must sound.

"Luck." He shrugs off my words, adjusting his glasses. "I was an orphan living on the streets of St. Kizis. Sleeping in alleys, stealing food... It was certainly not an easy life."

"That sounds awful." I feel for the guy. No kid should have to live like that.

"By the time I was eight years old, I was resorting to just about anything I could to survive." I can see that he doesn't want to go into more detail on what "anything" might include. "I had become quite the thief, but then one day, I made a mistake and stole from King Nachek."

"You did _what_?" I actually forget my composure, my jaw hanging open in shock.

"I did not realize who it was, at first," he defends his younger self. "It was still the early years in his reign. I simply saw a very nice-looking carriage parked in the city. That day, the king, queen, and consort were making a public visit to a local business... A bakery I believe. But I did not know that. I just saw something that was probably owned by someone with money and decided to break into it. I did not know what I was going to find, but I assumed there had to be something of value inside that would help me get by for a few more days."

"Then what happened?" I'm already worried for the young boy.

"I was caught almost immediately by his guards," he explains, still smiling slightly. "I was terrified, expecting the worst, to be thrown in the dungeon or even executed. But in reality, the king was kind and understanding. He and his spouses simply talked to me. They asked about my life and how I was surviving. I was expecting them to be angry, to punish me for my transgression, but instead they took me in. They brought me to live in the castle, gave me my own room, hired tutors, and the king even increased funding to the country's orphanages. And eventually, much later, he offered me the bite and made me a part of his pack."

"How old were you then?" I'm a little in wonder at his story.

"Nineteen, so over a decade after my attempted thievery," he answers. "It took some time, but by then I was confident in my place with the royal family."

"What was it like, living in the castle?" I ask, already wanting to know more about his own experiences living here.

"Difficult at first, and not just because of how different it was from living on the street," he says, his serious veneer starting to resurface. "Many of the members of King Nachek's court did not view me as a welcome addition to the castle. They were smart enough to not voice their displeasure directly in front of the royal family themselves, but it was not difficult to discover what they truly thought of me. They did not understand why the king would want to associate with such an urchin, a street rat, a—"

"Backwater peasant," I finish with Edgar's words for me at last month's court session.

"Yes," he agrees, sadly. "However, I did not let their opinions bother me— as I said, I knew I was where I belonged with the royal family. But because of my experiences, I have taken my role as the king's attendant very seriously. I ... apologize for the times my dedication to the role has perhaps made me seem a bit cold or out of touch."

"I think I understand." At least a little about why he seems so serious about what he does.

"I also want to apologize again for the events surrounding your arrival at the palace. I know first-hand what it can be like to be forced to suddenly engage with people so different from your previous situation." He regains his composure, story finished. "I know my methods may seem extreme at times, but I never intended to make you feel further alienated. I assure you, I only want what is best for the royal family and the kingdom."

"Thank you, Kamo," I tell him honestly, appreciating the explanation. I can't say that I completely get the guy, but it does help knowing a little of his story.

"Now, I believe the prince is waiting for you in the drawing room," he says, his mask fully back on.

"Yes, you're probably right," I agree. "Thanks again." And I hope he knows I mean for more than the towel.

I leave the bathroom and make my way back, feeling a little less shaken after hearing Kamo's history. I don't know if I feel as confident as he did, but I'm starting to get there. And I think I'm confident enough to make a decision about my place here with Max ... and what better way to share that than publicly?

Still gathering my nerves, I walk back into the room and spot Max across the room in our previously occupied seats. He smiles, his eyes already on me thanks to his werewolf hearing. That smile is all it takes to trigger the final burst of determination I need, and I march straight over, ignoring everyone else in the room but him. *I have no idea if this is right, but here goes nothing.* Instead of taking my seat, I stop in front of him and kneel at his feet, surprising not just him but everyone around us.

"Prince Makseka, Your Highness," I start, almost shocked by how steady my own voice is, "I have really enjoyed the time we have spent together these past few months, and I... I would like to accept the offer to become your consort."

He looks surprised by my words at first, but that quickly morphs into a bright smile. There's a moment of silence as everyone fully takes in what I've just said, but a moment later a *woop* of congratulations comes from some of the nearby guards—Max's friends—and then his parents begin to excitedly applaud. Everyone else in the room begins to politely applaud with them, no doubt already starting to gossip about this latest development. But I don't care about any of that—the only thing I can see right now is the way Max is looking at me.

***

"Are you sure you're alright?" Hannah asks me. "You seem nervous."

"What makes you say that?" I ask back, frowning. It's been a week since I publicly agreed to be Max's consort, and tonight is the night of the full moon. It's time for him to claim me. My collaring ceremony will be next week, and then the week after *that* is the Lavender ball—but let's deal with one thing at a time.

"Well, you've been pacing for the last fifteen minutes or so," Daniel keenly observes.

"I think better when I'm walking," I half-heartedly defend. "Are you sure neither of you knows anything about what's going to happen tonight?"

"Sorry." Hannah shakes her head no. "Like most pack things, this isn't an event we're asked for help with."

"Yeah, werewolves don't exactly care about their hair and makeup," Daniel points out. "We probably know less about tonight than you do."

"I tried to learn what I could about claiming in the library," I admit. "I found a few books, but they were all in a language I couldn't read, and I was too embarrassed to ask anyone around to translate them for me." I can feel myself blushing.

"Look at it this way: they've been doing this for hundreds of years, right?" He pauses, waiting for me to nod my head yes. "Well, in all that time, I've never really heard of this going wrong. You told us yourself: if the bite doesn't take, the worst thing you have to worry about is feeling sick tomorrow."

"Yes, I guess..." I agree, ignoring that Max's bite not taking means much worse.

"I think there's a little more riding on it than that, Dan," Hannah helpfully corrects. "But it still almost never happens. I don't think you have anything to worry about."

"I hope you're righ—" A knock on my door cuts me off, and when I open it, I find Alden on the other side. "Oh! Hello, sir, please come in." I quickly step to the side.

"Consort Blackclaw!" Hannah greets, bowing alongside Daniel. "It is good to see you this evening. Is there anything we can—"

"Come on. You know I don't need the formalities." Alden quickly works to disperse the pageantry. "It's good to see you both, but I'm afraid I need to speak with Peter alone before tonight's gathering."

"Yes, sir, of course," Hannah agrees with a nod of her head as she and Daniel make their way out of the room.

"Break a leg tonight," Daniel whispers as he leaves. "But not literally."

"Sir?" I start to ask as the door closes behind my friends. "Was there something in particular I needed to do to prepare?"

"Yes, actually, but I also just wanted to talk." As he speaks, he walks across my room, taking a seat on the edge of the bed. "Come, sit. How are you feeling?"

"Nervous." I see no point in lying to the man since he was once in my shoes himself and take a seat next to him. "What if... What if the bite doesn't work?"

"Well, I'm pretty sure that isn't going to happen," he answers with confidence. "But regardless, you shouldn't worry about something you can't control. If it doesn't take, then it doesn't take, and we deal with what comes next."

"What comes next?" I hesitantly ask.

"No idea," Alden responds with a dramatic shrug of his shoulders. "But Max seems pretty attached, so I don't think you're going anywhere. Does that help?"

"A little..." It *does* actually make me feel better. "So, what is it I need to do before the claiming? And then... I know Max is going to bite me, but what else is going to happen?"

"Let me guess: Max did not give you much in the way of specifics?" He huffs a laugh at his son's antics.

"I'm afraid not, sir." I shake my head. "I probably could have asked, though."

"Listen, from one consort to another: don't let them off the hook," he tells me with a knowing look. "Now, truth be told, there isn't a lot to tonight. After moonrise, there will be a small ceremony with you and Max before the king and the rest of the pack. After that, you'll be sent into the woods while Max waits about twenty minutes before he follows to chase after you—"

"He's going to *what?*" I stop him before he goes further. "Go back to the beginning. *I'm* going into the woods? On my own?"

"It's perfectly safe," he tries to assure me. "The pack regularly patrols the forest. They know every inch of it and everything that lives there. You'll be in no danger."

"But he'll be chasing me?" I remember the last time he chased me. I kinda liked it, but this time he's going to be all ... wolfy.

"He'll be 'hunting' you, per tradition," he tells me with a slight grimace. "And then once he manages to catch you, the two of you will spend the night out there together ... where he will bite you."

"All night?" I did not read about *any* of this.

"It's meant to show that Max is able to protect and provide for you, even at his worst—when he's the least human," he keeps explaining. "I promise that it's a lot more fun than I'm making it sound."

"Fun? Did you have fun at yours?" I ask, still unsure.

"I did." He nods. "In fact, I had so much fun that sometimes Sam and I still like to go out there and ... take walks together," he catches himself, his face tightening slightly in embarrassment.

"What... What should I wear?" *A pair of boots is probably more suited to a nighttime stroll in the forest...*

"Well, traditionally the person to be claimed wears ... nothing." Another grimace.

"I'm going to be *naked?*" My eyes are wide and my voice. "In the woods? All night?"

"Again, it's safer than you think," he starts to calm me. "There are spells that will keep you warm, increase your endurance, even make your skin tougher. It's completely safe. I *promise.*"

"If... If you're sure," I hesitantly agree. "What... What do I need to do to prepare?"

"First, you'll need to drink this." He pulls a small potion out of one of the pockets of his robe. "The wolfsbane potion to prevent the bite from fully affecting your body."

"Right." I eye the glass vial, a purple-colored liquid inside. "I guess I expected to take it later."

"Nope, best take it now, I'm afraid." He holds the vial up to the light. "It won't take long to kick in, but without it, you'll have no protection from the full effect of the bite—if you survived, at least. So, are you certain this is what you want to do? Because after tonight, there's no going back."

"I... Yes. Yes, sir, I am." I nod with more courage than I actually have. "I want this. I want Max to claim me."

"Then alright. Here you go." He nods and hands the vial over. "That potion is going to do a number on your stomach, which is why I wanted to give it to you while we're still up here with a bathroom—it's rough, but you'll thank me for that tomorrow."

I'm not sure I understand his meaning but accept the potion anyway.

"...Bottoms up, I guess." I uncork the vial and pour the liquid into my mouth. It tastes strongly bitter, almost enough to make me gag, but I manage to down it all.

"Sorry about the taste." *Must not have done a good job at hiding my reaction.* "Not really much they can do about that. Did you have any more questions while we wait for it to take effect?"

Considering the number of things that immediately come to mind, maybe I should have made a list.

<hr />

About an hour later, and with a stomach that has been completely emptied, Alden walks with me downstairs to meet the rest of the family. I wasn't expecting that kind of reaction from drinking the potion, but Alden was kind enough to excuse himself when I had to suddenly run to the bathroom, coming back a short while later to collect me. Other than that, I feel mostly like myself, other than a slight haziness at the very back of my mind. It's not strong, not like I'm going to start stumbling over my feet or words, things are just a little *off*.

Max, King Samoset, Queen Anna, and even Kamo are waiting for us in the gathering room near the castle's rear gate. No one says anything when we enter, but there is an energy in the room that makes things feel different. Max in particular almost seems like he's ready to bounce out of his skin early. He looks great, wearing much nicer clothing than I wore myself, given that we're both about to strip naked. He lights up when he sees me, so much that he almost seems embarrassed by it. Was he worried I'd change my mind?

After checking that we're ready, Kamo leads us into the forest, Max holding my hand the whole way. Maybe it's the potion or the way the others look at us, but things feel different as we walk from the castle to the clearing.

The rest of the pack has already gathered, several of them coming up to offer us their congratulations, but most seem happy to give us our space.

"You look good," I tell him as he pulls me closer.

"You look great," he responds, his eyes raking down my body. "And soon you'll look even better."

I blush at my implied nudity, but I just wrap my own arm around Max's waist instead of responding. It feels nice to just touch him and be touched right now, and I know there will be plenty of that later. His friends all make sure to say hi, and even Gala sounds genuine when she wishes us well. Not long after that, the king gets everyone's attention.

"We only have a few minutes, but I wanted to thank you as always for joining us here. Tonight, we celebrate my son claiming Peter as his consort." He pauses, turning to me and Max. "Though they have only known each other a short time, I can already see how strong their connection is and how it grows more every day. Makseka, Peter, you have the pack's full support behind you."

The gathered werewolves let loose with a few cheers and mock howls as the king finishes his short speech. The two of us receive a few more congratulations, but there isn't much time before moonrise. Soon everyone is splitting off to strip and prepare for the change while Alden gathers me to do the same. I shiver in the cool night air as I rejoin Max just before the moon rises, standing together naked while we wait. It feels odd, waiting naked around a bunch of other naked people, but still less strange than I did last month when I was one of the only ones clothed.

I notice it first with Max, his body freezing as the moon officially crosses the horizon, and then it's upon the entire pack. This is the closest I've ever been, so it's a struggle to not freak out as I watch as Max suddenly hunches over, falling onto all fours as his body starts to change. Fur starts to sprout across his back, his limbs shift, growing thicker and longer, and I'm not sure I'll ever get used to the sound of bone scraping on bone, but when it's over, he stands, my large, black, muscled, and fur-covered werewolf.

Immediately after the transformation, the pack engages in a group howl to the sky. After he finishes, Max takes a step toward me, somehow looking graceful even in his large, lumbering form. A few months ago, being surrounded by *literal* monsters like this would have scared the life outta me, but right now, as Max carefully wraps a large clawed hand around my waist and leans over to smell my neck, I feel surprisingly calm. At least about the werewolves.

After the rest of the pack shakes off the after effects of the transformation, they all begin to gather around us. King Samoset—I can tell because his fur color matches his hair, just like Max's—approaches us once more, though now in werewolf form. A clawed hand reaches out to grasp his son's shoulder, and while I can't exactly understand anything beyond some huffs and growls, he seems to be saying something to Max.

Max responds with some huffs and growls of his own before the king turns to me, Queen Anna and Alden circling around to my other side. Before I realize it, the king has pulled me in, all three wolves and Alden squeezing me into a hug. There are a few rumbles and growls, though all sound happy, and then I'm released, Max leading the pack in another group howl.

"Alright, it's nearly time," Alden gets my attention as a familiar face approaches our group.

"H-Hello, Kendra," I greet as I fight the urge to cover my naked body.

"Hello again, Peter." She smiles at me warmly. "I'm just going to help make sure your trip into the forest is a safe one."

She places both her hands on my shoulders and begins to speak under her breath. Her hands and eyes start to faintly glow, and then I feel the magical energy entering my body. It's a strange feeling I've only experienced once before when I was much younger. A traveling circus was passing through Weston and one of the acts was a sorceress who would cast glamour spells on all the kids. Violet got a pair of cat ears on her head, and I had my eyes changed to—you guessed it—a wolf's.

This is different though. The glamour was more focused, so I really only felt it in my eyes. These spells spread through my entire body. Almost instantly, my body seems to adjust to the temperature, and I'm no longer cold. As the casting continues, I notice the little bit of fogginess I'd been feeling is gone, and then it feels like my skin is getting thicker. Everything still feels normal when I run my hand down my arm, but it's like it's *tougher*, making my bare feet more comfortable on the hard ground.

"Alright, I think you're ready," Alden tells me as Kendra finishes.

"Best of luck," she tells me before she rejoins the rest of the pack.

Alden walks me toward the northern boundary of the clearing, along with Max, the king, and the queen. All eyes, human and wolf, are on us as we approach the edge of the forest. Before we reach the edge, Max's parents all pause.

"Remember, you're completely safe," Alden assures me as they hang back to give us a moment of privacy. "The rest of the pack will know to avoid both of your scents, so it will just be the two of you out there."

Max leads me the rest of the way, a clawed hand placed gently on my shoulder. Just as we reach the treeline, Max stops and turns me so that we're facing each other before covering my body with his own. I'm pressed close to his furry muscles as he rubs his face against my neck a few times before inhaling deeply, like he's worried he'll forget my scent. When he finally releases me and steps back, it's not just him, but everyone watching me as I turn and make my way into the forest alone.

It's strange at first, walking through the forest at night, naked and alone. Especially the naked part. It's eerie, much spookier than wandering through the castle's halls. I can hear every rustle of the leaves, feel every blade of grass under my feet, but before I know it, I start to relax with my surroundings. And I start to get an idea.

I know the tradition is that he's supposed to hunt and find me all by himself, but what if I did something to help him? I don't mean like just sitting around close to the clearing and waiting for him. I'm not gonna just give up. But what if I headed toward a place that was familiar to the both of us? Like, the spot by the river where we first…

It's a little far, but I'm pretty sure I know how to get there from where I am. Honestly, I'll be happy if I can just find the river, which shouldn't be too hard. And I'm not too worried if I *do* happen to get lost—I know Max will be able to find me. So after pointing myself in what I think is the right direction, I head off.

With a destination in mind, I move a little faster than before, pushing myself to get there before Max catches up to me. The more I think about it, about him following my trail and *capturing* me, the more excited I get, moving faster and faster until I'm practically running. At least as fast as I can without accidentally running into any trees. This is *fun!*

I'm not sure when I hear the first twig snap, but it's the second and third that make me realize that someone is following me. *Has it been twenty minutes already? Darn.* I try to keep running but curiosity gets the better of me and I slowly jog to a stop, turning to see a lumbering form in the distance.

"Max?" I call out, making him pause his steps. "I didn't think you'd catch up to me so fast."

I try not to sound too disappointed … and then take off as fast as I can in the other direction. I mean, he hasn't caught me yet, so why should I make it easier on him? A little giddy, I can't help the excited giggles I let out as I run away.

I'm not exactly sure how long I run for, but I keep going until my lungs burn. Max is behind me every step of the way, his claws digging into the earth as he bounds through the trees. When I finally hear water in the distance, I let myself stop, leaning against a tree to catch my breath.

"Okay, okay... You win," I tell him between pants. "You caught..."

I trail off as I take in Max's form once more. He's closer now, and thanks to reflection from the river, more well-lit, too. And now I'm not actually sure that's Max anymore. This close I can see that the color of this wolf's fur is more of dark gray, with brighter gray lines along his face. And his eyes, they're so dark they look almost black.

"Max?" I test anyway. "Or... I'm sorry. I-I don't know who you are." *If he's in the forest, he has to be a member of the pack, right? But Alden said they'd know to stay away.*

Instead of answering (although, how would he, I guess), this new werewolf takes a step toward me, one that feels menacing. It's not at all helped by the way he bares his teeth either or the low growl that starts to reverberate from his chest. *Is he about to...?*

I don't stop to consider anything except the alarms going off in my head. Instead, I turn and start to run again down the riverbank. Almost immediately, the werewolf lets out an angry snarl, the ground shaking as he gives chase.

Who is this werewolf, and why is he chasing me?! Is he trying to kill me!? I don't really have time to consider these questions much, as I am too busy *running for my life!* Knowing that the werewolf is right behind me and that I stand no chance against its speed, I duck into the trees, hoping the added obstacles will work in my favor.

Unfortunately, I'm still a klutzy human, and in my panic, I stumble, rolling onto the ground. I'm able to scramble back to my feet, just barely dodging a sharp claw that rips through the earth where I just fell. I shriek in panic as I keep running, even though I already know I don't stand a chance. This is the end.

I almost have a heart attack when I hear a wolf howl, one very, very nearby, only seconds before a second werewolf bursts through the trees ahead of me. It rushes past me, and behind me, I hear the sounds of two bodies hitting each other, turning just in time to see both werewolves tumbling to the ground. For a moment, I want to panic again until I see this new wolf's blue eyes—*Max!*

The two werewolves start to fight on the forest floor, snarling and clawing at each other. I'm glued to my spot, terrified of having the beasts' attention back on me. It's only when I dare to take a step back that a twig

snaps beneath my foot and both wolves twist their heads in my direction—
and after another moment of blind terror, I start to run again.

I can still hear them fighting behind me. It sounds like they're following
me at first, but eventually the noises of their battle start to fade as I get farther and farther away. I keep running until it feels like my legs might give
out, and I have to stop before I collapse. Seeing some bushes next to a large
tree, I quickly crawl my way under, curling up and doing my best to hide.

I wrap my arms around myself and squeeze my eyes shut, willing myself
to stop shaking. *What is going on? Is this supposed to happen? No one said anything about a second werewolf or that Max would have to fight someone! What
if he had caught me? It didn't seem like he was playing around.*

I don't know how long I hide for, but eventually I realize that the sounds
of fighting have stopped. I'm still too scared to leave my hiding place, and
it isn't long before I hear the heavy footsteps of a werewolf coming my way.
I screw my eyes shut when they reach me, scared to look up when I feel the
branches above me being pushed back. *Oh gods... please be Max, please be
Max, please be Max...* I finally dare to peek up, a pair of icy blue eyes looking
back down at me.

"M-Max?" I try, getting a quick nod in response.

I launch myself at him, wrapping my arms around his torso as I sob
against his chest. I feel his arms tighten around me, holding me as I cry and
nuzzling the top of my head. We just stand there, holding each other, as I let
all of the fear and terror pour out of me.

After my tears stop flowing, I feel Max's arms slide down my back until
they reach under my butt. Then, with little warning, Max lifts me, making
me wrap my legs around his waist. Barely able to see over his shoulder, Max
starts to walk with me in his arms, carrying me to our next destination.

I hear the sound of rushing water again as we approach the river. We walk
along the bank, the full moon reflecting off of the water, the forest silent as
a church. Eventually, we come to a stop and Max allows me to lower my legs
to the ground and stand on my own. When I look around, I realize we're
at exactly the spot I was first looking for. It seems like we had the same idea.
Before I can say anything to Max, he's walking toward the tree we ... had fun
under, bending over to reach into a hollow in the trunk.

"What's that?" I ask when I see him pull out a soft looking blanket. "Wait,
did you come out here earlier and leave that here? For me?"

I never would have guessed it was possible for a werewolf to look embarrassed, but it's a lot cuter than you'd expect. His ears go a little flat, and he

ignores my question. Carefully using his claws, he fans the blanket out onto the ground. Taking a seat, he pats his lap, asking me to straddle him again.

"Do you... Do you know who that was earlier?" I'm hesitant as I climb into his lap. "Or what they wanted?"

He shakes his head no, a sorry look on his face. *Well, that's not great.* Before I can say more, he hugs me close, nuzzling and sniffing at my neck, face, and chest. When he pulls back, he gives me another sad look, his eyes locked on my neck as he bares his teeth slightly.

"Oh, right." I remember the original purpose behind tonight. "You still have to bite me, don't you?"

Instead of nodding, he whines, his ears flattening against his head as he looks at my neck again. Almost like he's unsure. Or maybe he's just worried that I might have changed my mind after what happened with that other werewolf. And I do need to think about it for a minute because that was probably the single scariest thing that's ever happened to me. But ... would *not* getting bitten really change anything? I mean, if anything I'll be better able to defend myself after, right? And sitting here with Max, even when he's covered in fur and fangs... This is still where I want to be.

"Nothing's changed," I tell him confidently, one hand on his chest. "I still want you to claim me. I still want your bite."

His mood brightens a little when hears that, but he still looks unsure of himself. After a few more minutes of nuzzling, and maybe waiting to see if I'd reconsider, he pulls back again, a serious look on his face. He gently strokes a clawed finger down my face, his eyes locked onto mine, searching for any sign that I don't want this. Then, nodding to himself, he tilts my head to the left, exposing the right side of my neck.

He leans over and sniffs at me before his tongue licks a wide swath across my skin. Seemingly satisfied with the spot he's picked, I feel his mouth open as he lowers his jaw down, right where my neck meets my shoulders. The sharp points of his teeth scrape against me, making me shudder, but I fight to remain still. There's only a moment of hesitation before his jaw closes and his teeth pierce my flesh.

I immediately feel a sharp pain in my shoulder because duh, a mouth full of fangs just sank into my skin. Max releases his oral hold on me a moment later, his tongue darting out to lick over what I'm sure is a fresh wound. I can feel the blood starting to seep down onto my chest and back, but before I can react, the bite starts to feel warm. No, not warm, *burning*, a burning that spreads from my shoulder across my entire body, making me cry out, clutching onto Max's fur in pain. The pain grows every second, getting worse and worse until finally it feels like I'm on fire, and everything goes black.

CHAPTER 15

MAX

It's lonely at night in the forest. I realize that statement is probably true 99% of the time, but this is the first time I've felt lonely out here while being with someone else. Though to be fair, he is completely unconscious.

I've been holding Peter in my lap for over an hour now. He passed out right after I bit him, and he's been still and quiet ever since, other than the occasional twitch or pained-sounding moan. His body is warm, *really* warm, but I think that's a good sign that the bite is working. Changing him. There's still a knot of worry at the back of my mind that we're not out of the metaphorical woods yet, but all my wolfier-instincts are a lot calmer than I would have expected. I'm even feeling a little happy about what this means for the future.

Of course, those feelings of happiness are kinda ruined by the fact that Peter was nearly *mauled to death* by a strange werewolf. I'm so glad I found him when I did because if I had been even a minute later... The wolf was a good fighter. Strong, too, but I was able to hold my own and sent him running after getting a few good licks in with my claws. I wanted to chase after him, but I had a more pressing matter to take care of: Peter.

It wasn't too hard to find him, given how scared he was; I could smell him as soon as I started looking. I've never seen him so terrified before. It's exactly how I was worried he was going to react the first time seeing *me* change. But when I found him hiding, he didn't even hesitate to jump into my arms, fangs, claws, and all.

I seriously have no idea who that wolf was. Just based on what he looks like, he could be any of the dozens of black-with-slightly-gray haired werewolves I know. It isn't exactly an uncommon hair color among the pack. Though it's not the fact that I couldn't recognize him that's really bothering me. Sight isn't the first sense you rely on when in wolf form. What worries me is that I couldn't *smell* him. He had no scent at all. I couldn't have tracked him down if I wanted to. He's probably still out there somewhere right now, doing gods' know what.

It's not out of the question for someone to cloak their scent, and because it was so completely masked, I have to assume that magic was used. They could have done it themselves—it's difficult but not impossible to cast magic in werewolf form. They also could have just as easily gotten someone else to do it, or taken a potion, or even cast it right before moonrise. Who knows how long it even lasts.

None of that helps me right now. The first thing I need to do after the sun comes up is find my parents. They'll know what to do. We'll search the forest for any sign of who that wolf was, where he came from, and where he went. Any of the wounds I left will probably be healed by morning, so that won't help to identify him. Knowing Dad, he'll probably want to round up every wolf that fits the description. If we can't find the actual culprit, then hopefully we can at least find some kind of clue to point us in the right direction.

I still don't understand why they'd do this at all though. What was their goal? What could they gain from hurting Peter? Or... Shit, maybe Peter wasn't who they were trying to hurt. *Maybe it's you, the royal prince and next in line for the throne that they were trying to get to, you idiot.* But even if that is true, it still doesn't explain *why*. What does killing Peter change about anything?

Maybe it's not a wolf from the pack at all. Maybe he's some rogue, packless werewolf that just managed to wander into the forest after moonrise. He might not even have his transformations under control and just didn't realize what he was doing ... but with the way his scent was covered up, I really doubt it. I also find it hard to believe that a random werewolf would have even been able to make it into the forest considering how strict Dad is about making sure the borders are guarded and patrolled, especially on the full moon.

It's one of the reasons Dad, Grandpa, and every other ruler of Litkalaa has been so strict on who they turn. Dad has always taught me that I should only ever offer the bite to those I trust the most. Biting someone doesn't create some sort of magical bond, they're exactly as loyal to the person who turned them as they were before. Turn the wrong person and you risk them sharing the bite themselves and building up a pack of their own—possibly to overtake yours. It hasn't been a risk for hundreds of years, but it *has* happened.

"Ngh..." Peter whimpers in his sleep, one of his hands reaching out to clutch at my fur.

I tighten my arms around his back, turning and laying us down on our sides, my body covering most of his. I feel the worst for Peter in all of this. Ever since I met him, it's been one bad thing after another—and all of them because of me. But even after all that, even after he almost *died* tonight, he still wanted this. He still wants to be with me. I have no idea what that wolf was planning, but I'm not going to let anything hurt Peter. I made a promise to protect him, and I'm going to keep it.

There's a part of me that thinks I should just grab him, take him out of the forest all together, and wait out the rest of the night in the castle. Even hiding by the stables until morning might be a better idea than this. But another, bigger part is *screaming* at me to stay and protect my charge, to defend his unconscious form. We aren't even by the river anymore; it was too exposed. As soon as Peter passed out, I gathered him up along with the blanket and bag I'd packed and moved us farther into the forest. Right now, we're near a grouping of trees, one having fallen near some brush that I'm using to keep us hidden.

Even despite all the ways tonight has gone wrong... I'm excited. Not for dealing with everything that happened but for the future. The future I will have with Peter. I haven't even known him for a full three months, but I swear he's almost all I've thought about since meeting him. He's kind, caring, devoted... Everything I was hoping to find in someone. And he's pretty nice to look at too.

He's going to be so much stronger after this, so much faster. We'll be able to go on runs together without me needing to slow down or him getting tired. I wonder if he'd ever be interested in any kind of combat training or sparring? Knowing how gentle he is, probably not, but I bet he'll appreciate the extra strength when it comes to garden tending! And I'm more than okay with that. There's also plenty of other things we can do now that I no longer have to worry about being so gentle with him.

That may have been the reason I had originally planned to take Peter to that spot by a river. After the first time we fooled around, I thought it might make Peter feel a little more comfortable for round two. Not tonight, obviously. I'm not a creep. I doubt he'll be in the mood much come morning either after tonight's trauma. But when I think about the way he came untouched when I kissed him against that tree or how he moaned and writhed on the grass by the river... I have to adjust our positions so that I'm not grinding myself against him again.

Maybe it's just my wishful thinking, but I swear his scent has already started changing. Becoming muskier, more wolf-like. And it smells *good*. There's a part of me that's actually a little sad that I won't ever get to see what he'd look like as a full werewolf. His hair color, that slightly darker shade of blonde, almost golden, would make for a beautiful looking wolf. But I'm really not complaining because he's beautiful as it is, and no matter what, what we have will be special.

I know my mother and father love each other very much. They're always together, and I've almost never seen them fight. But the relationship between Dad and Papa is different. I see all these little moments they have, the looks they share, almost like they have a secret language sometimes. I want that too. I mean, I'd like to have what he has with Mom one day too, but I just ... don't quite see that for myself. I feel bad for thinking that way, but I'm not sure I can see myself being that way with *any* woman.

I do know that no matter what, the relationship Peter and I have will be special because it will be *ours*. And I can't wait for us to figure out exactly what that means. He just has to wake up first.

CHAPTER 16

PETER

I'm slow to wake up, first wondering where all my blankets have gone. As I feel around for them, I realize that it's not a mattress underneath me but grass and leaves, and the pillow I'm using is ... another person. My eyes shoot open as the memories of last night flood my mind, making me lurch to my feet.

The chase through the woods, Max rescuing me and fighting the other werewolf, being bitten... When I take a deep breath to calm myself, my nose is immediately assaulted with dozens of different scents. Overwhelmed, I stumble until I realize that the plants, the ground, the animals—I can smell them all. More than that, I can pick each one of them out individually. There's a patch of lupin flowers just ahead of me and what must be a tree leaking maple sap to my left, and just behind me is a musky, almost spicy smelling... *Max!*

He's laying on the forest floor, where he was just acting as my pillow. He's still asleep, his chest slowly rising and falling with his breath. He's also completely naked. So am I, which yeah, still weird. I let my eyes wander down his body for a moment before he shifts in his sleep, and I suddenly feel like I'm being creepy and have to look away.

I start to scan the horizon with my eyes. This isn't where I remember ending the night by the river where Max bit me. The memory makes me touch the spot on my shoulder, feeling the raised outline of Max's teeth.

We're still in the forest, and everything still mostly looks the same, but something feels different. *I* feel different.

The more I wake up, the more my senses do too. The first thing I hear is running water—the river. But when I look around, I can't see it anywhere. Then I realize I can hear animals... *a lot* of animals. Birds chirping, squirrels chittering, bees buzzing, and something bigger that sounds like it's snoring. Or at least it was—I turn around when I hear Max start to stir.

"Mmmmm." He stretches as he sits up. "G'morning."

"Morning." I give an awkward little wave.

He looks at me a little dopily, still waking up. He scratches his belly with a yawn before a look of realization crosses his face, and he freezes. Probably remembering everything from last night, same as me. He quickly jumps up and closes the distance between us.

"How are you feeling?" he asks, his eyes already roaming my body for signs that something is wrong.

"Good, I think?" I offer with a small smile. "All the smells and sounds are a little overwhelming."

"Don't worry. You'll learn how to filter them out," he assures me with a bright grin and a gentle hand on my back, and I find myself leaning in, seeking more contact. "Have you tried anything out yet?"

"No, I just woke up." I shake my head, confused. "Try what out?"

"Your newly upgraded body." He taps me on the ass before jogging ahead, bending over to grab his bag. "Come on. Let's go for a run."

"Right now?" I ask, following after him.

"Why not?" he responds over his shoulder, already picking up speed.

And then we're both off, starting our morning with a naked run through the woods. We gradually start to pick up speed, and before I know it, we're running faster than I ever have before. As the trees fly past me in a blur, I can't help a laugh of excitement.

"Isn't it great?" Max asks as we both slow to a stop.

"This is amazing!" I respond excitedly, not feeling even a little tired or winded.

"I know. Now let's see how strong you are." He grins, walking over to a fallen log ahead of us. To demonstrate, he bends down, lifting the log up with both hands before letting it drop back down with a heavy *thud*. "Try lifting that."

I walk up to the log, unsure if I can do what he's asking. I squat down and dig my hands between the log and the ground, surprised at how easy it is to get my hands underneath it. Then I'm equally surprised by how light it feels when I try to lift it. I struggle a little more than Max did to bring it all the way up to my chest, but once I do, I drop the log to the ground with another excited laugh.

I know everyone told me these things would happen, but it's still so different to actually experience for myself. With strength like this, just think of how easy work would be on the farm. Plowing fields, carrying crops, heck, I wonder if I could lift one of the horses! I gotta show Momma and...

I catch myself, remembering that it's been over two months since I've heard from anyone in Weston. I start to think about writing a letter, telling them about the claiming, even inviting them to the collaring ceremony next week, but the more I do, the sadder I feel. If they didn't bother responding to any of my other letters, why would they care now? I look up at Max, who is watching me with concern. I ignore the thoughts of home, instead focusing on the sound of the river in the distance.

"Hey, Max?" I ask him softly.

"Yeah?" He steps forward, still looking worried.

"Race you to the river!" I shout before taking off.

It's not immediate, but a few seconds after I start, I hear a swear from Max behind me as he starts to give chase. Something about that makes me want to run faster, these new instincts urging me to try and win this game. Or maybe it's just that I want Max to catch me. Either way, this is fun!

It doesn't take Max long to catch up, and I can feel him practically nipping at my heels. Knowing that he can beat me on speed if he really wanted to, I start to duck and weave through the trees, trying to confuse him or at least give myself some kind of advantage. I'm not sure if it's working, but the annoyed, slightly-exasperated growls I hear from behind me make me want to giggle.

I can't believe how fast and strong I feel right now! I mean, I know I wasn't exactly a weakling before, but this is so much different. Maybe it's because I'm naked, but as the wind rushes past me, I feel as free as a bird. I can see the bank of the river just up ahead, pushing myself even harder to reach it first.

"No you don't!" Max growls behind me, just before he tackles me to the ground.

We tumble and roll on the grass, stopping just inches from the base of a tree. Yesterday, taking a tumble like that would have really hurt, I'd be bruised and scraped up for days. But now? All I do is grin up at the man currently laying on top of me. Before I can say anything, he stands, and after dropping his bag to the ground, scoops me up in his arms, bridal style. Then he walks us toward the river.

"*I* win," he tells me smugly before jumping in, still holding me.

I let out a very girly shriek as the cold river water hits my skin. His arms no longer holding me up, Max laughs as I flail around in the water for a few seconds before I manage to stand up, not even shivering from the temperature. Max, as naked and wet as I am, reaches over to wrap an arm around my waist, pulling me toward him and kissing me.

I almost slip on the river bed as I'm moved, but I quickly find my footing. I take a hold of Max's shoulders as we continue to kiss, his hands wrapping around my waist just above the water. As his tongue pokes between my lips, his hands start to wander lower, cupping my butt in his hands with a squeeze.

I'm not sure how long we make out there in the river, but eventually Max takes me by the hand and leads me to shore. Bending over to pick up the bag he brought with him, Max leads me to a soft patch of grass. He pulls out his blanket and spreads it on the ground before kneeling on top of it. He pats the spot next to him before holding out his hand for me to take, and I join him.

As we lay on our sides together, we start to kiss again, and things quickly turn hot and heavy. I can even hear Max's chest rumbling every time he growls under his breath. Without warning, Max flips us so that I'm on my back with him on top of me. He looks down at me, a cocky grin on his face, as he slots himself between my legs. After starting with my lips, he moves toward my ear and neck to do the same.

"You're all mine," he says breathlessly before nipping my ear. "And now that I've caught you, I can do whatever I want with you. Right?"

"Yes... Yes, sir," I answer as best I can, unsure if I want more or less of the bursts of pain and pleasure that come with each bite.

"Good boy," he responds, lifting up and locking his eyes onto mine.

His pupils are completely blown out, only a thin rim of blue around the black circle of his pupil. He looks hungry, aggressive even, and I feel ... like I'm exactly where I need to be, underneath him. Just like I said, I feel caught, but I'm not afraid. Actually, I'm feeling a *really* strong urge to bare my neck, so I do.

Titling my neck like that gets Max to growl, and after fisting both his hands in my hair, he's right back to chewing on my shoulder. He bites me, sucking the flesh into his mouth and running his tongue over it, again and again. I know I'll probably be covered in bite marks, but that thought only makes me want more, makes me want to show them off.

As he continues to tease my neck, I feel one of Max's hands leave my hair and move down to my chest. His fingers squeeze my left pec before seeking out my nipple. He starts teasing it, gently running his finger tip over it before giving it a small flick, the dueling sensations making me writhe underneath him.

He leaves my neck and moves down my body, using his mouth on my other pec. I squirm again when I feel his sharp teeth on my nipple as he bites at my chest. The hand on my other nipple finally releases me, sliding down my chest and stomach until it reaches my groin—and then it skips past that to delve between my legs.

I let out a squeak of surprise when I feel Max's fingers start to delve between my butt. He's slow, gentle even, but it still feels weird when I've never had anyone doing *that* before. I make another noise when his finger comes into contact with my hole, and I finally realize what Alden meant about thanking him later for the potion last night. *Are we really going to...?*

"Can I..." Max starts, looking up at me over my chest. "I... I want to be inside of you. Would you—"

"Yes," I answer before he can finish, blushing at how eagerly I agree.

Max doesn't say anything, just gives me a warm smile and pushes himself up so he can reach back into his bag. He pulls out a small glass vial, one filled with a clear liquid, uncorking it as he rejoins me, pouring some out into his hands. It looks slippery, almost like oil.

Back at my side, Max pulls one of my legs over his own, spreading me wide. He brings his slick hand down under my balls, his slippery fingers sliding easily across my skin to find my entrance. He circles my hole with a single finger, teasing and rubbing before he starts to push inside.

I gasp when I'm finally breached, unused to the feeling. It's not quite painful, different but not bad. With his free hand, Max turns my head to face him, kissing me again while he gently continues to probe my hole. As he pushes farther inside, I can the burn of my muscles being stretched, never having been used like this before.

One finger becomes two, and I whimper as they both sink into me to at least the second knuckle. It's a little hard so see exactly what's going on at this angle, especially when the slight pain just makes me want to close my eyes. The whole time, Max continues his gentle kisses, watching my face carefully for signs of pain. I know Max is big, but when he starts to insert his third finger, I start to wonder just how much stretching I'm going to need.

"Alright," Max says with a small kiss on my shoulder a minute later, gently pulling his fingers from my butt, "I think you're ready... if you think you are."

"Okay." I nod, nervous and unsure of what to do. "I trust you."

Max takes the lead and thankfully doesn't comment on my obvious confusion. With me still on my back, he rises to his knees and kneels between my legs. He takes me by the calves, lifting them to hang over his shoulders and placing a gentle kiss on the inside of my thigh. He uncorks the bottle again, and I can hear the *schlick* of his hand as he runs it over himself, his cock hanging over my own.

After tossing the bottle to the side, he shifts forward a little, adjusting himself so his slick cock is now pressing against my ass. My hole twitches involuntarily, especially at the thought that I'm somehow going to take all of *that* inside of me. My nerves must be obvious because I hear Max chuckle, looking up to see him placing a kiss on my other thigh.

"It's okay. Just relax and breathe," he tells me, running a hand over my knee. "I'm going to start very, very slow. If you ever need me to stop or want me to pull out, just tell me. We don't even have to—"

"I want it," I blurt out, blushing at my own eagerness.

With another huff of laughter, Max reaches down and takes aim. I feel his head brush over my hole, my whole body tensing involuntarily. Max just lets it sit there, waiting for me to relax before he starts to press forward. I tense up again when the head starts to push against me, grabbing onto the grass at my sides as I try to breathe and keep myself calm.

I'm unprepared for when the head of his cock finally pops in, the sudden increase in pressure and pain forcing a low grunt from me. Even this already feels like too much, and I almost start to panic until I look up at Max. His expression is split, half-concerned, while also looking... I don't know how else to say it: really, really horny.

"Remember to breathe," he instructs gently.

I take a deep breath, and then another, and as they start to even out, I can feel myself relaxing. Max must feel it too because he presses forward, sliding an inch or two deeper before I tense up again. We repeat this five or more six times until I can feel Max's body pressed all the way against mine—meaning he has to be all the way inside of me.

"*Fuck*, you feel so good," Max says like it's taking all his power to not move. "How are you doing?"

"I'm... I'm okay, I think." It's hard to describe exactly how I'm feeling right now. "It doesn't hurt. There was a little pain at first, but now I mostly just feel really ... *full*."

"You can thank your new werewolf powers for the higher pain tolerance." He kisses my thigh again. "Still, let me know if it gets to be too much, okay?"

I nod my head, and that's all Max needs to start really moving. He pulls back just a little, which is a very strange feeling, and when he pushes back in, I'm right back to feeling so full I'm overstuffed. He pulls out a little farther on the next stroke, and I feel this strong burst of pleasure from *somewhere* inside of me, just for a second. It happens again on his next stroke, and just about every stroke after that.

I hear a high-pitched moan, and it takes a second before I recognize that it's coming from me. Max keeps up the slow pace for a while, waiting for me to relax again before gradually speeding up, his eyes watching my face closely. Once things are moving a little more steadily, Max lets my legs drop from his shoulders to his arms, allowing him to bend over me. His eyes are still blown out, and I swear he even looks a little wolfy, like his teeth are longer and his facial hair thicker.

"I can't tell you how happy I am to be able to say that you belong to me now," he tells me in a low, husky voice. "You're *mine*," he says before diving in for a rough kiss.

Unable to respond with more than a muffled moan, his fucking gets faster, and a little rougher, too. I'm not expecting it, but when Max nips at my neck, I just want him to bite me again, harder. I can hear our noises start to get louder, more animalistic, like we really are two wolves rutting in the forest.

That isn't the only thing I feel. There's also this pressure inside. Not like the full feeling I get when Max presses all the way in to the balls—that's still happening too. This is something else, something extra, but I don't know what. It just keeps building with every stroke of Max's cock until finally it feels like too much, like my whole body might explode ... and then it does.

"Holy shit, what was *that*?" Max asks as lights start to burst in my eyes, kneeling up straight and holding me by the backs of my thighs.

"I... I don't know." It feels like I came, but when I look down, I'm still hard against my belly, and while I'm a little sticky, not nearly as sticky as I should be.

"...Do you think you can do it again?" Max asks devilishly.

"I might ... need your help," I try to say as sexy as I can between breaths.

It's enough for Max, whose grip on my thighs tightens as he starts to rock himself in and out of me. He pulls out more and more with each stroke until he's practically using the entire length every time he thrusts in. Before I know it, that pressure starts to build up again, and as my toes curl and my eyes roll around my head, I feel myself cum again.

Max lets out a roar of triumph before a look of concentration crosses his face. He's no longer using his full length, but his thrusts are coming faster and harder. He covers my body with his as he pounds away at me, our sweaty chests sliding against each other. Even if his mouth wasn't near my ear, with my new abilities I can hear his breath getting ragged until he stumbles in his rhythm and presses in as deeply as he can. Then, with a growl and a bite to my neck, I realize that he's cumming.

And oh boy, is he. I can feel him inside me, filling me up with a searing warmth. His hips continue to hump forward in short, abortive thrusts, like he's trying to bury himself even deeper, if it were even possible. I've never felt so full in my life. I can barely think straight right now, my unfocused eyes staring up at the sky through the treetops.

Max lays on top of me as we catch our breaths, allowing my legs and feet to fall to the ground. The angle causes his softening cock to slip out of me with a wet *squelch*. I grimace at the feeling, but Max quickly distracts me by flopping onto his side and pulling me in to cuddle.

We just lay there for a while, catching our breaths, naked and covered in each other's sweat and other fluids. I bury myself in Max's furry chest, smiling when I feel him nuzzle the top of my head. After-sex cuddles feel almost as nice as the sex itself. Almost.

"Oh my gods, that was..." Max stops before finishing, pulling away enough to see my face. "How was it for you?"

"That was amazing," I answer without thinking. "Is it like that every time?"

"Probably not *every* time, but that is the idea," he says with a laugh. "Did you cum twice?"

"It... It felt like I did." I can already feel my body turning red. "But, um, I'm still ... really hard."

"Yeah, you are." To emphasize, he reaches down and gives me a squeeze. "Well, if you give me like fifteen minutes, I can be ready for round two. Or if you want, we could head back to the castle and give a bed a..." He stops, his eyes going wide.

"A what?" I ask, confused.

"The other werewolf from last night," he answers with realization. "I got so caught up in the excitement that I completely forgot. Sorry baby, we have to get back so we can tell my family."

"No, you're right." Neither of us says anything about the way "baby" makes me blush. "Let's go."

Now that I'm faster, it's a much shorter run back to the pack's gathering site than it was the last time we spent the night out here. Most of the pack has already left, with only a few stragglers still waking up. From what Max tells me, it's pretty common after a claiming for the two people involved to spend the morning after together like this in the forest, so most of the pack cleared out early.

We get dressed as quickly as we can, politely saying our thanks to the people who come up to congratulate us. Despite knowing the obvious, no one makes any comments about how we spent the morning, but it's still a little mortifying to walk inside and realize every werewolf we pass can probably smell what we've been up to in the woods.

We head straight for his parents' room once we're inside, walking up flight after flight of stairs. Once again, my new werewolf powers come in handy, not feeling even a little tired by the time we reach the top. The guards outside what must be the royal bed chambers greet us with a smile, but after seeing the serious look on Max's face, they both step aside to allow him access to his parent's bedroom door, to which he gives three rapid knocks.

"Son!" King Samoset himself opens the door, still wearing just a robe. "We didn't quite expect to see you this early. Congratulations on—"

"Someone attacked us last night," Max blurts out, the guards at our sides looking over with alarm.

"What?" The king's face immediately falls. "Come inside."

He steps to the side, allowing the two of us to enter the bedroom. Alden and Queen Anna are both seated on a couch near the fireplace, still wearing their own morning robes. Hearing and seeing their son so upset, both make to stand, the five of us standing together at the center of the room.

"What's this about?" the queen asks.

"You were *attacked*?" Alden clarifies.

"Not me. Peter," Max clarifies. "When I went out after him last night, there was another werewolf already hunting him. And I mean *hunting*—he was not playing around. If I hadn't found them when I did, he could have..." He growls to himself, his hands clenching tightly into fists.

"Hey, I'm okay," I tell him, feeling the need to plaster myself to his side and loving the way he wraps an arm around my waist in response.

"A werewolf attacked Peter?" the king asks in shock. "Who were they? Did you get a look at them?"

"I don't know." Max shakes his head. "I mean, I saw him, but I don't know who it was. Dad, I couldn't even *smell* him."

"He had no scent at all?" He waits for Max to shake his head again before continuing. "Magic. Do you think it was someone from the pack?"

"I don't know," Max answers, sounding a little defeated. "We didn't exactly stop to chat, but if he was in the forest..."

"Then a rogue werewolf is unlikely," the king finishes with a frown. "What did they look like?"

"It was a man. His hair was black with a little gray," Max says without much confidence.

"That could describe a quarter of the pack." Alden grimaces. "Almost everyone between ... thirty-five and sixty."

"I don't understand why someone would do something like this." The queen comes over to put her arm around my shoulders.

"I am sorry this happened to the two of you on what should have been a very special night," the king apologizes to the both of us. "I promise we will find who is responsible and bring them to justice. I'm going to get my best men on this immediately."

"Thanks, Dad," Max says with a nod, not sounding very hopeful... So, I'll just have to be hopeful for the both of us.

CHAPTER 17

"Oww."

"Hold still. I'm almost done."

It's been over a week since the full moon, since Max claimed me with a bite after I was attacked by that unknown werewolf. As soon as we finished talking to him, the king got to work on finding the culprit. His first order of business was gathering the people he trusted the most, his kingsguard. Or at least most of them.

These knights are probably closer to the king than anyone, and while that didn't completely absolve them, most were free of suspicion. Only two of the five fit my and Max's description—an older male with black to graying hair, and of those two, one is actually missing at moment—Max complained about wishing his Uncle Achak was here because apparently, he's their best tracker. That only left Sir Dakota, who was more than willing to answer all our questions and even be monitored by his fellow knights until the culprit has been found.

Kamo also joined us, which after learning more of his history with Max's family makes sense. He's the king's advisor, and his advice is to begin questioning the men of the pack immediately. He also recommended that we avoid allowing news of the attack to spread, wanting to avoid causing a panic in the city. Which I guess makes sense, but I still can't help but notice the man's own black, slightly graying hair.

I think the main reason for wanting us to keep quiet about this is the Lavender Ball, which is only five days away. It's going to be my second public appearance as Max's consort because today is my first—the collaring ceremony! Max assured me that it's mostly just a show for the public, mainly the court.

After talking about it with him, I did end up writing home again, inviting my family and friends to come today—but it seems like my letters were ignored, just like all the others. But it's okay. I'm fine. Really! I'm excited for tonight—or I will be, as soon as Daniel finishes ripping things out of my face.

"Oww!" I repeat as he plucks another of my eyebrow hairs.

"Okay, done." Daniel wipes his tweezers on a small cloth. "You're lucky you're blonde, unibrows are a lot less noticeable."

"He did not have a unibrow," Hannah defends me from behind my chair. "But if you're done, move so I can finish his hair."

Even though it's only for a single night, these two have been up here preparing me for almost two hours now. Trixie dropped off my outfit earlier, which is thankfully very different from the flimsy gold thong I wore the last time I was presented as Max's consort—which, from what he told me, is exactly what used to happen. My hair has been cut, my face shaved, and I'm even wearing a little makeup—Hannah says I have nice cheekbones.

"Almost done," Hannah assures me as she finishes styling my hair with some sort of cream. "I know this is different from the claiming, but you must still be excited."

"Max doesn't seem like he wants to make a big deal of it, but you know, I really am," I confirm with a small smile.

I won't say it out loud, but there's a part of me that hopes that once everyone in the court sees Max put that collar on me, they'll finally start to think of me differently. I know that's not realistic, but I can't help it. I'm also really excited about the collar itself, for very, very different reasons.

"He must care about it a little bit, seeing as they gave you your own two bodyguards," Daniel complains, gesturing his head to the door of my room.

As a safety precaution, I've had a pair of guards assigned to protect me—specifically the two guards that were stationed outside the royal bedroom the morning after I was claimed, to keep the information from spreading. Mika and Timothy—they're both non-werewolf humans and have been very nice, but it's still weird to have them follow me everywhere I go. They stopped Hannah, Daniel, and Trixie all at the door so they could inspect everything they brought with them. I guess they're worried that someone might try to sneak in something that could hurt me, which wasn't something I was really worried about *before*, but now...

"Yeah, something like that." I wish I could tell my friends more about what's going on, but until we figure this out, I'm not supposed to say anything.

Right after the knights were assembled, I went with Max and King Sam into the forest to the area I was attacked. There was obvious evidence of Max's fight with the other wolf, claw marks gouged into the ground and on the sides of trees. With my new, stronger nose, I can smell my and Max's scents all over the place. Mine is pretty consistent, strong and almost damp—the smell of fear, I would learn. Max's is equally heavy but more erratic, with a peppery spiciness—anger.

Sadly, we didn't learn much beyond confirming that the attack had happened. Without any other leads, the king and his guard put together a list of the pack members who fit the description given by me and Max. Those interrogations have been going on all week with Max even personally sizing them up in their shifted forms, but so far, we haven't found them.

Still, not *everything* has been bad. Every night, Max takes over for Tim and Mika as my personal guard, which has been very easy for him to do seeing as we've been sleeping in the same room. We spend almost all our time together as it is, though I guess we are usually pretty ... distracted.

Even though we were just in danger, it hasn't taken very long for the, uh, mood to strike us again. In fact, we pretty much went up to Max's bedroom as soon as we got back to the castle after taking everyone out to the forest. Round two turned into round three, and then four... I'm really glad Max's bedroom walls are soundproof, even though I'm sure Mika and Tim know exactly what we're up to when those doors close.

"Okay, done," Hannah declares after looking at my head from all angles. "Let's get you dressed."

I might be the prince's consort now, but that doesn't mean I'm somebody who suddenly needs other people to dress him. It's not a complicated outfit, a nice shirt and pants, polished leather shoes, and a shiny gold belt. The only thing I actually need help with is the shirt, both Hannah and Daniel making sure I don't mess up my hair or rub off any makeup onto the shiny blue silk by accident.

"Looking good," Daniel tells me, eyes going from the shirt to the black pants below. "Tight in all the right places."

"Thank you." I blush, and despite my best effort, steal a peek in the mirror at my back. *They do make my butt look pretty nice.*

"You look *great,* Peter," Hannah says, turning to her partner with a smile. "Which means *we* did a great job."

"We always do a great job," Daniel replies cockily when there's a knock on my door. "And right on time too!"

"Consort Peter, are you ready?" Kamo asks as he steps in to collect me.

"Yes, I think so," I answer after checking all the buttons on my shirt again.

"Wonderful." He nods, turning to the other two people in the room. "Thank you for your work. The king and queen have invited the both of you to attend the collaring ceremony and reception."

"Free food? I'm in," Daniel declares without much thought.

"Thank you, sir. We'd love to be there," Hannah accepts with a little more class before pulling Daniel out of the room. "Come on. We need to change."

"The ceremony will begin shortly," Kamo starts to instruct as my friends leave the room. "We will be walking down to the throne room, which is currently filled with members of the public eager to watch the proceedings."

"How many?" I never really considered how many people might actually show up.

"The room was nearly filled when I left to retrieve you. When you enter, you will proceed down the carpet until you reach the throne platform, where you will kneel," Kamo continues. "Prince Makseka will stand at the top of the steps, where his father will speak to those gathered. The prince will then proceed down the steps to your side, where the king will ask the two of you to affirm aloud your commitment to each other. The prince will then lock his collar around your neck, I will announce you to the public, and the two of you will exit the throne room together, rejoining us shortly after in the dining room for dinner."

"Okay." I think I can remember all of that. "Is there anything else I should know?"

He shakes his head. "All you need to do is focus on the prince."

After a few more minutes of waiting, and a quick trip to the bathroom because being nervous always makes me have to pee, I walk with Kamo down to the castle's ground floor, my two guards in tow. He leaves me with them in a small waiting room near the throne room, double checking that everything is ready before returning to collect me.

"When they open the doors, proceed down to the thrones like we spoke about," Kamo tells me, standing me in front of the closed throne room. "Try not to let your nerves get the best of you. I shall see you shortly... Congratulations, Consort Peter."

"Thank you, Kamo," I say with a little surprise as he turns and quickly walks away, probably to run around to the back entrance to the throne room.

I stand there waiting, two guards in front of me on either side of the door, and my personal two behind me, making me feel a little claustrophobic. Before I can worry about that, trumpets start to blare from inside the throne room. There's what sounds like some muffled speaking, a pause, and then more trumpets, which seem to signal the guards that it's time to open the doors.

I instantly see that the room is packed, probably as much if not more than it is during court sessions. The back half is filled with people standing while the front has rows and rows of filled chairs. A piano begins to play, everyone's eyes are on me as I walk down the aisle, and it takes a lot of effort to not freeze up or start looking around. I can make out a few familiar faces, but it's mostly a sea of strangers, so I keep my focus on putting one foot in front of the other.

This feels so much stranger than my claiming night, and I was naked then. This is the most formal event I've ever been a part of. Just like I'd heard, the whole thing almost seems like a wedding. If I had said *that*, would my parents have wanted to come?

I stop when I reach the platform, the instruments finally dying down. Max and his parents are all ahead of me, each in their thrones with Alden kneeling next to the king. Seeing his posture, I drop to my knees and do my best to copy it. As I do, Max stands from his throne, standing at the edge of the platform and waiting for his father to do the same at his side while his mother and Alden stand behind them.

"We have a tradition in this kingdom," King Samoset begins his speech. "One between wolf and non-wolf, guardian and attendant, protector and the protected. Nearly four-hundred years ago, my ancestor, then known only as Chief Wyman, accepted the offer of King Andrew Durenholtz to become this nation's new king and for the werewolves of his tribe to watch over them as its protectors."

"Though they are gone, we have continued to honor this tradition every generation," he continues in his well-practiced way of speaking. "Today, we are here to celebrate the continuation of that tradition as my son reaches another milestone on his journey to one day be your future king. Son, I am very proud of the man you are becoming."

A small amount of applause breaks out as father turns to son, and then both begin to step down the stairs toward me. Just behind them, I see Oliver, carrying a pillow in both hands. Though I can't see the top of it, I am pretty sure I know what it's carrying. Seeing Max, his father, and the collar all coming toward me at once is overwhelming, and I can feel my breath start to get heavy, but before I can panic, Max is at my side, his hand gently squeezing my shoulder.

"Peter Lambert," the king speaks, standing in front of the both of us, "you are a fine young man, and it is an honor to welcome you into the Blackclaw family."

"Th-thank you, Your Highness," I reply nervously.

"Peter," he starts again, "do you swear to serve my son to the best of your ability, to obey him when it is required, and to support him when it is needed?"

"I-I do, sir." I nod, my throat dry and my heart pounding.

"Makseka, my son," King Samoset turns to Max, "do you swear to watch over Peter, to protect his well-being, to take care of and defend him?"

"I do, Father," Max answers, squeezing my shoulder again.

"Makseka, please collar your consort." At the king's urging, Oliver steps forward, holding his pillow in front of Max.

From the pillow, Max picks up a golden chain, each link shining in the sunlight streaming through the room's large windows. Hanging from the end of the chain is a pendant, also made of gold, molded in the shape of a sun with four swirling arms of light. As Max brings it even closer, I can see that the front of the pendant is imprinted with letters "PB"—Peter Blackclaw.

"I designed it myself," Max whispers as he lowers himself to wrap the chain around the back of my neck. "I hope you like it, Sunshine."

The chain is so long that he actually wraps it fully around my neck once before bringing the free end around to the front and connecting it to the lock that sits on the back of the pendent, a keyhole at its center. When it clicks shut, it's like a bolt of lightning runs through my body, the hairs on my arms and neck standing straight up. It seems like the same has happened to Max, the rest of the world fading away.

"Rise, Consort Peter Blackclaw!" King Samoset announces, bringing us back to the throne room.

The next few moments are a bit of a blur. The room breaks into applause as I stand, the trumpets once more blaring their song as Max takes me by the hand and kisses me. We share a brief moment with his parents on the throne platform before Max pulls me out of the room through the back door to the waiting room his parents normally use. The guards open the doors for us automatically, closing them once we are inside, and then we're alone.

"I'd say that went pretty well," Max declares while stretching his arms over his head and turning to face me. "What about you? Doing okay?"

"Yeah, I think so." I nod, still a little dazed. "It kinda feels like we just got married."

"Well, we kind of did," Max admits. "We've basically been werewolf-married since I claimed you. I guess we still need to officially move you into my room, huh?"

"I guess." I shrug, seeing as I've basically already been living there for over a week now. "It's not like I have that much stuff to move."

"Which is my fault for taking you away from your home." Max frowns, taking my hand in apology. "I'm sorry they didn't answer your letters."

"It's okay. Really." I ignore the pang of sadness I feel at none of my friends or family from home being here. "I guess I just never expected so many people would be watching."

"People love a spectacle," Max replies, taking my hands in his. "Can't blame them though. You look great."

"Thanks," I say with a blush. "You do too."

Without really thinking about it, my hand reaches for my collar, holding the pendant in my hand and running over it with my thumb.

"Do you like it?" Max asks with hesitation, referring to the pendant.

"I love it," I answer, still touching it. "You really designed it yourself?"

"Yeah... Like a week after you got here," he sheepishly admits. "I'm glad you like it. It's enchanted to never rust or break, and the lock can only be opened with the key."

"Where's the key?" Not that I'm planning on ever taking it off.

"Right here." Max pulls back his right sleeve, revealing a small gold chain around his wrist, a gold key dangling from it. "It's enchanted the same way. If you ever want me to take it off—"

"I won't." I don't bother letting him finish. "So, what happens now?"

"Well, we have a little time to ourselves while everyone moves to the dining room," Max explains. "I can think of a few things we can do to keep us busy."

"Like what..." I decide to try something out again, "...sir."

"C'mere, you," he says with a growl, pulling me by the collar.

We kiss standing in the center of the room, our mouths hungrily seeking each other out. Max wraps his arms around me, running blunt nails down my back as his tongue invades my mouth. It's not hard to imagine them as a pair of sharp claws, the thought making me moan and press myself harder against him. I wrap my own arms around his neck while his hands move down lower to my ass, squeezing me roughly.

I'm not sure exactly how long we're kissing for. At some point, we move to the couch, where I straddle Max's lap while he bites and sucks on my neck. Just as I start to wonder how long it might take hickeys to heal, a knock at the door makes us both jump in surprise.

"Hope you boys are decent," King Sam's voice rings through the room, though he doesn't open the door more than a crack. "It's time for dinner."

"Just a minute, Dad," Max tells his father after reluctantly pulling away from me. "We'll have plenty more time for that later."

I climb off his lap, and we both stand, adjusting our clothes and waiting for certain body parts to stop swelling. Not that it matters, 'cause as I'm learning, it's pretty easy to smell when people are "in the mood." Once we're decent enough, we exit the waiting room, finding Max's parents (and many guards) outside waiting for us.

We walk together to the large dining room, which has even more tables added on either side of the large one at its center. Max and I are once again announced as prince and consort, the room applauding as we are seated at a table of our own with the royal family seated together at the head of the large table not far away. There are so many people in the room, it's hard to not want to shrink in on myself, their eyes watching our every move.

For the next several hours, we sit there while just about everyone else takes the opportunity to speak with and congratulate us. Well, they mostly talk to Max, but it still feels good to have people come up and wish me well—even if they were just gossiping about me a few weeks ago. Who am I kidding? They're probably gossiping about me right now.

It's not all strangers though. Trixie, Hannah, and Daniel make sure to come say hi, and Oliver gives us a nice congratulation as well. Still, it's a pretty stuffy affair, just sitting there all night. There's decent food, roasted beef as the main course, but it's all just a little too boring. I kinda wish we were running through the woods again.

"Alright, I don't know about you, but I think I'm about done with all this for the night." Max looks over to me, speaking like he was reading my mind. "Wanna get out of here?"

"Uh-huh." I nod yes, still overwhelmed by our surroundings.

"Come on." He stands, offering me his hand. "Just need to say goodnight to my parents."

The king and queen are dealing with their own well-wishers crowding them with Alden in a similar position as me, most people not speaking to him directly. He doesn't look bothered, but maybe he's just used to it by now.

When people see the prince approaching, they quickly wrap their conversations up, taking a step back for the family to speak together.

"Mom, Dad, Papa," Max says when we have the appearance of privacy. "Peter and I were going to call it at night if that's okay."

"Of course, son." The king smiles and nods his head. "Thank you for allowing us to celebrate your union today."

"It was a beautiful ceremony," the queen comments next. "I hope you both will remember it for years to come."

"Enjoy the rest of your evening, boys," Alden says to us last. "We love you."

"Love you all too," Max says with a grin, squeezing my hand before leading me away.

We walk from the room hand in hand, and though no one says anything, I can feel them all watching us. I breathe easy once we're in the hall, when it's just the two of us and the guards. We stay silent, still holding hands, as we climb up the castle to Max's—no, *our* bedroom. As soon as we're inside, Max starts to strip.

"Can finally get out of these," Max says to me as he starts to unbutton his shirt. "Don't you hate having to dress up?"

"I dunno. I think sometimes it can be nice to look nice," I answer, untucking my own shirt.

"Well, you look nice in everything," he flirts, "and even better in nothing."

I blush, too shy to flirt back and take off my clothes at the same time. I manage to slip off my belt when Max surprises me from behind, wrapping his arms around my waist and kissing my neck. I turn to face him, our mouths and tongues struggling to meet. It's a little awkward to keep taking off my clothes like this, but I manage to keep going until the both of us are naked—except for my collar.

"So you really like it?" he asks, taking the chain in his hand.

"I told you I love it, *sir*." I try to make the *sir* sound breathy.

"Good boy," Max growls, his grip on my collar tightening until he uses it to pull me forward, crushing our lips together again.

Gosh I love kissing. Seriously, I could do this all night, Max's naked body pressed to mine, his coarse, dark body hair scratching against my softer blonde. But I've also learned that there's also a lot of other things I like too, and so even though it's tough, I break our kiss again. Max looks confused until I lower myself to my knees in front of him.

"*Good boy*," he praises again when I take the initiative, leaning forward to nuzzle at his crotch.

I take a big inhale after I bury my nose in his fur. I swear, he smells *so good* down here, like concentrated sex. I start to leave open mouth kisses on the base of his shaft and the heavy sack below. Before I can get too involved, a hand suddenly tugs me by my hair, pulling me away and forcing me to look up.

"Open," Max gives me the single worded order while swiping over my bottom lip with the thumb of his other hand.

I immediately obey, not fighting the hand in my hair holding me in place while Max inserts himself into my mouth. He's thick, and I force my jaw open even wider so I can avoid scraping with my teeth—it's been nearly two weeks, and I've been practicing. Still, as he starts to slide himself in and out, I have to concentrate on not gagging each time he hits the back of my throat.

He moves faster and faster, thrusting in and out of my lips almost like it was my other end. It gets harder and harder not to gag, and I can feel the spit that's been pooling in my mouth starting to drip down my face. The hand in my hair has been a steady pressure, never pulling or tugging, just making sure I stay exactly where my prince wants me.

"Such a good boy for me," Max whispers above me. "Practically made for this."

He pulls out of my mouth with a wet and unexpected *slurp*, leaving me with my mouth hanging open, silently asking for more. Instead of giving it to me, the hand in my hair releases me and helps me to stand. Max hungrily kisses me, plunging his tongue in before I can even react, before pulling away and spinning me around to face the bed.

"All fours on the bed," he orders next, "and use the charm."

"Yes, sir." I rush forward to obey.

The roles are still new to us, and so is the charm he's talking about. As I climb up, I reach for it on the stand next to the bed, a black stone disc about half the size of my palm, its edges perfectly round and smooth. Max introduced me to this not long after the night of my claiming. I don't fully understand how it works, but when I touch it to my stomach, the charm cleans out my downstairs regions in a much more pleasant way than that wolfsbane potion did. I'm not supposed to use it too much though.

Already on my knees, I slide the charm to the side of the bed after I feel the familiar tingle in my belly, falling to my elbows. The first few times I was in the position felt almost shameful, my most sensitive areas completely exposed, to be ogled and on display. I *still* feel most of those things, but now I'm starting to like the way all that shame makes me pulse between my legs.

I hear footsteps behind me just before two hands reach for my ass. They squeeze and spread me wide, exposing me to the air and making me the rest of my body turn red. I feel a puff of breath against my butt, seconds before Max lowers his mouth to my hole with a noisy slurp. I lose my balance in surprise, my chest falling to the mattress and helping to muffle my moan.

Max has done this a few times to me now, and I've loved each and every one of them. His tongue is very different from the other parts of his body, wet and flexible, stretching me just enough to let me know it's in there. Fisting the sheets in my hands, I press back as much as I'm able, urging Max to give me even more.

A finger joins his tongue, slowly slipping into my hole alongside it. A second later, the tongue pulls out and a second finger replaces it, followed by something wet sliding down the crack of my ass—Max must have grabbed the oil. He works me open on his two fingers before adding a third, getting more used to this kind of treatment every day. All three fingers leave me next and my hips are grabbed with both hands, pulling me back and adjusting my height at the edge of the bed. I can feel Max stepping up behind me, his upper thighs brushing against my rear.

"You ready, boy?" he asks, tapping his cock against me with one hand.

"Yes, sir," I answer quickly, already eager for more.

"Good boy," he tells me just before he takes aim.

I'm happy to tell you that there's almost no pain when he enters me, just a small pinch during the first stretch. I'm pretty sure we've done this every day since he claimed me, but I'm still just as excited as the first. I bite my lip as I feel every one of his nine inches (we measured) slide into me. When he's seated all the way to the base, he gives the side of my ass a few rough smacks, making me whimper and moan, once again glad that these walls are soundproof.

He starts slow and steady, allowing me the time to get used to it. Faster healing apparently means I tighten up a little more than usual, even after doing this regularly, but I still love it. Once he's moving faster, I start to push back to meet his thrusts, earning myself a few more spanks that each send another jolt of bliss through my body. I've got my face to the mattress, using it to muffle my sounds, when I suddenly feel Max lean over and pull me up by the shoulder until I'm back on my hands.

"You gettin' tired on me already?" He grabs and tugs my hair roughly when he asks, already starting to fuck me faster.

"N-No sir," I manage to stutter out between all the dueling sensations.

With his hand in my hair, Max gets even rougher, his hips loudly smacking against my ass each time he pounds back in. My dick hangs heavy between my legs, bouncing up and slapping against my belly. With Max focused on using every inch of his length, the pressure I feel that means I'm about to cum dry starts to build. I try to bring my legs together in a feeble and involuntary attempt to stave it off, groaning loudly when it washes over me anyway.

"Love making you do that," Max says cockily, releasing the hold on my hair so that he can reach under me for my cock. "Wanna cum again?"

"Yes, sir," I answer quickly, spreading my thighs wider so he can more easily reach.

"What was that?" He spanks me roughly, slowing his thrusts and losing his grip on my dick. "Doesn't sound like you want to cum."

"Please let me cum, sir!" I beg, which quickly turns into babbling. "Please, I'll do whatever you want, sir. Just make cum, pleasepleasepleaseplease." I start to bounce my ass back toward him in an attempt to please him and hopefully earn my reward.

"That's better." He rewards me with a firmer grip around my shaft.

He starts to jerk me in time with his thrusts, partially bent over me so he can reach. This means his thrusts aren't quite as big or rough as they just were, but the little bursts of pleasure I feel each time he slides over that nice little spot inside just behind my balls make my cock twitch. I can hear how wet I am, the wet *schlick* of my foreskin sliding back and forth over the head. I can feel my balls start to draw up tight, my cock somehow getting even harder just before I groan, unloading all over the sheets below me.

"There's a good boy," Max coos, pumping my dick as it pulses with every shot. "My turn."

He releases me, barely giving me a moment to steady myself before he's back to fucking into me fast and hard. I grip onto the sheets to hold myself in place as he fucks his way to his own orgasm, his thrusts strong enough to knock me from the mattress. Everything still feels good, but his strokes are starting to push that good feeling into overstimulation. But I want sir—Max—to finish, so I focus on keeping myself steady and staying nice and open for him.

I'm unexpectedly and unceremoniously pushed forward onto my stomach, forcibly pulling me off of Max's cock. A second later and the bed shifts as Max climbs over me. I don't even have a chance to look behind to see what he's doing before he's already lined himself up and is sliding back inside me. With his full body weight on top of me, he starts to fuck me rapid fire into the mattress, forcing a series of squawks, gasps, and groans from my mouth that would sound more at home in a barn than a bedroom.

Max's mouth seeks out my shoulder, biting down roughly on my claiming scar as his arms slide down under my armpits and lock my body to his. This new position does the trick and after a few more thrusts that feel like he might fuck me *through* the bed, he finally cums, the liquid heat spreading through my body as he fills me, growling around my shoulder and worrying it with his teeth. He releases me when he's finished, licking over the sore spot he left on my skin.

"That will never not be amazing," he says confidently, nuzzling the back of my neck.

"Th-thank you, sir." I have to turn to the side so I'm not mumbling.

Max manages to roll us both on our side without ever letting himself slip out of me, still hard after all that. He trails his hand up and down my chest and belly as we cuddle together, the exhaustion of the day (and probably all that sex) finally catching up with us. I'm out before I even feel Max slip out of me, my last thoughts of how nice he feels still snuggly inside.

CHAPTER 18

"**...A**nd so, because the lycanthropic curse has already 'primed' the body's cells for transformation, cellular regeneration is increased to between two and five times the speed of a non-lycanthrope."

"Which means they heal faster."

"Correct, Peter," Mrs. Koplat praises. "That is why even when not transformed, werewolves still heal more quickly."

"That also happens to people who only receive a claiming bite, like me, right?" The scrapes on my legs I got from helping Queen Anna with her rose bushes earlier this week were healed by the next day.

"Also correct," she confirms. "Now I'm afraid that's all the time we have for today's lesson. I need to get home and begin preparing for the Lavender Ball tonight."

"I understand, Mrs. Koplat." I nod, gathering my notes and standing. "I probably need to start getting ready too. Thank you for the lesson, and I hope you enjoy the ball."

"You as well, Peter." She bids me goodbye, gathering her materials as I exit the room with Mika and Timothy following me out.

The days following the collaring ceremony have been pretty quiet. We're still no closer to finding the mystery werewolf who tried to kill me— everyone who's been interviewed so far has been able to account for their whereabouts that night with other pack members. While I haven't felt like

I'm in any danger, it's still a little nerve wracking knowing there is someone out there who apparently wants to kill me.

My guards take their places on either side of the door as I open it to enter Max's—*my* bedroom. I'm still getting used to calling it that, but Max insists that it's just as much mine as his. I officially moved in the day after I got my collar, not that I had much to bring with me. Just clothing, my notes from my tutoring classes, and a few other items I've been gifted since being here, plus the bag I first came with. I technically still have the other room to go to or sleep in if I ever want, but I haven't seen a reason to yet.

Max had a second desk added for me, placing it next to his own against the room's eastern wall. The huge four poster bed is against the north wall, which is large enough for four people to sleep in comfortably. There are a couple of couches around a small fireplace, and in one corner sits a lounge chair. The closet is almost as big as the room itself, as is the bathroom that features a huge stone tub sunken into the floor. Max and I have already enjoyed it together a number of times.

I add today's class notes to the others on my desk, where I keep them organized by class. That's when I notice the framed picture next to them, the drawing of me and my parents from the Weston Harvest Festival. I pick it up, the metal frame a solid weight in my hands, running a thumb over the still slightly creased paper within. Max must have framed this for me after I showed it to him.

"Is that everything?"

"I think so." I nodded. "Oh, wait, my bag, it's under the bed."

"I got it." Max bent down, reaching under to retrieve it.

A loose piece of paper fell from the bag's unsecured flap as he pulled it out. He picked it up, unfolding it to reveal the charcoal drawing of my family that was made ten years ago. I'd almost forgotten that I brought it.

"What's this?" He looked at the drawing curiously before handing it to me.

"That's me and my parents," I explained, taking the paper but not stopping him from looking. "We're at Weston's annual harvest festival."

"How old were you?" he asked with a smile, eyes focused on me in the center.

"Nine, maybe ten?" I couldn't remember exactly. "It was a long time ago."

"It looks like you were having fun." He nodded, letting me fold up the drawing again.

"We were," I confirmed. "The harvest festival was always a good time."

"Maybe we can go back for the next one," he offered as I slid the drawing back in my bag.

"Yeah." I nodded, doing my best to act excited instead of hurt at the memory.

I'm torn. Part of me loves it, knowing that Max did it for me, even surprised me with it. But another part of me just feels hurt and angry when I see that picture. Angry enough to do something about it. Before I lose my nerve, I grab a blank piece of paper and a pen and sit down to write.

Momma and Daddy,

This is probably the fifth letter I've written you without getting one back. And I just want to know why? Are you mad at me for not staying? For leaving you alone on the farm? Just because I moved away doesn't mean we're not still a family.

I just want to hear from you to know you're okay. If you don't respond to this letter, I'm coming to see you, whether you like it or not. If the problem is something you can't write about in a letter, then you can say it to me in person.

Your son,

Peter

I read over the letter twice to make sure there's nothing else I want to add, but it really is that simple. If my parents aren't going to come to me, I'll go to them. And I'll check in on Violet while I'm there, too. Determined to see this through before I can change my mind, I fold up the letter and march out of my room.

"Do either of you know where the castle's postmaster is?" I ask my two guards.

"I do," Timothy says with a hand up. "We could take you there now if you'd like, sir."

"Please and thank you." I'm still getting used to being called sir.

Before now I'd just wait for one of the castle staff to pick it up during their rounds, but I'm going to put this letter in the postmaster's hand myself. Tim and Mika lead me all the way down to the castle's ground floor, back towards the kitchens. We reach a room with an open door, an office with a large table at its center, stacks of letters and packages on its surface. A young elf and human both seem to be sorting through the piles while an older gnome stands at his desk off to the side when he sees us walk in.

"Young Consort Blackclaw," he greets me warmly. "What can I do for you today?"

"Hello, sir." I'm still getting used to my title too. The fact that I share it with Alden hasn't helped make things less confusing, either. "I have a letter I need to send to Weston."

"Ah, a lovely village," he comments with a knowing nod and out-stretched hand.

"Have you been there before?" I ask as I pass him the letter.

"Many years ago, when I was only a postboy making deliveries myself." I watch as he steps over to his desk and stuffs my letter into an envelope. "Beautiful countryside. I've enjoyed seeing the name crop up recently on some of our deliveries out of the castle."

"Those have probably been to my parents." The money and my previous letters. "That's actually who I need to send this to."

"Of course, I should have their names in my records..." He flips through a small leather-bound book. "Ronald and Mary Lambert of Lamplight Farm?"

"That's them," I confirm. "How long will it take to reach them?"

"Parcel delivery can take some time depending on the volume," he explains, taking a pen to write on the envelope. "But a letter could be there in three or four days. Possibly faster, but I will need to check to see if we have any hounds trained for a route to Weston. We haven't sent any letters there in some time."

"You use dogs to deliver mail? That's so..." His final words finally reach my brain. "What do you mean you haven't sent any letters to Weston? Why not?"

"Well, because there haven't been any to send," he answers simply, looking at me curiously. "Not for many, many years."

"None?" *That doesn't make any sense. I've sent a bunch!* "Are you sure?"

"Positive." He taps on the side of his head. "I may be getting older, but I've still got an excellent memory. The only things that have left for Weston have been the packages sent once a month courtesy of the royal family."

"Is this where all of the mail in the castle is gathered?" I point to the table filled with letters. The human and elf have continued to work, though I do catch the elf giving me an odd look.

"Yes." He nods. "Anything that goes out of the castle passes through this room first. Letters and packages from the staff living on the castle grounds, orders for the kitchen and other supplies, even the royal family's personal correspondence. After we gather and sort it here, couriers for the city's post-master collect them and process them for delivery."

"Do you collect everything in the castle yourself?" I don't *think* this man is lying to me, but what happened to my letters?

"Heavens no, that would take up almost all of my day," he answers with a laugh. "The heads of staff take it upon themselves to gather together the mail from those they oversee and deliver them here."

"Who collects the mail for the royal family?" I have a sinking feeling in the pit of my stomach. "Or their guests?"

"That would be master Kamo," he informs me, watching me with some concern. "Is everything all right?"

"Yes, everything's fine," I lie, not sure if I should reveal anything. "But could I get that letter back? I just remembered something I need to add."

"Of course, Consort Blackclaw." He hands it back. "Was there anything else I could help you with?"

"No, thank you." I shake my head. "I'll be back with my corrected letter tomorrow."

"Then I shall see you tomorrow, sir." He gives me a small bow as I turn with my guard and exit his office.

"Do either of you know where the prince is right now?" I ask Mika and Timothy. "I need to talk to him—it's important."

"I last heard he was with the royal tailor, sir," Mika informs me.

"Could you take me to him, please?" I ask, both guards nodding before Mika leads us away.

My body is almost moving automatically as we walk the castle halls, my mind running a hundred miles a minute. None of my letters reaching home would explain why I haven't gotten a single response. And if that is the case, it's not hard to figure out who is responsible. I really thought that we were starting to understand each other after our talk during the last court session, but I guess Kamo still views me the same as he always has.

Mika knocks on the door, waiting to hear the "come in" before opening it for me. The first thing I see is at least a dozen or more mannequins placed around the room, each in various states of dress. A wooden divider blocks off one corner while another wall is lined with a rack of clothing. Max stands on a stool near a mirror against the room's far wall with Trixie next to him on the floor on one knee, needle in hand as she does something to Max's pants.

"Peter," Max says my name with concern, "is everything okay?"

"No." I look behind me, waiting for Timothy to close the door before I continue. "I think Kamo might have been the werewolf who tried to kill me."

"*What?*" He's completely thrown by my accusation, his eyes immediately moving to Trixie, who up until now had no idea about any of this. "What makes you think that?"

"Aside from the fact that he's hated me since I got here?" I reply with a little sarcasm. "I just came back from seeing the castle postmaster. He says that *none* of my letters back home have passed through his office, and I'm pretty sure Kamo was the one in charge of collecting them."

"Shit." Max's eyes go wide. "Maybe that's why you haven't heard back from anyone."

"That's what I was thinking too." I nod, the thought bringing me a little bit of comfort. "What do we do?"

"I'll talk to Dad," Max replies confidently. "I promise we'll get to the bottom of this, but it might have to wait until after the ball tomorrow."

"I know." I hang my head, not liking the frustration I'm feeling.

"Just try to have fun tonight, okay?" he offers with a sad smile. "We'll figure this all out, I promise."

After Max and I explain the situation to Trixie, she's nervous but understands the need for secrecy. I'm not any less frustrated, but there are things I need to do myself before the ball, so I leave Trixie to finish Max's outfit. I head to the spa, where despite having just cut my hair last week, Daniel and Hannah spend over an hour fixing me up again. After that, they send me to Trixie for my own outfit while they work their magic on Max.

Finished with our pre-ball preparations, we meet in the hallway just outside our bedroom. The outfit Trixie has made for me is amazing, as her things always are, but it isn't until I see Max in his that I fully appreciate them both.

He's wearing a black jacket over black pants, his buttons, belt buckle, and even crown all made of shiny, polished platinum. His shoulders and pockets are lined with an equally shiny material, and a lavender colored sash extends from his right shoulder to his left hip. My outfit is very similar, except that it is my shirt that is silver with the accessories and accents colored black. I don't have a crown, but I do have a sash like his, crossing my chest in the opposite direction.

"Wow," Max says as we meet in the middle of the hall. "You look amazing."

"So do you," I answer with a blush, loving how our outfits match. "Trixie did a good job."

"She certainly did." He nods before turning slightly and offering me his arm. "Shall we?"

"Ready if you are." I slip my arm through his.

"I know there's a lot going on right now," he says as we start walking, our guards following behind us. "But remember, tonight is supposed to be fun."

"I'm sure it will be," I tell him, squeezing his arm with mine. "Especially if you're there."

We are headed for the castle's ballroom, which takes up almost the entire third and part of the fourth floor. I haven't actually been inside it before. We don't use the main entrance, instead using the guarded back stairwell reserved for the royal family, which exits right next to one of their usual waiting rooms.

Inside are the king, queen, and consort, each of them dressed to the nines. Their wardrobe is coordinated to match like ours, Trixie having taken the lavender theme even further, the queen's dress and men's tops all sharing the same light shade of purple. Before we are forced to make small talk, Kamo enters and I freeze. I swear I can feel my blood actually starting to boil until Max rubs the small of my back, silently reminding me to stay calm.

"You all look spectacular," he tells us, clasping his hands. "If you are ready, the ball awaits!"

He leads us back into the hallway to a set of ornate guarded double doors just a few yards away, the sounds of a crowded room just on the other side. When the guards open the doors for us, the noise increases tenfold, and I realize just how many people are here. Kamo enters first, and there is a brief pause before a trumpet sounds, and he begins speaking.

"Presenting His Royal Highness King Samoset Blackclaw, Queen Anna Blackclaw, and Consort Alden Blackclaw." At Kamo's words, Max's parents all step into the ballroom, Alden and the queen on either of the king's arms, to what sounds like an adoring crowd.

"We're next," Max tells me, squeezing my hand before getting us into position.

"Also presenting His Royal Highness Prince Makseka Blackclaw and Consort Peter Blackclaw." *That's us!*

Together, we step through the doorway and into the ballroom. More specifically, the top of a flight of stairs overlooking the ballroom. It's easily the biggest room I've ever seen; I think you could fit my house in here. Around the edge of the room are dozens of tables, each overlaid with a lavender table-cloth and a vase of flowers by the same name. That seems to be the color of the evening, paper streamers hanging from the ceiling and most people's clothing also matching. A huge, ornate chandelier hangs over the center of the room, the floor filled with couple after couple dancing away. The music is being played by a small orchestra set up toward one side of the room, near some of the large ceiling-to-floor windows that line the walls.

"Ready to have some fun?" Max asks after seeing the amazement on my face.

"Uh-huh." I nod, still taking everything in.

Max's parents have already proceeded down the stairs ahead of us, and we follow after them. We head for a table that's a little smaller and more secluded than the others with places set for the five of us. Max pulls out my chair for me, but before he joins me, he flags down a server with a tray of wine glasses, grabbing one for us both.

"You'll see some people carrying snacks, but dinner won't be served for another hour or so," he tells me as he hands me a glass. "Until then, there's not much to do but drink, talk, and dance."

"Sounds like the dances we had back home." I take a sip of the wine and try not to grimace. The ale in Weston tasted way better than this.

"Does that mean you like to dance?" he asks, drinking some himself. On the opposite end of the table, people are already trying to speak with the king.

"I, uh, guess I did. I haven't danced in a really long time." And *never with another man.*

"Would you like to?" he asks next, looking toward the dancefloor.

"Right now?" People have been staring at us since we came in. There are already people lining up on the other side of the table just to speak with the king and queen. "I don't think I know any of the kind of dances you do at something like this."

"They're not too complicated." He smiles cockily. "Besides, you have me here to teach you."

"Okay." I bite my lip, torn between feeling excited, nervous, and just wanting to make him happy.

"You can finish your wine first," he teases. "Might even help."

I do, and it does. After downing my glass in record time, it only takes a few minutes for the familiar warmth of alcohol to spread through my body. I'm still completely terrified of making a fool of myself, but at least now I can feel a little drunk while I do it. After checking that I'm ready, Max stands and offers me his hand, pulling me onto the dancefloor.

People automatically part as we approach, clearing us a path toward the room's center. Happy with our placement, Max turns so that we are facing each other, taking one of my hands and placing it on his shoulder. Then, taking my free hand in his and putting the other on my waist, we start to move.

"Just follow my lead," he instructs, like it's the easiest thing in the world.

The music being played isn't very fast, but people are still moving with much more grace than I ever have. I spend the first few minutes staring at my feet, paranoid that I might step on Max or someone else by accident—which I end up doing anyway, of course. I also trip over my own feet a couple of times and even accidentally bump into a woman wearing a huge hoop dress, but eventually I find the rhythm in Max's steps.

I'm not doing it *well*, but I am dancing. Excited at my progress, I meet Max's eye and receive a proud grin in return. The next thing I know, the two of us are spinning around the ballroom together. We take a couple of breaks, Max's choice of dance changing each time the music does, but after the first time, I'm a lot less worried about learning as I go. The extra wine we have during those breaks probably helps too.

"You're a natural," Max praises. "Getting hungry? Should be having dinner soon."

"Food sounds good," I agree, not that I'm in a rush to stop this.

"I'm glad we got to do this now," he says as we continue to dance. "After dinner, I'm probably going to have to spend a little time playing politics like my parents have."

"It's okay." I'm disappointed, but hopefully we'll get to do more of this too. "I know you have to be a good prince for your people."

"Just for a little bit," he confirms with a smile. "Really, it's mostly to give my parents a chance to enjoy themselves, too."

"That's sweet." I look over at our table, seeing even more people lined up than before.

Thankfully, they all disperse once dinner begins. The first thing we're served is a small plate of this biscuit-like thing made of potatoes, onions, and fish. After that comes a salad, followed by a chicken breast served over roasted potatoes, our servers never letting our wine glasses go empty the entire meal. Dessert is a slice of chocolate and cherry cake, and even after that, there are trays covered in cheese being walked around to go with all the wine everyone is still drinking.

The dinner break does give the king a chance to dance with both Queen Anna and Alden, Max taking over the line with whichever of them isn't currently with King Sam. There's some disappointment, some people even going back to their seats, but those who remain are excited for face time with *any* of the royal family. Even when the king comes back, they mostly talk about themselves, bragging about the accomplishments of themselves and their family while Max just politely nods his head through all of it. It's boring, but the wine makes it easy for my mind to wander.

At least the first part of the night was fun. Even this stuffy kind of dancing is fun, once you get the basics down. Still wish I was better, though. Maybe I could get dance lessons? When I turn to ask that out loud to Max, I'm distracted by the people next in line to speak with him: Charlotte and Edgar Halfdan.

"Prince Makseka, it's so wonderful to see you," Edgar greets with a bow while his sister curtseys at his side.

"Nice to see you two as well," Max lies to the siblings. "How is your night going?"

"It has been absolutely splendid, my prince," Charlotte says in a breathier voice than she needs. "But nothing would make my happier if you would please grant me the honor of a dance."

"A dance?" The request throws Max, who looks from Charlotte to me and then Alden sitting on the other side of the table, who nods. "Of course, Charlotte, I'd be happy to dance with you."

He gives me an apologetic look before he stands, taking Charlotte's offered hand and leading her to the dance floor. Edgar watches them with a pleased smile, giving me and Alden a small bow of the head before he walks away, having gotten what he came here for. With only the two consorts at the table, the remaining people waiting to speak with the king or prince disperse, leaving us to each other's company.

"I honestly don't know why that girl still tries," Alden says as soon as the coast is clear. "But his father donates a lot of money for things like repairing the roads and bridges in St. Kizis, so Sam likes to stay on their good side."

"I understand," I tell him. "I know he's got to make nice with his people."

"Are you enjoying yourself tonight?" Alden checks in with me next. "I know this can't be what you're used to."

"It's different but still a lot of fun." I nod. "I've never danced like that before."

"My first ball was fun too," he shares. "Once I got over my nerves—"

"Sorry to interrupt," a tall woman says, doing exactly that. She's got shoulder length brown hair, and rather than a dress, she's in a suit not unlike my own. Actually, I think I recognize her from the stables.

"Nina!" Alden says with excitement, standing and hugging the woman before sitting back down. "Peter, this is my sister Nina, the castle stablemaster."

"It's very nice to meet you." I take her offered hand. "I've seen the horses you keep. They're incredible."

"Thank you," she accepts confidently. "I've heard a lot about you, too, and I hope living in the castle is agreeing with you. As I said, I'm sorry to interrupt, but I wanted to see if my brother wanted to dance."

"No, you wanted the chance to corner me so you could complain about Dad without me running away." Even as he says it, Alden stands. "Excuse us, Peter."

"Have fun." I watch as they walk away, Nina already talking excitedly to her brother.

Out on the dancefloor, I can see the king and queen smiling warmly as they happily move in each other's arms. I also see Max and Charlotte, and the poor girl may as well have hearts in her eyes with the way she stares at him. For his part, he looks like he's having fun... but I already know he was having more fun with me before.

"You know he's still going to get married one day." Edgar's voice makes me jump, not having heard him creep back up to the table when I wasn't looking.

"What?" It takes a moment for me to even understand what he's talking about. "Who said anything about marriage?"

"He may care for you, even make you his consort," he continues, ignoring my question, "but you will never be his wife."

"Oh yeah?" It's probably (*definitely*) the wine talking, but I really don't feel like sitting here and listening to this guy insult me. "Well neither will your sister, seeing you don't have anything to offer besides a pair of tits and that stick you have jammed up your ass."

I don't know what comes over me, but the words fly out of my mouth without even thinking as Edgar's face turns red in anger and humiliation. Feeling confident and not wanting to give him the chance to respond, I push my chair from the table, storming away to the nearest balcony and not once looking back.

Thankfully, I'm alone. Outside, the air is cool, the moon above only half full. I lean over the edge of the balcony, looking into the forest behind the castle and trying to calm down. I should have known I wasn't going to make it through the night without *someone* being an asshole.

"Hey." Max surprises me, leaning over the same balcony. "Are you okay?"

"I'm fine," I tell him, not sure I want to go into detail.

"It looked like Edgar said something shitty to you," he says next. "Do I need to go beat him up?"

"No, you don't need to beat him up." I shake my head with a shy smile. "He was just talking about how I'll never be your wife."

"And I suppose he thinks his sister will be?" He looks over his shoulder into the ballroom, unimpressed.

"Something like that," I grumble. "I ... might have said all she had to offer was a pair of tits."

Max slaps his hand over his mouth to hold in a guffaw of laughter. "I bet he *loved* hearing that."

"No idea. Walked away before he could respond," I admit bashfully.

"That's awesome," he tells me with a grin. "Still, I'm sorry. He shouldn't be talking to you like that."

"It's okay," I say with a shrug. "I still had a great night."

"Yeah, but it's been kind of a crappy day," he continues, taking one of my hands. "With everything going on, I know the moment is probably ruined, but I just really wanted to tell you... I love you, Peter."

The "L" word doesn't register right away, and after an almost agonizingly slow realization of what Max just said, it hits me.

"I... Max... You..." I start to stutter before finding the words. "I love you, too, Max."

Without another word, he takes me in his moonlit-arms and kisses me. The music and noise all melt away as Max's scent, taste, and touch surround me, becoming my entire world. I can barely remember we're even *at* a ball when we finally pull apart.

"You wanna get out of here?" Max asks, looking from the ballroom on one side to the forest on the other.

"Are we allowed?" I don't know what the rules are for this stuff yet. "Won't your parents be upset?"

"Nah, we've been here long enough." He shakes his head. "We danced, we ate, we made nice with the public. No one will even realize we're gone."

"How are we going to manage that?" Even if there was a secret passage in the ballroom, how would we use it without somebody seeing?

"By going over the balcony," Max answers while looking over the edge at the ground.

"*What?*" I look down with him.

"We're only on the third floor." He shrugs. "We can make that no problem. Werewolf strength, remember?"

"Are you sure?" I look between him and the ground between the castle and the forest nervously.

"Completely." He nods confidently. "I'll go first. That way I can catch you. Even if we *do* get hurt, we'll heal right up."

"Okay..." I really don't like that response, but he seems confident.

After first checking to make sure no one is watching, Max climbs up and swings his legs over the balcony. Dropping to his hands first, I watch nervously as he releases his grip and falls, landing on the ground in a crouch. After dusting off his hands, he stands, looking up to me and holding up a thumb before urging me down.

Here goes nothing. I copy his movements as best I can, not nearly as graceful as he was. When it's time to let go and fall, it takes me a few tries, and when I finally do, I stupidly close my eyes and then panic about not being able to see where I'm falling. Thankfully, Max manages to catch me anyway.

"We might have to start you on some agility training," he comments while setting me on my feet.

"I don't know that I'll ever get used to jumping from a third-floor balcony," I say as I regain my balance. "So, what do you want to do now?"

"I thought we could go for a walk," he answers, taking me by the hand and leading me into the forest with a knowing look. "At least until we're far enough away from the party."

I grin, taking his hand as we walk farther into the woods. The fun I had dancing, the wine I drank, even the energy I felt after telling off Edgar, all of it combines into an excitement that turns our walk into a run, the trees soon flying past us. With a growl, Max pulls me to a stop, taking me by the shoulders and pushing me up against a tree before kissing me.

"W-Wait," I sputter between kisses, "I don't want Trixie to get mad because we messed up the nice clothes she made us."

"Then I guess we better get out of them," Max replies with a wiggle of his eyebrows, already reaching for his sash.

The two of us start to strip, leaning in to steal the occasional kiss. He's not even halfway down his shirt when something makes Max freeze. Before I can ask him about it, I hear it myself—footsteps, heavy ones, coming this way.

"Get behind me," Max orders quickly, putting himself between me and whoever is getting closer. "Who's there?" he asks loudly to the trees.

We don't get an answer, but the footsteps keep getting louder until it becomes apparent that there's more than one of them. Still hiding behind Max, I watch as not one but *three* different werewolves emerge from deep in the forest. As they continue to take step after menacing step toward us, I realize that these werewolves have no scent, and worry about just how much trouble the two of us are in.

CHAPTER 19

"Peter, you need to run."

"What? I can't just leave you—"

"Run back to the castle and get help," Max tells me, his voice getting rougher, like he just swallowed a bunch of gravel. "I'll hold them off for as long as I can, just go. *NOW!*"

He barks the single worded order over his shoulder, his fangs already elongating. As he turns back to our approaching attackers, he finishes shifting, his muscles bulging until they rip through the fabric of his clothes. As he leaps at them, the shredded tatters of his ball outfit falling to the grass, I remember to spring into action. *Run!*

I turn back toward the castle and take off, the growling behind me quickly growing into angry roars. I'm worried for Max, outnumbered three-to-one, but I try not to think about that. He told me to get help, so I'm going to get help. Even as strong as I am now, I wouldn't have stood a chance in that fight. I don't even *know* how to fight, but if I can't use my strength, at least I can use my speed.

Those aren't the only things that got better after the bite. With my improved hearing, I do my best to try and keep track of Max's situation. I think I can make out his growls over the other three, but as I get farther away it starts to fade. But while Max gets harder to hear, another wolf seems to get easier—a lot easier: one of them is chasing me.

The thought sends me into a panic, pushing me to run faster. Of course Max wouldn't be able to hold them all off—I just hope he's still okay. I also hope that this wolf doesn't manage to catch up to me before I reach the castle. I just have to get to the back gate. Once I'm inside there will be plenty of guards to—

I stumble to a stop as I reach the castle's rear gate, the one we usually exit from on the full moon. Except it's not open, the large wooden doors sealed shut, and without a guard in sight. I rush forward and try in vain to pull the doors open, but they barely budge even after trying with all my might. *Why is this closed? Where are the guards? Who would—Kamo!* My earlier revelation comes crashing back to me.

He basically runs the castle; it wouldn't be hard for him to order this gate to be closed. Had he planned this whole thing? Was he watching us at the ball? Did he know we'd leave for the forest and have these other wolves waiting for us? I don't have time to wonder about too much because I can hear the other wolf still getting closer—I have to find a way inside.

Running around to the front of the castle is going to take too long, and I'm not even sure I know the way. But I *do* remember where the secret entrance Max used to sneak us out of the castle is. At least I think I do.

I rush down the castle wall to the section I'm sure we came out of, my hands desperately seeking out the brick I need to press to get the door to open. I hear the werewolf off to my left, having just reached the castle gate themselves, when the stone under my hand finally gives away and pushes in. I quickly squeeze myself through the open passage, pushing the stone wall shut behind me.

I can hear the werewolf approaching the other side of the wall, and I quickly move away. I don't even take a second to breathe—there's no time. I have to get out of here and get help, but that's easier said than done.

I am able to see a little better in the dark now, but without a light source, I still find myself stumbling into walls and on steps. I don't even know any other exits except the one in the library, so I'll have to run down to the ballroom from there. If I can remember the right way to go. I'm passing through one of the small rooms on my way to the stairs I'm *pretty* sure lead to the library, when a low growl freezes me in my tracks.

"H-Hello?" I stutter out as I nervously turn toward the noise. "Is someone there?"

In the dark, dusty room, I watch as a hulking figure rises from behind an old crate. The werewolf growls menacingly as it stalks toward me. *How are they already here? How did they know where to find me?* I don't get an immediate answer to those questions as I nervously try to back away.

"I knew you would be trouble," a familiar voice behind me says before something hard hits me on the back of the head and the world goes dark.

"I think he's finally waking up," a new voice says somewhere to my right.

"Nnngh," I moan as I feel the throbbing pain on the back of my skull.

"Get away from him!" Max shouts—*Max!*

My eyes fly open, my mind catching up on the events of the last hour or so—plus however long I was out for. I try to move my arms but find them chained together behind the back of the chair I'm tied to, the cold metal links digging into my skin. Even with my new strength, I can't break free of them. A look around reveals a room that from the looks of it is still in the castle. There's a desk just to my left, so we must be in some kind of office, but I'm a lot more interested in the people filling the room than the furniture.

Four of them stand around us, eyes glaring at me menacingly. The two right next to me are human, a man and woman, with another human man just across from me next to an elf woman I recognize from the mailroom. I can't smell any of them, so I think we've found our mystery wolves, not that it's of any help now. Behind them, tied to a chair just like me, is Max, his blue eyes watching me with concern.

"Max!" I cry, struggling in vain against my tied wrists as I try to reach him.

"Peter…" he manages to get out, smiling sadly.

He looks terrible. He's completely naked, his skin a sickly pale color, with dark circles under both of his eyes. Shiny metal chains wrap around his shoulders and neck, the skin underneath looking raw and chafed. I can even hear a slight sizzle, the smell of burnt flesh wafting from him. *Silver.*

"There. Are you happy now?" that familiar voice from earlier asks from behind me, its owner walking around to my front. "He healed just fine without the silver."

"Mr. Longfellow?" I'm confused to see the old man, my and Max's history tutor, standing in front of me.

"Nice to have you back with us, Peter Lambert," he tells me with a menacing smile. "Or should I say, Peter Durenholtz."

"What?" *Durenholtz?* "I don't understand."

"Ugh," Longfellow grunts in frustration and turns away. "Are we really going to have to do this? I recognized you the second I saw you."

"I told you! He doesn't know what you're talking about." Max struggles in his seat, a hand on either side clamping onto his shoulders to hold him in place. "Neither of us do."

"Oh, I wouldn't expect *you* to know anything," he says dismissively, turning so he can face us both, his arms crossed over his chest. "With your mixed blood, it would have been a miracle if you had picked up on any of this interloper's secret plot."

"What the hell is *that* supposed to mean?" Even in pain, Max manages to sound righteously angry.

"It means that your father, much like many of your ancestors, was content to *breed* with outsiders!" Longfellow snarls in anger, pausing and taking a deep breath before he calmly adjusts his glasses. "We have been working for some time to try and rehabilitate your bloodline. We had high hopes for your grandparents with the way your grandfather insisted on observing even our oldest traditions, but in the later years of his rule, it was clear that he had gone soft. Not that replacing him with the feckless ruler of your father was any better, and with you it has become apparent that you are all a lost cause. No matter. We will be sure to install a new, *true* werewolf king in your place."

"What are you talking about?" Max looks as confused as I am—but much, much angrier. "Do you *really* think you're going to get away with this? The *second* I get out of here—*Oof!*" Max grunts in pain as the elf's fist connects with his stomach.

"We've been getting away with it for hundreds of years. What makes you think this will be any different?" the older man says with a sneer before turning to face me. "Now to deal with *you.*"

"Mr. Longfellow, I don't understand," I repeat to the older man who looks at me with a level of anger and resentment I've never seen. "Why are you doing this?"

"You're good. I'll give you that," he says with a chuckle, reaching toward the desk and picking up a small stack of papers. "I must have read over these letters dozens of times and still can't crack your code."

"Code?" *What is he talking about?* "Why do you have my letters?"

"Did you really think you'd be able to get word to your allies without anyone knowing?" He waves the stack of letters in front of me before nodding to the human I recognized from the mailroom. "I had Carmen intercept everything before the postmaster knew they even existed."

So I *was* right—mostly. I guess I owe Kamo an apology, if I ever see him again. Despite the apparent danger, my heart soars at the conformation that my friends and family haven't been ignoring me. Then it sinks that it also means they probably think I've been ignoring *them* for months.

"I don't know what you're talking about," I try to reason with the man.

"I assume that 'Momma' and 'Daddy' are your leaders," he says while reading through the stack of papers. "And you were clearly working to try and bring them and the rest of your group into the capitol."

"What? No, they're just my par—"

"Were you hoping to launch an attack during the collaring ceremony? That never seemed like Ava's style," he mutters, mostly to himself. "Probably just an attempt to install a few spies on the staff without anyone noticing... This friend with the sick father. More allies of yours?"

"Who's Ava?" I plead, confused.

"Drop the act." Mr. Longfellow rolls his eyes. "Even if I hadn't *immediately* recognized your mother's hair color, your scent is just like the both of them. I *knew* she was in hiding. I just had no idea where. Until now."

"I swear I don't know what you're talking about!" I guess I have my mom's hair color, but nothing else he's saying makes sense.

"I was always curious how she was able to overcome the sterilization effects of the claiming bite," he continues, watching me with curiosity. "I suppose I'll have to ask her myself now that I know where to find her."

"Would you give it up already?!" Max growls angrily. "He already told you he doesn't know what you're talking about! You can *hear* that he isn't lying!"

"I wouldn't expect someone like *you* to understand," Longfellow responds dismissively. "It's a wonder you were ever able to grasp my lessons at all!"

"The second I get out of these chains, I'm going to rip your throat out with my teeth," Max says with a flash of his not-yet-fangs.

"Oh really?" Longfellow asks, unimpressed, before turning to the elf at Max's side. "Carmen, if you would?"

Without even a nod, the elf turns and gives Max a punch to the stomach, knocking the air from him in a loud grunt.

"Fuck... You..." Max tells them both a few seconds later.

"Again," Longfellow orders, the elf striking Max across the jaw this time.

"Max!" I cry out. "Stop hurting him!"

"Why do you..." Longfellow trails off, his eyes searching me for something. "Don't tell me you *actually* care about him?"

"Of course I do!" *Why is he doing this?!*

"Hmm." His eyes narrow suspiciously at my answer. "Well in that case... Gustav, assist Carmen."

"No!" I shout as the human joins in with the elf in brutalizing Max.

"There's only one way this stops: tell me about your plans," he offers me a deal, one I can't actually take.

"I keep telling you I don't know about any plans!" I appeal to him again.

"Hmm. We'll see." He shrugs, leaning against the desk as he watches the others work.

Gustav and Carmen take turns as they beat Max. He doubles over each time their fists connect with his stomach, and what started as a trickle of blood from his mouth splatters on the wall behind him each time they punch his face. I struggle in my bonds, begging them to stop.

"I told you—this only stops when you tell me everything." He waits for an answer, and when I don't have one for him, he pushes off from the desk in a huff. "Have it your way."

He raises his hand for the two to pause, and I breathe a sigh of relief. It's short lived as I'm forced to watch as he turns to the desk, sliding a simple wooden box toward him and opening the lid. From inside, he pulls out some sort of tool, two of them, a thick wooden handle attached to a thin, long rod with a pointed end. If you ignored the handle, they'd almost look like knitting needles, the metal shining brightly in the light of the room. As he takes one in each hand and walks menacingly toward Max, a sinking feeling in my stomach tells me that they're probably made of silver.

"Tell me what you and your mother have been planning." He flips one of the tools in his fist, holding the pointed end down over Max's leg.

"I... I don't know!" I shake my head, already crying. "Momma and I haven't planned anything!"

He rolls his eyes at my answer—then stabs the needle down into Max's thigh. He howls in pain as the metal pierces cleanly through his skin, the muscle underneath sizzling against the silver. Longfellow wriggles the handle, watching me for a reaction as Max cries out. He walks to Max's other side and repeats this on his second thigh, and every time I so much as struggle in my chair, hands clamp onto my shoulders to hold me in place.

"You know I'm going to find out everything anyway," he tries to reason with me. "As soon as we are finished with you here, we ride for Weston to this 'farm' of yours to take care of the problem ourselves."

"How many times do I have to tell you that I don't know what you're talking about?!" I shout, tears of fear, sadness, and anger streaming down my face. "I don't know what you want from me!"

"The truth!" he shouts at me. "You and I both know that you don't belong here!"

I shut my eyes at his words, feeling my anger build and build. I am so *sick* of people like him telling me where I don't belong. Sick of hearing his stupid and confusing questions. Sick of watching him hurt Max. I just want to *Make. Them. Stop.*

"Uh, sir?" The woman at my left sounds afraid.

When I open my eyes, it's like the room around me is growing smaller. Then the wooden legs of the chair beneath me snap, forcing me to stand and breaking the rest of the chair when I do. Everyone in the room seems to freeze as they all look up at me—way up—with fearful and confused eyes.

"He's a werewolf?!" Carmen shouts.

"Don't just stand there!" Longfellow orders angrily, already starting to shift.

I don't. I'm not sure what comes over me, but with my anger still fueling me, I spring into action. Before they can shift themselves, I turn to the humans who were guarding me, using my claws to fling the woman against a stone wall, and the man out of the room's only window. With them taken care of, I face the three people still standing, the ones who would dare to hurt my *mate.*

Still only mid-shift, the elf makes a perfect first target, my fangs sinking cleanly into her arm. She shrieks as I lift and shake her in my jaw before I fling her against the same stone wall she was just splattering Max's blood on. Someone jumps on my back next—the last of Longfellow's guards, and another person to hurt Max. Without even thinking, I leap straight up, flipping so that I land on my back—and him—with my full weight. While he's still stunned, I roll and quickly heave him out of the same window I broke with his buddy just a minute ago.

And that just leaves Longfellow. The man stands between me and my still bound mate. In his fully shifted form, I recognize him as the werewolf who tried to kill me during the night of my claiming. Only he looks so small now. *Why was I ever afraid of him?*

He attacks first, leaping at me with heavy swipes of his claws that I easily deflect before knocking him back. Roaring in anger, he comes at me again—leaving himself completely open for my own claws to rake down his neck and chest. As he stumbles backward, I strike him again on the side and knock him to the ground. Before he can recover, I leap on him, the room shaking as I land on the stone floor.

I pin his arms by his head, his strength no match for mine. He snarls and barks up at me, spittle flying from his jaw as he struggles to free himself. I can smell the rage pouring off of him, barely covering the fear he feels over his current predicament. I can also still smell Max and his pain, his burning flesh, making my own anger surge. Max's words, his threat, suddenly flashes in my mind, and before I can think, my jaws are clamped around Longfellow's neck,

Before he can so much as move, before he can even register that my teeth are there, I rip the flesh away from his throat and fling it to the side, Longfellow's blood still warm in my mouth as he gurgles angrily beneath me. His arms struggle in vain, growing weaker and weaker until he finally stops making any sounds of movement altogether. Having properly avenged my mate, I howl up at the ceiling in satisfaction.

"Peter?" I turn to find Max watching me with a mix of worry and awe, still tied to his chair. "Is that really you?"

I nod, quickly moving to help him, kneeling so that I can more easily reach him.

"You're so big," he says with wonder. "I knew you'd make a gorgeous wolf."

As I reach forward to try and find a way to break his bonds, the sight of my hands—my *claws*—covered in golden colored fur—makes me pause, Max's words hitting me like a brick. I'm a werewolf. An actual werewolf. A big one, too, able to wrap my hands entirely around Max's thigh. How... How did this happen?

The events of the last few minutes start crashing back next. The anger, the violence... *Oh gods, Longfellow!* I look over to the man's corpse and the red, pulpy mess of his neck, having transformed back into human form in death. I did that. *I did that! Why did I do that?!* I start to panic, my breathing turning ragged as I struggle to take in oxygen.

"Peter?" Max asks with worry, still chained and impaled by silver. "What's wrong?"

I killed him. I may have even killed the others. How high up are we? I didn't think before throwing them out the window. They're probably lying down there right now, their bodies even more mangled than Longfellow's. The more I panic, the harder it feels to breath, and I can hear myself whining as I double over on my knees.

"You have to calm down," Max tries to soothe me. "You have to *breathe*."

I want to listen to him, really, I do, but it's hard to get my brain and body to follow through. Spots start to cloud my vision when I dare to look over at the two people I threw against the wall. But before I can even worry about whether or not they're alive, I slump over, and the last thing I hear is the *thunk* of my head hitting the floor.

CHAPTER 20

MAX

"Hello? What was that noise?"

"In here! Quickly!" I call out.

"Prince Makseka?!" the guard cries out in surprise when he forces open the door, then he takes in the rest of the scene. "What is... What happened here?"

I know I should be thankful that the noise from the fight attracted some attention, especially with the ball going on, but the only thing I'm worried about right now is Peter, who is currently a giant, hulking werewolf. The guard and I watch in quiet fascination as the body covered in blonde fur begins to shrink until all that's left is an unconscious and naked Peter on the stone floor. Then the guard notices the rest of the room and decides it would be best to call for reinforcements before quickly getting me out of my chains. I tell as much of the story as I know to Captain Ulman, the head of castle security, who moves to quickly apprehend the other attackers both outside and in—well, except Longfellow.

Of course, this all means that the Lavender Ball is forced to end much earlier than usual, not that the attendees are told why as they are guided out of the castle. Instead, my parents are alerted to the situation while I'm brought to the castle's infirmary with Peter, where the castle's current on-call physician, Dr. Mira, receives us with shock. She immediately moves to help me, but I insist she examine Peter first. He still hasn't woken up, and I'm worried that something might be wrong. I'd also like to know if there's any evidence of his shifting because I've never seen anything like it myself.

Longfellow's accomplices are brought to the healer as well, each of them secured with silver cuffs and a team of knights standing guard. I can already hear Captain Ulman interrogating them in the next room as Dr. Mira finishes looking at the wounds around my neck. Everything should heal just fine, but I'm not going to be able to feel calm until I find out what exactly is going on. I'm sitting at Peter's bedside when my parents are finally let in, and I find myself explaining things so fast I can barely even understand myself.

"Max, slow down and start from the beginning," my mother requests as calmly as she can.

"Peter and I had just snuck out of the ball," I start again. "We were out in the forest, where we *thought* we were alone." I'm very thankful when none of my parents ask *why* we were out there.

"And then you were attacked?" Papa asks, looking over a sleeping Peter.

"Yes, by three werewolves." I nod before pointing to the next room. "They're some of the people Captain Ulman currently has in handcuffs. I saw them shift myself. This whole thing was planned. They were working with Longfellow."

"I just don't understand what he wanted with you." I can see Dad fighting the urge to start pacing while he thinks. "He's been your teacher for years. Why do this now?"

"He was more interested in Peter than me," I start.

"Sire!" Kamo suddenly bursts into the room. "I apologize for the intrusion—and I am happy to see you in better health, my prince—but a messenger just arrived at the castle gates. Sir Hebert has been located!"

"Really?" Dad looks shocked. "Where is he? And what happened to him?"

"He is currently in a small, recently established township called ... Richardtown, I believe?" Kamo scans the paper in his hand. "The circumstances around how he arrived there and where he has been for the past few months are ... a bit more complicated. I've already asked one of the mage knights to verify his location."

"That's wonderful news," Mom adds.

"It is." Dad nods. "And we can worry about retrieving him after we finish dealing with our current issues. You were saying about Peter, son?"

"Just that Longfellow was more focused on him than me," I continue my explanation.

"He kept asking him about things he didn't know about. Something about plans and someone named Ava."

"What?" Kamo asks suddenly. "What was that name?"

"Ava," I repeat. "He seemed to think that was Peter's mother's name. Why?"

No one says anything, but Kamo and all three of my parents share a way-too-obvious look.

"What did Peter say to him?" Dad asks instead of answering.

"I told you; he didn't know what the guy was talking about." I narrow my eyes. "*Why?* What's going on? Who's Ava?"

"I... I don't know, son," Dad finally answers, though I know it's not the full truth.

"Dad, he... He shifted," I continue, telling them of yet another of tonight's surprises. "He shifted into a wolf form twice as big as I've ever seen. Papa gave him the wolfsbane potion himself. How is that even possible?"

"He *what?*" Kamo sounds in shock, his head practically spinning with the information. "That... That should *not* be possible."

"I think we will need to speak with Peter himself," Papa suggests. "Tonight just became far more complicated than we could have predicted."

"Can you please let us know once he has woken up?" Mom asks one of the guards assigned to the room.

"I'll tell you," I say instead. "I'm staying right here until he opens his eyes." I don't know what any of this means or what sort of secrets my family is keeping, but I trust what Peter was saying, and I'll do whatever it takes to keep him safe.

CHAPTER 21

PETER

"**S**on, you need to eat something."

"I'm not hungry."

"Starving yourself isn't going to make him wake up any faster."

"I'm not starving my— He's waking up!"

My eyes blink open to an unfamiliar ceiling, the voices of Max and his father in my ears. I sit up slowly with a groan, feeling like I just got done sleeping for a solid week. As I rub the sleep from my eyes, I see that I'm in an unfamiliar room, one with several beds. Max is here, as are his father, Kamo, and ... a lot of guards.

"Max?" I croak out, nervous with how everyone is staring at me.

"Right here." Max quickly pulls his chair closer to my bedside. "I'm so glad you're awake."

"How long was I asleep?" My entire body feels sore, like I spent all day working in the fields.

"About twelve hours," he answers with a frown. "Can you remember anything that happened yesterday?"

"We went to the ball, and then we snuck out, and then..." I trail off as the memories unlock.

I remember the werewolves that found us in the forest, and then one of them chasing me as I ran back to the castle. Sneaking in through the secret passageway, getting caught by Longfellow, watching him hurt Max and then… My eyes shoot down to my hands, checking for fur or claws. *I'm a werewolf!*

"Good, you *do* remember," Max says after seeing my reaction.

"How… How did I do that?" I ask in confusion.

"We were hoping you could tell us that." The king steps forward, his guards following closely.

"I told you, Dad. He doesn't know anything about it," Max insists, taking my hand.

"I'd still like to hear it from him," the king responds as he turns to me, at least looking apologetic. "Peter, how were you able to shift yesterday?"

"I… I don't know." I rapidly shake my head. "I-I swear, I've never done anything like that before. I have n-no idea how I—"

"I believe you." He calms me with a raised hand. "You were here for two full moons before your claiming and did not show any signs during either. Still, I don't understand how something like this could happen."

"Perhaps the claiming bite unlocked something that was already there?" Kamo suggests, thinking. "Though that still leaves the question of his parentage."

"What about my parents?" I'm nervous as I remember some of Longfellow's accusations.

"What is your mother's name, Peter?" King Samoset asks me carefully.

"Mary. Mary Lambert," I answer honestly.

"And does the name Ava mean anything to you?" he asks next. "Ava Hebert? Ava McCormack?"

"No, sir." I shake my head again. "I don't know anyone by those names."

"Sire," Kamo starts, standing next to the king, "while I suppose it is possible she was using magic to alter her appearance, I can confirm that the woman I was introduced to as Peter's mother did not appear to be the late Ava Hebert. She did not appear to recognize me at all."

As Kamo backs up my story, I remember the guilt I felt when I learnt the truth behind Longfellow's meddling. At least the accusations I made yesterday didn't go past me, Max, and Trixie, Mika, or Tim. Then I remember why I was upset about the letters to begin with.

"Max, my parents…" I start to explain. "My letters never made it home because Longfellow had someone snatch them before the castle postmaster could even see them."

"He interfered with the castle's mail?" Kamo questions.

"Yeah, some of his accomplices worked in the mail room," Max confirms.

"They haven't heard from me since I left," I bring it back to the reason I brought it up. "They have no idea about anything that's been going on. I have to go home, I have to talk to them."

"I agree," the king surprises me by answering. "Which is why we are leaving for Weston this afternoon."

"We are?" I respond in confusion.

"*We*?" Max follows up,

"I am afraid there are still too many questions I need to hear the answers for myself, so Kamo and I will be accompanying the two of you," he explains. "However, before that, we need to determine the level of control you have over this new shifting ability of yours."

"You looked amazing," Max interjects, squeezing my hand. "I've never seen a werewolf that big. I didn't even know we could get that big!"

"What can you remember about the transformation, Peter?" King Sam questions me directly.

"I... I remember getting angry," I start to explain, struggling to remember clearly. "Longfellow and the others were hurting Max, and I was screaming at them to stop. Then I... I think the room started to shrink. I remember looking down over everyone else."

"Were you still in control of your actions?" is his next question, watching my face closely.

"I-I think so?" I offer nervously.

"He was," Max says with confidence. "He only fought back against the people who attacked us, and he was trying to untie me before he passed out."

"Hmmm." The king looks me over, thinking. "Your scent has not changed, and you appear to have all of your mental faculties. Do you feel any different?"

"No," I answer after a moment. "I feel the same way I have since the claiming bite."

"That's enough for me, for now at least." The king nods confidently. "Max, I'm leaving you and your guard to watch over him. Watch for any changes in his abilities, and perhaps try and help him learn to control his shifting before the next full moon."

"Given that he is able to shift at all is an anomaly, I am curious to see how it affects him, if at all," Kamo speculates, scratching his chin. "Please monitor him closely, my prince."

"Of course." Max nods his head.

"The two of you would probably like some time to talk alone." As the king says this, everyone else in the room seems to stand up straighter, turning toward the door. "We need to leave in a few hours, so don't dally."

"We'll be ready, Dad," Max assures his father, who leads the procession of guards out of the room, leaving us alone. "How are you feeling?"

"Okay, I think," I answer honestly. "What... What happened last night after I passed out?"

"I've never seen a werewolf hyperventilate before," he says with a chuckle. "I think once your brain caught up with what was going on, you freaked out. It wasn't long after you went down that guards burst into the room and discovered everything. You changed back into human form while they were untying me and securing Longfellow's collaborators."

"Oh gods, I hurt all those people..." I cover my mouth in shock as I recall the violence. "I-I *k-killed* Longfellow."

"Peter, *breathe*," Max tells me as he runs a hand down my back. "I know it's a lot to process, but everything is okay. Just try and remember that if you hadn't stopped Longfellow, he would have killed us *both*."

"W-What about the others?" I ask hesitantly.

"Everyone else is alright, even the people you threw out the window—which looked *badass*, by the way," he explains, still holding my hand. "Dad and his kingsguard have already started interrogating them, trying to figure out who else in the castle has been working with them."

I try to find some comfort in Max's words, but my mind just keeps replaying the violence of last night. Not just what was done to us, but what I did to everyone else. Seeing that I'm still upset, Max stands next to the bed.

"Scooch over." He pushes against my side, urging me to slide to the side as he climbs onto the small cot, wrapping his arms around me.

"I can't undo what happened," he tells me, kissing the top of my head. "But you saved us, Peter, and I'm going to do whatever it takes to return the favor."

Max and I lay there for a while, just cuddling, until we need to get moving. The castle doctor already gave me a clean bill of health, so all that's left to do is get ready for our trip to Weston. *Home.* It'll be at least two days of travel, and just as long coming back, so I pack enough clothing for almost a week just to be safe. Comparing the clothes I came here with to the soft, tailored silks I normally wear these days leaves me with a weird feeling in the pit of my stomach. *Can I even call Weston home anymore?*

I'm finished before Max, and I can't hide my laugh when I see the three different bags he's stuffing his things into. For some reason, I think he might be nervous about seeing my parents again, which is cute. I know I shouldn't be, but I'm still surprised when the castle staff carries our bags down for us. Just seems like a waste to basically have superstrength and not use it.

Alden and Queen Anna are downstairs to wish us goodbye as we load into our carriages. We're taking three, one for the king and Kamo, one for me and Max, and one to carry the knights who aren't driving. From the concerned looks on all their faces, I'm pretty sure everyone is up to date on what's going on, but no one says anything about my furry transformation.

The first day on the road is uneventful. We drive straight on until dark, long past sunset, before making camp, a lot like we did on my trip out of Weston, except this time the king is here too. He seems happy to "rough it" with the rest of us, though his tent *is* bigger than the rest of ours—it even has a little awning over the entrance.

Dinner is a simple stew, one that was cooked at the castle and packed into an enchanted jar to keep it warm for our journey. After eating, I sit around the campfire with Max and his guard, the young wolves each trying to help train me on how to shift. Not that any of them are having any success.

"Do you remember waking up after your claiming, and all the new instincts you suddenly felt?" Gala tries first. "Try focusing on those."

"No, what you need to do is think about your body changing," Thomas suggests next. "Imagine yourself shifting, your bones and muscles stretching, the fur growing on your skin. That's what I do."

"He probably can't even remember what he felt like in the moment," Aria says with a tone that doesn't sound like she's mocking me but isn't entirely supportive either. "He was barely a wolf for fifteen minutes."

I close my eyes and try to do what they're saying anyway. I concentrate on those wolfy-instincts, the urge to run, to chase, to be with Max and the pack. Then I try Thomas's idea and imagine my body growing, sprouting fur, fangs, and claws, but still, nothing happens. Sensing my frustration, Max leans over and throws his arm over my shoulder.

"Don't stress out about it," he tells me. "It'll come to you, and we've got plenty of time to practice."

I know he's right. There's a part of me that feels disappointed, but there's another that feels ... relief? Just thinking back to the night before, to the things I did while shifted, makes me shudder. What if I can't control myself?

We don't stay up much later than that and are up early the next morning. We reach the outskirts of Weston in the early evening, and as I stare out the window, I find myself wondering what Momma has cooking for supper on the stove. That and what everyone's going to think when they see me back.

From a distance, the farm seems as normal as it ever was, but once we get closer, I can see how much things have changed. Almost all of the fields have been tilled, with only the land near the barn still having grass over it.

There's six or seven people working in the fields, and none of them look like my parents. As we pull through the farm's gate, one of these ranch hands approaches the carriages as they come to a stop.

"Can I help you gentle—" The man stops in shock, falling to his knees as the king exits the first carriage. "Your Highness!"

"Mr. Grover?" I ask as Max and I exit our own carriage. "Is that you?"

"Peter?" Mr. Grover's head swivels around to me, surprised again. "I had no idea you would be coming... Your parents will be so happy!"

"Are you working here now?" I continue, not expecting to see one of my former teachers working on the farm.

"For a couple of months," he answers with a nod, then freezes when he remembers who is here with me. "Your Highnesses, how can I—"

"Please, there is no need for the formalities." King Samoset offers a hand to the man to stand. "We are here to speak with Mr. and Mrs. Lambert."

"Of course, Your Highness." Mr. Grover stands without taking the hand, and bows. "I can just go—"

"Peter?" Before he can do anything, Momma walks out onto the farm-house porch.

"Momma!" I exclaim, rushing over to her and embracing her.

"Mary, what's going— Peter!" Daddy quickly joins the hug after he follows Momma outside.

"Oh, we've been so worried," Momma tells me, almost in tears. "We had no idea what or how you were doing."

"What happened, son?" Daddy sounds less tearful but no less concerned. "It's been months since you left, and we didn't hear a word. Not until a day or two ago, when the news about your, ah, collaring left the capital."

"I am so, so sorry. I swear, I tried to write to you a bunch of times, but there was someone who—" I pause when I remember why we're here and that I probably shouldn't blab about everything outside. "Actually, can we go inside? I'll explain everything. There's a reason we're here, something we need to talk about."

"'We'? Who else is here with—" Daddy's face does the same thing Mr. Grover's did when he finally notices the king and prince over my shoulder. "Your Highness!" Both of my parents quickly separate from me to give the man a bow.

"Please, we're practically family now." King Samoset easily disarms my parents, taking one of Momma's hands and kissing the back of it. "But I'm afraid your son is correct. We are here to discuss something important that would best be done in private."

"O-Of course, my king," Daddy responds, straightening his posture. "Please, everyone, come inside."

Momma and Daddy lead the king, Kamo, Max and me all inside, along with half of the knights. They position themselves around the room as a defense while the other half stand guard on the porch. The six of us take our seats around the dining room table, my parents watching me with worry.

"Now, son, what's this all about?" Daddy asks after we're settled.

"Well, like I was telling you, I tried to write home, but there was someone who stopped me," I start to explain. "They stopped anything I wrote to you from ever leaving the castle."

"Why would they do that?" Momma asks next.

"They thought I was someone else ... or related to someone else." I steady myself before I ask what I do next. "Momma, Daddy... do you know anybody named Ava?"

The reaction is immediate, both of my parents freezing and sharing a look.

"Where... Where did you hear that name?" Daddy sounds hesitant when he asks.

"So you *do* know her?" I take their response for confirmation. "Who was she? This person said... They said she was my mother."

Neither of them says anything further, continuing to share strange and even fearful looks.

"I'm sorry, but it is clear that you two know something," King Sam speaks up. "And I am afraid we cannot leave until we know what it is."

"We need to tell him, Ron," Momma finally breaks their silence.

"I know that. I'm just thinking," Daddy responds with a huff before taking a deep breath. "Son... it was almost twenty years ago, when it was just me and your mother here on the farm. It seemed like your average day, the both of us out in the fields taking care of the crops, when we saw a woman exit the forest, before she slumped over the fence around the property."

"She was young and injured," Momma says next. "And very, very pregnant. So pregnant that she went into labor almost as soon as we got her in the house. She wouldn't even let us get a doctor. We had to help her through the birth ourselves."

"She told us her name was Ava, and that she was in danger. But she wouldn't tell us anything else," Daddy continues. "The labor was ... difficult. She was already so weak, and after the baby was born... it seemed like she knew she wasn't going to make it."

"She asked us to take care of the baby." Momma sounds sad as she shares. "Peter... that baby was *you*."

"Wh... What? I... I don't understand." I sit there, stunned. "I'm... I'm not your real son?"

"Of *course* you're our son!" Momma says, the tears having finally broken through.

"We're sorry for not telling you." Daddy's crying too. "She said that for your safety, we could never tell you the truth, or anyone for that matter. We weren't even supposed to repeat her name."

"She was pregnant..." The king's statement manages to draw attention away from the shocking revelation.

"You knew Ava, Your Highness?" Momma asks, wiping her eyes.

"I did." It's the king's turn to explain. "As you said, it was twenty years ago when I last saw her. I first met her through a man named Kojak Hebert. He, along with his younger brother, were members of my newly christened kingsguard and good friends."

"Ava and Kojak had been seeing each other for some time by then," he continues. "Some thought it was odd when she made the unconventional choice of being claimed by Kojak, but I never thought much of it because it made them happy. Less than a year later, my parents died, I was made king, and Kojak was promoted to the kingsguard."

"Ava had become a good friend as well by then, especially as I grieved my parents," the king says somberly. "But right around then, Kojak told us she had become sick, and I began to see less and less of her in person. Though I now suspect they may have been trying to hide a pregnancy."

"Are... Are you saying this Kojak person is my ... father?" I ask nervously, my mind still reeling. "But I don't understand. If he claimed her, how could she—"

"I think that is what we are working to uncover now," the king answers before I can finish. "How was she able to become pregnant at all, let alone hide it? There was so much mystery around their deaths..."

"What happened?" Max presses on.

"They had left the capital together on a vacation," King Samoset continues. "They were just visiting the countryside, hoping the change of scenery might improve Ava's supposedly failing health. It was so mundane that I barely thought anything of it. And then we received the news that they were attacked by a group of bandits. Bandits who were prepared with silver weapons and magic. We only ever found Kojak's body for burial. We searched for Ava for months, to no avail, and eventually just assumed she had passed."

"She made it as far as Weston," my father confirms sadly. "She looked at least six or seven months pregnant. We did our best to care for her, but she was so weak, and she wouldn't let us get her any other help."

"I had to stay home and avoid being seen for months after while Ronald went into town telling everyone I was pregnant," Momma adds. "Then after Peter was "born" we had to pretend that he wasn't already three months old, which wasn't easy considering how fast he grew!" She sniffles, smiling at the memory.

"Peter... she's buried in the family graveyard," Daddy says to me. "She's in the grave we told you was your Aunt Eveline... Would you like to go see her?"

The request catches me off guard, and I look from my sad parents to Max, unsure of what to say. But this is a decision I'm going to have to make all on my own.

"P-Please," I give my answer with a shaky voice, already feeling unsteady. "I-I think I'd like to see her."

With a sad nod, my parents are the first to rise from the table. They lead us out the back door, past the barn, and through the fields. A few of the new field hands watch as we make our way, most likely distracted by the king. I see some familiar faces, but no one I know as well as Mr. Grover except for one person—Ricky. *Why is he here and not on his own family's farm?*

We make our way to the northwest corner of our land where the Lambert family graveyard is located, where the Lambert's have buried our family and pets for decades. Or at least that's what I thought. As we come to a stop in front of what I previously thought was my Aunt Eveline's grave, I'm not sure what I'm supposed to feel. *Does Aunt Eveline even exist?*

"I can't believe she's been here this whole time..." King Samoset says wistfully at my side.

"Dad, do you think we should maybe...?" From the corner of my eye, I see Max gesturing back toward the farmhouse.

"Of course," he says from behind me. "Peter would probably like to be alone for a moment."

"We... We're so sorry we kept this from you, Peter," Momma tells me, still crying.

"We'll be right inside if you'd like to talk," Daddy says sadly with a hand on my shoulder.

I can't do much more than nod numbly as I stare at the gravestone. I can hear the others start to step away, leaving me alone. But before he can leave, I reach out and take a hold of Max's hand.

"Stay with me, please?" I ask, unsure of how I even found my voice.

"Of course, Sunshine." He squeezes my hand, standing with me in silence before the grave of the woman who is apparently my real mother.

CHAPTER 22

"Are you sure you don't want some privacy?"

"No, I don't think so." I shake my head, still holding Max's hand. "I'm not really sure what I should do. Or feel."

"I don't think there's a wrong way to feel about this." He squeezes my hand. "I wish I could give you some advice but this is new to me too. Maybe just try talking to her?"

I stare at the gravestone, just trying to think. What do I say? I'd never even heard the name "Ava" until yesterday. I have no idea who she is, other than my birth mother, apparently.

"H-Hello," I nervously start. "I... I guess you're my mom. That feels weird to say, seeing as I already have Momma. I... I wish I knew more about you, that I could talk to you. There's a lot of things that I don't understand. Like what I am, or why those people were after me, or why they were after you in the first place. I just..." I trail off and shake my head. "This feels stupid."

"Not helping?" Max asks with a frown.

"No. It's not like she can hear me." I sigh. "I have even more questions than I did before we came here, and it seems like everyone who might be able to answer them is already dead. I don't even know who I am anymore. I mean, my parents aren't even my parents."

"Speaking as someone with a parent they're not actually related to—yes, they are," he assures me. "They raised you, they love you, and they want what's best for you. The only reason they even kept this from you was because they were trying to protect you."

"I wish I knew what they were thinking back then," I admit sadly.

"Well, why don't you ask them?" Max offers, sounding upbeat. "I'm sure you have a lot to catch up on anyway."

"Yeah, maybe." I don't sound nearly as convinced.

The two of us walk back to the farmhouse together, finding our parents once again sitting around the dining table. Whatever discussion they were having stopped as soon as we approached the door. Standing in the living room, it's hard to get a read on what Momma and Daddy are feeling from their faces other than "worried."

"Welcome back, boys," King Sam greets us. "We'll be staying for dinner tonight. Peter, I was just telling your parents that, assuming these revelations are true, though your parents have passed, you may actually have a still living relative. An uncle, your father's younger brother."

"Uncle Achak?" Max asks at my side.

"Correct, son." The king nods and faces me. "Sir Achak Hebert. I wonder if he might be able to shed some light on things. After going missing for many months, we finally received word yesterday as to his location and condition."

"Which is great news!" Max says, standing. "Dad, why don't we and the knights go out onto the porch and figure out what we need to do to get him home?"

The king looks confused before he sees the way his son is looking between me and my parents. "Of course, son. Great idea."

Every one then stands and marches out of the front door, silent except for the clinking of armor and heavy boots hitting the wood floors with a *thud*. That just leaves the three of us, and I take a seat at the table opposite the both of them. *Why does this feel so awkward?*

"So..." I start after no one else says anything.

"Peter, we're so sorry," Momma sounds near tears. "We thought we were protecting you."

"We were scared that someone might come and try to hurt you or take you from us," Daddy continues. "But we were also scared of what you might think of us if you knew that we weren't really your parents."

"You *are* my parents," I respond without thinking, Max's words still in my head and heart. "And you'll always be my parents, no matter what. I love you."

"We love you too." Momma rushes around the table to hug me.

"I just wish I knew more about my *other* parents, too," I admit.

"So do we." Daddy stands and walks around to join my mother in hugging me. "We always wondered about the woman who brought you to us, but we were just so happy to have you with us at all."

"I... I can't have children, Peter," Momma says next, making me turn my head. "Not of my own."

"We only learned that fact a few months before Ava appeared," Daddy continues. "By then, we had resigned ourselves to the fact that we wouldn't ever have a child."

"But then we found you." Momma sounds like she might cry again as she kisses the top of my head. "Even with all the tragedy around how you came to us, we were just so happy to have you here with us."

"It felt like you were where you were meant to be." Daddy puts his arm around Momma's waist.

"We had to hide you those early months, and it wasn't easy explaining how I gave birth at home on my own," Momma explains with a sniffle. "But we weren't going to let anything take you away from us."

"No matter what, you will *always* be our son," Daddy says with finality. "We love you."

"And you'll always be my parents. I love you too." I stand, the three of us embracing, until we hear a knock on the door.

"Come in," Momma answers aloud, trying to dry her eyes.

"Sorry, am I interrupting?" *That's not Max or his dad...*

"Violet!" I call out when I see her. "It's so good to see you."

"Peter." She sounds less excited. "Did... Did Prince Blackclaw really just tell me to 'go ahead and knock'?"

"I guess he did." I say with a smile, moving toward her and the front door. "I'm so glad you came."

"Well, someone in town saw the carriages, and I figured I'd come look for myself." She's smiling but she won't look at me. *Crap, the letters!* "So are you just passing through on a visit?"

"No, not exactly." I'm trying to think of the best way to tell her what happened. "I know you haven't heard from me since I left. I'm really sorry about that."

"Yeah, usually when your best friend promises to write to you, you actually get a letter or two." She sounds disappointed and still won't meet my eye.

"I *did* write to you, really," I just go right into explaining it. "But there was someone in the castle that was stopping all my letters home from getting out."

"That sounds ... made up." She's finally looking at me, at least.

"No really, I swear!" I pleaded. "I literally wrote you and my parents *both* as soon as I arrived."

"It's true, Violet," Daddy defends me. "That's why the king and prince are here with Peter at all."

"...Really?" She's skeptical, but that's progress! "What happened?"

I give her a rundown of the events of the last few days, leaving out some of the more violent parts. And also the parts where I'm apparently now a werewolf and how close me and Max came to dying. Not sure hearing any of that would make her *or* my parents feel any better. I also share a little about what life in St. Kizis has been like, but there's something I'm more interested in hearing about first: her father.

"How is your dad doing, Vi?" I finally broach the topic.

"Oh! He's... He's doing better." She offers me a shaky smile. "The healer you sent has been great. She says the problem is a growth in his lungs... Something called a 'tumor.' We've been trying this kind of... magical therapy that is supposed to stop it from spreading."

"That's good to hear," Momma comments.

"It is, but..." Violet bites her lip. "There's only so much it can do, and in the meantime, it's making him even weaker. They say he's going to need an operation soon."

"An operation? What kind?" Daddy asks next.

"They have to remove part of his lung," Violet answers grimly. "That's where the growth—the tumor—is."

"They have to cut out his lung?" I say next, in shock. "Is that... Can they do that?"

"Dr. Hiram seems to think so," Violet confirms. "And he shouldn't have any complications afterward either. But it's not a guarantee, and I'm still nervous."

"I'm sure they'll do their best." I try to sound confident. "Max told me they sent the best doctor they had in the castle."

"Thank you so much for that, Peter." She sniffles. "This is the first time in a long time where I actually feel like there's hope."

"You're my best friend." I hug her. "There's nothing I wouldn't do to help you."

"And you know we're here for you too, sweetheart," Momma adds. "Would you like to stay for dinner? We're hosting royalty tonight!"

"Hun, I'm not sure we're allowed to invite other people to have dinner with the king," Daddy tries to inform her.

"I can when I'm the one cooking," she responds with her "no room for arguments" look.

"Thanks, Mrs. Lambert. I'd love to." She looks at the three of us, uncertain. "If you're sure it's alright?"

"Positive." I nod. "I'd want you to meet Max and his family eventually anyway."

"I've never met a king before," she says wistfully.

"We hadn't either before today," Daddy jokes before getting pulled away by Momma to help with dinner.

"Now that we're alone," I start as I watch my parents leave the room, "I have *so* much to tell you about."

"Yeah you do," she says while pulling me onto the couch. "You can start by telling me *all* about Prince Makseka."

"He actually prefers 'Max,'" I start, already thinking about my prince. "He's... He's really great."

"He must be if just mentioning him makes you smile all goofy like that," she teases.

"He's sweet, and smart, and a good listener," I begin to describe him. "He's shown me all around the castle, and the city, and even the forest his pack meets in during the full moon."

"That all sounds great," Violet says while patting my thigh. "But how big is his—"

"*Violet!*" I hiss, looking nervously to the open door of the kitchen. "... Pretty big."

"I knew he had too much swagger to not be well hung." She nods confidently to herself.

"You know, he was actually jealous of you at first," I tell her.

"Of me?" She's taken aback by this info. "Why?"

"He said he could smell you all over me that first day," I say. "He thought you were my girlfriend."

"Seriously?!" She can't hold back her laughter at that. "Tell me about what it's like living in the castle. Ooo, and what happens on the full moon?"

I tell her all about my life in the castle, all the new friends I've made, and even my teachers. I also share some about the werewolves, at least the things that didn't seem private. She's excited to hear it all—she even *squeals* when I pull my shirt collar to the side and show her my collar and claiming bite. Around then, the banging of pots and pans in the kitchen start to get a little too distracting, at least to my ears.

"Wanna go outside?" I ask, offering Vi a hand up from the couch. "I want to hear about what's changed in town."

"Nothing too exciting," Violet says as we walk onto the porch. "People were happy to have the new doctor around—she's pretty much been busy every day. Most of the changes have happened here."

"Yeah, this place is very different." I spot Max and the others over by the carriages talking, with Max turning his head and waving to me.

"I still can't believe you landed a *prince*," Vi says as she watches the interaction.

"Me either." I shake my head.

We walk around the farm as we talk, wanting to see some of the changes for myself. In addition to all the new crops that have been planted, it seems like we've got some new animals too, another three cows and two young, healthy-looking plow horses. I make sure to say hello to my girls and give them and the horses a good petting. After that, we walk along the tilled fields, watching the farmhands hard at work.

"Is that Ricky?" I ask Violet when I notice the familiar farmhand once more.

"Oh yeah, you wouldn't know this, but there was a problem on his family's farm," Violet informs me. "A blight destroyed over ¾ of their crops. There was actually some worry over not being able to feed the town, but luckily your parents were already in the process of expanding their own fields. Since they lost most of their harvest, Ricky's family needed money, and your parents offered him a job here."

He's facing away from us, standing with two other men, the three of them talking animatedly. Deciding to say hi, we approach them, just as they all start to laugh. Unfortunately, when I hear what they're saying, I freeze in my tracks.

"—probably thinks he's better than the rest of us," one of the men finishes, and it's not hard to figure out who he's talking about. "Not sure why he came back here."

"Your guess is as good as mine. Maybe the prince finally got tired and decided to send back his new whore!" Ricky jokes loud enough for even Violet to hear.

All three of them break into laughter again—at least until they see an angry Violet stomping their way with an embarrassed me standing behind her. Ricky stops laughing too, confused by their reactions, when he gets an angry shove on the back of his shoulder.

"Seriously?" Violet asks angrily when he turns around. "That's how you talk about one of your *friends*?"

"Violet, Peter!" He looks nervously between the two of us. "I—I—"

"If he hadn't left, you wouldn't even *have* this job." She pokes him in the chest. "Maybe you should remember that."

"O-Of course," he stutters with wide eyes. "I... I'm sorry."

I don't know what to say, just standing there dumbfounded and hurt. When he sees that he's not getting a response, all three farmhands quickly pick up their tools and scurry off to find something to do as Violet watches them all leave.

"I can't believe that asshole sometimes," she mutters as she comes back to me.

"Is... Is that what people in town are saying about me?" I ask her, the title of "whore" stuck in my head.

"No, not at all," she tries to assure me. "Some people are just jerks and love to gossip."

"I guess." I'm not really buying it, but I'm not sure what I could do about it anyway.

With my farm tour over, we make our way back to the farmhouse. I notice that Max and the others are now just milling about around the carriages. Max sees us and starts trotting over before we reach the porch, a smile on his face.

"Hey!" he greets, then notices my expression. "What's wrong?"

"Nothing." I shake my head, even though he probably can tell I'm lying. "Max, I want you to meet my best friend, Violet."

"I've heard so much about you." He's full of charm as he takes her hand and kisses the back of it, just like my mother. "It's nice to finally put a face to the name."

"It's an honor to meet you, Your Highness," Violet says with more nerves than I usually see on her.

"Please, you're Peter's friend. Call me Max," he tells her.

"I ... will try," Violet hesitantly offers.

"You'll get used to it." I know exactly how she's feeling.

"So, Peter, we just finished discussing..." His eyes shift to Violet nervously. "Some of the ... recent events."

"It's okay. She knows," I tell him. She *is* my best friend after all.

"Oh, okay." He immediately relaxes. "Well, with everything that's happened, Dad doesn't want Uncle Achak to travel back on his own. He going to send some of the kingsguard to collect him—but I suggested that we go ourselves."

"Us? Is that safe?" It's not something I'd expect a prince would be doing.

"Totally," he assures me. "He's not in any danger, and we won't be going alone anyway. My own guard will be coming along with us. I just thought you might enjoy not being cooped up in the castle anymore, and this way you'll get to meet your long-lost uncle in person even sooner."

"Wait, like your *real* uncle?" Violet interjects.

"Yeah, my birth-father's younger brother." I nod.

"Uncle Achak is the captain of my father's kingsguard," Max explains. "He's been missing for a few months."

"You call him uncle too?" Violet asks skeptically. "Does that mean the two of you are ... related?"

The thought makes me turn to Max in shock, but he just laughs.

"He's not my actual uncle," Max continues explaining. "He's just close enough to my family that I called him that growing up."

"Good," Violet comments. "Congrats on not committing incest."

"Thanks, I think?" *Not sure how to take that.* "So the king is really okay with us doing this?"

"Well, I had to persuade him a little," Max admits. "I told him it would also be a good opportunity to see some of the world and stretch my dip-lomat legs. We'll be going in disguise—or at least not loudly announcing ourselves to everyone."

"That sounds like it could be fun." A chance to travel and meet some of my family. "I've never left Litkalaa before."

"You know, me neither." He takes my hand in his. "But you'll have me to protect you."

"Aww," Violet coos before poking me in the shoulder. "You better write to me on your travels."

"I will. Really this time, I promise," I assure with a laugh. "And as soon as we're finished, I'll come back to visit."

The three of us chat a bit more, and Max calls over his guards and friends to introduce them to Violet as well. Everyone is nice and friendly, and even Gala manages to not be her usual surly self. Once we notice the sky starting to get dark, we head inside for dinner.

Momma really went all out, cooking enough food to feed a small army—which with all the knights here, she basically is. She roasted two fat chickens, fried up a bunch of spiced potatoes in a huge skillet, and made a big pot of vegetable stew. I sit at the dinner table with Max, my parents, the king, Kamo, and Violet in an extra seat we pulled up, while the knights eat either on the couch or the porch outside. If that bothers any of them, they're too polite to complain, but I tell myself it's just because Momma's cooking is so dang good.

"...and we're painting the barn next week!" Daddy finishes telling me about more of the changes and upgrades coming to Lamplight Farm.

"The farm looks great," I tell him with a smile. "I can't believe we're finally using all that land."

"Next month's harvest will be our biggest yet," Momma adds. "And you can thank our last harvest for tonight's dinner."

"Everything has been delicious, Mrs. Lambert," King Samoset compliments, making Momma blush. "Peter, has Max already told you about his plan for the two of you to venture to the mainland yourselves?"

"What's that?" Daddy asks. "You're leaving the island?"

"Uh, yes, he has, sir." *I wasn't really expecting to talk about this over dinner.* "Momma, Daddy, Max and I are going to go to the mainland ... to find my uncle."

"But you just got here." There's sadness and worry in Momma's voice. "Is... Is that safe?"

"We'll be back as soon as we can." I hate that I've been away from them for so long, and I'm already leaving. "It's just ... I feel like this is something I need to do."

"We understand, son," Daddy says, though he sounds just as worried as Momma. "Just please be careful and come back to us soon."

"We won't be going alone," Max tries to reassure her. "And I promise to do whatever it takes to keep your son safe."

"Perhaps, once you've returned, we could arrange for you to come stay at the palace," King Sam suggests. "My wife and consort would both *love* to meet you."

"That would be nice," Momma politely accepts the invitation, even though I can tell she's still thinking about me.

"We can start planning as soon as we are back home," King Sam continues cheerfully. "We will head out in the morning."

"You're leaving already?" Momma almost drops her fork.

"Not Peter." Max quickly jumps in.

"Not me?" He's not going to leave me behind, is he?

"I thought you'd like to spend some time with your family and friends to catch up," he explains, covering my hand with his. "I'll head back and pack for the both of us, and then we can pick you up on our way to Blackport in a few days. Sounds good?"

"Yeah." I nod, smiling at the way he's already thought ahead for me. "Sounds good."

"I'll leave Ryse here with you, just for protection," Max continues.

"Mmm." The mostly non-verbal werewolf grunts in agreement from the couch.

"That's wonderful." Momma's mood has instantly lifted. "Your room is exactly how you left it."

"No it's not. You've been in there every week to dust. Oww." Daddy rubs his leg after Momma kicks him under the table.

The rest of dinner is fairly quiet. I think everyone is a little nervous to be dining with the king. Personally, I'm a little more curious to hear what *he* thinks of it, seeing how different it is from the palace. Has he ever eaten at a table this small before?

Violet excuses herself to go home, promising to come back tomorrow. The king, Kamo, and the knights all decide to sleep in their tents, setting up a small camp near the carriages. Max, however, asks to sleep in my room with me. It's not like my room is up to his usual standards, but it's sweet. My bed's not huge, but with some squeezing, we both manage to fit.

"So, how are you feeling?" Max speaks softly, spooning me from behind. "About things with your family."

"Okay, I guess," I say while staring out the window. "I think they're worried. That I might ... replace them or something."

"Seems like something they've probably been worried about for a long time." His arm tightens around my chest. "You'll just have to make sure they know that's not the case."

"Easier said than done." I sigh. "I have a *lot* to make up for after vanishing for almost three months without a word."

"You can get started on that tomorrow." His hands nudge at me to turn over and face him. "For now, I've got something else you can take care of."

He leans forward, our mouths meeting in a messy, open-mouthed kiss. Hands start to roam downward, grabbing at asses, dicks, and other appendages as our kisses turn hungrier and hungrier. We're both rock hard, but as we grind against each other, my old bed starts to creak loudly with every movement.

"Wait." I put my hand against Max's chest to stop him.

"What's wrong?" Max looks innocently confused.

"I don't think we can do this." I shake my head. "Even without werewolf ears, there's no way my parents won't hear us."

"Aww." He looks like a kicked puppy—until his eyes brighten as he looks past me. "Alright, then I have an idea."

"What idea?" I ask as he stands, offering me a hand up myself.

"We're sneaking out." He walks over to my window and lifts it open.

"What? I can't do that!" I say in a hushed whisper. "My parents would—"

"Peter, I know this is a thing teenagers do, but we're both adults," he reminds me. "We could walk out of the front door if we wanted. I just thought this was more fun."

"Oh." I deflate a little in embarrassment.

"None of that." He gives me a quick kiss on the lips before grabbing his bag and the sheet from my bed, stuffing them under his arm. "Now get your pants on." He winks.

We both carefully climb out of my window and onto the roof, then drop down to the ground as quietly as we can. As we walk away from the farm-house—and the werewolves sleeping on the other side of it—I watch Max's head craning around to find a suitable place for the two of us. When he lands on the barn and starts to lead me toward it, I stop him.

"Uh-uh." I shake my head. "It's going to smell exactly like a barn in there."

Instead, I lead him *around* the barn—to a spot where I noticed some extra hay bales laying out earlier. After pushing a few together to form a pallet, I take the blanket from Max and spread it over the top. Satisfied, I smooth it out with my arms and climb on.

"Wow." Max looks impressed. "Is this what you used to do with the boys in town?"

"What? No." I roll my eyes and offer him a hand. "You know you were basically my first everything."

"Uh huh." He doesn't sound convinced as he joins me on the makeshift bed.

"You were!" I insist, pulling him close. "But my parents *did* catch lots of other kids back here all the time, and I might have gotten the idea from them."

"I'll be sure to thank them personally." He gives me a predatory grin.

We quickly shuck off our barely-buttoned pants, tossing them off to the side so we feel nothing but skin on skin as he rolls me onto my back and covers my body with his own. We pick right back up where we left off in my bedroom, hungry mouths pressed tightly together. The more we kiss, the more precum I can feel leaking onto my belly as Max grinds our cocks together.

Pulling away with a twinkle in his eye, Max starts to kiss, suck, and bite his way down my body. He makes stops at my neck, shoulder, chest, and even belly button before he reaches his goal. Stroking me gently in one hand, he licks his lips before wrapping them around my cock. I bite my lip to avoid moaning too loudly, thrusting up into Max's mouth on instinct.

He bobs up and down on me effortlessly, never once gagging. I have a lot of practice ahead of me if I want to get even half as good as he is. I let my head fall back, closing my eyes and enjoying the warm, wet sensations of his mouth. When he finally pulls off, my cock is standing straight up, the wind chilling the still-wet flesh. *That means it's my turn.*

Flipping our positions, I find myself nuzzling against the furry forest that rests between Max's legs. I lick my way up his thick shaft, using one hand to hold him steady as he enters my mouth. I take him as far as I can without gagging, careful to avoid the scrape of my teeth. I feel one of Max's hands touch the back of my head, threading through my hair as he encourages me downward.

I suck him as well as I'm able, spurred on by every little moan I pull from his lips. I can feel the drool building up when I try to take him even deeper, not caring about the mess. His balls are a set of warm furry orbs resting in my hand, where I give him the occasional squeeze. I love doing this, love making him feel good.

Which is why I whine a little when he tugs my head off him, my mouth still open as I try in vain to get him back inside. Another quick tug brings me back to my senses, my eyes focusing on Max and what he is holding in his other hand: oil and a cleansing charm. *That's why he brought the bag.*

"You ready for what's next, boy?" he asks with a cocky smirk.

"Yes, sir." I nod my head quickly, holding my hand out for the charm.

While I hold the charm against my stomach and wait for it to work, Max pops the cork on the bottle of oil and drips some into his free hand. I watch closely as he strokes his slick hand up and down his cock, the pink-tan head poking through his fist each time he drags down his foreskin. It's only when he passes the oil bottle to me that I stop gawking.

I shuffle up our makeshift bed on my knees, pouring some oil into my own hand along the way. I reach behind me, bringing my slick fingers to my hole, unable to stop my nerves from making me clench up. Straddling Max's thighs, I close my eyes and take a deep breath, pushing a finger inside myself once I have relaxed. I slowly drive it in and out before adding a second one, and after a few more thrusts I decide that is enough for me.

I move farther up Max's body, letting his cock pass under me and then reaching behind to stroke it. Max is still hard as stone, his eyes heavy with lust. He bares his teeth, sucking in a quick breath when I give his shaft a squeeze. Then I lift myself up, press his cock against my hole, and push back down.

I whine in pain when the thick head finally pops through my entrance. Max's touch becomes light, not wanting to push me to take more, but that's okay because that's something I'm determined to do all on my own. Gritting my teeth, I sink myself down the full length of his cock, shuddering on top of his thighs as my body struggles to take it all.

"Whoa, slow down, babe." Max runs his hands over my shaking thighs, now fully seated on top of him. "We've got all night."

I don't argue with him, holding myself in place while my hole is stretched to its limits. I can feel Max's hands running all over my body, petting and stroking every piece of skin he touches. I can see on his face the way he holds himself back, fighting against the urge to just take me. *One day...* Inside of me, I can feel every twitch and pulse of his prick, making me shudder and groan with each new sensation.

When I'm finally relaxed enough, I start to roll my hips, sliding barely even an inch of Max in and out of my hole. Gradually, as the pain continues to subside (thank you, werewolf healing), I pick up speed, my hands gripping onto either side of Max's chest as I lift myself up and really start to ride. My own dick is heavy between my legs, slapping down onto Max's stomach with every bounce.

Max reaches a hand up, scratching a fingernail down my chest before pinching a nipple. I can't help but imagine that finger as a sharp, furry claw, and the rest of the beast attached to it. *Do I want Max to fuck me while he's shifted? Is that even possible?* I don't really care, the thought alone of being pinned down by my own personal monster sends my brain to new, horny heights.

The pressure that always comes before a dry orgasm has been building since I started bouncing on Max's dick. My fingers dig into his pecs, my whole body tensing up as I get close to the edge. When it finally washes over me, it's a struggle to stay upright, the muscle of my ass and groin pulsing as it washes through my body.

I slow down but don't stop, knowing my prince beneath me still has not finished himself. Knowing it'll just happen again before too long, I start using those same muscles to milk him, trying to coax the cum from his balls. Just from the way his eyes are screwed up tight, and how tightly his hands are gripping my thighs, I think he's close, and right now I want nothing more than to make him finish.

"Fuck..." he huffs through gritted teeth. "You feel so fucking *good!*"

At that moment, he thrusts up, clamping down on the tops of my thighs with a grip strong enough to bruise. I feel more than hear the low rumble in his chest, just before his cock starts to pulse and a sticky warmth begins to spread inside of my body. Still holding steady, I grind myself down against his crotch, trying to work every last drop of cum from his prick. When it finally feels like he's finished, I release the breath I've been holding—only to be quickly pulled down.

"You are so *perfect*," Max mutters against my skin as he kisses my neck.

He has me lay on my side next to him. His lips move from my neck to my ear just as his hand moves from my cock, gripping me in a hand slick with his own cum. He strokes me as his tongue plunges into my mouth, nipping at my lips. As he works me toward my own cumshot, I start to thrust up into his hand.

"There you go," he praises as my cum spills over his fist. "Good boy."

I can only whimper happily in response, burying my face against his skin to muffle all the noises I *really* want to make. I feel sticky front and back, exhausted and satisfied all at the same time. When Max pulls me against his side, I don't fight at all.

"I love you, Peter." His voice is husky and warm against my ear.

"I love you too, Max," I mumble against this collarbone, knowing he can hear me regardless.

The two of us lay together on our makeshift bed, sticky and sweaty. I know we need to get back inside (and try and get all the hay and cum off this blanket), but neither of us wants to move. As we lay there under the waxing moon, hundreds of stars twinkling above us, I find myself wanting to thank each and every one.

Book Club Questions

1. Does Weston remind you of any place you've ever lived or visited? Would you want to go back?

2. Has someone famous ever come through your place of business? How did you react? How do you think you would have reacted in Peter's shoes?

3. What did you first make of Max's offer to Peter? Would you have taken it yourself? Do you think he should have known better?

4. Have you ever had to move to a new place without any friends or family in the area like Peter? How difficult was it to settle in?

5. Because of the danger, the royal family is very strict about who they are allowed to pass the bite to. Do you agree with their position, or do you think they should relax their rules?

6. While attending the royal court, Peter is forced to deal with many people who think he does not belong where he is. How would you have handled them?

7. Peter spends a good portion of the book never hearing from his loved ones back home, thanks to someone else's machinations. What would you have done in Peter's shoes?

8. Throughout the book, people use secret passages to move in, out, and around the castle. Do you wish your own home had passages like that? Where would you put them?

9. At least at first, it seems like Kamo is out to get Peter. Have you ever had to work or live with a person you just didn't get along with? How did you deal with them?

10. Mr. Longfellow being behind things was intended as a surprise and Kamo a red herring. Were you surprised when the culprit was revealed? Did you suspect anyone else?

Author Bio

Dominic N. Ashen is an author and avid reader with a heavy focus on gay BDSM-themed erotica. After spending his youth in search of books with characters who were more like himself—queer ones, specifically—he decided to start creating some of his own. His stories star queer protagonists, most often gay and bisexual men, and feature heavy themes of dominance, submission, and all sorts of kinks. Dominic loves the fantasy, sci-fi, and horror genres with a penchant for writing longer stories where he is able to weave in the sex and kink right alongside the plot.

Website: https://www.dominicashen.com/
Patreon: https://www.patreon.com/dominicashen
Twitter: https://twitter.com/DomNAshen
Facebook: https://www.facebook.com/dom.n.ashen
Instagram: https://www.instagram.com/dom.n.ashen

More books from 4 Horsemen Publications

LGBT Erotica

Dominic N. Ashen
Steel & Thunder
Storms & Sacrifice
Secrets & Spires
Arenas & Monsters
My Three Orc Dads: a Novella
Before the Storm: a Novella

What Makes Me a Whore?
A Breach in Confidentiality
Back Door Pass
My European Adventure
An Unexpected Affair
Finding True Love
The Dr. Cage Chronicles

Eskay Kabba
Hidden Love
Not So Hidden
Signs of Affection
Deeply Devoted to Him
Honest Love
A Plane and Simple Connection

Leo Sparx
Before Alexander
Claiming Alexander
Taming Alexander
Saving Alexander
The Fall of the House of Otter
The Case of Armando

Grayson Ace
How I Got Here
First Year Out of the Closet
You're Only a Top?
You're Only a Bottom?
I Think I'm a Serial Swiper
Lookin in All the Wrong Places

Robert Lewis
Someone to Love
Someone to Come Home To
Someone to Kiss
Someone to Marry

LGBT Romance

AJ Buchannan
Orchestrated Love
Facing the Music

Eskay Kabba
Hidden Love
Not So Hidden
Signs of Affection
Deeply Devoted to Him
Honest Love
A Plane and Simple Connection

Lucas LaMont
Roman's Reckoning: Type 6
Mikaél's Moment: Type 6
Stephan's Resurgence: Type 5
Anastasia's Arrival: Type 6

Stormie Skyes
Check Yes, No, or Maybe

V.C. Willis
The Prince's Priest
The Priest's Assassin
The Assassin's Saint
The Champion's Lord

Fantasy, SciFi, & Paranormal Romance

Amanda Fasciano
Waking Up Dead
Dead Vessel
The Dead Show
Dead Revelations

Beau Lake
The Beast Beside Me
The Beast Within Me
Taming the Beast: Novella
The Beast After Me
Charming the Beast
The Beast Like Me
An Eye for Emeralds
Swimming in Sapphires
Pining for Pearls

Chelsea Burton Dunn
By Moonlight
Moonbound
Bloodthirsty

D. Lambert
Rydan
Celebrant
Northlander
Esparan
King
Traitor
His Last Name

Danielle Orsino
Locked Out of Heaven
Thine Eyes of Mercy
From the Ashes
Kingdom Come
Fire, Ice, Acid, & Heart
A Fae is Done

J.M. Paquette
Klauden's Ring
Solyn's Body
The Inbetween
Hannah's Heart
Call Me Forth
Invite Me In
Keep Me Close
Heart of Stone

Kait Disney-Leugers
Antique Magic
Blood Magic
Heart Magic

Kyle Sorrell
Munderworld
Potarium

Lyra R. Saenz
Prelude
Falsetto in the Woods: Novella
Ragtime Swing
Sonata
Song of the Sea
The Devil's Trill
Bercuese
To Heal a Songbird
Ghost March
Nocturne

Paige Lavoie
I'm in Love with Mothman
I'm Engaged to Mothman
Dear Galaxy

Robert J. Lewis
Shadow Guardian and the Three Bears
Shadow Guardian and the Big Bad Wolf
Shadow Guardian and the Boys
That Went Woof

Milton Keynes UK
Ingram Content Group UK Ltd.
UKHW021843050324
438930UK00015B/244/J

9 798823 202862